A MERCY OF WIDOWS

Marcy Lane

To Cindy,
Lovely to meet
you. Enjoy!

Best wishes
Marcy

Happy Toad Books

ISBN-13: 978-1-7387845-2-3

Cover design by: Marcy Lane (with Canva)
Library of Congress Control Number: 2018675309
Printed in the United States of America

To my family, past and present.

A MERCY OF WIDOWS

CHAPTER 1

Bad Luck

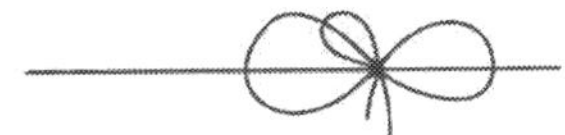

"Bad luck comes in threes." My beloved Hug's sayings, his Huggisms were usually apt, but not this time. From my current vantage, he'd miscalculated badly. After all, three months, one day, eleven hours and thirteen minutes ago, at age forty-seven, he died. And not a peaceful, reassuring death, but a haunting painful one, with blood seeping from all the wrong places, a complication of his fatal cancer. That stuff of nightmares might've been the end of his misfortune. I wasn't so lucky.

But today was supposed to be different, a new beginning, a fresh start. Wrong again. Still, I tried what Hug had asked, what I'd promised: I tried to move on. The three months had been his idea, a timeline he considered long enough for me to grieve my love, my loss, right?

"Take three months, Heddie," he'd said, "then pick yourself up, dust yourself off, and move on."

And today began promising enough. I'd hauled myself out of bed and lined up appointments with three prospective partners for the business I'd let languish after Hug's diagnosis. Pawsitive Pups—built over nearly two decades—had once been my passion. I resolved it could be again. I'd been creating an advanced course for my canine graduates, full of games and tricks to hone their skills. I envisioned a dog decathlon of sorts, with teams, points, and a winner's cup, full of tasty dog treats.

I loved dogs. I was good with dogs. I got dogs and they

got me. Humans? Not so much.

My meetings today had been a bust, even though Fella fulfilled his part. In his snazzy bandanna, Hug's black and white border collie showcased my idea to potential partners better than any words. He communicated his joy with his whole body, standing on tiptoes, his expressive ears perked in anticipation of every new game.

I returned home to Hug's yellow brick bungalow, where I jockeyed Dimples, my hail-stricken Honda Accord, back and forth closer to the curb. Hug's older Calgary suburb featured lots of three-storey spruce and pine, with squatter mountain ash and lilac nearby. The streetlights spotlighted the pummelling rain, and the windshield wipers swished like a metronome timing my efforts. At least it wasn't snow. Once in place, I gripped the steering wheel, rested my head in the cradle my arms formed, and let the disappointment of my failed plans sink in.

The inertia of my grief gripped me, anchored me in place for a moment like cement shoes. Nearer to his end, Hug had needed me day and night. I shelved my own plans, my own life to help. And I'd tried so hard, a desperate resistance fighter in his battle against cancer. But I failed. Cancer had won Hug and knocked me down for the count too. Living was hard enough. Doing it without him was unbearable.

Eventually, I got a grip on myself again, exited my car and hefted my backpack onto one shoulder. I tethered Fella to my waist to keep both hands free to carry my groceries. I collected my bags from the trunk, pleased I'd remembered my nylon sacks for this rare outing. I'd stuffed the bags full of rediscovered healthy foods, all nourishing my fresh start. Sweet ambrosia apples, a clamshell of baby greens, and even plain—ew—yoghurt. My one nod to my former junk food diet? A jumbo bag of flavoured popcorn.

I'd keep trying. For Fella. Because I'd promised Hug. Eventually for myself.

When my key didn't fit into the front door lock,

I assumed user error, even though I'd used that precise key hundreds, maybe thousands, of times. "Rackafrack," I muttered, brushing aside my hair, which was matted and plastered to my forehead. I put Fella into a sit-stay and plopped my groceries onto a dry spot on the veranda before trying the key again.

I fumbled with the lock for at least a minute before I spotted my sister-in-law in the living room window, standing still, watching me with a haughty curiosity. When Becky and I finally made eye contact, she dismissed me by flipping her hand—an inch short of a full-on insult. She pointed her French-manicured finger toward the street at a collection of stuffed garbage bags and sodden boxes. My favourite fleece flapped in the evening breeze, planted like a flag in the middle of the mound. I'd walked right past the whole ensemble without noticing anything off.

My teeth chattered—maybe from the cold or maybe from my nerves. "Hi, Becky," I yelled so she could hear me through the closed window. I waved and smiled, hoping I pulled off "friendly." "What's going on? Open the door, please?"

She shook her head. I could almost hear her dried pea brain rattling inside her bulbous skull.

I knew better than to argue with her. In her own mind, she was always right. "Is Stanley there? Can I talk with him?" Maybe Hug's baby brother would tell me what was going on.

When she ignored me, I swallowed my pride and called my best friend. Leah answered on the third ring.

"What's up?" She sounded distracted.

"Your prediction was right," I said. "Stanley's up to something. Can you come over?" Leah, a former lawyer and current death doula, had seen things more clearly than I had. My tunnel vision, with its focus only on Hug, had blinded me to his family's antics.

"Hold on," she replied. "I'll be right there. Let me handle this, okay."

I hung up, turned slightly away from Becky, and used

my body to shield my hands from her view. I flicked the camera app to video, and pressed record, and dismissed Hug's "two wrongs don't make a right" tsk-tsk reel playing in my head. I'd get audio, but I angled the phone so, with a rare bit of good luck, I might get decent video too. Perhaps they'd say or do something I—or more likely, Leah—could use to sort this mess.

Stanley joined his wife, and they stood in the window like thrift-store mannequins.

"Why won't my key work?"

Silent stares. I felt like a pinned cockroach inspected under a magnifying glass, scorched by their scrutiny.

I pounded on the door with my clenched fists. "Come on, guys. Let me in," I tried. "Joke's over. Funny. Ha. Ha."

They weren't joking, and I wasn't amused. I wanted to scream and emphatically stomp my feet, but recent hard lessons—especially with this pair—counselled me to restrain myself. "Please. What's going on? Why are you doing this?"

Becky crossed her arms, a signal I interpreted as resolution. But Stanley pulled back the sheer curtains and cranked open the window a crack. Maybe this was a promising sign.

"You knew this was coming," he said. "You got our letter." He moved to close the window and end our lopsided conversation.

I put my hand up, the universal "stop" sign, at least in dog-speak. "Wait a minute." He quit cranking the window closed, and I jammed my key between the pane and the frame, preserving a sliver of open air to let our voices carry in a sham of communication. "Let's be civilized. Talk to me. To start, what letter?" I didn't have to fake it. I truly had no idea what he was talking about.

"Don't give me that. I have your receipt." He reached into his back pocket and pulled out his wallet. From the billfold compartment, he removed and unfolded a piece of paper, then used his palm to press it flat against the window. "See. That's you?" He mock-studied it. "Appears you signed it."

I recognized my signature. Oh, that. “I never read it. Never opened it.”

“You receive a registered letter and don’t open it? Hard to believe.”

“No,” I snapped. “Don’t believe me? Go to Hug’s desk. Top lefthand drawer.”

Stanley disappeared for a minute and returned, waving a stack of envelopes.

“I can’t believe you.” He fanned the envelopes in front of his face. “You’ve got bills here dating back months.” He held up one emblazoned with “past due” in blue capital letters. A second read “final notice” in a red version of the same font. He shook his head, and I felt his judgement. His disdain.

Once upon a time, I’d been responsible, frugal, with money. But lately, I hadn’t possessed the energy, the wherewithal, to sort those bills. “I’ve been grieving,” I explained.

“I’ve been grieving too,” he said. “But I don’t get to shirk my responsibilities.”

“It’s not a contest. Now, can we talk about this? Please.”

“I’m done talking to you,” he scoffed. “I cannot—will not—let you bankrupt us both.”

“Pardon? What are you saying?”

Becky reached over and touched her husband on the shoulder, a placating gesture that he shook off. When he spoke again, his voice was quieter, his tone menacing. “I’m not getting into it with you. You’re impossible. I will be glad to be done with you.”

“You can’t just say that and not explain yourself,” I responded.

“Try me.” He sorted through the mail like a dealer at a blackjack table. One pile was for me, and I already recognized my unlucky cards. Once he finished, he disappeared for a second before nudging the front door ajar. He shoved the envelopes through the opening, and when I didn’t grab them fast enough, he tossed them onto the veranda. The ones strewn on the bottom got soggy and stuck together.

Fella leaned in to investigate.

"Leave it," I said, and he did.

"You better grab those. You've got bigger troubles than me. One there is from the provincial court. What else have you done?"

"Nothing." I set aside their missive for closer inspection and shoved the rest into my backpack for later. I ripped open the envelope, removed the paper, and read "eviction notice." According to the legalese, I should've left two days ago—exactly three months after Hug's death. "You're kicking me out?"

They were standing at the window again, stony faces matching their hard hearts.

"We gave you lots of notice. More than you deserve." Stanley moved his face closer to the open window.

"More than I deserve? What do you mean?" My voice was shrill, and I drew in a deep breath, trying to suck in some self-control along with the oxygen. This was not the happy future Hug had promised.

"Think on the bright side, all the positives in your life. This could be a new beginning," Stanley soothed. "You're still young and you've got your health. Hugh meant for you to live your life. Be happy."

"Bright side? What bright side? The love of my life is dead. I don't have a job and now you're kicking me out. Where will I go?"

"I really don't care. Hugh will not saddle me with you for the rest of my life." He swatted his hand like I was a bothersome fly. "You've freeloaded here long enough. Today, that ends. I will not pay your way for one more second." He pounded the wall with his open palm. "Go ruin your own life," he snarled. "I won't let you ruin ours."

"I've got rights too. You can't do this."

"You have no rights to Hugh's estate," Stanley replied. "Don't believe me? Get a lawyer and I'll see you in court." He spoofed a nasty laugh. "Get yourself a two-for-one deal on whatever other pickle you've gotten yourself into."

I ignored his taunts. "You never respected me. You hated that Hug spent time with me. Loved me."

"Loved you?" He blew out a chortle. "He didn't love you. Hugh used you. You were convenient. Occasionally fun. And when he was sick, you were cheaper than a nurse."

I stared at him, open-mouthed. I had no rebuttal, no way to prove Hug's esteem.

"Did he marry you? No. Did he write you into his will? No."

"I will never forgive you for this," I said.

"You are not the injured party here," Stanley replied. "I'm perfectly within my rights. You, on the other hand? You're the one who won't be forgiven." We stood close enough for me to see the red veins in his bulging eyes. "You hurt him, caused him to suffer. You let him down when he needed you most."

I was too angry, too hurt to cry. "You're wrong, Stanley. You're black-hearted and greedy." It was decent bluster, but I deflated like a popped blimp.

Some neighbours emerged from their houses to investigate our ruckus. The old woman across the way came out wearing a tatty cardigan over her paisley housecoat and socked feet in canary-coloured flip-flops. I waved, a gesture of habit rather than courtesy. She recognized me, waved in answer, turned her back on my disgrace, and shuffled back into her house.

Stanley stared at me for another minute, his hatred distilled into a single scowl. Then he dropped the curtains and didn't bother closing the window. No need. I'd become insignificant.

I wondered what to do next, but I'd used up all my fight. I sank onto the veranda to wait for Leah, and curled up like an exposed woodlouse, my arse on the cold concrete and feet planted on the top stair. Fella imitated my posture and I leaned into him, holding him close while gently petting his neck. The rain dribbled down my cheeks, but this time, I didn't bother to brush it aside.

Hug might've wanted me to have a good life, with no wallowing in the past and no regrets about our lost future. But move on? What did that even mean?

CHAPTER 2

The Deal

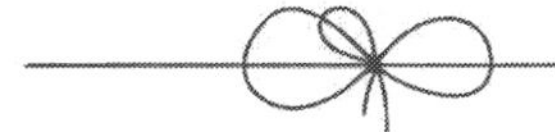

Fella and I moved from our perch and stood on the sidewalk next to my belongings while Leah expertly parked her minivan.

Once Leah joined me, I handed her Stanley's letter to decipher. “Eviction notice, eh? Interesting, but wrong. You weren’t a tenant.” She pointed to an indented paragraph at the top of page one. “Says here Stanley is the executor of Hugh’s estate. Did you find his will?”

Bea and Emm waved at me from their car seats in the middle row, and I waved back, a pasted smile on my face. “No and I looked everywhere.”

“Seems Stanley found it. Probated it too. Did he give you a copy?”

I shook my head.

“What about Hugh’s video?”

“I couldn’t find that either,” I admitted.

“Okey dokey. I’ll get this sorted. You stay put.” Leah marched up the path to Hug’s house and rang the bell. I watched rather than heard their conversation. Gauging by her gesticulations, Leah remained unconvinced by Stanley’s explanations.

When she returned to me, Leah put her hands on her hips and examined my belongings. “He’s got it, alright and he’ll get me a copy. He also says you made it harder for him to wrap up Hugh’s estate?”

"What? I have not. Today's the first time we've talked since the memorial." I didn't mention I'd dodged their several calls and emails. I was done with their harangues. "Can you fix this mess?"

She stared at me bug-eyed before her gaze dropped to the ground. "It's not my skill set. Some death doulas help with clients' estates, but I prefer to bring in the experts."

"But you used to be a lawyer," I squeaked.

"Years ago. I've forgotten too much." She paused long enough for me to wonder whether I'd said something wrong. "Besides, I'm too close to you, to Hugh." Her sigh did little to buoy my confidence. "Plus, I've got a better idea. Until we get this sorted, you'll stay with me and the girls." It was more of a command than an offer, but her sing-song tone reminded me to watch my tongue around her eavesdropping children.

"I can't do that," I said. "I'll find a hotel or something."

"With Fella?" she asked. Her raised eyebrows emphasized her winning retort.

"There's gotta be another answer. Maybe I'll pitch a tent right here." I stomped my foot to mark the location. "Call CBC. Play the widow card."

"Please be sensible, Sweetie. You'll freeze to death." She glanced at the rain now mixed with snow. "Let me give you a break." Leah turned and glared at the window where Stanley and Becky had resumed their watch. "I can't resurrect Hugh, but I won't let them have the ultimate word."

I wasn't yet ready to erase the pity from my party. "Where?" I mentally inventoried the rooms in her century-old house and came up short of any extras. "I'm too old for couch-surfing."

"In the suite." She and her husband Jake had spent the equivalent of a year of my income converting her basement into a comfortable one-bedroom abode. They had installed not one, but two proper egress windows, and carved out a separate entrance with its own shelter from the worst of Calgary's weather. "We fixed it up for something like this."

I raised my arms and let them drop. "I can't pay rent," I admitted, gritting my teeth to hold back tears.

"I know," she replied.

The girls released their seatbelts, climbed out of the car, and scuffed soggy fallen leaves into a pile. I toyed with some myself before adding to their collection.

Leah watched us. "You've got to let me help." She paused, and I didn't reply. "Let's start by getting these boxes out of the rain. Girls, over here, please."

"You're giving up? Doesn't moving all this weaken my position?"

"Your stuff will get ruined out here," she said, ever practical. "And Stanley won't budge. He's decided."

I huffed my last protest before digging into my task.

Leah had brought along plastic bins, confirming that she had anticipated this ending to my story. She hauled her totes from her cavernous hatch and handed me a blue one with a snap-on lid. "Is this everything?" she asked as we shuttled boxes and bags from the sidewalk to my car.

"Dunno. I think so. I ditched most of my furniture when I moved in with him."

Bea picked up a smaller box and shrieked when its contents plummeted to the sidewalk. I rushed over and knelt next to her. Fella, tethered to my waist, slurped Bea's cheek. "Ew," she said and wiped his slobber with her pink-mittened hand.

"I have an idea," I said. "Would you take care of Fella for me?"

She offered a hesitant smile.

I unclipped Fella's leash and handed it to her with both hands. "You'll need a firm grip." Beyond the child's view, I signalled Fella to "stay." He plopped his arse onto the sidewalk and leaned into the child. I ruffled his ears.

Emm helped me transfer some books, my toothbrush, and various toiletries from the sidewalk to a bin. Leah retrieved *Grief Recovery Workbook*, her gift to me early in post-

Hug. "Did you complete the self-assessment?"

I nodded and hoped she didn't notice the book's pristine spine. At least I'd removed the cellophane wrapping.

"What did it say? You're still in the denial stage, right?" Leah was clearly persuaded by her expert opinion. She held aloft another book bristling with Post-its. "What's *Doodle Notes*?" She didn't await my answer before tossing both books into the bin.

I crammed my belongings into Dimples' trunk, backseat, and miscellaneous crannies while reserving the shotgun seat for Fella.

Leah scooped some composting leaves from the crevice between the hood and the windshield and flung them onto the road. "Jake would tell you to remove these." Scoop and fling, she finished the job. "They'll stain your paint."

She ran her hand along the pitted surface of the car's hood. "You should've set me loose on that insurance company." The hailstorm had marred every inch of my trusty car about a month after Hug's diagnosis. The thick black clouds had rolled in like some biblical reckoning, darkening the noon sky before wreaking their damage. I'd heard the clamour but decided against scrambling to protect my car with collected blankets and cushions.

"It was easier to change his name." From Beau to Dimples. "He still runs."

"You can't sell it, liquidate it, to help with your bills. Not looking like this." She'd changed her approach but not the topic.

I held up my hands, palms up. It was time to surrender. I'd been fighting something or other for so long. "I already owe you so much." I lifted another box, positioning my hands to avoid another mishap.

Once Dimples was full, we started filling Leah's ancient Plymouth Voyager.

"Jake and I, we want to help," Leah admitted.

Stanley was gone, but Becky remained at the window,

still and ethereal, camouflaged by the reflection of the few remaining leaves fluttering in the breeze as she watched us work.

I ignored Becky and put one hand on my hip. "When did you have time to talk this through with Jake?"

Leah gave me a tentative smile. "Never mind that now."

I watched the children, and a good idea began to form, a win-win. "What if we trade?" I suggested. "I could be like a live-in nanny. Take the kidlets to school in the mornings. Care for them after school until you get home."

Leah's face brightened. "That's a wonderful idea."

I continued, "Save you on babysitting costs."

She chuckled. "You can stop negotiating. I'm already persuaded. Part-time nannying is a fair trade for room and board."

I noticed she'd upped her offer. "You feeding me too? You need remedial lessons in bartering."

"The basement kitchen is not well-equipped. Besides, you cook too many curries," she said, wrinkling her nose.

"Turmeric is healthy."

"And messy. Stains everything."

I tutted. "It's an antioxidant. Anti-inflammatory too." With that topic exhausted, I asked, "What about Jake?" Jake was her equal partner in all things, and especially in parenting their children.

Leah picked up the second to last box from the pavement. "His clinic needs him more. They're short-handed since one vet went on mat leave. Listen, I'm not handing off total care of my children." She glanced at me again, eyes wide in exclamation. "I'll still get them ready every day, get their dinner, put them to bed." She brightened. "If you're home, it'll be less disruptive for everyone when I get called out at night." Most of Leah's clients didn't die during daylight hours. Midnight callouts often meant piggy-backing the sleepy children across the back alley to their room in Jake's place.

I shook my head. "I still hate this. A year ago, I had a life.

Today, I live off my best friend's handouts."

"That's not true."

"You don't really need me. You and Jake managed your lives, your kids, your abodes, your wonky schedules, for years without me."

"It'll be healthier for you to live with us for a while," she admitted. "You need to talk to somebody, process your feelings, move on."

"I'm trying," I bleated. "I spent all day drumming up support for a new business concept. Fella's old daycare said they'd hire me in an instant, but it's only minimum wage." I needed a bit more.

"You're over-qualified for that job."

"I'd train them too," I said defensively. "The dogs would leave my care better behaved than when they arrived."

"Maybe train my kids? I'd love for them to behave as well as Fella." She laughed and used both hands to muss their hair. "It's settled then?"

I felt part relief and part resignation. "Yes." Then, I remembered my manners. "Thank you, Leah."

I moved to shake her hand, cinching the deal, but she pulled me into an embrace. In a moment, the girls joined our huggle.

CHAPTER 3

Unpacking

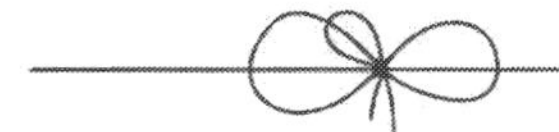

"Welcome home," Leah said. I realized she was trying, but it didn't feel like home.

The suite looked like a museum to Leah's past, a furniture-based chronology of her life. Her mother's colonial oak kitchen set formed the centrepiece of the room, and I recognized the tattered futon from our dorm at university. Her kids had claimed the space as their own and filled it with their toys and forts, crafts and chaos.

Leah read my mind. "We'll clean-up this mess. Make room for you. Children, can you pile your toys in one corner?"

They did as they were asked, but it was a bigger job than they could handle, so their efforts dwindled, and I resolved to finish their chore later.

"It's beautiful," I assured her. "I'll be very comfortable here."

Leah hugged me. "It'll be okay, Heddie, I promise. Right now? We'll let you get settled."

The girls reluctantly followed their mother up the stairs.

I was grateful for my brief return to solitude. "Good night," I called toward their receding footsteps. "Bed bugs, etc."

I discovered my backpacks jammed into the first box I opened. Hug used to say I owned the world's largest collection of backpacks. Not even remotely true; I just had more than he did. I still had the thick canvas one I used while at school, the

University of Calgary's logo faded from hard use and too many washes. Now, it was only suitable for day hikes. My favourite was my work pack—lightweight, waterproof, and adorned by amusing smiling daisies. Emm and Bea helped me choose this most conservative of the store's selection, nixing the more flamboyant options. Besides being cheerful, this pack glowed in the dark—a distinct advantage when working outdoors on dark winter evenings. My human-students located me easier when I strapped a lit-up beacon to my back. The dogs just followed their noses to my pocketful of treats.

I dumped the lot onto the carpet. I sorted them, lining them up on the floor of the front closet, while Stanley's nasty words rolled around my head like burdock burrs, catching and ruining anything nice, threatening my composure. I jammed the rest of my packs into the closet higgledy-piggledy, tucking in a stray strap so I could close the door. I looked around for my suitcase, and then unpacked enough essentials for the morning.

I glanced at the digital clock on the microwave. 7:55. Exhausted, I went to bed anyway. My chores would wait for tomorrow.

CHAPTER 4

Disguised

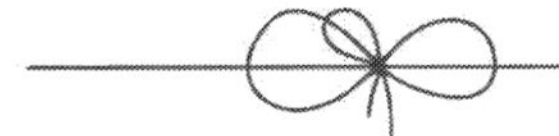

"Wake up, Sleepyhead."

I groaned and opened one eye. Leah stood at the foot of the bed, clenching a mug of something steaming. I sniffed the air and confirmed coffee. She moved it closer, luring me with it the way I taught dogs new tricks.

I groaned, and she laughed. "That's coherent. Meet you in the kitchen." She beckoned me to follow her.

I flipped my legs over the edge of the bed, shoved my feet into my slippers, and plodded after her. "I could get used to this."

"Excellent." Leah sat at the kitchen table and flipped through the stack of ignored mail, dry again following Stanley's abuse. "You should open these," she counselled. "Uh-oh." She straightened in her seat and held a white envelope up to the light. "Can I open this one?" she asked when her x-ray vision failed her. She didn't wait for my go-ahead before she stuck her thumb under the sealed flap and ripped through the paper. She fished out a folded page and read its contents. "Oh no," she exclaimed. "You've got to get moving." She handed me the paper, which I held at arm's length to skim without my glasses.

"What is it?"

"A jury summons. For today." She tapped the backside of the paper still in my hands and rattled it. "Good thing I opened it." She picked up the envelope and examined it back and front. “When did you get this?”

“Yesterday. In all the mail Stanley gave me.”

“You had to know it was coming,” she snapped. “Juror certification would’ve happened weeks ago.”

I shrugged. Sure, I had completed that form, full of hope, like a job application. I even bought a stamp and submitted it, snail mail, within the required timeline.

“You won’t get discharged now.” She scowled. “You’ve got to go in. No excuses. No-shows get charged with contempt of court.”

“I don’t want to go to jail,” I admitted.

“You’d probably only get fined.” She stood swiftly, and the envelope fluttered to the floor. “I’ve got an idea. Hop in the shower. I’ll be back in a few minutes.”

I slurped my coffee, burning the roof of my mouth before I complied with her instructions. A few minutes later, I clenched a beach towel around me with one hand and ineffectually rubbed my hair dry with the other.

Leah stood in the open doorway. “Put these on.” She held an armful of clothes to within my easy reach.

I dropped the towel and grabbed the proffered T-shirt. I shook it out and examined the middle finger emblazoned in sequins on its front. “No way. I can’t wear this.”

She sighed. “I’ll be in the kitchen. Put that stuff on and come sit down.” She chuckled a little too gleefully. “I’ve got quite the costume planned for you.”

“What good will it do?” I asked, tugging the shirt over my head. “You said it’s too late.”

“The rules say you must go in, but you can avoid getting chosen.” Something clattered in the other room. “I’m glad I’ll never be a juror.”

“Why not?” I grabbed some clean socks from the pile of clothes I’d lazily plopped on top of the dresser.

“No one wants that duty.”

I didn’t contradict her. “Okay. But why can’t you be on a jury?”

"People on all sides of the law get excused. Lawyers, cops. Judges too."

"But you're not a lawyer anymore."

"They excuse has-beens like me." She paused. "Lots of others get excused too. Seniors. Criminals. Sometimes, people who'd lose wages."

I cat-walked in front of her and she stifled a laugh. I waved my hand up and down my body to showcase the rude T-shirt atop paint-stained oversize sweatpants. I bent over and snapped at the elastic cinching the pants around an ankle. "Whoever thought this was attractive?"

Leah ignored my commentary. "Sit here." She patted the back of a kitchen chair, and I obliged her. She pulled another chair closer and sat down in front of me. "Close your eyes."

Something feathery touched both eyelids, then something greasy coated my lips. She rubbed circles on the apples of each cheek. "This might hurt," was my only warning before she yanked first one and then a second hank of my hair.

"Open your eyes." She leaned back to examine me, her features twitching merrily.

"You're too happy about all of this."

"Go look in the mirror. You look fabulous," she chortled.

I went to the bathroom and yelped at my reflection. "I can't go out like this. I look ridiculous." I wiped at the blue smear over one eye. "This stuff won't come off. What is it?"

"Face paint," she said, holding aloft the jars. "And that's the point. No one will choose you now."

I rubbed the fist-sized disk of flamingo-pink paint on one cheek. "You made me look like a clown. An ugly, unfriendly clown." I grabbed my damp towel from the floor where I'd dropped it and rubbed vigorously. To no avail.

"Leave it alone," she said. "Soap and water will get it off tonight."

I winced. "I can't do this. I'll be the laughingstock."

She stood, hand on one hip. “Heddie, sweetie. Don’t be mad. I’m trying to help.”

Realizing the truth in her words, I packed my backpack for the day.

I inspected each in my collection to find the prettiest, most presentable one for today’s job. Calling it “professional” was a stretch. It was black nylon and very durable, with no distracting logos. But the teal and yellow seaming around its pockets identified its owner—me—as a rube in the world of office towers and cubicles.

I jammed it with my winter kit and my indoor shoes. I certainly did not want to sit around a courtroom all day, steaming hot feet crammed into my otherwise trusty Sorels.

“This outfit will work,” Leah stated. “Lawyers don’t know much about potential jurors, so they rely on how you look.” She waved at my ensemble. “This outfit tells everyone you want to be excused. Of course, everyone recognizes this game, but it’s effective. No one wants someone who’d rather not be a juror.”

When she turned her back, I stuffed a plain black T-shirt and leggings into my kit.

“Now, for your backup plans, in case all the lawyers overlook your appearance.” She laughed again and shook her head. “Unlikely. But still. Backup plan one. Tell the judge your situation.”

“Which part?”

She scowled. “Well, start with your part-time job. You can’t pick up my kids from school if you’re at the courthouse.”

I nodded.

“If that doesn’t work, tell them you’re a recent widow.”

“Almost-widow,” I corrected.

“Close enough. So you don’t have a marriage certificate. Who cares?” She sounded exasperated. “The judge will probably excuse you on that basis alone. No guarantees. But probably.”

“Close only counts in horseshoes,” I muttered,

dismayed to find myself repeating one of Stanley's expressions.

She ignored me. "Your backup plan twice removed? Tell them you're related to Stanley."

"Why would they care?"

You'd think I'd grown a second head. "He's a bailiff at the courthouse."

I'd never asked about the details of his work, although I'd seen him strutting around in his uniform enough times.

"Relatives of courthouse staff don't get exempted outright, but lawyers and probably the judge would prefer someone totally disconnected from the case. And the law."

I stared at her, nodding in apparent agreement while the barest hint of an alternative plan edged into my brain.

CHAPTER 5

First Impressions

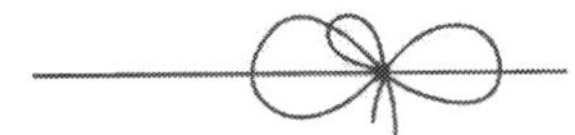

Upon arrival at the courtroom, a grizzled bailiff—not Stanley—took my summons before inspecting me up and down. "I need to look in there," he said, gesturing to my backpack.

I handed it to him, and he plopped it carelessly onto a table. He unzipped the compartment, rifled through its contents, and hauled out my doodle pad with its accompanying zipped baggy of coloured pencils. "What's this? It's not kindergarten. You need to take this seriously."

Who did he think he was, lecturing me? "Doodling helps me remember things. Grounds me," I replied. "Keeps me focused." He remained unpersuaded, but I refused to explain the brain science to this hack.

He pointed to a square box in the bottom corner of my summons. "This is your number. If you're selected, they'll call this number. Memorize it." He sniffed disdainfully before he opened one of the double doors to admit me.

This early bird got to choose a prime seat. The designer of the room's hard oak benches must've favoured hair shirts and self-flagellation. I spurned those and beelined instead to the cushy office chairs along the back wall. Soon enough, I had close company.

During the first couple hours, a man with a fuchsia fauxhawk roosted next to me. When he sat down, I gagged from the stench of his body odour mixed with the distinct overtones of pot. My nose suffered every time he twirled his chair in dizzying circles.

"Looks like we received the same advice," he said, smirking.

I sniffed my armpit to confirm his error. "Not quite."

I ignored him for the rest of his stay, despite our proximity and the many lulls in the selection process. Instead, I people-watched and studied my surroundings. The raised oak panelling on all the walls, with its bevelled edges and mouldings, was too old-fashioned for my taste. Despite my neighbour's olfactory assault, I only mustered food-oriented descriptions for the room's colour palette. Honey, butterscotch, caramel. Nougat. Almond. I should've packed a snack.

Eventually, Fauxhawk's number was called. He pivoted upright immediately and collected his sloughed belongings. The only female bailiff, who stood in the far corner, yelled, "Present." If he hadn't budged, she would have yelled, "Repeat the number," a couple more times until the dozing jury candidate clued in. Someone always responded. Eventually.

As soon as he vacated his seat, another man grabbed it. I expected he was after the comfortable seat rather than my company. He was approximately half my age and dressed normally in black jeans and an untucked white button-up shirt, with a down jacket in my favourite shade of peacock blue slung over his arm. A waft of cedar and cinnamon healed my nostrils.

"Fancy hairdo."

I tittered, pretending he was funny. "You like it?" I batted my eyelashes and used my open palm to bounce my hair and accentuate Leah's ridiculous styling.

He laughed with a rich belly laugh, drawing stares from nearby guards. I warmed to him.

"This was my friend's idea," I admitted.

"You look like a clown, but more Pennywise than Bozo." He studied me almost clinically. "Well, they won't choose you.

Not looking like that."

"I'm having second thoughts." I shared too much with this affable stranger.

"You want to be a juror?" He looked incredulous. "I've talked to nearly everyone here and you're the first I've found."

"Sure. I've got nothing better to do." I felt my face flush.

"You do realize they're selecting for a murder trial?"

"Doesn't scare me." Au contraire, the idea intrigued me. "I've been around my share of dead bodies."

He blinked several times. Like he'd just met a serial killer. He rolled his repurposed office chair away from me, but the close quarters contained his progress.

"My husband."

His mouth opened as he scoped the corners of the room, seeking his escape.

"No, listen. My husband died of cancer." I laughed—cackled, more like—and immediately regretted it. Hug's death wasn't funny. "He wasn't murdered."

The scaredy cat relaxed.

"I tried to prolong his life. Cure him." Why did I explain myself to this man? "I nearly bankrupted both of us in the process."

"This could be the right trial for you after all. This victim also had cancer, but his wife killed him instead of curing him."

"Wow. That's wrong," I admitted. "Why would someone do that?"

"Her Defence lawyers claim he was in unbearable pain, that she ended his suffering."

"What do you think?" I asked, intrigued by his insights.

"Me? I think it was a publicity stunt. They both worked as lobbyists for the new euthanasia laws. He was sick, sure. But his murder brought a lot of attention to their cause." He shoved his hand toward me. "I'm Axel. I'm a journalist."

I shook his hand. "So? I'm a dog trainer."

"Listen. I know too much about this case. If I get called

up there…" He pointed to the front of the room where a bevy of lawyers winnowed the keepers. "I'll work it so they don't choose me. I want to cover this story on my substack."

I made a mental note to figure out what a substack was, but nodded knowingly despite my ignorance.

"If you get chosen, let me interview you?"

"What's in it for me?" I asked.

"Depends on your views about the legislation." He smiled with the sincerity of a scorpion. "This case could make my career."

I didn't even know my views about euthanasia, assisted dying, whatever it was called.

A polite few minutes later, I collected my things and excused myself to go to the loo. I studied my reflection in the bathroom mirror before I squirted soap onto my hands and plied it all over my face. A splash of water and a bit of rubbing fermented a generous lather. I splashed the suds from my face and down the drain, admiring the lavender hue blending from the frothy pink and blue swirls. Residue from the paint still stained my face, so I scrubbed it with gritty commercial-grade paper towels, giving myself a painful facial. When I finished, I felt like I'd sandblasted my skin. I slipped into a stall, where I removed the offensive clothing in favour of the outfit I'd secreted into my backpack. I also loosed my hair from their antenna-like ponytails and finger-combed it into a presentable do.

"That's better," the bailiff said, as he held the door open on my return. "Glad you reconsidered."

I chose a different seat, far from my original associates —one of the empty pews where I could sit by myself.

When they finally got around to calling my number, they had to repeat it twice.

CHAPTER 6

Jury Selected

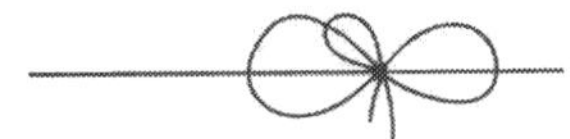

#maidissin

MAID Murder Trial Starts Tuesday

By Axel Spinnewyn

Fourteen jurors, including two alternates, formed a jury today to try Molly Agnes Hopewell for the death earlier this year of her husband, Maxwell Gerald Taylor. Ms. Hopewell, a former lobbyist who helped get Canada's euthanasia laws pushed through, stands accused of murdering her husband when he did not qualify for an assisted death under the Medical Assistance in Dying (MAID) legislation.

Police charged Molly Hopewell with first degree murder.

Peter Parker, the Crown Prosecutor on the case, said, "The evidence is clear. Molly Hopewell murdered her husband, Max Taylor. Justice will prevail. I will see to it."

Ms. Hopewell's Defence attorneys refused to comment.

Comments

Axel Spinnewyn - *I'm the moderator. I'm creating a forum for healthy discussion and debate. Play nice, people. I will delete nasty comments.*

L'eagle - *Surprised this is going to trial. Molly gave Max mercy.*

Olivia - *Message deleted.*

Axel Spinnewyn - *Really, Liv? Already? Get a grip.*

L'eagle - *Parker should recuse himself. He opposed the MAID legislation from the start. This is vengeance, not justice.*

Superhero – *Maybe Parker's doing what he can. Why didn't he charge her with second-degree murder? Would've been much easier to prove.*

Axel Spinnewyn - *Evidence, L'eagle? What are your sources?*

CHAPTER 7

To Me

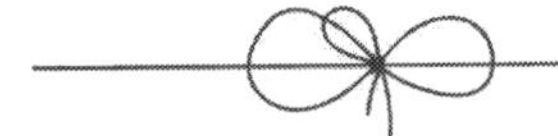

In the late afternoon, I left the courthouse with lots of time to pick up the kids. I texted Leah these glad tidings and walked, picking up Fella from home on route. The kids' school was on 14th, a busy street by anyone's standards; plus, it flanked one of the few steep hills in Calgary. Drivers heading north stripped their brakes to stay below the thirty-klick speed limit. A high chain-link fence circumscribed the yard, and a volunteer monitor kept the students on the safe side of the barrier.

"Fella!" Bea scrambled toward me dressed in a two-piece snowsuit that made her look like a Teletubby.

I unclipped Fella's leash, maintained my grip on his harness, and ignored the signage plastered on the fence posts proclaiming the schoolyard off limits to dogs. Fella loved a job, and any old job would do.

"Say hello to Bea," I said, and released his harness. Once given a task, nothing except a replacement job could distract him. He pounced forward, excited both to be free and to greet one of his favourite people. He stopped in front of her, giving her a full-body wiggle and his own version of a toothy grin. Some people, unfamiliar with goofy dogs who spent too much time with their humans, mistook such an expression for a threat. Understandable mistake. But his eyes remained soft and happy, and his tail flipped back and forth, wagging the dog. Still, a grinning dog was an amusing if not a pretty sight.

Bea slammed herself onto her knees.

"Oomph," I muttered on her behalf. "You'll regret that when you're my age," I prophesied.

She grabbed Fella's head with both hands and, unperturbed by dog slobber, pulled him toward her for a sloppy kiss. He obligingly returned her affection. She wrapped her arms around his neck and Fella's backend pranced, jumping back and forth from his child-tether, delighted in his restraint.

Behind the wigglers, a staid purple Teletubby tromped my way, aloof to her sister's antics. Leah enjoyed matching outfits for her girls, each in their current favourite colour. Emm had decided a week back that seven-year-olds don't play with dogs anymore, a notion I hoped she'd soon outgrow.

Greetings over, we all walked home up 14th. Conversation was difficult over the din of traffic, so I diverted us onto Bagot, a quieter side road.

Bea's endless babble and Emm's morose shuffle were interrupted by a panicked shriek, "No, Pixie, come back! Help!" A well-dressed woman stood on her doorstep only a few feet away, with her front door ajar and her hands full of grocery bags and a briefcase. A leash dangled from her fistful of treasures and swayed under the weight of its empty collar.

A white fluff ball raced past us—a Komondor, about three months old, still little and pre-dreadlocks, hell-bent for 14th and the oblivious man and child walking hand in hand toward us. The puppy reached the couple and snatched an orange mitten dangling from the child's coat sleeve. Several tug-o-war tosses later, the child and pup went sprawling. The puppy bounced to resume her game and vigorously shook her stolen catch.

The woman dropped her bags onto her stoop and tottered after her puppy in impractical high-heeled boots. I paused long enough to assess the problem, the potential calamity, before I reacted. I bent over Fella, unclasped his leash, and bade him, "To me, Fella, to me."

Fella reacted immediately. Bursting into action, he raced down the sidewalk toward the pup. Fella reminded me of a cartoon dog, moving in a blur as each stride propelled him momentarily airborne where his taut body hung parallel to the sidewalk. He reached the pup within seconds. His first attempt to wrangle the gadabout was to block her path, stopping in front of her and staring her down. But this puppy was no sheep and moved to sidestep the blockade, even after Fella crouched in his border collie prowl and buffaloed a convincing snarl.

I kept my eye on Fella while I tried to calm the woman. "My dog will get her," I promised.

Fella proved my point when he picked the pup up like a kitten and transported her back home bodily. The pup maintained her grip on the child's mitten, even as she contorted and squirmed in Fella's grip.

Fella deposited the pup at my feet. I picked her up, smoothed her ruffled fur, and handed her back to her owner.

The father right-ended his child, and the two travelled the remaining distance to join our gathering. "I'll take that," he laughed, and reached for the mitten. But Pixie was not into sharing. I fished a sealed baggy of stinky treats—chopped-up wieners and cubes of cheddar—from my coat pocket and waved it under her nose. Pixie considered my offering a fair exchange and dropped the mitten.

"How did you do that?" the woman exclaimed. "She never does what I want."

"Heddie's smart," Emm said. "She trained Fella. He got ribbons for a fetching contest."

The other child hid her face behind her father's thigh.

"Hi, Tilly," Emm said. She glanced at me and explained, "Tilly's in my class." Emm let go of my hand and stepped toward the cowering child.

The child sniffled a smile. "Uh-huh." The girl's flattened features and upward-slanting eyes revealed she had Down Syndrome. She stared wide-eyed at Fella and the puppy.

"Fella, here," Emm said authoritatively, and I admitted

to feeling an ounce or two of pride. I'd trained both dog and girls well. To Tilly, she said, "Pet him. Fella won't hurt you. He's a good dog."

The child tentatively reached forward, her hand stopping a few inches over Fella's head. Impatient, Fella stretched himself to his full height, so the child's hand cupped the crown of his head, and he shimmied forward to receive his praise. Tilly squealed, this time in delight, and petted Fella's head gleefully.

"Who's a good boy?" Emm said with considerable emotion for a girl who'd recently sworn off dogs. I smiled, glad that phase had been mercifully short-lived.

Our good deed done, we resumed our trek. "Race ya," I said, and we trotted home.

CHAPTER 8

Peace Offerings

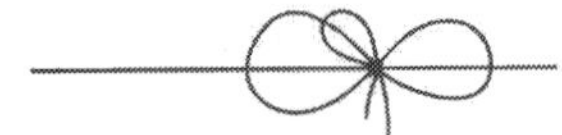

"Heddie, dinnertime," Leah tempted me upstairs. What was I now? Her guest? Roommate? Employee? These days, I felt most like her project—but I just wanted to remain her friend. Her best friend.

I covered the phone microphone with my fingertip. "I'm on a call. Be up in a sec." I returned to my negotiations. "So, we got a deal?"

Sam, the owner of Fella's former doggy daycare, heaved a great sigh. "You drive a hard bargain."

I glommed on to my opportunity. "Thanks, Sam. You're a doll. You still got the better end of our arrangement. Fella's no trouble, especially in trade for me working your Saturday shifts."

She laughed. "See you both on Monday."

After I disconnected the call, I stretched by lacing my fingers together and raising my arms above my head. I leaned backward slightly and groaned at the physical pleasure of the movement. I examined myself in the mirror on the far wall, smoothed my hair and my clothes, and braced myself for what I needed to do next. "Here we go," I said, flopping Fella's ears playfully. I grabbed the sack laden with peace offerings and clomped up the stairs.

"Hi again, children." I peeked around the corner from the kitchen into the dining room and waved at the kids. Leah assigned them the nightly chore of setting the table.

Emm, the tip of her tongue between her lips emphasizing her concentration, carefully folded paper towels and placed one under the knife and spoon at each setting. Bea was less attentive as she lobbed the plates like they were frisbees.

"Oy, careful there, Bumblebee," I said.

The child giggled and took more care with the remaining dishes.

I pivoted toward the kitchen, where I playfully hip-checked Leah away from the stove and used my free hand to waft the aroma of her cooking toward my nose like a culinary smudging. "Smells great. How can I help?" I plopped my grocery bag onto a clear spot on the counter and examined Leah's efforts. "You feeding the entire street?"

Leah ignored my observation and stepped back. "What's this?" She placed her spatula on the side of the pan, angling it so it didn't slide in.

"Just a contribution to dinner," I said.

She hauled out a container of sun-dried olives, my personal favourite, plus samplers of salami and cheeses. And a box of animal crackers for the kids. She smiled her thanks. "Wash some carrots and celery, add these, and put them out? Dinner's almost ready and the children are setting the table."

"I saw that. Fine job too," I hollered loud enough for them to overhear. I grabbed the vegetables from the fridge crisper and the colander from the drying rack and settled into my task.

Leah opened a drawer, pulled out a folded apron, and tossed it to me. "Put this on. I see you ditched your favourite T-shirt." She chuckled too loudly at her little joke.

"Hardy har-har."

Fella wedged himself between me and the counter, his head peeking around my legs as he watched the goings-on in the kitchen.

"Out of the way," I said and pointed to the dining room.

He glided under the table and rested his head on his front paws. He remained vigilant, ready to scrounge any dropped snack. "Shoulda called you 'Hoover.'"

Leah turned back to the stove, where her confection sizzled and snapped over medium heat. "Before you start that, pour us some wine?"

"Bad day?" I asked.

Leah angled herself so she could face me and talk without burning our supper. She sighed deeply and smiled. "Nah. Not bad. Just normal. Busy. I'm helping a young mother right now. Ovarian cancer. Her family's in denial." She still wore her work clothes, a circumspect charcoal suit. Her cream silk blouse, unbuttoned at the neck, revealed her talisman—her mother's single-strand pearl necklace. She'd donned an apron, my gift to her when she switched careers, emblazoned with "I'm a Death Doula because Life's a Miracle."

I reached into the built-in wine rack above the counter and hauled down the first bottle I touched. "Red okay?"

"Perfect. We're having something like chicken cacciatore—really chopped chicken and peppers with tomatoes and spices. Lots of garlic. I don't know if it'll pair or not, and I don't really care."

I eyeballed two eight-ounce glasses. "I have something to tell you, and you won't like it," I said, nudging the olives and the wine toward her. "They picked me. I'm on the jury."

"What? How? I don't understand." She shook her head. "Those costumes always work."

"I know, eh." I kept the rest of the story to myself.

She stirred her pot vigorously. Splashes of tomato sauce flecked the stove and the once-pristine backsplash. "When do you start?"

"I go in on Monday, but the trial starts in earnest after Thanksgiving."

"That soon?" Her stirring picked up speed. "I'll have to make new arrangements for the kids," she said.

"Sorry," I said, and meant it.

"It's not your fault," she soothed. "What trial?"

"I didn't catch the woman's name. The accused." I

repeated the new jargon I was learning. "First degree murder, though. They selected juries for three trials total."

Leah handed me the spatula. "Here. Stir."

I did as she said.

Leah grabbed her phone and flicked, swiped, and thumbed it before looking at me. "Ouch. I think you're on the Hopewell trial. That'll be no good for you." She pulled at her hair, and it fell free from her all-business chignon. "Let me think. I gotta fix this." She paced the few steps across her kitchen. "Maybe they'll cancel the trial."

"Why would they do that?" The rising panic in my voice revealed my true thoughts.

"Usually when the accused accepts a plea." She waved her hand in a little circle, as though lassoing her explanations together. "Sometimes the prosecutor just drops the charges. That'd be the right outcome here anyway." She twisted her pearls around her index finger and pinched the skin on her neck. "The euthanasia case though?" She shook her head. "You really have rotten luck. Nothing's ever easy for you. You won't even talk to me about death, dying. Grief. How will you fare in a roomful of strangers?"

My problem-solving was interrupted when Bea came into the kitchen. "Which country?"

"Huh?" we adults asked in unison.

"Which country? We learned about Japan in geography. They got volcanoes there."

I turned the burner off under the cacciatore and led the questioning. "I still don't understand, kidlet."

"You're studying youth in Asia." She enunciated her syllables like I was deaf. Or dim. "Which country?"

I stifled a laugh, but the joke was on me. How do you explain death to a ten-year old?

Leah saved me. "Oh, honey. Euthanasia is a grown-up word. Do you remember when Thumper got sick? We put him to sleep. Euthanasia is the fancy way of describing that." Leah studied her daughter's face. Her comprehension. Her composure.

Tears filled Bea's eyes and threatened to spill down her cheeks. Their bunny's death had been traumatic for both girls. I hoped Leah didn't see my own trembling chin. I grabbed two tissues from on top of the microwave and handed one to Bea. "Y'all did the kind thing, Bea," I said, my voice cracking from the effort of self-control. "Thumper hurt and wasn't going to get better."

She inclined her head. "I hurt too. I miss him."

"Yes, kidlet. I know." I reached out and smoothed her hair, hoping my touch provided some consolation, before I changed the subject. "Help me put the food out?"

I inspected the spread and noticed something missing. "What'll the kids eat?" I wasn't joking. Animal crackers would only carry them so far, and both kids were in a white food phase. Potatoes worked, preferably French fried. Boxed mac and cheese, but only the kind with white cheese powder. Eggs, sometimes.

On cue, Jake strolled into the kitchen. "They're coming with me. We're going fancy—Mickey D's."

"Really? It's not your night."

I'd already discerned the rhythm of Jake and Leah's complicated lives. They'd always maintained separate addresses—defiantly so—since their wedding day twelve years ago. Many thought the setup strange, ill-advised, but those folks quickly found themselves excused as friends.

"Nope." To the kids, he said, "Do you mind?"

In answer, they ran circles around him, squealing like he was the ringleader at a circus.

To me, he said, "They don't mind."

Leah wiped her wet hands on her apron. "Thanks, Tiger," she said. She grabbed his face with both hands, bent his head closer to her own, and pecked Jake on the lips. "I owe you one."

"Three hours enough time?"

"Should be. Can you get them to do their homework

too?"

"Sure. Hey, shrimps, let's go. Your friend Ronald has Happy Meals with your names on them."

Once the house was quiet again, I addressed the elephant in the room. "Enough time for what?"

Leah regarded me. "Remember? Dee's coming over."

My hackles raised as I smelled an intervention. Why else would Hug's inept lawyer be coming to dinner? "Well, it's your house. You can invite over anyone you please." I recognized my ingratitude.

"Sweetie, I'm only looking out for you."

I sucked in my breath. Only Leah got away with calling me "sweetie." It was also her tell, and she used it to preface all disquieting conversations.

"She's too late to fix her mistake," I said, maintaining my pout. "Hug's dead."

"It wasn't really a mistake," Leah said. "Wrapping up Hugh's affairs was complicated."

I rubbed my temples in anticipation of a long evening. "Well, she left me in a fine mess."

Leah reached out to touch my shoulder, but I pulled away. "It wasn't Dee's fault, but she wants to negotiate a fix."

Ding-dong. Leah was saved by the bell.

"I'll get it." I jogged to the door, careful not to slip on the hardwood. A few years ago, I might've slid intentionally and claimed to polish the floor. My mother would've scolded me. Leah's mom, Charlie, would've joined in.

A woman, mid-forties like me, stood on the doorstep. Her chin-length bob sparkled in the light from the outdoor sconce. I wondered if she used that purple shampoo and added the product to my mental list of things to try.

"I never want to see you again." I offered her a broad smile, even though I wasn't joking.

"Hi, Heddie," she said. "Glad to see you too."

I stood aside to admit her into the foyer, and she handed me a paper bag. I peered into it and spotted two bottles of wine. “You brought goodies.”

Dee removed her winter gear, and we joined Leah. “Look what Dee brought.” I displayed the wine like a hard-earned trophy.

“I’m glad you could make it,” Leah said. “Now we wait for Stanley.”

“Stanley?” I couldn’t believe my ears. “Why is he coming?”

Leah eyed me cautiously. “I told you. Dee wants to negotiate a truce between you two. You both need to be in the same room.”

I crossed my arms. “You’re springing this on me now?”

The women exchanged a look I couldn’t decipher. Leah stepped forward and reached for my forearm, but I twisted from her grasp.

“You can’t gussy this up. It’s an ambush. I don’t want to see him.”

Leah stared at me for a long minute, her expression sour.

“Well, at least don’t let on about my jury duty. I’ll tell him myself when I’m good and ready.” I needed at least one secret up my sleeve.

“Jury duty?” Dee asked.

“I’ll explain later,” Leah responded, and studied a bottle from Dee’s sack. “They really have funny wine names these days.” Her laugh sounded forced.

“I choose solely based on the labels,” Dee replied.

I splashed wine from the already-open bottle into a third glass and handed it to Leah’s guest. “We’ll save your bottles for later.”

Stanley arrived, while I still pouted.

CHAPTER 9

Broken Promises

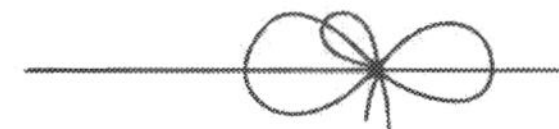

"My obligations go beyond death. My clients die knowing I will do my best to right their wrongs and keep their promises. I'm like the executor of their loose ends." Leah delivered her speech following a surprisingly pleasant meal where she allowed only small talk to accompany each of our courses.

We four sat around the table—plates empty and bellies full. Leah stood to clear the spent dishes. Dee gripped our second wine bottle and asked me with raised eyebrows whether I wanted more. I signalled my definitive answer. Leah had cannily stationed Stanley at the head of the table, and he sat there like a toad, hands folded over his belly, conceit overshadowing his face. Fella lay next to me and used my right foot as his pillow.

"Shall we get down to business?" Dee asked. "We must discuss Hugh's wishes."

"We all know what Hug wanted," I answered.

"Stop calling him that. Hugh hated it," Stanley announced, as though only he knew the truth.

Leah poked her head around the corner from the kitchen. "You're misinformed, Stanley. Sure, Hugh indulged Heddie at the start, but he warmed to her endearment."

Stanley's face reddened but he didn't rebut.

Dee refilled her glass. A drop of red wine slid down the outside of the bottle, its escape slowed by the label. "As you both know, Hugh hired me to update his will." Dee dabbed at the bottle with her napkin and sloppy polka dots bloomed on the white cotton. "We started drafting it about a month before he died. When he was still in the hospital. I don't normally meet people outside my office, but I made an exception for him."

"How?" I asked, still sluggish.

"I don't understand, Heddie. What are you asking?" Dee said.

"I didn't see you."

Leah poked her head around the corner again. "You couldn't be present. For legal reasons."

"But I was always there," I cried.

"Sweetie, not always. Remember when I booted you. Told you to take Fella for a walk? Get some fresh air?"

How could I forget? Hug had been in the hospital sometimes for weeks on end, and I'd hated leaving him there alone. By then, I understood our time together was finite, had a best-by date. But also, bad things happened whenever I left. His doctors possessed an uncanny knack—like hateful harbingers—of sharing bad news when I wasn't around. If the doctors appeared when only Stanley visited, I never got reliable reports. Hug tried to explain things later but messed it up; he was stressed, possessed no background in medicine, and retained little of what doctors said to him.

That's why Leah had subbed for me. When doctors dropped in, she recorded their revelations on her phone and sent me the files afterward. After listening to each attachment, I scurried to the internet for explanations. That's how I learned Hug was dying.

Leah had sent me a file, careful not to editorialize, although she had to know. She'd spelled out his latest complication in her text message—a good thing, as the garbled recording made it impossible to decipher the medicalese. Disseminated intravascular coagulation—DIC for short. The internet, with questionable bedside manner, translated the abbreviation to "death is coming."

"You didn't record Dee's meetings?" I said. What game were they playing?

Dee answered, "I didn't allow it. In troublesome cases, when we expect challenges," she glanced sideways at Stanley, "independent client meetings stand up better in court. No chance for coercion or influence. Everything must be confidential." Dee adopted the same stare Hug's doctors had used when they doled out precise information to answer only unambiguous questions. "We had to keep the meetings private."

I hung my head to avoid anyone's scrutiny. "Do you have the new will? Can they chuck Stanley's version?" I struggled to find the right jargon. "Overruled?"

Dee raised her hand to silence Stanley's maturing outburst. She shook her head, her lips taut. "Hugh tried, but he couldn't manage it."

My renewed hopes evaporated.

"Don't concede yet," Dee said. "He gave me detailed instructions. For one thing, he wanted you to have his house."

"That's not what his will says," Stanley interrupted. "I'm the executor." He glared at me. "He left everything to me." When I said nothing, he continued, "That means I do what I want with his house. In fact, I already started liquidating his assets."

Dee interrupted him. "Stanley, you have an opportunity to do the right thing here. You know what Hugh wanted."

"I already did my bit. I paid her way for the last three months. That's a bigger boost than I ever got, and it's not my fault she frittered it." His jowls jiggled, accentuating his indignation. "Besides, Hugh's house is conditionally sold. They should confirm the sale in a week."

"What? You had no right," I exclaimed.

"I have every right." He drawled his syllables. "You're stuck, Heddie, stuck in place. You need to get unstuck."

Dee shook her head. "Hugh wanted you and Heddie to share his estate."

"Too bad you can't prove it." Stanley crossed his arms and leaned on the rear two legs of his chair. "Besides, I let her keep Hugh's dog." He nodded in Fella's direction. "I won't even require her to buy it from the estate."

"Good of you," I sniffed.

Dee pulled out a sheaf of folded papers from her purse. "Hugh initialled his instructions, although as usual, the notes themselves are in my handwriting. Still, they should be sufficient to establish your brother's wishes." She slid the notes across the table toward my brother-in-law. "My notes would not meet probate standards. But as executor and sole beneficiary of a will you know is outdated, you can voluntarily share your bequest."

"I'll take those to my lawyer." Stanley tried to snatch the papers, but Dee pulled them back.

"I'm happy to send your lawyer pictures," Dee said. "If he wants something more official, I will make him a notarized copy."

Stanley and Dee held a quiet showdown with their eyes, neither budging from their positions. Stanley broke eye contact first. "Don't bother. I already know what he'll say. He'll tell me I have no legal obligation to do whatever you've written on that paper."

Dee carefully refolded the document and secured it back in her purse.

"Besides. How do I really know that's what Hugh wanted?"

"What are you saying, Stanley?" Dee's eyes narrowed and her tone chilled the room. "Are you challenging my credibility?"

"No, no," Stanley stammered. "It's just... Nothing he wrote in those last weeks made any sense. And I've already probated his will. I'm his executor," Stanley reiterated. "I inherit everything."

I threw my hands up, exasperated. "Can't we hire a referee?" I glanced back and forth between the combatants. Somebody had to see the sense in my suggestion.

Leah answered, displaying her loyalty from the safety of her kitchen. "That's a terrific idea."

"I know a mediator who owes me a favour," Dee added. "I'll see if he's available."

"I think it's a terrible idea," Stanley interrupted. "I'm not spending more money to resolve my brother's estate. My lawyer said you all are being..." he hesitated before enunciating, "... dilatory."

Dee's lips curled when she spoke. "Stanley, you may be within your legal rights to do what you're doing. Your moral obligations, though? That's different." She removed her notes again and snapped several pictures with her phone. A ding from Stanley's pocket followed a few more finger swipes. "Now, you have evidence your brother wanted you to proceed differently. Govern yourself accordingly."

"I'll think about it," Stanley retorted, before making a hasty retreat.

After Stanley's bad-mannered departure, we three women remained. "What did he mean about Fella?" I sat cross-legged on the floor and hugged Fella protectively in my lap.

"Technically, Fella belongs to Hugh's estate," Dee explained. "Stanley can decide where he goes."

"Why does he hold all the cards? He won't decide things in my favour. And it's..." I struggled for the phrase, "... a 'conflict of interest.' You know, where someone chooses an option that benefits them."

"I know what 'conflict of interest' means," Dee said, somewhat harshly.

"What happened? Why didn't he update it?" My voice was thick and betrayed my emotions.

"I visited Hugh three times, but he was never

competent enough to execute his will. In hindsight, maybe I should've videoed him giving me his instructions. He was lucid that day. But none of us knew how quickly he'd decline." She grimaced as she considered her missed opportunity that had cost me my future. "I prepared the documents, but he couldn't sign them. On my second and third visits, I waited half the day, using Hugh's room as an impromptu office. I wanted his meds to kick in."

"Hug was lucid right to the end." Despite myself, I cried. I hated crying in public.

Leah had retaken her regular spot at the head of the table. "Heddie, sweetie. You know he wasn't. The hypercalcemia, well, it impaired his judgement."

His blood had been like sludge. "Those drugs helped. The ones they give old ladies with osteoporosis."

"They did," Leah said. "But their benefit didn't last, and I couldn't align Dee's visits with a window of lucidity."

"They could've challenged it anyway," Dee acknowledged. "His doctors would've had to admit his disease frequently impaired his mental capacity. As a stopgap, I advised him how to complete a holographic will. I hoped he'd write it down when he was lucid. Even if I wasn't around."

"His handwriting was always terrible. Illegible." I sad-smiled, remembering. "Did I ever show you his cheat sheets?" I'd saved them, a reminder of his creativity, where Hug had painstakingly crafted incomprehensible half-thoughts into half-sentences.

Leah stared at the floor, so I shifted my position to address only Dee. "Doctors asked the same questions day after day. Things like, who's the prime minister? What's today's lunch? What's today's date? Hug grilled the nurses for the answers and wrote them on a tissue box. When he got stuck, he'd grab a tissue and consult his notes."

"Ha. Clever," Dee said. Leah didn't react. She'd heard this story before.

"So don't tell me he wasn't competent."

"It wasn't his fault," Leah said. "He tried so hard, Heddie. You need to remember that. Focus on that."

"That's why he accepted another blood transfusion," Dee added. "He hoped to buy himself enough time to update his will."

I bawled, but turned my head so Leah's guest didn't see the worst of it. One of them—probably Leah—wedged a tissue into my fist. The platelet transfusions had been tedious affairs, requiring a full day's prep while they thawed the frozen blood, and twelve hours lying in bed connected to an intravenous pole while they transfused. He suffered through four transfusions, hoping the DIC would correct itself. Apparently, sometimes it did. No one mentioned that cancer patients rarely enjoyed such happy results. We'd greeted each transfusion with elation, a false hope of artificial wellness because diseased cells won every scrimmage.

"I wish he'd just given you a ring," Leah said.

I still couldn't express that regret aloud. "He did." I waggled my finger to display his carved silver gift from one of our trips to Vancouver Island.

Her distracted gaze betrayed her assessment. "I mean—I wish you'd gotten married."

"Your marriage would've rendered all this moot." Dee waved at Stanley's now-empty chair. "Marriage nullifies all previous wills. Hugh would've died without a valid will, intestate, but you'd get spousal rights."

I had different reasons to wish we'd gotten married. Then, our relationship would have been clearer—my rights to grieving established, his commitment to me conclusive. "We just didn't get around to it."

The truth is, he did propose. Maybe it was real or maybe not. I'd rarely fantasized about marriage proposals, but when I did, I imagined something like skywriting, or the life-changing question baked into a fortune cookie, or at least a bent knee in a posh restaurant with a pianist playing Pachelbel's single hit.

It hadn't even been a good day. His doctor just told him there was no cure for his disease. No more treatments. He promised to keep Hug comfortable, to manage his pain while we all waited for his body to malfunction.

Hug's latest oncologist had acted like a glib salesman for a pyramid scheme rather than a medical professional conveying the worst news. He'd talked fast, injecting flashed smiles into his sentences. He'd walked briskly and unapologetically into the room where we'd waited for over an hour, not bothering to announce his arrival by knocking first. He bounced into the room with his white coat flapping behind him like a superhero cape and his sidekick-student trailing a foot behind. I disliked him before he opened his mouth.

The doctor's broad smile had revealed straight and probably recently whitened teeth. I think he fake-baked or sprayed-on his tan. His blue eyes sparkled—but not with sincerity. His false bonhomie made me suspicious. I think Hug was, too, as he fluttered his hand in the air until he found mine. He grabbed it and held on tight.

"I am going to say a word that no one wants to hear." The doctor paused for us to consider our options, but his timing was off, leaving us no room to guess. "Palliative." He projected a word that should only be whispered.

Thinking about it now, months later, made me want to slug him hard enough to require dental repairs. At the time, though, something somewhere, some protective instinct, reminded me to take my cue from Hug. I could see he didn't understand. He didn't realize he'd just received a death sentence.

"It's not about the quantity of life. It is about quality." The doctor sold hope to the hopeless, a false hope hiding a bleak present and a hostile future.

Later that night, just after I'd prepared him for bed, Hug had proposed. By then, he'd googled enough information to understand the doctor's meaning. His proposal may have been an act of desperation, some sort of bargain with me or the universe to forego his cherished freedom for some additional life. He'd already given up hope for a better life, and now he'd settle for a longer one.

My response? I'd said, "Yes. Let's. As soon as you get better." But, of course, he never got better.

"I would've shown Stanley more compassion," I announced, changing the subject. "If I'd been in charge of Hug's will, I mean."

"No doubt," Leah said. "We need to find that video Hugh left you."

I had a gazillion pictures, and treasured them all, even the unfocused ones or those with his eyes half-closed or his mouth agape. But video would've captured his movement, his expressions. His voice.

Dee smiled. "What's on it?"

"Don't know, exactly," Leah explained. "He wanted to say his goodbyes. I setup my equipment for him. A tripod to hold his phone and a switch he could press when he was ready to record."

"It's probably on his laptop," I blurted. "Password protected."

"He wrote a password on a sticky for you," Leah said. "I taped it to the fridge after it kept falling off."

"Was the paper orange? That disappeared months ago." I hadn't grasped its meaning, but I didn't remember tossing it. "Doesn't matter anyway. I don't have access to his fridge anymore."

Leah and Dee exchanged looks that excluded me. "I can petition Stanley to snoop around for it," Dee said.

I didn't want to take bets on her success.

CHAPTER 10

Love Me, Love Me Not

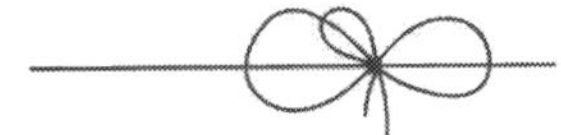

In the middle of the night, I sat in my borrowed kitchen, my laptop atop the scratched table. I was determined to find that video.

But first things first. After Hug died, I had set up notifications to alert me to new messages added to his online condolence book. These reminders were unnecessary, as I compulsively read and reread the messages every day. At the start of the post-Hug era, the alert chattered like spoons in the hands of an accomplished musician, but the staccato slowed as the shockwaves of his death stilled. Most people had moved on. I remained hopeful I could too.

My body served as my clock, marking the time: my back pinched from my poor posture, my butt numbed from the well-worn seat, and my eyes ached from the strain of staring at the screen. I tried to force myself to get up and turn on the overhead lights, but I wouldn't budge.

I studied my reflection on the screen, my loss written in the new creases on my face, like parentheses around my mouth, shaded by the reflected words of kind condolences. I felt some relief—perhaps even so-called 'consolation'—realizing others missed him too. I was not alone. Of course, Stanley missed him, probably as much as I did—although I'd never admit that to him. Certainly Fella missed him too. Whenever I hauled out one of Hug's coats, Fella came over to investigate. Sometimes, he had wagged his tail to greet Hug's memory. Other times, he curled up like a jellybean on a nearby mat.

Leah said I needed to talk about Hug. I needed to reminisce about our happier times, and shove aside all the sick-Hug and dead-Hug memories that clogged my heart like congealed chicken fat. I could not rejoice in our happy times together, not when I failed him, failed us, so badly.

I couldn't bring myself to share our memories, speak them aloud. They were private, mine alone now that he'd died. Who else could appreciate my souvenirs? Like the time we nuzzled on a threadbare loveseat at his rustic Kananaskis cabin, sipping toddies while we admired the sun-dappled poplar leaves. Or when we danced to the latest Sia song, spotlighted by then-Beau's headlights, in the middle of a midnight rainstorm. Or when we lingered over the perfectly dressed coffee he brought me in bed, my legs still tangled in the sheets after an absent-minded morning romp. I wished I'd savoured our happy moments. Shoulda coulda woulda.

One message read, "I miss you every day." Becky had signed it. I knew only one Becky—Stanley's Becky. I assumed she'd signed the book to put her emotions on display. What did she know about missing him? I didn't think about Hug once a day, or once an hour, but virtually every waking moment, and many dreaming moments too. His absence was like a phantom limb, my ghost heart always present and breaking.

"Goddamn shit for brains." I pounded the table, and Fella jumped to investigate my commotion. I moderated myself, waiting to hear if I'd disturbed the house's occupants. I heard no creaks or groans from the wide plank floorboards or insistent demands for a contribution to the swear jar.

I read and reread messages like, "Heddie, our deepest condolences. We just heard of Hugh's passing and our hearts go out to you. Call us. Love, Jen and Paul." Or, "Heddie, words cannot express the depth of our sorrow at Hugh's passing. Please know our thoughts and prayers are with you. Love, Gord and Ted."

But one message rankled. "See you later Gator. I already miss your laughter and wise ways." It was signed "WD." I came back to it again and again, doubt blinding me to all common sense. Its secrecy—the implied intimacy—grabbed my guts and twisted. Who was this WD? Why hadn't she signed her name? I just knew it was a "she". Even his closest friends, those entwined in his life, signed with their actual names.

I studied the message now through the filter of recent revelations. Was WD in the will? Had Hug loved me at all? I hated mistrusting him. His condolence book contained over 100 messages. Dozens addressed me directly. But reassurance from these acquaintances was no substitute for any heartening from Hug himself.

"How dare she?" I slammed the screen down on my laptop as an exclamation point to my anger. Regret blanketed me. I tentatively reopened the computer and found no damage. Relief that my tantrum had left no long-lasting effects gave way to chagrin at my rashness. I resolved, once again—story of my life—to do better.

I felt ugly. And unloved. Unlovable. Telling myself to shut up didn't help. Had I lived a lie? The irrational part of my brain gained a stranglehold. Hug couldn't even defend himself, declare his innocence of alleged crimes. Would I have believed him?

I needed a balance sheet to calculate our love, catalogue my proof. Some rummaging in the children's corner of the suite unearthed blank paper and crayons for my brainstormed list, evidence for and against. I labelled it, "Love me, Love Me Not," and decorated it with daisies, each with an odd number of petals.

The most obvious proof? He told me so. Neither of us had spoken the magic words during the healthy-Hug years of our relationship. "I love you" had gotten muddled with our middle-aged baggage of too many hurts, insults, disappointments. I hadn't said the words aloud because I didn't want to chase him away. He was a catch, and I was not. I feared, if I said too much too soon, he'd vanish. His explanations also sounded like excuses.

He spoke the words first. He made up for years of neglect in his last months, punctuating every conversation with "I love you." His words were a healing salve, and I hoped he'd intended that.

So what about this WD? Was she as close to him as her message suggested? Pretended. An old girlfriend? Had she visited him after he got sick? I'd been by his side almost the entire time, like we'd Velcroed ourselves together. Near the end, in his weakened condition, he hadn't the strength or stamina to admit his own guests. So if she hung around, I'd probably met her.

In the "for" column, I jotted "every holiday weekend times six years." Also, I'd met his family—well, his surviving family. Both his parents, like mine, had died long before I arrived on the scene. I saw photos of adorable Hug and almost-cute Stanley when they were boys. Hug had photos of me, of us, on his fridge framed by a heart magnet. He had a different photo, one with us and Fella, on his file cabinet at work.

This WD had to be sick, twisted, with a warped sense of right and wrong. I'd heard of diseases where people connected themselves to strangers' troubles. Perhaps she was one of those poor, sad folks with no meaning in their own lives, so she'd borrowed my sorrows. Anonymous and online was a terrible combination, too often amplifying the voices of the bitter and the messed up while muting the balanced and circumspect.

I tapped at the keyboard again and brightened when a fledgling idea hatched in my head. I displayed none of my usual fine judgement and trust for my deceased beloved when I hacked his email account.

I obviously knew his email address, so it wasn't difficult to find the webmail browser and enter a username: HFields. Simple. The trouble was his password. Movies made it look easy to hack an email account with a girlfriend's or pet's names. I tried my name in its iterations. Fella's too. With no luck. After a few failed attempts, a button labelled "Hint?" appeared on the screen. Eagerly, I clicked it, and chuckled in surprise when I read "hyphenated Honda". I knew that answer. I typed "Beau-Dimples", and just like that, broke into his account. And, just like that, I wished I hadn't.

I went through three months of routine emails, spam, and phishing before I spotted it. The subject line read, "MAID Appointment", and the email was dated six days before he died. The sender, some doctor I'd never met, wrote, "I confirm the postponement of our MAID appointment. Please contact me to reschedule the procedure for a more suitable time." I typed the doctor's name and MAID in the google search box and discovered he was one of Calgary's medical professionals willing to provide a patient with an assisted death.

I had no idea how to interpret this email. I checked Hug's sent folder for clues, and that's when I found the other email. He'd addressed the last email he ever wrote, five days before he died, to "Wendy Darling." The message was brief: "I need to see you. Time has run out." I couldn't find any reply. The moniker on her Gmail address, wdd-calgary, was no help.

I lost it. Completely overreacted. Lots of people gave nicknames to their friends and acquaintances. But Hug named everything. I did, too, and it was that bit of whimsy that first attracted me to him. My system was random, whatever caught my fancy: Barney for my old purple Ford, Abacus for the state-of-the-art tablet Hug gave me last Christmas. His system was more elaborate, one I'd only pieced together through observation. He used the first letter of an item's name to limit the range of options. Working or macho items got hard-sounding men's names—like Sarge for his brother's Suburban or Arnold for his own Aerostar. Prettier items got women's names—like Kiki for his Killarney house or Sonia for his stereo.

In his later years—perhaps an early warning sign of the cancer that would kill him—Hug had suffered from what someone dubbed tip-of-the-tongue syndrome. He remembered people's faces and weird details about them, especially what kind of car they drove or their favourite Tim Horton's beverage, but he could not remember people's names. He'd get close. Mary for Marilyn. Dave for Devon. Wilson for Willis. In the presence of his faltering memory, Hug replaced names with exuberant greetings using generic nicknames. His favourite for men was Sport. His favourite for women was Boss.

Darling, though? That's not generic. Hug never called me Darling. Or Dear. Or Love. He chafed at such tags and would've gagged, coughed, fake-barfed at such a stodgy choice.

Convinced I'd found a rival, I clicked "forward," pasted her address into the "to" box, blind-copied myself, and wrote her from his account. "Who the hell are you? And why did my late husband call you darling?"

Fella stirred himself from my new bed. He stretched before coming over to rest his head on my lap. I stroked his ears and wondered how long I'd have to wait for a reply.

I looked at my unfinished list of pro's and con's. I added "he lied" and "affair" to the con side, before I crumpled the sheet and tossed it into the recycling bin. I'd given up everything to help Hug, and none of that mattered. Because, truth be told, in the end, Hug had plain given up. Conceded. Succumbed. How could I forgive him for that?

——— ○ ○ ○ ———

I couldn't sleep, so I tiptoed upstairs and waited for Leah on her couch. That seemed a better option than waking her in the middle of the night for answers.

"Did you know?" I ambushed her as she walked, bleary-eyed, from her bedroom.

"Know what?"

"About Hug's MAID application."

"I'll be right back," she said before she stepped into the bathroom and closed the door.

When I heard the shower running, I stood to make coffee. I sat at her kitchen table, coffee in hand, by the time she emerged, hair damp, and wearing a plush housecoat.

"Did you help him with it?" My leg jiggled, and I couldn't stop it.

"He applied on his own." She met my eyes. "I didn't even witness it."

"Why didn't you tell me?"

"I thought you knew. Stanley did too." Leah poured herself a coffee before she sank onto the chair opposite me.

"Well, I didn't, and you all should've talked to me about it." My hand shook, so I set my cup onto the table.

"Hugh should've. It was his decision, and so he needed to discuss it with you." She sipped her coffee gingerly before blowing on it to cool it. "One good thing has come out of all this. You're not in denial anymore. You've definitely progressed to the anger stage of grief."

I huffed, unintentionally confirming her assessment. "How many stages are there?"

"Five. You cycled through denial and depression right after Hugh's death. Now, anger," she pointed at me with her hand. "Last is bargaining and acceptance." She stood and moved to the fridge. "Will you help me make breakfast?"

I hesitated at her invitation. "Nope," I decided. "Fella needs his walk." I tapped my thigh to beckon my dog and slammed the front door on my way out.

CHAPTER 11

Do-Over

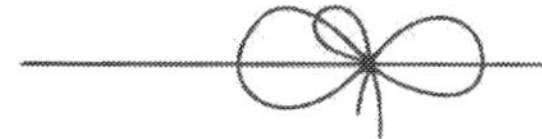

"I still can't believe my costume failed." A fake smile crimped Leah's face.

Leah reluctantly agreed to drive me to the courthouse after I'd dropped Fella off at his daycare. He had enjoyed our trek, snuffling through the freshly fallen snow, even as the unshovelled sidewalks threatened my punctuality and my do-over.

"Never failed me before." Leah's tone suggested everything was fine, but her fists clenched the steering wheel precisely at ten and two and I knew irritation always improved her driving. I guessed she hadn't forgiven me either. "The judge should've let you off."

I smiled. "Lots of people got similar advice. The room was full of rude T-shirts. Obscene. Ripped. Filthy." The presence of children restrained more colourful descriptions. "They didn't fool anybody, and certainly not the judge."

"He's probably seen it all," she admitted. "Do you have a favourite?"

"Yes," I chuckled. "One guy had bright pink hair glued like a shark's fin."

She laughed. "Men's costumes are generally less elaborate. Most often, they just don't shower." She held up her hand and enumerated her points by bouncing her thumb against each of her fingertips, and I wished she'd put both hands back on the wheel. "Or they put on too much aftershave.

One way or the other, they reek. Unshaven. Greasy hair, ripped dirty clothes, no deodorant, the whole nine yards."

"The room was rancid with someone's BO."

"Probably lots of 'someones.' Cleaning up afterward is the staff's least favourite job." She twisted toward me while turning the steering wheel and narrowly missed sideswiping a line of parked cars. "What about Stanley? You know you're going to run into him."

"I haven't seen him yet. But I like the idea of him on clean-up duty." I grinned so hard my jaw ached. "I think the guy with the fancy hairdo showed up stoned."

"That's unwise. He could've been fined. Even spent the night in jail."

"I think it was only pot." I wasn't defending the guy, but he'd seemed decent enough, even if too chatty. "The room was almost empty by the time I got called. They selected jurors for three trials, and mine was last."

Leah checked over her shoulder before switching lanes, and I wondered how I'd ticked her off again.

"You taking a different route?" I asked.

"I don't follow," she said.

"You missed their school," I said, ever helpful.

"It's a PA day, remember? I arranged a field trip." She frowned at me, but I didn't take her bait.

A flickering blue glow washing across the children's faces explained their uncharacteristic silence. A thin white cord leashed one of each of their ears to their tablet.

Leah drove north on 14th. I never took 14th, preferring to zigzag my way through the one-way streets of the quieter Beltline.

"I think that's beet juice," I said, practising my small talk to fill the silence. I pointed to the brown smear dirtying the crystalline snow on the road. "It's supposed to be a greener alternative to rock salt." Learning random bits of trivia usually improved her mood. Mine too. Not today.

The plows had already passed this way, leaving hillocks

of dirty sludge piled down the road like misaligned medians. The painted lines identifying the four lanes remained obscured, making them easier to ignore. Drivers acted out their frustrations using a rude form of charades against a soundtrack of horns. The driver of a battleship grey Mercedes gave us the finger.

"How rude." I pointed out the offender next to us in the slow lane.

Leah pulled her lips back in an incomplete smile. "It'll happen." She paused a long while and I let the silence hang. "Sweetie…"

I held my breath and braced myself for another lecture.

"Did you use any of our backup plans?"

Salt stains widened on my boots. I needed to clean them. And coat them in protector goo. Did beet juice stain? "I didn't really have a chance," I admitted this half-truth.

"I should've gone with my gut," she said. "Maybe if you'd had another part-time job. Maybe something at Jake's clinic? Better yet, something in Dee's law firm. I bet they would've excused you then."

I shook my head, no. "One of my fellow jurors is a legal secretary." She had sat on the other side of me at the selection, opposite Fauxhawk. I never caught her name but had learned many other vital statistics. Like, she hated her job and wanted to retire. She was also widowed, and we'd gushed over all we shared.

Leah flicked on her turn signal before switching lanes.

"The judge didn't allow questions about people's jobs," I added. "One fellow mentioned something, and the Crown guy pounced to ask him more. But the judge shut it down." I tried to recall other observations she might find interesting. "Seniors fill up my jury."

"Interesting. Seniors get to choose whether they get exempted."

"Both lawyers used challenges to boot candidates. Some folks seemed relieved when dismissed. Others looked miffed."

"I get that," Leah said.

"The judge claimed these decisions weren't personal. Sometimes it felt personal, though." The judge had excused one fellow after he answered their questions in thickly accented English. He claimed to understand the judge perfectly. The judge had responded, "Your fellow jurors need to understand you too," before dismissing him. That seemed personal.

"There's still a chance they'll cancel your trial." Leah flicked her signal on and slipped into the drop-off zone in front of the science centre. "Kidlets, we're here," she announced, loud enough to be heard over their movie.

"I'll run them in," I said, unclipping my seatbelt.

"Stay put. I'll be back in a minute." Leah hustled the kids out of the car and through the front door.

When she returned, her mood had lifted. Leah twisted in her seat to face me. "Well, if you're stuck doing this, let me look at you."

I'd considered my outfit carefully, and hoped it said: just an ordinary person here, a little down on her luck but doing her best and capable of hearing all the evidence—despite Leah's beliefs—and rendering a just verdict. I'd ironed my khakis and polished the dark brown tie-up brogues I'd retrieved from the depths of one of my crates. One of Hug's hand-me-downs, a white button-down shirt, was too big even though I'd gained weight since he died. I'd topped it with a charcoal vest from some long-forgotten suit. To finish my business-casual ensemble, I'd rolled up the sleeves tidily, tucked the shirttails into my pants, and sported a brown pleather belt. I'd even tamed my hair into a so-called messy bun. And used packing tape to pull Fella's hair off my cloth coat, which I unzipped now and opened for Leah's inspection.

She applied her keen fashion sense to my attire. Herself, she could've walked right out of a Holt Renfrew catalogue. Only we two knew most of her clothes came from

Winners, a few choice consignment shops, with an occasional lucky find from Value Village.

"You kind of look like Annie Hall," she said.

"Is that a compliment?"

She smiled, somewhat patronizingly. "Can you reach my satchel?"

I twisted in my seat and stretched far enough to grab her bag. "Oof. What's in here?" I half-dragged, half-lifted it between the seats and plopped it into her lap.

"Treasures." She rummaged in it until she found a jewel-toned scarf. "Wear this today."

I took it from her and wrapped it around my neck.

"No." She reached over, and after several complicated moves, like she cast a spell, she patted a tidy knot flat on my throat. "That's better."

"Why are you helping me?" I asked.

"Consider it armour in case you meet Stanley. It costs more retail than he earns in a week."

"Ouch. Take it back," I said, grasping one end of the scarf to unravel her knot. "You know me. I'll dip it in curry or something."

She touched my hands firmly, stilling them. "Take it. I didn't pay full price."

A horn sounded behind us, reminding Leah that other parents also had children to drop off. She jockeyed the car a few feet forward, closing the gap between us and our release back into the wilds of Calgary streets. "Did any of the other costumes work?"

This time, I kept up. "Yes. Most of them got excused." All except Fauxhawk. His number had been called about twenty minutes before mine, and out of costume, he hadn't recognized me when I joined his ranks.

Leah switched lanes unexpectedly and not one of the neighbouring cars reacted. The time on the dash clock read 8:17. I could've walked faster.

"The judge was impatient by the end," I said. "Lots of

people wanted out of it. Some people didn't get paid from their jobs. He let them off."

"That's legit. A boss can't fire you, but they don't have to pay you. Fifty bucks a day does not cover lost wages."

I turned away, ashamed. I was sick of being perpetually broke and wanted the stipend. "Lots of people had plane tickets and he let them go too."

"You had a generous judge. It's risky, but if people are loaded and really want out of service, buying a plane ticket for a few days after selection can work."

"I think some explanations were valid."

"Yes." Her agreement sounded half-hearted. "You know, there's still hope. When you go in, speak to the assigned bailiff. Explain your situation. The judge might listen. Okay?" Hope gilded her face.

"Yes." I wasn't lying, not exactly. More placating.

Leah always knew when I hedged. "Promise? Pinky swear?"

I collected my thoughts. "No. Actually, I want to be a juror."

Leah pursed her lips. "The media's all over this case. They'll start doing background checks on the jurors. Start trying to predict how you'll all lean." She paused. "There's one journalist—"

I stomped my foot, an ineffective gesture within the confines of the car. "Stop." I cut her off. "I don't want to hear anything more about it. Nothing."

Leah opened her mouth to continue.

"That's enough," I said. "Maybe this will help me process my feelings," I said, mirroring her use of the phrase.

Her withering look asserted that she knew best. "Doubt it. You've got enough of your own troubles, and don't need to borrow someone else's."

"Shouldn't I be the judge of that?"

"Okey dokey," Leah muttered, mostly to herself. "We still have the slight problem of after-school care for my girls."

She glanced at me, then relented. "I'll arrange something with Jake. The trial probably won't last longer than a month."

I also caved and admitted a fuller truth. "I probably won't get to do this anyway, so you're fretting about nothing."

"What do you mean?"

"I'm number thirteen, just the spare. I gotta show up today, but they'll probably send me home once everyone else clocks in." A considerate friend would've led with this detail.

Leah breathed out a heavy sigh. "Yes, they rarely need the alternates. This entire case is a mess. The assisted dying law is changing all the time, but Max Taylor's situation didn't fit anywhere."

"I know you think I'm nuts, but I hope I get it. I hope somebody else, one of the first twelve, gets excused. Then they'll have to choose me." Leah protested, but I shook my head. "Truth is, I'm bored and I'm curious. Probably read too much *Nancy Drew* as a kid."

Leah pulled the car into a loading zone cut-out and put on her four-way emergency flashers.

"It'll get me out of my own head for a while."

"So be it." Leah smiled. "If you stay on, we can do lunch more often. Crabby's Diner?"

"I hope to see you there," I admitted, even to myself.

I left the car, shutting rather than slamming the door, and hoisted my backpack onto one shoulder. Even its weight didn't subdue the bounce in my step. "I hope I don't get sent home." I spoke the words aloud, glancing around to see if anyone overheard me. They'd probably think I'm crazy. Or, maybe, because I dressed so business-like, that I yakked into earbuds. I picked my way along the sidewalk, jumping hopscotch between the sanded and salted patches to avoid the ice. I turned to wave goodbye to Leah, but she'd already slipped back into traffic. I waved anyway, just in case she glanced back in her rearview mirror.

CHAPTER 12

Security

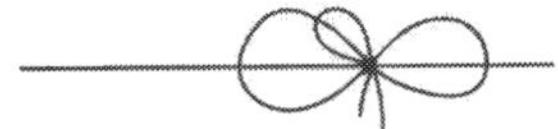

I moved toward the roundabout entrance of the new courthouse. As I walked past him, aiming to cover the few remaining steps to the entrance, the cop's face transformed from amused, charmed, to severe. He held up his arm like a toll gate. "This area is off limits. You need to stay in front of those pylons." His voice was disappointingly shrill. I scanned the area where he pointed and saw a ring of retractable cylinders serving as fortifications—but against tanks, not pedestrians. On foot, I could easily skirt the barricade. When I hesitated, the cop said, "Please move to the other side of the pylons."

I gestured to the crowd. "I'm not one of them. Look, I need to be in there." I didn't mention I was late.

"What capacity?" he said, checking out my attire. I think he sniffed at me in disdain, but then again, maybe the chilly air gave him a nasal drip.

I drew myself up to my full height but was still shorter than my interrogator. "I'm a juror."

"Got your summons?" he asked as if I'd uttered some magic word.

I swung my backpack to the front. "In here."

We stood close enough for me to count his nose hairs. "Show it to security. Please use the centre door."

Inside the building, courthouse security resembled the airport's setup. Three lines snaked through the airy foyer toward three pairs of glass doors all propped open with rubber stoppers. A sign at each entrance itemized what could and couldn't remain in bags. I headed toward a fourth shorter line that moved faster. When I got to the front of the queue, a guard said, "Credentials, please."

"What credentials?"

"Are you security-cleared court personnel?" he asked, already uninterested in my answer.

"No."

"Please use one of the other three lines," he said. When I didn't shuffle off immediately, he beckoned over my shoulder. "Next."

I got the message.

I moved over to the next nearest line, calculating its endpoint to avoid butting. Guards stood next to each set of doors and reminded us to remove all electronics from our bags.

After the heads-up from the cop outside, I now wore my backpack like a papoose. I unzipped the primary pocket where I normally stashed my tablet and phone. A commotion two lines over added to the existing clamour of everyday chatter. Voices raised, putrid with expletives. Glass, stone, and chrome made attractive building materials but weren't renowned for their sound-dampening qualities.

Then, I heard him. "Sir, please leave." Stanley staffed the coffin-like x-ray machine and focused on the brawny bald man next to him.

"You're not worried about this thing." Baldy sounded like a Jedi beguiling his opponent as he held aloft an intimidating knife with an impressive, serrated edge. "You gotta locker somewhere to stash it?"

"No. If I take it, you won't get it back." Stanley sounded calm, firm. In control.

After more blue air, Baldy left in a huff, complaining he'd be late and vowing to talk to management.

I arrived at the front of my line.

"Hello, miss." The elderly security guard just made my day. I couldn't remember the last time I'd been called "miss."

I pulled out my devices and placed them in one scratched plastic bin and then shoved my backpack and coat into a second. The trays moved toward their inspection slowly on the conveyor. I struggled to open the latch on my Fitbit to remove it for screening too.

"No need," the guard said. "Just raise your hands above your head when you walk through the machine." He indicated the open tunnel of the metal detector and raised his own hands up to demonstrate his instructions.

I read his name tag, clipped at an angle and centred over his shirt buttons. Otherwise, his uniform was exactly what I expected—clean and ironed, with creases on his pant legs and even his shirt sleeves. "Thanks, Roy," I said, smiling at the man. "Who're all these people?" I asked, mostly to be chatty.

"MAID protesters." Roy looked at me kindly, like I was a bumpkin. "Medical Assistance in Dying?" He held out his hand, palm-up. "MAID. You know, euthanasia."

"I call it 'assisted dying.'"

I looked out the wall of glass toward the milling crowd. Some of their members were stomping their feet. I recognized the bullish behaviour as an effort to keep warm rather than any threat or warning. Someone close-by started a chant, "Justice for Max." A few more voices repeated it, but the slogan wasn't pithy enough to catch on.

The guard behind this line's x-ray machine squinted at the image, disquiet darkening his features. "Roy, look at this."

Roy studied the display and did his own share of squinting. To me, knowing the answer full well, Roy asked, "This yours?"

I nodded.

"What's in it? Can I look?"

"Sure," I said, realizing I had no choice.

Roy motioned for me to join him at a long table he'd cleared of everything except my backpack. I walked through the metal detector, hands in the air like a hold-up, and joined him.

Roy examined the x-ray on the display again before unzipping my pack's main pocket. He hauled out my cleats. "What are these?" he asked.

Given this scrutiny, I was relieved I hadn't brought my work pack, preferring not to explain gnawed bones or meat treats to anyone outside the dog world. "Cleats," I said.

"Like, for golf?" He looked outside in disbelief, presumably at the inclement day.

"No. Like grips. Crampons. So, I can walk on ice."

His understanding seemed mixed with a bit of approval. "And this?" He pulled out a tangle of metal poles, loops, and bungees.

"Walking poles," I said. "Also for walking on ice."

He smiled kindly. "We're okay here, Joe," he assured the x-ray technician.

While I restowed my belongings, I asked, "Can you give me directions?"

"Where are you headed?"

"I'm supposed to be in court today."

A troubled expression crossed his face as he considered whether he'd misjudged me.

"I'm a juror," I added.

His shoulders relaxed. "What case?" Roy asked.

"Hopewell. Rex versus Hopewell."

"Did you know 'rex' is Latin for 'king'?"

I nodded. Did he know "euthanasia" was ancient Greek for "good death"?

"It was a big to-do when Queen Elizabeth died and we switched everything over to reference King Charles."

I smiled and added his trivia to my mental repertoire. Hug believed small talk was how strangers found topics in common for discussion. It seemed Roy and I shared a penchant for trivia. And maybe etymologies.

I thrust my juror's instructions toward him, the crumpled sheet now more trash than treasure. He removed it from my hand and smoothed the paper flat. "You're late," he said. He unclipped an old-style walkie-talkie, the size of a brick and probably as heavy, from the belt cinching his pants around his ample waist. "I'll call Clemence. She's your jury guard. She'll need to escort you."

"I'm really just a spare," I said. "Number thirteen."

"You're still late." He depressed the button on his walkie-talkie. "Roy to Clemence." He pronounced her name "Clay-mints." I thought of the unwrapped gritty, gooey glob of candies at the bottom of my grandma's purse.

The reception was staticky. After a moment or two, a woman with a thick French-Canadian accent responded, "Clemence here." She pronounced her own name correctly.

Roy showed dexterity, pressing the button when he needed to speak, and releasing it to listen. All conversations could benefit from this sequencing, a sharing caused by the limitations of this gear. "I got one of your jurors here. She needs an escort." He added, "Please." He let the button go, and then blushed before depressing it again, and mumbled, "Over."

"What's the name? Over." The static sounded like a Rice Krispies ad.

At Roy's raised eyebrows, I leaned toward the walkie-talkie. He pressed the button and I announced, "Heddie Wright." Remembering who I dealt with, I corrected, "I'll be listed as Henry-Etta." Then, because it was fun, I added, "Over." Our relay was flawless.

"She's on my list, but I'm tied up here. Can you bring her up? Over."

"On our way," Roy said. "Over."

"You know our new room assignment? Over."

"Yes. Over." To me, he said, "Miss, please follow me."

"We moved?" I asked.

"You're now in one of the bulletproof rooms."

"Why?" I asked too shrilly.

"Because of them," Roy said, pointing at the protesters.

We'd almost made it out of the lobby when I heard fast

squeaking steps behind me. "Heddie, Heddie." I recognized the phlegmy wheezing of my not-brother-in-law.

I turned around so he could catch up. "Oh. Hi, Stan."

"Stanley," he corrected, emphasizing the second syllable.

I smirked, pleased I'd pushed his buttons. "Fancy seeing you here."

"You know each other?" observant Roy asked.

"Yes—" I started to explain our connection, but Stanley interrupted.

"We go way back," he said, waving his hand dismissively. "I heard you on the walkie." He waved his device. "Whatcha doing here?" he asked. A hometown tone camouflaged his poisonous nature.

None of your beeswax. "Oh, I have some business here. Roy is taking me to my appointment." I cupped my hand lightly in the crook of Roy's elbow.

"You stalking me?"

I gawked at him. "Stalking? No."

Roy chortled. "You got some imagination, Stanley."

"Don't butt in, Roy. You do not know what's going on here."

Roy frowned but turned away, affording us some imaginary privacy.

"You shouldn't come to my workplace," Stanley said.

"I have a right to be here."

"Okay, then. What are you doing here?" He put his hands on his hips and drummed his fingers.

"Don't worry. I'm not here to fight you."

"I know how courts work, Heddie." He waved his left hand up and down his body to show-and-tell his uniform. "I do work here."

As a juror for a day, my window for tormenting Stanley was small. I was considering some witty rejoinder when Roy raised his hand to silence us both. "I'm escorting her upstairs and we're late. You guys catch up later."

On cue, one elevator door dinged open, and Roy and I stepped into it. I gave Stanley a half-smile and a quick little wave as he stared open-mouthed at our departure.

CHAPTER 13

Lucky Thirteen

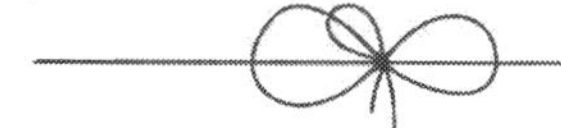

Roy happily passed me off like a baton to Clemence, who ushered me to the jury room.

"My name is Clemence."

I'd deduced that.

Clemence reached out, wooden and unceremonious, to shake my hand. She was an elfin woman with grey hair worn in a no-nonsense spiky do. Even in my sensible boots, I stood at least six inches taller. "I'm the lead guard for the trial, although I have some back-ups."

I scuttled behind her, barely able to keep up as she strode down seemingly endless hallways. A ring of keys clipped with a carabiner through her belt jangled at every step, making her sound like a high-prancing horse festooned for parade day. I was grateful she guided me. My crumpled instructions were indecipherable, describing labyrinthine twists and dead-ends, hidden doorbells and warrens of hallways. And they were obsolete. The new jury room behind the bulletproof courtroom was on the twentieth floor, behind two locked doors and down a bleak corridor on the windowless backside of the building.

In the pictures I'd googled to prepare for this day, the new courthouse looked luxurious, even grand, with its marble entries, plush carpets, oak panelling, gleaming glass. It presented a mosaic of high-tech modernity alongside stable tradition. But they reserved such palatial aesthetics for the public view. The hidden areas, I discovered, were utilitarian —and to quote Hug, "fugly." The final corridor leading to the jury room was one such secreted space. Concrete walls were painted stark white but bore scuffs at shin height from carelessly wielded mop buckets and handcarts. A well-worn path down the middle of the steel grey linoleum—the kind from a roll rather than stick-on tiles—left a dulled trail flanked by shinier shoulders. Fluorescent lights hung directly from the ceiling, drooping wires exposed among the rest of the building's guts.

I must've sighed, because Clemence asked, "You okay?"

"Yes, thanks." I didn't feel the cheer I forced into my tone.

"You were late, so we rush."

Two narrow tables, the sort with a fake-wood top and sturdy metal legs, flanked the entrance to the room like squat sentries. A dog-eared copy of a Louise Penny mystery lay atop the far one, spread open and face down like a passed out drunk. I leaned over to skim the back cover. I hadn't read this one.

A tattered cardboard box sat on top of the nearest surface. One of the box's corners aligned precisely with the edges of the table. Inside the box were several plastic envelopes tied with cords wrapped around oversized buttons to seal them closed. Each sported a worn label in the top-left corner where someone had printed numbers using a black sharpie. Someone, probably Clemence, had arranged the envelopes in order, one through twelve. No thirteen.

Clemence reached around me, exaggerating her movements so she didn't invade my personal space, and pulled a clipboard from the front of the box. She wrapped a blank front page over the top, covering the metal clip and revealing a short, typed list on the page beneath. When I leaned over to scan the list, she hugged the works closer to her chest to prevent my snooping.

"What's your name again?" A whiff of stale cigarettes invaded my nostrils. Clemence waited for my answer, pencilled eyebrows raised.

"Heddie Wright."

She ran her finger down the list and then back up again, double-checking her facts. "I see a Henry-Etta Wright."

"That's me. No one calls me that, though. And lives to tell the tale." I grinned at her, aiming to be playful, cheeky. Perhaps teasing could scratch her prickly veneer.

She lifted the corners of her mouth in an imitation smile. "I cannot change the list." She replaced the cover sheet, smoothing it in place. "It is the official juror roster. Names on it are from the electoral rolls and tax records. They use your official name, your legal name." She smiled more sincerely this time. "But I will try to remember and use your preference. Mostly, I will just call you Number Thirteen. Thirteen for short." She pronounced "th" like a "t," so it came out "tirteen." Even her accented English was better than my French.

"Now, please remove all your electronics, and I mean everything. Recording devices too. We permit none of these items in the jury room." She glared at me as if staring could uncover stashed secrets. "You're a spare, so you don't have an envelope." She pointed to the spot next to the box. "Put your belongings here. They are safe with me." I recognized this was a well-practised recitation.

"What about breaks and things?" I didn't hide the rising alarm in my voice. I couldn't remember the last time I'd been separated from my phone. Thumbing my phone was my comfort in social and other difficult situations, and she was about to thrust me into a roomful of strangers. Worse? There'd be no compulsive checking for Wendy's reply. Or consoling myself with Hug's online tribute book.

"I expect you won't be here that long. You will probably be excused."

I sighed in agreement. I removed my Fitbit and tried to hand it to her. She tapped her finger on the open spot on the table and I placed it there instead. I rummaged through my backpack and set my tablet and phone next to my watch.

She unclipped her collection of keys, which now reminded me of a jailer's ring, and flipped through each key with a practised rhythm until she found the right one to unlock the door.

Clemence hip-checked the door open for me and then remained in the doorway like a jam. I had to sidle into the space, pressing myself against the doorframe to pass her.

Eleven faces turned to stare. Not twelve, which surprised me. One seat, on the far side of the table, was empty. The long, narrow space took its design cues from the hallway. It was small, even puny. The painted concrete walls were probably blast-proof. Opaque windows along one wall bathed the room in natural light, despite the obscuring privacy film. At least this room was carpeted.

An older man, thin, bottled blond hair poking from the edges of his fluorescent tuque, sat at the nearest end of the board table. Several plates were scattered on the surface, alongside folders, clipboards, notepads, and pens—the tools of the juror's trade. This man's plate contained rinds from oranges and melons and the end bits of croissants.

"You're late," he said.

I inspected him, looking for any sign confirming his right to chide me. Seeing none, I tsked.

Clemence ignored him. "Please sit in one of those chairs." She pointed at two of the metal fold-up kind used for assemblies in school gyms. Some genius had positioned them in front of the kitchenette counter bearing an assortment of fruits and pastries. I could think of several reasons I didn't want to be that close to goodies.

"Can I sit there?" I gestured to the empty seat at the table.

"No. Number Nine is meeting with the judge and counsel. That's her chair," Clemence said.

"Isn't there another spare?" There'd been two of us at the selection.

"Fourteen was excused already."

I found a clock behind me on the microwave that helped me mark the time wasted waiting. We sat like that for nearly ninety minutes.

Three loud raps on the door silenced the chatter in the room. A clatter of keys in the lock was followed by the door swinging open. "Good," Clemence said. "When I knock, please stop all discussion." She peered over my head at the two plastic trays of food, presumably taking inventory. "It won't be long now." She closed the door and locked us back in.

A few minutes later, three loud knocks silenced the room again. This time, when the door opened, it wasn't Clemence. A thirty-something woman dressed professionally in a navy suit walked in. Drying mascara marred each cheek and her polished veneer.

Clemence stood behind the woman in the open doorway. "You can wash up in the restroom." Clemence pointed toward a hallway just past the far end of the kitchenette. "Down that hall."

Clemence propped the door open with her right foot and waited for the woman to return. The room was silent except for the breathing of its occupants and the occasional creak of a twirling chair. Somebody tapped a pen as though marking off the seconds.

The woman reappeared, face scrubbed and presentable. She collected her coat from the closet behind the door.

"Thank you for your service," Clemence said.

The woman nodded at those of us remaining in the room and then left.

Clemence stepped into the room and announced, "Number Thirteen, can you please move to that seat?" She pointed to the comfortable chair I'd earlier coveted. "You're Number Nine now."

Just like that, I joined the jury.

CHAPTER 14

Frank: Weathervane

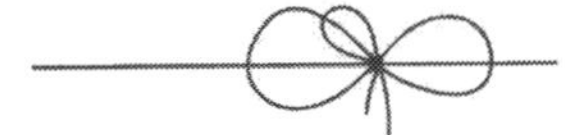

"Let me be clear," Frank Dodge said, addressing his legal opponent. "You'll be judged twenty years from now as the asshole who put this woman in jail. An unenviable legacy. I can't believe you're pushing this case. The legislation is a moving target and has already been amended twice since it was enacted."

Frank carried a newspaper under his arm. Before this meeting, he had folded and refolded the paper, making it compact while still displaying the relevant article. He'd studied his image in the full-length mirror hanging on the back of his office door, trying out several positions for his newsprint prop until he felt satisfied. The headline needed to be upright and readable, and his nonchalance couldn't look contrived. He felt a little slimy resorting to this dirty trick, but he was fast running out of options. He glanced at the paper out of the corner of his eye to confirm his elbow framed the headline for the op-ed piece. The piece's author, a distant friend from law school, had proposed the letter congratulating the Trudeau government for posthumously pardoning George Klippert. He would have paid her well for her handiwork, but she said no. Instead, she expected a role in Molly's Defence. Arm's length. Backroom. Out of the spotlight. Then, last-minute and without explanation, she'd bailed.

"What have you got there?" the judge asked. Frank couldn't have timed the judge's observation better if he'd tried.

His client had been lucky to draw the name of the only gay judge on the bench. At least Justice Sol Forrest was the only openly gay judge. Statistics suggested there were others —but they kept their private lives private. He couldn't blame them. Even in this so-called modern age, homophobic trolls abounded, hiding behind the false anonymity of social media. Forrest didn't seem to care, but he enjoyed the support and reassurance of a loving husband of thirty years, roughly fifteen of which were legal.

"Oh, this?" Frank examined the paper, feigning indifference, the pounding of his heart reverberating in his ears while he composed his face into studied ease. Frank handed the judge the paper.

Sol unfolded the page and began reading. Did he blanch? Frank couldn't be certain in this light. The judge refolded the paper using the same creases Frank had created, but placed the packet so the relevant page was face down on his desk.

"My uncle heard that case," Sol said.

Frank already knew this tidbit and was counting on the judge to note the parallels between the cases. Stella Askew, his second chair, had dug up the information that the judge's maternal uncle had been one of two Supreme Court judges who wrote dissenting opinions in Klippert's failed 1967 appeal.

"Oh?" Frank glanced at Peter to assess his reaction, but realized he remained clueless about the meat of their conversation. "Your uncle was a great man. I will consider my life well-lived if I'm able to accomplish half as much."

Sol smiled, acknowledging Frank's compliment.

"Which case?" Peter Parker asked.

"George Klippert. The last gay man imprisoned in Canada simply for being gay. In the late sixties." Frank hopped onto his soapbox. "Public attitudes were changing even as Klippert was convicted. The government reformed the laws themselves two years later, reclassifying consensual gay sex so it was no longer criminal. But Klippert remained jailed for another few years and was only pardoned fifty years later. Klippert was long dead by then, and I doubt his family rejoiced when his innocence was acknowledged."

Frank studied the faces of his colleague and the judge. Neither connected the dots. "Legislation was changing then too. Klippert got caught in the middle and was imprisoned under obsolete rules. I think those rules were ill-considered in the first place, but that's a discussion for another time."

The judge monitored Frank closely.

"There's a strong parallel between Klippert's and Molly's cases. They were both tried just as the legislation, and public opinion, was changing."

"You manipulative sonuva—" Peter said.

Frank smirked, knowing he'd blocked all Peter's rejoinders. What could he say? Peter wouldn't dare trek through the political minefield Frank had constructed. "You must admit, Klippert's and Molly's cases share a lot in common. What's criminal today could become legit tomorrow." Rules about death and morality changed constantly. Abortion was legalized. Gambling was now allowed, and even provided lucrative revenue streams for governments. Pot was legalized.

Frank stared at the judge and believed he saw appreciation, even admiration, so he persisted. "George Klippert suffered terrible timing. Imagine? He was convicted and imprisoned only two years before the laws changed."

The judge had not taken Frank's bait. "I know what you're doing, Frank," Sol said. "Ingenious. But it won't work. Not in my courtroom."

Frank persisted. "Peter has a choice here. Prosecutions covered by other legislative reforms—such as pot possession, even trafficking—declined in the years leading up to its legalization. The prosecutors," Frank pointed with his whole hand at Peter, "noted public opinion was changing. No one could support sending someone to prison for five years for a couple joints, like in the seventies and eighties. Prosecutors stopped enforcing the letter of the law and instead waited for the law to catch up." Frank stared wide-eyed at his colleague, hoping he'd see reason. He perched on his tiptoes and willed himself to lower his heels so he would stop telegraphing his thoughts and feelings. "You could do the same here, Peter."

"Fat chance." Peter's eyes dilated into lusterless pebbles and Frank understood his colleague remained stubbornly stuck in his position. "No one died in those situations. Plus, Molly Hopewell knew the consequences of her actions. She wants to be a martyr to her cause. I'd hate to disappoint her."

Frank glanced at his client sitting silently in the corner and winked. Peter had fallen straight into Frank's trap.

Peter continued, "If the laws change enough to decriminalize your client's actions, she can apply for a pardon. I'll even pay the 600 bucks for the application fee. The MAID legislation has changed, sure, but still requires the patient to decide for themselves. Max Taylor couldn't give his final consent and he never prepared advanced consent. Period. Your client took matters into her own hands, and I can prove it." Peter stood straight, shoulders back, head high, like he marshalled a parade.

Frank moved over to the wall and leaned into it, seeking the reassuring pressure against his spine and kidneys. Maybe he had another infection. He'd get dried cranberries on his way home. "The public is often more humane than our laws. I'm convinced our jurors, as weathervanes of public opinion, will side with me."

Peter stood and started pacing back and forth in front of the judge's desk. "Poisoning your spouse, no matter the reason, will never be legal," he declared.

Not for the first time, Frank wondered where Peter had finished in his class rankings. No professional ever told you where they graduated in their class. Doctors didn't tell you how many misdiagnoses they'd made or how many of their patients had died before their time. Same with lawyers. At least websites abounded where patients reviewed doctors, although Frank doubted medicine informed many of the commentaries. Rather, he suspected patients gave poor reviews if they disliked the diagnosis, higher reviews if they thought the doctor was cute, and highest reviews if they thought the doctor was an eligible match for themselves or a loved one. Frank had never heard of a similar site ranking lawyers' skill. *We'd probably sue anyone who tried.*

"I must prosecute. Your Honour, please educate my colleague. It's the law. Even if Ms. Hopewell killed her husband with the best of intentions—and there's lots of evidence to suggest the contrary—it's still murder." Peter trained his beady eyes on the judge but kept glancing toward Frank.

Forrest scowled. "Peter, please don't tell me how to do my job."

Frank smiled smugly. *Bad move, Peter. Another point for Team Molly.* "You don't really want Molly anyway. She's a small fish. You really want James Bell."

"That's not true," Peter said. But his eyes darted to see whether Forrest picked up on the comment. The judge's countenance betrayed nothing.

"Bell is the big fish here," Frank continued. "Molly is just the lure, a helpless guppy pinioned on your hook."

"James Bell did not murder Max Taylor. He was in Ontario when Max died. He may be—how did you describe him?—the Morgentaler of euthanasia. But he was not involved with this crime."

Frank smirked. "You looked into his alibi?"

Peter opened his mouth and then closed it. He stared ahead, his eyes darting between the faces of everyone in the room. "Of course, we did."

"Who funded the investigation?" Frank asked. "Your church?"

Peter exhaled. "This has nothing to do with my church, and I resent the insinuation."

Frank glanced at Forrest, who'd leaned back in his chair

to let the feud play out.

"Oh, I'm sorry. My mistake. I thought those protesters were yours," Frank said insincerely. "Somebody's funding them. Too many are paid provocateurs."

"What's your evidence, Frank?" Forrest asked.

"They're not hiding it, Sir. Some placards have logos in the corner, like they fundraised to get the signs printed. They probably ran a GoFundMe campaign." He'd made his point and let the topic drop. "What can we do to avoid Molly going to jail?" Frank asked, even though he already knew Peter's answer.

"Nothing." Peter's pugilistic expression meant business.

"Peter, think about it," Forrest interjected. "Now might be the time to get creative." He shook his head sadly. "This trial is already a media circus and it's becoming the source of political fodder." He picked up an inch-thick stack of pink and yellow squares and waved it. "Today's messages. And just about this trial. Some lobbyists. The usual journalists. Even politicians. For and against the charges."

Frank suspected the politicians were responding to his call.

"Have you seen the blog?" Frank added another layer to the conversation. "Its hashtag is 'maidissin.' Sounds like a porn site."

Molly, demure and polished, cracked up.

The judge covered his mouth to stifle a cough, then flipped open his laptop and quickly found the blog. Peter and Frank moved to the proprietary side of the desk to peer over his shoulder. The first thing to pop-up was a photo of Max's tearful mother and taciturn father. The caption read, "She didn't let us say goodbye."

The judge scrolled to the next page. "Jury Selected."

"I was right." Frank pointed to a "donate here" button on the bottom of the page. "I wonder how many seniors they've swindled."

No one laughed. His quip was too close to the truth.

"But," Peter wheedled, "Max wasn't a candidate for assisted suicide under the legislation. Not even under the updated law."

"The legislation failed them. And I fear that Dr. Bell pushed this issue, even though he knew better, and it's Max and Molly who are paying the price. Bell certainly found himself a sympathetic couple to use as patsies." Frank shook his head slightly before noticing that Peter watched him intently. "The jury might still acquit, despite the law. Like Morgentaler."

The judge stood, face red and flushed. "Enough. Do not play those games in my courtroom, Frank. Do you hear me? One mention of jury nullification, directly," he waved his hand toward his tablet, "or indirectly, in the blogs? Or newspaper editorials? Well, you'll leave me no choice. I'll declare a mistrial. And I'll see you charged with contempt."

CHAPTER 15

Ashes to Ashes

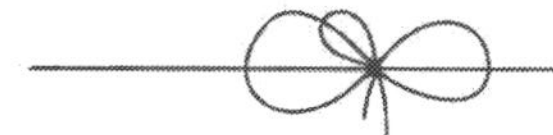

The phone quacked and I smiled, amused by my cheerful ringtone.

"Hello?" I didn't recognize the number on call display but answered anyway. Leah, Jake, and the kids had headed out to Nelson to visit his parents for the Thanksgiving weekend, and I half-expected her to report their safe arrival. She'd invited me, of course. I'd considered going, but instead, I prioritized my friend's quality time with her actual family.

"Hi, Heddie. It's Becky." She sounded like she spoke through a scuba helmet, and hearing her voice set my teeth on edge. "I wasn't sure you'd answer." I probably imagined her disappointment.

"Oh, hi." I added updating Becky's contact information to a mental list of chores I'd surely forget.

"How are you doing?" She didn't let me answer. "Anywho, I'm reaching out to mend fences between us. Let's all move on past our last encounter."

A long silence followed, and for once, I didn't fill it. One Okanagan. Two Okanagan.

"Anywho." She rushed past any chagrin, right into the reason for her call. "We're having people over for dinner. We'd just love for you to come too."

"Will I know anybody?" Besides Stanley.

"Oh, yes," she gushed. "The last guest just confirmed." There was a long pause before she added, "We want everyone to be here."

"Who's 'everyone'?" I asked.

"All Hugh's friends. Everyone important to him."

"I'm so glad you thought to include me," I said icily, before adding, "Sure. When?" My need for company on my first Thanksgiving without him controverted any common sense or self-preservation.

"I should have mentioned that first. Tonight, six o'clock."

I looked at my watch. Only ninety minutes to shower, dress, and get halfway across town. Even if I drove, I'd barely make it on time, and I couldn't remember when I'd last refuelled Dimples.

"That's not much time."

"Sorry." Becky did not seem to notice my criticism. "We head out tomorrow for the rest of the weekend. See you at six then?"

I checked to make sure I disconnected the call before muttering, "Selfish, mean-spirited, insensitive bastards." I double-checked the phone. Yup, still disconnected. I placed it on the counter and hoped I'd remember where I left it when I headed out. Despite myself and my justified anger, I wanted to see Hug's friends again. I even liked most of them.

——— ∘ ∘ ∘ ———

Even happy firsts and lasts were trouble, all bittersweet —an expression I only understood after he died. But now I felt it viscerally, with my gut twisting at the hurt of recollecting the happy moments alongside their irretrievable loss. Like when we first met, our first date, our first trip, or even the first time we made love.

I never understood "viscerally," either, until his disease. I was happy the day they told us there was "no visceral involvement" of his cancer. Before getting too jubilant, though, I checked with the doctor—a young one, probably an intern, still enthused about answering questions—who had confirmed it meant his organs were cancer-free. So far, in my growing experience, I'd learned cancer itself rarely caused death; instead, "complications" of cancer killed. I imagined the disease as construction zones in the body with impassable detours for essentials like oxygen and blood. Everything gradually stopped working efficiently. And then stopped working. Period.

Hug's disease progressed through so many unhappy anniversaries. The first time I spotted lumps on the side of his neck. Or his first biopsy with its misleading positive result. Positives and negatives were reversed in medicine, like some sort of mirror universe where positives were wrong and negatives were preferred. More dates like his first radiation treatment. Then on to surgery to strengthen his cancer-laced bones. Worse dates were when they told us his disease was incurable. When he'd suffered enough. When he said he was ready to die.

I knew his lasts too. Like, the last time he drove his car or visited his brother or walked Fella. Of course, no one recognized lasts at the time—particularly at the start of the end. Labelling required hindsight.

Leah promised that these unhappy details would blur, blend, even dissolve over time. Unfortunately for me and my impossible post-Hug do-over, the details remained indelible. Living them etched them permanently onto my heart. And my heart was like an elephant—strong, steady, loyal. And it never forgot.

We spent our last Thanksgiving lying next to each other, holding hands, watching the snow fall.

"I want to feel normal again," he had said. "Lie next to me?"

How could I refuse? We both already hated the hospital bed, even though it was necessary, with its many options for positioning him just so. What we hated was the isolation, the fact that we'd kiss good night and then go off to separate rooms. The long nights of those last months seemed darker, more ominous because I slept alone. But his bone metastases, "mets" in medical shorthand, caused such pain, he fidgeted and repositioned for elusive relief. One night, I'd shoved some bogeyman in a nightmare and pushed my fading love in real life instead. He'd screamed. The rest of that night and the next, Fella and I slept on the couch—a solution Hug wouldn't accept indefinitely. Leah arranged for the hospital bed soon after, and I admitted it was the right decision.

I had studied the bedroom, stuffed with too much furniture. Where to begin? Older houses, such as his, had puny rooms unsuitable for our modern super-sizes, with king-sized beds, walk-in closets, and huge flat screens. Our sleigh bed, made of heavy wood, was handsome and impractical, occupying most of the floor space with only a narrow passageway around it. Even I barely avoided stubbed toes when navigating the room, and the space was utterly impassable for Hug with his indispensable walker. Rearranging the furniture to accommodate his infirmity required a sequenced plan. I moved a dresser, shoved aside a nightstand, nudged the bed, and widened his path. Of course, he preferred the bedside furthest from the door. Plus, everything was heavier than middle-aged me should move on my own.

But I figured out a trick. The only thing I had to my advantage was the hardwood floors, shiny and smooth from their recent refresh. I found four old facecloths and lifted the corners of the dresser enough to wedge cloths under each leg. A sensible person might've removed the drawers first. My only excuse, because I was indeed a sensible person, was the rising panic roiling inside me like toxic smog and obliterating all rational thought. The cloths did the trick, even with the laden drawers intact. I slid the furniture around using my bulk and gravity to full advantage, and didn't even mar his floors.

It took me over an hour to accomplish the feat. But it was worth it.

We watched that snowstorm through the bedroom

window while lying propped on plumped pillows. Feathery flakes floated from the sky, covering the branches of the fifty-odd-year-old spruce in front of the window. Streetlights illuminated the dark scene, making the taupe-purple sky glow and the snow glisten.

That Thanksgiving was the last time we laid together, side by side. It already hurt him too much for me to rest my head on his shoulder. My favourite place. My safe place. Instead, we held hands. I wished I'd paid more attention to those moments.

——— o o o ———

I arrived a few minutes late after traffic snarls slowed my impatient progress. At the edge of the property, I spotted Hug's friends gabbing in a grove of trees. I parked Dimples and strolled over, self-conscious with every step—conspicuous and silly in my inappropriate heels. My only excuse for the footwear was the weather had been decent, balmy for October, when I dressed. I should've listened to Hug, whose chief forecast was "if you like the weather, wait five minutes." I watched, dismayed, as darkening clouds emphasized my poor fashion decision. I shivered in the dropping temperatures and hoped someone noticed my shoes played up the cheerful teal hints in my dress.

I promised myself I wouldn't stay outside long. I picked my way through the grass, trying not to slip and create another spectacle, and joined Hug's friends as they examined the remains of the year's vegetable garden. The frozen yellow flowers of squash plants would never bear fruit, another reminder of our impossibly short growing season.

I waved, surprised at how glad I was to see them. We exchanged hellos all around, punctuated with head nods and abashed smiles. I stood off to the side, not wanting to interrupt their conversation, and feeling like a stranger among these familiar faces. People paired off, examining different parts of the yard, and so snippets of several conversations intersected and collided into an incomprehensible jumble. I could mostly discern Stanley's voice, but I still didn't understand.

"Dug a hole..."

"Ready to plant..."

"Compost from the potato garden."

Stanley—and to a lesser extent, Becky—spent their summers outdoors puttering. Stanley's attention showed, with baskets bursting late in the year with fuchsias and baby's breath. He'd planted some fall mums a few years back and they faithfully produced mounds of burgundy, orange, and yellow flowers every year—sometimes past Halloween.

People slowly made their way toward the house. Stanley's dog, Dagwood, charged out to greet us, barking threateningly while wagging his tail. Dagwood thought his job was to chase visitors away, but he struggled between his duty to protect his pack's turf and his desire to be petted. Petting usually won out.

"Where's Fella?" Becky asked.

I eyed her suspiciously and decided against informing her of Stanley's promise to let me keep him. "He's at Leah's. Probably on the couch." I laughed, but it wasn't a joke. Everyone knew Fella owned the couch. "Possession is nine-tenths of the law"—yup, another Huggism.

Becky laid out a smorgasbord of hors d'oeuvres. This subtle technique told everyone where she wanted us to congregate, and people obediently funnelled toward the food-laden table and chose positions next to their favourite delights.

"We're casual today. I cooked a turkey, but nothing else traditional," Becky explained.

I sniffed the air, and amid the tang of rosemary and sage, I caught cozy hints of cinnamon and cloves. "Smells like pumpkin pie too."

"Oh, yes. It's not Thanksgiving without pumpkin pie." She smiled politely before joining her other guests.

Conversation was free-flowing and wide-ranging, even if I had little to add. I felt happy and relaxed for the first time in months, surrounded by people who just got it. I didn't need to explain myself because they all missed him too.

○ ○ ○

"We want to plant a tree in Hugh's honour. A Thanksgiving tribute." Appearances suggested Becky was speaking only to the nucleus of women in her immediate vicinity, but her volume also included me.

I glanced up from my now-empty paper plate to catch the expression on Becky's face, and I failed to decipher the slight hardness, determination, of her eyes and the set to her jaw.

I think Becky expected resistance, but I didn't give it to her. I didn't object. And, given my own actions, how could I raise a ruckus? I'd already planted several shrubs—an ever-blooming lilac, a forsythia, three boxwoods, and a rhododendron—all in his honour. I even planted a prairie rose, but that was more for me. Unfortunately, they were all on his property and now out of my reach. I hadn't even thought to include anyone other than Fella, completing each planting quietly, unceremoniously. No chatter—except from magpies and chickadees—accompanied these memorials. No prayers or even moments of silence either, as that wasn't my style. I'd simply remembered Hug, recollecting some shared joke or fond expression. Once, I'd listened to one of his playlists while I dug and dressed a hole and planted the shrub. I bawled that time, but every other planting was waterworks-free.

I realized what was really going on when I returned from my car with a shawl. Stanley scurried like a rat out of his house, carrying a small cardboard box. Intuitively, with no observable explanation, I knew beyond a doubt Stanley carried Hug's ashes and intended to spread them in the hole for the tree. He moved quickly, beetling along their driveway, sticking to the shadows of the house. I moved quickly, too, more quickly than I thought possible in my flimsy shoes. But he was faster.

"Don't you do it," I said outside his hearing. "Please, at

least wait until I get there."

I turned the corner and saw the cluster of them standing around the open hole, two of them taking pictures. A telltale grey-white smudge against the dark exposed dirt told me everything.

"No," I said. "Stop." I grabbed the nearest elbow—Becky's, it turned out—to avoid sliding on the grass.

"Heddie, behave," Stanley whispered.

"Please, don't," I cried. "I've got nothing left of him."

"It's not your decision, Heddie," Stanley said. "Mine is a better option than leaving him in a coat closet. Besides, his friends are all here."

I fell to my knees and crawled to the hole, desperate to reclaim some of Hug's ashes.

Stanley intercepted me and blocked my progress with his legs. "Stop. You're making a spectacle of yourself."

The men plopped the tree into the hole, threw in shovels full of dirt, then stomped on their handiwork like they were dancing on his grave. They stood for selfies, grinning wildly, patting each other on the back, posing around the tree, looking like they'd bagged a prized seven-point elk. I stayed huddled on the grass and watched their antics, increasingly overwhelmed by my powerlessness. They hadn't even waited for me to say goodbye.

After that, one of the women helped me up and I scampered away as fast as I could. She yelled for me to "Drive safe" as I drove away. My voice cracked when I yelled back, "I'll try." I hoped I saw none of them ever again.

I glanced in the rearview mirror as I drove away. The group still huddled around the tree, drinking beer and wine, all smiles. Unleashed, Dagwood sniffed the ground and cocked a leg over Hug's tree. Becky spotted him but made no move to guide him elsewhere. I groaned and kept driving.

I was in no shape to drive. I bawled uncontrollably, a curtain of tears obscured my vision.

I phoned Leah first, hands-free, of course. "Leah!" I

wailed, and told her the whole story. Or, at least, enough of it to cause alarm.

"Sweetie, you need help. Pull over somewhere safe and talk to me."

I followed her instructions and pulled off at a random offramp from Deerfoot Trail, stopped on the shoulder, and started my hazard lights.

"Can you get to Dee's?"

"Dee won't see me." I sniffled and wished, not for the first time, I stuffed all my backpacks with such essentials as tissues.

"She'll see you," Leah promised.

"It's Saturday night on a holiday weekend. She'll be busy. If she's even in town."

"She's home. I just texted you her address. Copy it into your GPS. I'll call her and let her know you're on your way."

"Okay." I started hiccupping.

"Heddie, it'll be okay."

I bawled again. "You keep saying that, but it keeps getting worse. When the worst has already happened, how can it keep getting worse?"

CHAPTER 16

Dee: Consolation

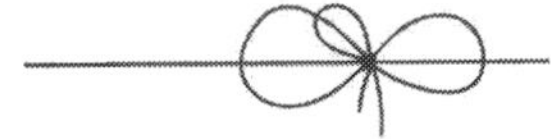

Heddie had selected the recliner from Dee's presented options and now sat almost prone. "They're just so nasty."

When Dee left her former firm, she'd toyed with the idea of converting her basement into an office where she'd see clients. But she'd smartened up and instead rented space on 17th, just off Crowchild Trail. She knew her business would eventually prosper, but in the meantime, she accepted some shady cases just to pay her bills. Heddie was her first client she invited to her home, an emergency response to Leah's plea, a one-time favour.

For the next ten minutes, Heddie recounted her version of the evening's events. Dee sat back and listened, her mouth stuck in a single note of astonished antipathy.

Heddie's voice hitched. "They didn't ask me. They just did it." Heddie teased fur from the chair upholstery and rolled it between her fingers. "I know Stanley loved him. But so did I." She stuffed the fur into her pocket. "Stanley didn't even bother himself when Hug was sick, dying. I could've used help with Hug, but Stanley only came around when he felt like it."

"Are you sure they didn't ask you? You didn't miss something?"

Heddie croaked. "I miss lots, but not that. Hug wanted nothing fancy. No cemetery with a preachy headstone. Only a park bench somewhere pretty."

"Where have his ashes been all this time?"

"In Hug's foyer closet," Heddie said. "Seemed as good a place as any."

Maybe she could help Heddie reframe the situation. "Planting his ashes under a tree is better than storing them in a closet, forgotten. Under a tree, they create a living tribute."

"Forgotten?" Heddie squeaked. "His death ripped my life apart. Stanley's life was merely interrupted."

"Losing a sibling is also hard, even if they weren't close. If nothing else, a brother's death reinforces one's own mortality."

Heddie shrugged. "They were close enough."

"People grieve differently." Dee wondered how many more platitudes she could dish out.

Heddie sneered. "I can't visit Hug now. They'd arrest me for trespassing."

Dee shook her head. "They wouldn't go that far." She spoke with a conviction she didn't have.

"But, as the saying goes," Heddie continued, "'you make your bed, you lie in it.'"

"You'll have to translate that."

"I got what I deserved. My comeuppance," Heddie answered.

"You think you deserve this?" Dee worked to get the frustration out of her voice, dismayed by the quantity of nonsense filling this woman's head.

"What if I'd paid more attention? Hug first spotted those lumps on his neck months before his diagnosis. He joked about mumps, about becoming infertile." Heddie paused and looked questioningly at Dee. "What if I'd gotten him to a doctor earlier? Would it have made a difference?"

"There's no way to know."

"I didn't save him. In the end, I couldn't even help him. Sure, I got him to the toilet on time. No accidents. But I couldn't help him in any meaningful way."

"Hugh was an adult, responsible for himself."

"I didn't even google it, when I first saw that lump,"

Heddie said. "I google everything, any question that flits across my pea brain. I just accepted his self-diagnosis. Mumps. I didn't google it until months later, after the doctor pointed it out, after it was too late."

"Cancer killed Hugh. Not you. You know that, right?"

Heddie nodded unconvincingly and studied her big toe sticking out through a hole in her right sock. "I should've been more insistent, caused more of a stir. Losing my partner, my ampersand, was difficult."

Been there, done that, Dee thought. Aloud, she said, "Ampersand?"

"It used to be Heddie and—ampersand, get it?—Hugh. Now it's just me. Nobody else."

"Why don't you call him your 'husband'?" Dee needed Heddie to spell it out.

Heddie's eyes popped and she pressed her hands into the armrests. "I'd be lying. I've paid a steep price for spurning that piece of paper."

"'Ampersand' is just so unusual," Dee said. "If not 'husband', why not 'significant other'?"

Heddie wrinkled her nose. "Nothing quite fits," she huffed. "'Boyfriend' was ridiculous at our age. 'Manfriend' felt contrived. 'Soulmate' didn't work, because we weren't religious. 'Lover' was too much information in polite company. 'Partner' was okay but still sounds like a business transaction. 'Friend' was true, but incomplete. 'Companion' was insulting. 'Beloved,' true and tragic. 'Spouse' sounded like mealy mouthed legalese, hiding more than sharing. 'Fiancé' sorta works but he never gave me a ring. Sometimes I settle on 'husband', but 'ampersand' is my favourite."

"You've thought about it a lot," Dee acknowledged. "I lost my husband—my ampersand—too."

Heddie closed her eyes. "I've had to think about it. Everyone knows I loved him, but I'm not sure he felt the same way." A slight tabby with golden eyes jumped into Heddie's lap. "Oof. I didn't see you coming." She reached out to stroke the cat who accepted the attention.

"That's Mercy," Dee said. "Her brother's around here too. Somewhere." Dee leaned back, smoothed the skirt on her lap to create inviting real estate, and smooched the air. "Justice, here, boy."

A fat cat scurried around the corner, paws slipping on the uncarpeted floor.

Heddie laughed, a rich, throaty, well-practised sound. "He's ginormous."

The cat launched himself from across the room. Dee braced herself for impact, and her chair still rolled back when he landed. Justice curled himself up, and both cats serenaded the women with purring.

"I'm a cliché, I know," Dee said, acknowledging the cats. "I adopted them both from the Meow Foundation after Todd died. I blame Leah."

"How so?"

"Todd died suddenly ten years ago. Brain aneurysm. I got lost too, and Leah helped me find my way again."

"That's Leah's superpower," Heddie acknowledged. "Giving me Fella was the best thing Hug did for me. You think I'm bad now? Can you imagine me without him?" Heddie shook her head vehemently to dispel the notion. "Why Mercy and Justice?"

"I was young. Just finished articling. Took everything too seriously. They were originally called Beauty and Beast, but somehow these moral principles seemed better than fairytale characters." Dee paused. "Enough about me. I looked over the eviction notice Stanley gave you." She fiddled with a paper clip from her desk. "Unfortunately, until I see Hugh's will, I can't be sure, but everything seems in order. Stanley is too careful. He would never evict you without proper authority."

"Hug called him persnickety," Heddie said. "But, hey, Leah said the same thing about you."

Dee snorted, aware of her growing reputation. "Do you want to fight Stanley over Hugh's estate?"

"Stanley won't see reason," Heddie asserted. "Leah said I had a slim chance. But she also said it'd be expensive. I don't have the money to spend on a maybe."

"Mediation is probably a better alternative. Cheaper, with more flexibility in developing workable solutions." Dee opened her laptop and logged into her work account. It only took a minute to find and open the folder she needed. "With your go-ahead, I'll start prepping materials to brief a mediator."

"I can't pay you," Heddie said. "I promised Hug I'd move on. I'm glad he's not around to see how spectacularly I've failed."

"You're just at the start of this journey, Heddie," Dee said. "I'm still grieving Todd, and he died a decade ago."

"I'm not sure I even want to 'move on'."

Dee rolled her hand for Heddie to elaborate.

"I'm afraid I'll forget him." Heddie looked down and shrunk into herself. "I don't want to forget him. Besides Fella and a few pictures, I have nothing left of him. I don't even have a place where I can visit him." Heddie tapped her forehead with her finger. "I have to safeguard him in here."

Dee reached over and flicked the switch on the floor lamp. She let the silence hang in the air. "I'll do it pro bono, my way of making amends for my earlier mistakes." Dee picked up a blank notepad and pen. "To start, what's your full name?"

"Henry hyphen Etta Wright. No middle name." She smiled. "I'm named after my father. Well, my mother too. Combined. He died before I was born."

"That must've been hard too. His name was Henry?" Dee was stunned by her inane question, but she needed to find a way to break through her new client's protective shell.

"Henry was his middle name. His first name was Marion. Like John Wayne, but before he got famous." Heddie smiled impishly. "You see why Mamma used my dad's second name?"

Dee shook her head.

"Marion-Etta?" Mischief brightened Heddie's features, and Dee caught a glimpse of what Leah saw in her.

Heddie laughed, mouth open and head back, and Dee smiled despite herself.

Dee opened one of the documents on her computer and started skimming the information.

"Is that about Hug?" Heddie clunked her chair closed and leaned over to investigate.

Dee realized her mistake too late. "It's confidential." She closed the computer. "I'll build up your case, but first, I need to ask several questions. For example, how long were you together?"

Heddie stared at her for several moments before she turned her gaze and resumed petting Mercy. "Not long enough. Never long enough," Heddie said. "We dated about six years, but we only lived together for ten months."

"Two months longer and you would've had more rights. No matter what the will said."

"Sorry, but that's old news." Heddie paused.

"What's the value of his estate?" Dee asked.

"Leah guesstimates about $100,000. After they sell his house, pay off his mortgage and taxes," Heddie said. "He had some savings. RSPs. No pension. His Killarney house was his nest egg." Heddie kept talking, although Dee didn't need further explanation. "Real estate is an excellent investment, and he bought his place twenty years ago."

Dee stared ahead and sat entirely still except for her fidgeting fingers untwisting the paper clip. "Until we get this sorted, stay away from Stanley. Okay?"

Heddie shook her head. "I can't. I'll probably see him next week."

"Why?" Dee asked, puzzled.

"I have jury duty and he's a bailiff at the courthouse."

"Well, that won't work." Dee stood, sending Justice plummeting to the floor, where he landed squarely on all four paws. Dee didn't notice, and instead paced back and forth across the small room. "Which trial?" Heddie was slow to answer, so Dee jumped in. "Rex versus Hopewell?"

Heddie nodded. "You trying to get in your 10,000 steps?" Heddie asked, then thumped her knee at her own joke.

Mercy jumped from her lap and moved over to join her brother on the couch. The two animals curled into each other, making it difficult to distinguish one from the other. Mercy started cleaning her brother's head.

"You know her? Hopewell?"

"Yes, I knew him too." Dee spotted Heddie's growing concern. "They're not clients or anything. We just travelled in the same circles. The world of death and dying, even in a big city, is small," Dee said, and resumed pacing. "Okay, I'll have to rethink this. I'll get back to you with a game plan."

CHAPTER 17

A Present

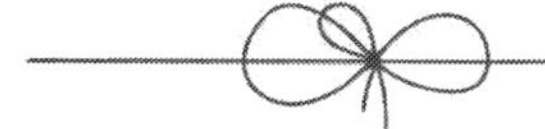

Leah handed me a package wrapped in brown paper and decorated with a white frilly bow. "Here. Maybe this will help."

I put the pot I was drying into the cupboard where it belonged before I wiped both hands on my apron and took the present from her. "Me? Why?"

"Open it and I'll explain."

I unstuck the tape from the wrapping and unfolded the paper to reveal a hard-covered book in my favourite shade of peacock blue. I rifled through the numbered pages, which were otherwise empty except for a grid of fine dots.

"I hope you'll use it to jot down your thoughts, what's going on in your head."

"A journal?" Oh, goody. "I love this colour." Mamma taught me to always say something nice.

"It'll help, Heddie," Leah said. "Trust me. I'm not your counsellor, but I am an expert in dying and grief. You're probably suffering from something called 'complicated grief.'" She stared at me unflinchingly, unapologetic.

"Probably?"

"People get assessed when they haven't moved on after a year." She picked up her wine glass from the counter.

"It hasn't been a year," I said, pleased to skirt her label. "Hug died three months, fourteen days ago." I checked the clock on the wall and kept mum about the additional thirteen hours and twenty minutes since his death.

"Thank you. You just made my point," she said. "This kind of rumination, even three and a half months later, is unhealthy. You need to process your thoughts and feelings, or you'll never find your way again."

I nodded.

"Besides, I suspect Stanley's latest antic set you back." She snorted unattractively. "As if he hasn't already caused enough trouble. Lots of science suggests journaling can work almost as well as therapy. Will you try it? Two pages a day."

What did she think my doodles were all about? Why were her solutions the only good ones? "Cheaper too." I clutched the book to my chest.

"Journaling can help you through the trial too," she added. "It was already going to be tough. Especially for you. But after Stanley's latest stunt—"

"What do you mean?"

"You know what I mean. Stanley should have at least consulted you about Hugh's ashes."

"I mean about the trial."

"The subject would be difficult for anyone." She gripped the tea towel in the hand resting on her hip. "But harder for you. You still need to process your grief, and given your views about MAID, about assisted dying—"

"People keep falsely accusing me, and you've all got it wrong," I snapped. "Hug didn't want to die."

"Hugh didn't want to leave you. But he was dying. It's not like he had a choice."

That's where I thought she was wrong. Hug and I made so many choices. Me, not wanting to rock the boat and push him to visit a doctor sooner. Him, giving up when there might've still been a chance. At least he had second thoughts and cancelled his appointment.

"When Hugh wanted to die... you objected."

I howled. "Of course, I objected." He couldn't leave me.

Leah exhaled and touched the journal. "Listen, this

might help. Promise me, you'll try it?"

"Pinky swear," I said, and hooked my curled little finger around hers. I knew she meant well.

CHAPTER 18

So it Begins

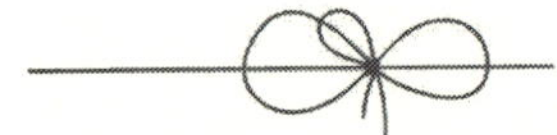

"All rise." A bailiff boomed our arrival, his deep baritone filling the enormous room. We followed Clemence and shuffled into the courtroom in a row, imprinting like ducklings behind our Mamma. The courtroom was packed, and I felt like an unpopular kid arriving late to the prom.

We walked single file, each to our assigned seats while two hundred-ish pairs of eyes studied our movements and expressions. I took tiny steps, careful not to tread on my neighbour's heels. I stepped up the three stairs to our fenced platform and then wedged myself into the narrow gap between the railing and the chairs. I clutched my numbered clipboard with its yellow-lined notepad like a shield. The judge, the lawyers, and the audience waited patiently while we filed in, took our seats, swivelled to get comfortable, and assembled our materials. We made quite a spectacle, twelve people jigging this odd line dance.

The courtroom was more than I expected, even with all my googling. Divided up like a playing field, everyone had their assigned roles and many had assigned seats. An oak-spindled railing with a swinging gate in the middle fenced the territories. Court officials, including jurors, stayed on one side, while the audience, heavily spiced with protesters, remained on the other. This courtroom, smaller than the one where they held jury selection, was also fifty shades of hated beige.

Determining the pecking order of the room's occupants

was easy. I eyeballed the heights of our various platforms and podiums. We, the jury, got a raised platform along one side of the room. Our platform was lower than the judge's bench, which towered over the room and afforded him the eagle-eye view of all. I didn't think our space was higher than the accused's directly opposite us, but ours was roomier. Hers was more like a scaffold; ours was like a stage. The witness box occupied that in-between level, a few inches taller than the jury platform, but several feet lower than the judge's. Everyone else, from the audience to the court reporter, even the lawyers and the clerks, were planted firmly on the floor.

Our chairs also defined our importance. Most of the guards had to stand. Clemence got to sit—on a metal chair recognizable from my Number Thirteen hours. I couldn't see the judge's chair, but I imagined it like a comfortable throne. Minus the jewels. All the clerks and lawyers sat in wheeled, high-backed office chairs, pulleys and levers visible underneath for adjustments to accommodate every physique.

We, the jury, sat in assigned seats and Clemence made sure we all knew our place. My spot was in the front row, two up from the witness box. I enjoyed an unobstructed view of the entire courtroom, except for one important design flaw: I needed to turn my head so that my nostrils aligned with my left shoulder to see the witnesses or the judge properly. It was a painful posture to maintain for long.

We sat in upholstered armchairs, each with an adjustable writing surface that slid into either the left or the right chair arm, depending on one's handedness. My neighbour was left-handed. He switched his writing table from one side to the other. It was so stuck, he had to wriggle the pole out of its socket inch by inch. After that, we spent too much of our time bumping elbows.

Once we were all seated, the judge began. "Good morning, ladies and gentlemen of the jury. I note you are all present." His voice sounded all rounded and warm, like the narrator in a high-budget documentary.

"I am Justice Solomon Forrest. I thank you for joining us today. Yours is the most important role in our judicial system, with many complex responsibilities. You have all committed to trying the accused and deciding a verdict based on the evidence. The accused, Molly Agnes Hopewell, faces charges of first degree murder for the death of her husband, Maxwell Gerald Taylor." He shifted in his seat, angling his torso toward us, and I realized this whole show was for our, the jury's, benefit.

The officials, even the clerks but not the guards, wore long, black robes with stiff, white collars that made them look like penguins at a fancy ball. What was a group of penguins called? A raft. A colony. A huddle. A waddle. Ha. I doodled "waddle," shading the lettering to create a three-dimensional marquee.

Two long tables flanked the privileged side of the banister, and two penguin-people sat at each one. Two bald men, both round—with round heads and round torsos—sat at the table for Crown counsel. The Defence's table was occupied by a man, roughly my age, and the only female lawyer in the room. I sketched the penguins in their positions.

"First, though, I will explain what happened with Number Nine."

I raised my head when I heard my new name.

He nodded at me, and in a softer tone said, "Pardon me, ma'am. The original Nine."

Someone's cell phone rang a chirpy tune. I held my breath while the guards scanned the audience to find the source of the offence. That's when I spotted Stanley, standing in a corner and craning his neck to stare at me. I pulled my lips into an acknowledging smile and then turned to watch the courtroom antics.

The audience lined up in neat rows on long, carved, wooden benches. More onlookers crowded on Max's side, behind the Crown counsel, the side nearer to the jury box. I assumed it was Max's parents seated in the first row, grim expressions on their dour faces.

A woman in the back row of Molly's side waved. "Sorry, it's me." She dumped her purse on the bench beside her, found her phone, and silenced it mid-ring.

"On that note." The judge paused. I recognized at the same time as everyone else, the judge's attempt at a joke, and we all chuckled dutifully. "Please turn off all devices. Not on vibrate. Powered off." He waited while about half the audience rummaged in their pockets and purses to comply.

Once everyone settled, he resumed. "The original Number Nine had personal considerations she was reluctant to share in open court. When she arrived for orientation last week, she conveyed her misgivings to your jury guard." He nodded at Clemence. "The juror wrote a statement outlining her situation, and when I read it aloud to counsel," here, he waved his arm indicating both the Crown and the Defence, "all parties agreed the juror candidate could be excused, and her written statement entered into the trial record." He brushed his hands together. "This morning, we are starting a trial that will likely last three weeks."

A penguin at each of the lawyers' tables watched us and scribbled notes. I squirmed and recrossed my legs tidily at the ankles, uncomfortable with this fishbowl scrutiny.

"During this trial, you will hear difficult and technical evidence. Please pay attention to the evidence as it is presented."

Spartan workspaces for the underlings who supported the proceedings—keeping records transcribed and evidence organized—were sandwiched at the foot of the judge's bench. There was no mistaking who was boss. The court reporter and the clerk occupied their own long table amid the equipment of their jobs. The court reporter sat with enviable posture, straight-backed, elbows and knees at right angles, feet firmly planted. She likely never even broke a sweat as she wrangled each spoken word, every *eh* and *um*.

"You are responsible for assessing and deciding the

evidence of the case. I am responsible for judging the law. I will provide you with instructions on how you must interpret the law." The judge wore a simple ring, probably platinum, that flashed when he waved his hands. "You do not need to concern yourself with sentencing. That's my job."

Several jurors took notes. I created elaborate doodles.

"The Crown will present his case first. He is required to prove the guilt of the accused. Remember, in our judicial system, the accused is innocent unless proven guilty. That means that the onus is on the Crown to prove guilt. The Defence will present their case once the Crown has concluded."

The lead Defence attorney wore formidable cowboy boots with pointy toes poking out from beneath his trouser legs. Thick wedge heels added two inches to his height. The stitched pattern was too floral for the insecure and I bet the price tag for the boots was too steep for the uncommitted.

"A reasonable doubt does not mean absolute certainty. Indeed, absolute certainty is impossible to achieve. Instead, you are required to be reasonable in your review and apply common sense to what you hear."

The junior Defence lawyer nodded her agreement with those instructions. Grouchy might be her resting face. Next to her, her associate seemed engrossed with an open file on the table. I studied the pair for any signs of intimacy and catalogued a collegial fondness but nothing more.

"Finally, I need to issue you a word of caution. I expect this case to be controversial and to generate considerable interest and divergent public opinions. You may have already encountered the journalists and protesters outside the building." I looked up but couldn't pinpoint his focus. "Do not—I repeat, do not—read newspapers, social media, watch the news, or converse with anyone other than your fellow jurors about this trial." He lowered his voice slightly, forcing me to lean forward to listen. "I cannot stress this instruction too firmly." He punctuated his warning with a pause. "Please refrain from watching all news or analysis about this trial."

I scanned the crowd again. A couple I'd pegged as reporters smirked at each other. I didn't see any computers or tablets and certainly no cameras. Several people scribbled swiftly in notebooks. That's when I spotted my neighbour from jury selection, Axel, the aspiring journalist. His peacock blue coat glared like a blue light special.

"You, as jurors, will have to be diligent—careful—to ensure you try this case based only on the evidence you hear in this courtroom. Nowhere else." Sharp, enunciated syllables replaced any kindly notes in his voice.

Axel wrote fast. He shook his wrist, probably to work out a kink, and caught me watching him. For a moment, his mouth and eyes rounded in surprise, then he waved and offered me a half-smile. I turned away and worked hard to ignore him, surprised he recognized me dressed presentably in street clothes.

"If you let outside information cloud your judgement, you will cause a mistrial. A mistrial means we need to start the process over with a new jury." The judge made eye contact with each of us. The zigzagging glances—front row Number One, back row Number Two, front row Number Three, etc. —continued until he'd stared each of us down. My left hand covered my doodles.

"I need to warn you. Failing to follow these instructions may result in harsh consequences for you. Trials are expensive."

I nodded solemnly, committed to do my bit.

"For now, you will be allowed to go home to your families."

A uniformed guard was stationed every few feet around the room, wearing no-nonsense expressions and watching the goings-on. They mostly stood still, like pillars stabilizing the structure. Occasionally, they strolled from one side of the room to the other, hands uncomfortably clasped behind their backs.

"You will find parts of the evidence troubling. I

apologize in advance." Again, the judge's voice softened, making him harder to hear. "Jurors can access complimentary counselling services once you have rendered your verdict and the trial has concluded. Your jury officer has information about these services."

I jotted down a reminder to ask Clemence for details, then shaded the loops in my letters.

"With your counsellor, you may talk about the details of this case, anything on the public record. But refrain from talking about the jury's deliberations themselves. Despite what you may have seen on TV, your deliberations must always remain confidential."

Opposite us, on the far side of the booted lawyer, in her own box, flanked by two matronly women I pegged as her guards, sat the reason we all convened. I had paid little attention to the news, too defeated by my own drama to make room for anyone else's. But I didn't see a villain when I examined Molly Hopewell, the haggard woman dressed in a winter white sweater set and pearls seated on the other side of the courtroom. Her slightly curled, brown-ish hair, flecked with grey at the temples, and cut into a soft bob suggested more schoolteacher than murderer.

"We will take a brief break now. Thank you for your presence and careful attention. Jurors, you will now be escorted from the courtroom."

"All rise," the same baritone voice boomed. I enjoyed getting heralded in and out of rooms.

We stood almost as one and filed out of our spaces in our predetermined order. Clemence directed us out the back of the courtroom, down the ugly hall, and into our room. As soon as I escaped the courtroom, I chattered to my neighbours.

"What d'ya think?"

Any response was cut short. "Silence," Clemence said. "No talking outside your jury room."

CHAPTER 19

Howdy

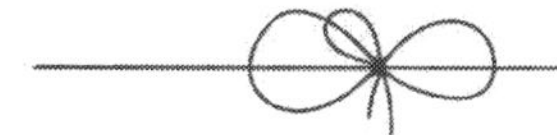

What was a group of jurors called? Not a flock. Too ordinary. Not a murder, although that amused me. Not a parliament. Nobody'd give us that much authority. A chattering? Yes, that was apt.

I waited for a lull in the half-dozen conversations. "Hi, everyone." A few heads turned my way, but Motormouth at the end of the table seemed deaf. "Hi." Silence. "Can we introduce ourselves? My name is Heddie."

On the far end of the room, someone had created a seating chart by affixing a flip-chart sheet to the wall with masking tape. Whoever ripped the sheet—probably not Clemence, given the ragged edges—started their artwork in blue marker. When that colour dried out, they started over again with green. One name marked each end of a sloppy rectangle drawn in the middle of the page. Five more names were written along each side, but someone had neatly taped a looseleaf sheet over the original Nine's name, replacing it with mine. Henry-Etta.

Motormouth donned a tuque, leaving wisps of hair untucked. "Dad wanted a boy?"

"Original." I sneered at him before locating his name on the flip-chart. "Phillip, yes?"

"My friends call me Phil."

"Phillip, then." I pronounced Number One's name "Fill up," rounding my lips with the "p" and popping them to close the second syllable. He didn't correct me.

I sidled through the narrow gap between our table and the wall to the seating chart and selected the licorice-scented black marker from the collection nested in a coffee tin to scribble out my given name. I printed H-E-D-D-I-E neatly overtop. No last names here. Yet another jury rule.

Phillip curled his lip and wrinkled his nose like a single puppet string animated his face.

Number Twelve said, "Never mind him." The teenager wore more makeup than a drag queen, complete with false eyelashes, rouge, and foundation.

"You old enough to be here?" I grinned.

"I know, eh," she said. "I just turned eighteen. Happy birthday to me."

I pointed to the diagram. "You wanna change your name too?"

"I go by Mandi. With an 'i.'" She stood, and in her high heels, she towered over me. The marker squeaked as she printed her preferred name with a heart over the "i."

I cocked my head, Fella-style, to examine the chart. It needed some anchors to orient us all. I grabbed the brown marker. Yum, cinnamon. First up? A door with an impressive chain and padlock in the bottom left corner, closest to Phillip. I drew the kitchenette near the door, complete with microwave, clock, and trays of treats, then the hallway next to the kitchenette with the all-important bathroom sign.

I turned and faced the entire room. "Anyone else want to change their names while I'm at it?" I held up a fistful of markers to show I meant business. "How about we also share a snippet about ourselves?"

Murmurs in every octave told me to proceed.

"I'll start. I'm a dog trainer, and I specialize in helping families welcome and integrate rescued animals." I wrote a number nine beside my name on the chart and drew a floppy-eared dog as my icon or symbol.

"My dog needs training," piped up a tattooed man

midway down the opposite side of the table. "Got him during the lockdowns, and I can't leave him alone."

"Hey," my left-side neighbour said, "me too."

Another juror added, "Me three."

I scurried to my seat, where I grabbed a fistful of crumpled business cards from the front pocket of my backpack and doled one out to each new prospect. The cards offered scant information, containing only my company name, *Pawsitive Pups*, work email address and my cell phone number. "Call me when we're done here."

My left-side neighbour, Number Seven, studied my card. "How about I go next? I'm Brad. My wife brings home the bacon. She's a rocket scientist. Literally." He peered at us through his horn-rimmed glasses. He wore a short-sleeved button-up shirt with a single breast pocket stuffed with a plastic pocket protector and pens. His ensemble gave him a nerdy vibe. Less wholesome Clark Kent, more Willy Loman. "I stay at home with our twins. They're twenty months old now, and a handful. Two handfuls."

I wrote a seven and drew wooden blocks with the ABCs for Brad.

"Your turn?" I pointed to my right-side neighbour, Number Eleven, to go next.

She busily crocheted a delicate baby blanket in gender-neutral shades of yellow and green. "I'm Ruth. I'm retired now, and happily collecting my pension. I was a nurse and worked mostly at the cancer centre. Nowadays, I teach knitting and crochet classes at high-end yarn shops. Doesn't pay the rent but helps replenish my stash." She Vanna-ed her blanket for our inspection.

I drew a ball of yarn and a crochet hook next to her place on the chart. "I thought seniors got exempted from jury duty?" I said.

"The judge offered me a pass, but I didn't take him up on it." She beamed a sunny smile. "This might surprise you, but I've always wanted to be a juror."

"You shouldn't be here." Phillip's eyes bulged slightly.

"Pardon me?" Ruth said.

"It's a conflict...a conflict of interest for you to be here."

"How so?" The question came from Number Ten, the tall woman seated across from me and whom I'd met at the selection. She resembled an aging Olive Oyl, with a dyed black bob atop a black and white buttoned-up cardigan and blouse ensemble.

Phillip crossed his arms. His pinched mouth made him look like a dried apple doll. "She might know some witnesses."

Number Ten chuckled. "You watch too much TV. They can't excuse everybody who might know somebody. Then nobody could be jurors. Six degrees of separation, right?" She flipped her hair out of her face, a gesture that elongated her ropy neck. "My turn? I'm Toni, and I'm a legal secretary." Directing her gaze at Phillip, she said, "Any more words of wisdom?"

He shook his head and strummed the papers in his folder.

Toni ignored him. "Lawyers and the rest might never be jurors, but we peons get called." I smiled at her word choice. "Besides. I mostly work on wills and such. Sometimes real estate deals. I never get to work on criminal cases."

I wrote ten and "Toni" in neat cursive. Her icon was the scale of justice.

I continued around the table, as self-appointed emcee. "Mandi, sorry, we skipped you."

She waved, then held her hands up to frame her face. "I just started at Mount Royal University. I'm in Open Studies right now, but I want to be a news anchor." I could see it. When she stopped giggling, her diction was crisp.

I put a number twelve and a corded microphone next to Mandi's name. "You could've got off. The judge excused lots of students." Some had complained about getting behind in their coursework or missing midterms, and the judge was sympathetic to them all.

"I want to be here. My profs even encouraged me. I'm taking a Social Justice class and including this experience somehow in my final assignment."

"Careful there," Toni warned. "Jurors need to follow lots of rules. For one, we can't talk about anything that happens in this room." Toni waved expansively, a gesture that emphasized the room's diminutive size.

"I'll be careful," Mandi enthused.

I used the marker as a pointer and felt like a majorette. "Can we go this way around the table? It looks like we got even numbers on Toni's side, and the odds on my side."

Number eight stretched various body parts behind his designated chair. "Remember me?" the tattooed man asked. "We met at selection." His shirt, a tight brown button-down, stretched across his chest and accentuated a burly physique. "We both look different," he said.

I shook my head. "Sorry?"

"At the summons? I wore my grandpa's turtleneck and kinda looked respectable." He laughed. "Except for the hair."

I still didn't place him.

A colourful geometric tattoo circled his neck and climbed into the bristle of his hairline. Insects twined into the pattern, a ladybug and what appeared to be a monarch butterfly. Some stubble on his head cast a pinkish hue and unmasked my fuchsia fauxhawk companion.

"You missed a few spots," I blurted.

He rubbed his head. "Always do. I'm Jim, by the way."

"What do you do?"

"Can't you guess?"

Spotting a dare, I studied him from head to toe. "You're a tattoo artist."

"Correct. Well done." He seemed pleased.

I drew a hearted "Mom" tattoo next to his name.

The next woman, Number Six, spoke up. "I'm Ingrid. I'm a schoolteacher, but I retire next summer. Finally." She exposed her gums when she smiled. "I'm sick—sick to death of other people's kids," she confessed. "Time for me to retire."

"Any plans?"

"No. Just looking forward to gardening and grandkids. Two outta three retirement Gs. I'll skip golf."

I wrote a six next to her name and drew daisy-like flowers with smiling faces for her icon.

Norman, Number Four, sat near the far end of the table. His physique was less pear-shaped and more gourd. "I'm a truck driver." I marked a four next to his name.

"What kind of truck?"

"Kenworth."

I drew a steering wheel with the initials KW in the middle as his icon.

The next man's buzz cut made his head square. That, combined with his blue khakis and pale-yellow shirt, reminded me of SpongeBob. He was even a little bucktoothed. "I'm Adam. I'm a massage therapist."

That information generated considerable enthusiasm.

"I'm happy to help each of you." He pulled a thick wallet from his back pocket, heedless of the misalignment caused by raising one buttock an inch or two higher than the other, then flipped a business card toward each of us. He seemed pleased with my stick figure knock-off of da Vinci's Vitruvian Man as his symbol.

Next up? "My name is Phil. I was a rancher, but I sold my place a year back and moved into town."

I wrote one next to his name. I only circled Phillip's name rather than changing it and hid my self-satisfied smile.

"You could've gotten out of this too." Toni, the legal secretary, hadn't forgiven him.

Phillip's face reddened. "I'm not old enough."

Oops. I also thought he was well into his dotage, with his pasty complexion, sagging gut, and pinched face.

"That judge was an ass," Phillip claimed.

I considered then dismissed this observation. Maybe near the end, when the judge had too many seats to fill and the number of potential jurors dwindled.

"He could've let me go." Phillip's icon was a stick figure trying to lasso a horse.

"You should've spoken up before they excused Fourteen," Toni replied.

Before anyone could answer, the next man spoke. "Hi, my name is Steve," he said, too cheerily. "I'm a salesman. Heavy equipment to ranchers." Steve studied Phillip, turning his head back and forth at exaggerated angles. "I'm sure we've met. Wanna do lunch?"

Phillip sat stone-faced, and I almost felt sorry for him.

"Don't worry. I talk a lot when I'm excited, and I'm thrilled to be here. I work on commission, so financially, well, I'm sure you can imagine." Steve was about my age and seemed pleasant enough, even if a tad oblivious. By my guess, nearly half the jury stood to lose wages.

I wrote three next to his name and drew a tractor with a grinning figure in the driver's seat.

"My turn?" His neighbour waved broadly, arm over her head. "I'm over the moon to be here. Super exciting, eh Steve?" Number Five elbowed her neighbour and winked, unfazed when he wheeled out of range. "I'm Pat. This is my fourth summons but my first trial. I never made it this far before." She rubbed her hands together, unable to contain her glee. "I got selected once before, but the guy pleaded guilty, so no trial."

"That happens a lot," Toni said. "Very few cases get this far."

Toni seemed to know more about criminal trials than she originally let on.

Pat lowered her voice. "Now, I can check this off my bucket list."

Phillip abruptly stood and inspected our snack pickings.

I ignored him. "What do you do, Pat?" I asked.

"I'm an aesthetician."

Say that word aloud three times fast. I drew well-coiffed hands with long fingernails and added a few fireworks just because.

Knock, knock, knock.

Phillip remained at the counter, his back to the room. "Quiet, everybody."

The chatter continued.

Phillip banged the counter and the stack of plates clattered. "Shuddup."

I used my fingertips to close my gaping mouth. "Wow. Did you forget your manners at the ranch?"

"Clemence said." He turned to Clemence, who'd just opened the door.

She stared at him and licked her teeth with her mouth mostly closed. She offered no preamble. "We're headed into the courtroom in a few minutes. Please get ready." She scowled at Mandi, who chewed and clicked bubblegum. "No gum in the courtroom."

Mandi ripped the corner off one page in her notepad and wrapped it before tossing it overhand into the bin.

Clemence turned to Phillip. "No gum and no hats."

Phillip sighed and rolled his eyes. "My head gets cold."

She stared. "Hats are not permitted in the courtroom. Please leave it here."

He opened his mouth, readying himself to protest.

"Sir, remove your hat." Her tone erased any courtesy. Phillip slumped before ripping off his beanie and tossing it onto his chair. His comb-over was out of place, with thin ringlets flopping around his ears.

Clemence wasn't finished with her rules. "This time, when you go into the courtroom, you must be silent. No talking."

"What happens if we need something?" I asked.

"Take what you need with you." She glared at me.

"It's dry in there," I said. "I might get parched."

Clemence moved over to the counter and opened the bottom cupboard to reveal a case of water. She hoisted it out, placed it on the floor, and squared it to the wall. "Grab some water." She glanced at me. "If something else comes up, write a note and send it down the row to me. I will decide how to handle the question. If you need more paper or another pen, I will pass it to you."

"I'm prepared," Brad said, patting his overstuffed breast pocket. Goody Two-Shoes.

She continued, "If you can't hear the testimony or see the evidence, I will ask the judge to make accommodations."

"Thank you," I said, satisfied by an actual answer.

"She told us all this before," Phillip said. "Oh, right. You were late."

Clemence ignored him. "I keep this door locked." She swung the open door back and forth. "Your belongings are safe here. When you are in this room—in the mornings before court or during breaks in the trial—if you need out, or if you need to talk to me, knock on the door. Knocking is how we communicate. For now, when everyone is ready to go into the courtroom…" She cocked her head, inviting someone to finish her sentence.

Mandi played along. "We knock on the door?"

Clemence pointed at Mandi and graced her with a rare smile. "Exactly." Clemence turned, left the room, closed the door, and, true to her word, locked us in.

We created plenty of commotion, all abuzz in our excitement. I considered our crew, the people assigned with hearing the evidence and deciding a woman's fate. We were evenly split, six men and six women. I think our economic backgrounds positioned us all as middle class. No rich folks here and no desperately poor ones. But our age profile leaned heavily toward the geriatric.

My fellow jurors and I milled close to the door. "We ready?" I asked.

Bobbing heads answered me.

Mandi bounced on the balls of her feet. "May I?"

I laughed, enjoying her spirit. "Sure."

"Here we go," she squealed, and began our service with her *knock, knock, knock*.

CHAPTER 20
Crabby's Diner

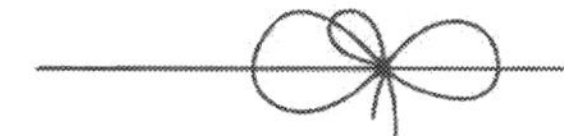

"Heddie."

I turned toward the voice calling my name, knowing full well there was only one me in any crowd. Ruth jogged along the slushy sidewalk and waved one arm over her head like a lucky cat at a Chinese takeaway. Fortunately, she'd didn't tote her crochet project. I inwardly cringed at the thought of making small talk for the next hour and waited for her to catch up.

"Are you dining with anyone?" she asked. She wasn't out of breath.

"I'm meeting a friend." Short. Succinct. Would she get the message?

"Can I join you?"

I tried a different approach. "Is that allowed?" Maybe, just maybe, she didn't know all our rules yet.

She glanced from side to side. "I think it's okay." I looked around, too, seeking her I-spy target. Maybe she sought other paired jurors traipsing off to find their own lunches? Or a bailiff to question on the finer points of our rules? "We can't talk about the case. We all need to be together for that."

I wrinkled my nose at the image of us crowding into some local eatery. Or finding twelve seats together during the lunch rush hour. Or watching Phillip eat, knowing he undoubtedly talked with his mouth full and picked his teeth in public.

I swung my arm like a semaphore directing traffic and beckoned her to follow. "I'm meeting my friend around the corner. You can join us."

I led Ruth to the diner that could've been teleported from the fifties. The black and white tile floor shone with polish and love. Purple, the royal shade, was the colour picked up in the Formica tables, the poofed gingham curtains, the upholstery on the vinyl benches along both windowless walls and the stools stationed uniformly around the counter. Chrome was the other accent, visible in all furniture legs, appliances, catching the glare from the fluorescent lights and bouncing it back off the shiny floor.

I held my arm out like an open door, and Ruth moved into the room.

I spotted Leah, already seated in a c-shaped booth in the furthest corner of the noisy room, facing the whole restaurant. She sat alone in that ubiquitous pose of the solitary with their smartphones. "Leah," I called and waved.

She looked up and I pointed at the top of Ruth's head, pumping my arm. Never a slouch, Leah interpreted my impromptu sign language and slid over to the disdained in-between seat. Leah's neat chignon reflected in the mirror behind her, and not for the first time, I envied my friend's poise. Beside her, I always felt like the ugly duckling.

Ruth slid into the booth and introduced herself. "Heddie asked me to join you."

I shook my head, wide-eyed and vehement, just out of Ruth's view.

Leah's return greeting featured a tight-lipped smile, but she didn't give me away.

I shucked my backpack from my shoulder and sat down onto the smooth bench, scooting across its length. It was a tight space, and I sat perpendicular to the table with one leg propped up on the seat. I preferred my back against a wall, but Ruth had already claimed that prize as her own.

Leah handed us each one of the tattered menus, stained

and creased by hard use.

"These things are a health violation." Ruth wrinkled her nose like she handled a fouled diaper.

"The food is delicious and cheap," Leah responded.

Ruth skimmed the choices. "What do you recommend?"

"Most people like their soups." Leah pointed to the dusty chalkboard propped on top of the counter. "They change their list every few days to take advantage of whatever's fresh and locally grown."

Soon, the place was jammed.

"Is it always so busy?" Ruth asked. "It's Tuesday."

"It's a favourite of almost everybody at the courthouse," Leah said. "I came here too, in my former life."

I quickly glanced around and didn't recognize anyone.

The server snuck up on me and placed a third setting on the table. "Hey, Leah. Been a long time," she said, smiling, her wrinkled cheeks folding like pleats. "Bruschetta?"

"You know it, Crabby. Thanks."

"Chef'll make it fresh the way you like. Extra tart." The woman had to be eighty years old, hunched over like a question mark, nimble despite her years and posture. I glanced at her name tag. "Sondra." Now I was confused. Shouldn't it be Crabby?

She turned to me. The server's uniform—her apron, cap, and the edging on her skirt—matched the curtains. "What would you like to order, ma'am?" Uh-oh, I'd gone from miss to ma'am in a week. Still, it was better than hon. Or shug.

"I'll have the soupe du jour," I said, pronouncing the French phrase like a Quebecker. "Please," I added hastily. I was more annoyed by the ma'am-calling than I realized. "Thank you," I added for extra measure.

Ruth placed her order before Crabby/Sondra could ask for it. "I'll have the potato leek soup too," she said. "I need rib-sticking food in this weather." She offered a toothy grin, eyes bright.

Crabby/Sondra twirled on her heel, taking our orders to the invisible chef.

"Will you excuse me?" Leah said. "I need to use the facilities."

Both Ruth and I moved to let her out, but Ruth was faster.

Once Leah was out of sight, Ruth filled the silence with our taboo subject, the only thing we shared. "What do you think about the trial so far?"

I rummaged around my thoughts for something appropriate to say within the limits of our rules. "It's not at all like the movies."

Ruth laughed. "I need dramatic music to cue the important bits."

I smiled in response. "Our oaths surprised me."

"What do you mean?"

"Most of us affirmed. Only one person swore on the Bible. The tattooed guy. Er, the heavily tattooed guy."

"Oh, Jim? He's tame." Ruth pondered for a moment. "But you're right. I hadn't noticed."

"There are lots of Bible verses on the protesters' signs, so I'd expected a similar showing on the jury," I admitted.

"What about Mandi?"

I didn't remember anything specifically religious from Mandi's mouth.

"She wears a crucifix," Ruth explained. "Flashy."

"That's a fashion statement," I said. "She makes her own jewellery."

Crabby/Sondra interrupted us to slide water glasses across the table to each of our spots. She didn't spill a drop.

"What I hate is the repetition," I said. "We hear the same thing over and over."

"Some people still don't get it," Ruth noted.

She was right. Most people were on the ball, but not Phillip. "I'm not sure how to help Phillip keep everything straight."

She shook her head. "I think he's got chemo-brain."

It was my turn to be surprised. And nosy.

Crabby/Sondra interrupted us again by tossing a basket of rolls onto the table. Next, she slid across a bowl of butter balls and a short stack of side plates, and both nudged to a stop next to the bread. I gaped at her, and she winked.

I grabbed a roll, warm from the oven, and passed the basket to Ruth. She held up her hand like a shield, so I set it down again.

"During my career, I saw closeup how chemo affects people. He lost most of his hair," she said.

I felt ashamed about my earlier appraisal of his hairdo but as an excuse, I had no experience with chemo. Hug had died quickly, just over a year after diagnosis. From my current vantage, his was a death sentence from the beginning. No point in chemo. Just some surgery. Radiation aimed to reduce the worst of the bone lesions. A bunch of pills, mostly for pain. Lots of blood transfusions. Many hospitalizations. And almost daily tests. "Maybe it'll get better? As he heals from his treatments?"

"We'll see." She didn't look convinced.

"I don't know why he didn't ask to get excused. Lots of others got off jury duty. For flimsy reasons."

Ruth stared at the basket of bread and hesitated before grabbing a roll. She ripped it into bite-sized pieces and buttered each morsel. "I love how organized the jury selection was. But that orientation video..."

I picked up the spoon from my place setting and rubbed off water spots with my napkin. "I liked how they assigned us all numbers. We get to be anonymous. No one knows who we are, and especially not the accused."

Ruth nodded too vigorously. "Lots of people there were protesters."

"Huh? I didn't notice them." That was the truth. "How'd they get past the guards? I had to show my summons before they let me in. Like an admission ticket."

"Security was lax," she snapped.

Leah returned, and I slid out of the booth to let her in. "What'd I miss?" she asked.

"Oh, we compared notes," Ruth said. "The whole thing's quite fascinating so far."

"You're a juror too?" Leah asked. "On the Hopewell case?" I'm sure Leah had already guessed but sought Ruth's confession.

"Correct." Ruth looked too pleased with herself, given the gravity of our trial.

"I used to be a lawyer," Leah said, then she spelled out why she inserted that fact into our conversation. "You're not supposed to be talking about the trial. Not in public, that's for sure." Now it was Leah's turn to inspect our neighbours, looking for any sign they found our conversation more scintillating than their own.

Ruth clamped her mouth closed.

We were saved by the arrival of our food. Mine was the size of a tureen, thick with hefty chunks of potato and leek and topped with crisped bacon and onion bits. I rummaged into my backpack, grabbed a hair clip, and pinned back the loose tendrils that always escaped their bonds. I glanced at the mirrored wall to inspect my image. This updo emphasized my cheekbones—my best feature. I blew on a spoonful before testing it, my taste buds blooming with the rich umami from the creamy blend.

Leah frowned at something behind me. I turned to look and spotted Stanley crossing the room.

"Surprise, surprise. Fancy meeting you here," he said.

"Thanks for popping by." Leah's voice was flat. "I hope it wasn't inconvenient."

I readied myself to protest, but Leah held up her hand to quieten me.

He placed a neatly folded plain brown sack on our table. "It's fine. I pick up takeout once or twice a month anyway."

I couldn't believe Leah had gone behind my back again.

"This is becoming a bad habit. You invited him here after what he did last weekend?"

Ruth proffered her hand, which Stanley took. "Pleased to meet you. I'm on the jury with Heddie."

"You too?" Stanley dropped her hand like she had warts. "I hope you'll do a better job than she will."

A sharp punt to my calf cut off any tirade. "Stanley," Leah began, "Heddie, please be kinder to each other. You're both having a rough go."

"Is that your professional assessment?" he asked, his tone sarcastic. "She's got impulse control issues."

"We all grieve differently," Leah said.

"Uh-huh. Whatever." Stanley turned his attention back to me and he looked like a scolded child. "Listen, I came by to apologize. Some of the stuff I said the other day, well, it was uncalled for."

Too little, too late. I crossed my arms and waited for more. "Your words were nasty, sure, but your actions were far worse. Harmful."

He sniffed at me. "I also need to give you this." He reached into the left breast pocket of his handsome flannel coat and removed a packet of paper wrapped in blue cardstock. "Here's Hugh's will. As proof."

Leah straightened in her seat. "I'll take that." She reached past me and nudged my outstretching arm aside to grasp the bundle of legal papers.

"It's for Heddie." Stanley pulled his arm back just enough that Leah got a fistful of air. A couple of his curls were plastered onto his forehead, making him look like an oversized Cabbage Patch doll.

Leah held her hand out. "Give it to me." Stanley held the papers poised in midair. Leah thwacked his hand, but he maintained his grip. Leah grabbed the papers, too, and both clenched them in a tug-of-war.

"Stop," I cried. "You'll tear them."

Stanley released his grip, but Leah had braced herself.

No undignified sprawling displays for my champion.

"It's only a notarized copy. The original is in for probate." He seemed too tickled for a man presenting the Last Will and Testament of his only brother. "You've been served."

"Don't be an officious cretin," Leah said. So much for playing nice. She flipped through the pages, scanning quickly, with too much head shaking.

"What did Hug say?" I asked. Bile burned the back of my throat, and I worked hard not to retch.

"Would you stop it?" Stanley interjected. "His name was Hugh—Hugh Fields. Stop calling him Hug."

I banged the table with my clenched fist. The salt and pepper shakers clattered when they fell over, and several patrons adjusted themselves to rubberneck. I righted the spices, but not before tossing a bit of salt over my shoulder. I turned to face Leah and thereby gave Stanley the cold shoulder. "Leah, tell me."

"It's not good, not good at all." She regarded Stanley and Ruth as if just remembering our observers. "We can talk about it tonight."

"I'm giving it to her as a courtesy." Stanley faced Leah and squared his shoulders. "She doesn't have any right to it. As you can see, she's not in the will at all."

"I've had enough of all this." I moved to leave the booth, and Leah placed her hand on my arm. I couldn't tell whether she was reassuring or restraining me.

She refolded the papers and zipped them into her purse, securing everything safe from pickpockets and my prying eyes. "It'll be okay, Heddie, I promise. I will make this all okay."

"Don't make promises you can't keep," I warned. She should listen to my voice of experience.

Stanley picked up his lunch bag and turned to leave. "I'll see you around."

Not so fast. He had the social graces of a gnat. I twisted to face him. "You've gotta lot of nerve."

"Shush. You're making a scene," Stanley whispered.

Don't shush me. "I'm making a scene? You dropped this on me in public." I felt the heat rise from my belly. Red was not my colour, and blotchy even less so.

"I tried to reach you."

"Really?" My volume rose with each syllable. "Is that all you got? I gave up everything for Hug, to care for him properly. The way he needed. I'm left here grieving, broke. And, thanks to you, homeless." No calls. No casseroles.

"Leah invited me," Stanley replied.

"Neither of you considered warning me. Send me a text, 'Hey Heddie, I know your husband just died, but he screwed you. Left you nothing.' Something like that?"

"You weren't married," he said, still whispering. He glared at me, his eyes protruding like—what? Like hemorrhoids, because he was such a pain in the butt.

"Close enough."

"Close only counts in horseshoes," he said, spraying spittle at every sibilant.

"Enough, you two." It was Leah's turn to slam the table. Fortunately, all the condiments remained upright.

Stanley didn't look chastised. "Get Dee to contact her mediator friend. We need to settle this once and for all."

"I'll be in touch. You should leave now." Leah swept her hand, and miraculously, he left.

"That'll teach you to invite him anywhere," I said, rightfully indignant. "Did you learn your lesson yet?"

For once, Leah looked chagrined.

"Why does he think you'll do a bad job?" Ruth latched onto the wrong topic.

Leah spoke for me again. "Stanley thinks Heddie's loss is too recent. And too complicated."

"That's not quite right, Ruth," I said. "Stanley thinks I'm against assisted dying. He thinks I talked Hug out of an easier death."

"Did you?"

"No. Hug and I never talked about it." Not explicitly. A social worker brought it up once, and I shook my head at the wrong time. Most misunderstood gesture of my life. But I wasn't saying no to an easier death. I was saying no to any death, to his dying. Totally different.

Ruth did not acknowledge my comment. With a lurch, she jumped up. "Heddie, we've got to go. Hustle or we'll be late." She clapped her hands. "Chop, chop."

I raised my arm to grab Crabby's attention, and we all dropped enough cash on the table to cover our bills.

When I stood to leave, I spotted Axel hunkered in the booth behind us. Granted, and in my defence, his back was to me, making him barely visible to my distracted eye. I recalled our lunch-time conversations and tried to put all our tangents back into place. I really wished we hadn't talked about the trial so much. I really wished my encounter with Stanley had been more private.

"Damn," I said only to myself.

CHAPTER 21

Dear Diary

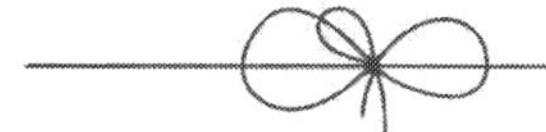

My skin crawled—*heeby jeebies*—at the sound of the pen scratching against the paper.

Dear diary.

My first words on the first page of my new journal were already wrong. I struck out the offending word, then doodled lines and flourishes to draw an open frame.

Dear ~~diary.~~ Hug.

That was better. He and I were the ones who needed to talk things through.

Everyone says you should have given me a ring. That we should have gotten married. Why didn't we?

My handwriting was slow, the quality of my letters poor.

I know we talked about it.

After his death sentence, I'd opened our house to our friends and family. I was already exhausted and greedy—exhausted from the months of vigilance and loss, greedy for his diminishing time. Leah broached the idea and we held a living wake for him, with a last goodbye.

You wanted to know why I shut-off the cuckoo clock? Its ticking reminded me of the bomb about to explode our lives apart.

He'd received visitors three afternoons in a row. I

scheduled most of them, reaching out to everyone through a mass email—"come say goodbye." I arranged the roster so no enemies overlapped, so he didn't get overwhelmed. But someone forwarded my message like a morbid chain letter, and I lost control of the guest list.

You left me with lots of unanswered questions and now, they're unanswerable.

"How did you meet?" Roberta asked. She was the third ex to pop by in as many days. I personally wouldn't have invited them, but Hug seemed pleased to see them all, and I couldn't deny him.

"He hired me to train Fella."

At the mention of his name, Fella opened his eyes and lifted his head from where he'd been resting in the crook of Hug's legs. I stroked his head and he dozed again.

"Bobby, excuse us. Heddie, can you help me to the loo?"

"Oh, she's promoted from dog-sitter to orderly?"

"Leave her alone," Hug said, defending me for once.

Why didn't you give me a nickname? I gave you one. Everything and everyone important in your life got a handle. But not me.

Roberta blushed. "I'm sorry, Hugh. I meant nothing by it. But she's a keeper. You should marry her."

You studied me after her comment, her challenge. Were you trying to gauge my reaction, what I wanted? I wish I'd spoken my mind.

I turned my head away and focused on my task. I transferred Hug from the bed to a wheelchair, and then wheeled him the short distance to the bathroom.

I didn't want you to see my hope, my eager longing you'd act on her suggestion. That you'd choose me.

He boomed like a sportscaster, his jolly voice detailing each movement with a running commentary. "Hugh Fields swings his legs over the bed and sits up. Carefully. And he wraps his arms around his lover. Because he loves her. He stands with the support of his love. One step. Two steps. Swing into the chair."

Stanley overheard everything, and his peevish reaction threatened to sully Hug's contrived party.

I really don't know why you left Stanley in charge. He never liked me. How can I build a new life without you when he keeps knocking me down?

Once Hug was comfortably snugged into his bed again, I left him in the company of some cousins and escorted Stanley to the living room for a much-needed heart-to-heart. The living room buzzed with the guests' lively chatter and laughter, a disconcerting contrast to Hug's sick room.

"What gives, Stanley?"

I was bolder then when I thought I had rights, when I thought you'd keep your promises too.

He and Becky stationed themselves on a couch along one wall. They behaved as though they were royalty and we were their serfs. He lolled in his seat, his legs splayed like a horseless rider with his arms resting outstretched along the couch's frame. They sat within easy reach of the snacks arranged on a low table in the middle of the room and helped themselves to generous portions heedless of the diminishing quantities left for everyone else. Fortunately, Leah replaced items as needed.

"You don't want to get married." It was more an order than an observation. His face was all screwed up, with both a rumpled nose and pursed lips. In the dim light, I couldn't tell whether his ruddy complexion was anger or high blood pressure. In hindsight, his eyes already possessed a reptilian quality.

Leah stepped between us, employing a technique I'd used countless times with a timid dog whose confidence I needed to boost. "Why not? They love each other." Leah's hands clenched into fists at her sides. "And it would be the right thing to do."

"Hugh doesn't believe in marriage," Stanley replied, the corners of his mouth lifting into a smirk.

"What does that matter?" Leah asked. "He should do it for her." She pointed at me with her thumb, like she was only a hitchhiker in the debate.

"She doesn't believe in marriage either," Stanley said, his chest swelling in triumph. He turned his gaze to me. "Tell her."

"It's true. I didn't think I needed marriage." I whispered these words, hoping my voice didn't carry. "That was before..." I stopped mid-sentence to muster my courage to tell everyone: Hug was mine and I was his.

"Stick to your principles, girl." He advised me against marrying while seated next to his wife.

"Principles change," I replied. "My boyfriend is dying."

"I know that," he said. "He's my brother."

"This isn't a competition," I said without knowing I'd repeat those words. Truth was, I was there every day and every night for Hug, while two or more weeks often elapsed between Stanley's visits. "Calling me his 'girlfriend' is just so inadequate. So incomplete. I want more."

His lips curled into a snarl. I think he found me disgusting. But dogs snarl before they attack, so it could've been a warning.

"I need to take care of myself," I said accurately. Even amid all that emotional turmoil, I was prescient.

Later, Leah followed me into the bathroom so we could be alone and out of everyone else's earshot. "I wish I'd talked with you about this before." It was the first time I noticed her wan face, her red-rimmed eyes. "Tell Hugh." I shook my head almost imperceptibly and tried to look away, but Leah used a bent forefinger to raise my chin so I couldn't avoid her gaze. "Stanley does not care about you. He will not do right by you."

Leah called it, but you knew him even better. Why did you leave him in charge?

Tears welled in my eyes, but I willed them to remain within their banks. "Remember when we used to make fun of women who got married and changed their names?"

"Yes," Leah said.

"I have a list of women's funny married names. Rude names. Unfortunate names."

"Yes."

"Now here I want to get married."

"You're trying to hold on to him. You love him."

"I feel so ashamed." I used my sleeve to wipe a tear from my cheek. "Now, look at me. Such a hypocrite."

"You want a commitment from him." She paused. "You can't have him for a long time. But you want him to tell the world he was yours for a while."

You were mine. Weren't you? There's nothing with this Wendy person, right?

I leaned against the counter, getting the rear of my dress wet from countless dripping hands. I covered my face with a hand towel to hide my ugly cry and patted around with the other, looking for a tissue or paper towel. She placed a crumpled wad into my hand, retrieved from her pants pocket. I used it to wipe my eyes before noisily, and with some satisfaction, blowing my nose.

"I don't even want a ring," I whispered. "Got enough jewellery, thanks." I watched Leah's reaction. "I just want him to choose me."

I split my time unequally between tending to his needs and the wants and whims of the well-wishers queued to send him off. Some were curious, probably there to dispel rumours. Others may have thought we exaggerated his disease or prognosis. Most came in disbelief. I understood that response best. It was all so extreme, so incomprehensible. So random.

We lived the opposite of a miracle—an anti-miracle.

I never told you how I felt. You weren't too tired that night to extract your impossible promise from me, and the next day, you died.

CHAPTER 22

Arguments

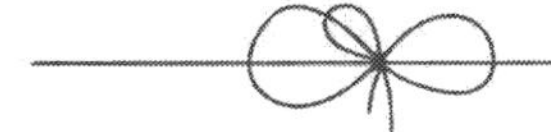

Brad gave me the stink-eye when I jostled him, and I wheeled my chair hastily away. Both lawyers at the Crown table watched our commotion, matching round eyes and mouths conveying their distaste.

That's when I dubbed them Tweedledee and Tweedledum. Unkind? Yes, probably.

Once we settled, the judge began. "Ladies and gentlemen of the jury, I see you are all present."

How many times would he repeat the same spiel?

The court reporter acknowledged the judge's assertion, and I realized he stated the obvious for her benefit.

"We all know you have lives of your own…" He spoke gravely, like some Shakespearean over-actor. I nodded, pretending to share his version of my reality.

"The charge against the accused is first degree murder, a crime that requires the Crown to prove both premeditation and planning." The judge's face was animated, and his expressions punctuated his sentences. When he stressed something, he raised his bushy eyebrows and opened his eyes wide like he feared we'd miss his meaning. He turned slightly in his chair. "Mr. Parker, would you like to begin?"

Tweedledee—Twee-dee for short—emerged from behind the nearest table. "Yessir." He strode the four steps to the lectern in the middle of the room and placed a jumble of papers onto the stand. Twee-dee grabbed the mic stand with both hands and adjusted it. High-pitched squeals cut his wrestling short, and I knocked my notepad off my table when I covered my ears.

Unruffled—in both costume and attitude—the clerk moved to a metal box resembling a DJ's equipment where she twisted knobs and pushed levers to stop the screeching.

From behind his left ear, Twee-dee pulled a pencil. He used the eraser to flip through some pages before settling on his starting point. "Welcome." He beamed at us as though greeting fond friends after a long hiatus. "My name is Peter Parker." He paused, then chuckled. "Yes, just like Spider-Man."

Polite laughter circulated the room like a foul smell.

"Just as Uncle Ben said to Peter, 'With great power comes great responsibility.' That is my motto for this case and the reason we are here. The power in this context is the power of life and death under Canada's MAID legislation. MAID? That's Medical Assistance in Dying." He bounced his pencil like the dot over karaoke lyrics, emphasizing each syllable.

"The responsibility for wielding this incredible power lies with the dying. Only the person dying can say 'yes' or 'no.' 'Now is the time.' Not their parents. Not their siblings. Not their children. Not their spouses." Here, he turned to stare at Molly in the prisoner's dock. She held his gaze without seeming pushy, but she looked away first.

"When legislators created this law, they strove to prevent abuse of the power of death by asking for verbal consent at several key points. The patient needed to be lucid, aware of his situation, aware he was asking to die. Know what death meant. One of those points—safeguards—was just before injecting the medicine to end the person's suffering." He studied us rather than his notes, and I realized he didn't need to read his speech. His messy notes were a prop.

He turned toward the judge. "Your Honour, may I present exhibit one?"

A fine assortment of holes adorned Twee-dee's ear lobes. I imagined they were remnants of a past life, former badassery, and my estimation of him improved.

The judge nodded. “Madam clerk, please distribute copies of exhibit one to the jury.”

The clerk handed us each a small packet of papers.

The judge continued, “Please mark your juror number and the exhibit number in the top right-hand corner of every exhibit you receive.”

The scratching of a dozen pens on the papers broadcast our compliance with his instructions.

The Crown flicked an image onto the television screens. The colour photograph showed a man, head back and mouth open, caught in mid-laugh. His black hair was streaked with some grey, mostly at his temples. Brown eyes, alert and happy, scrunched in clusters of wrinkles. I thought I heard someone gasp. Molly? She stared straight ahead blankly. Nope. Who then? I couldn’t tell.

“May I introduce Maxwell Gerald Taylor. Max to his friends and family. Max was diagnosed with breast cancer when he was only fifty years old. Yes, men can develop breast cancer, too, and it’s usually fatal, often diagnosed too late. But Max was one of the lucky ones. His cancer was treatable, and he responded well to the therapies his doctors prescribed.”

I searched the audience for the source of the quiet sobbing. The elderly woman I’d tagged as Max’s mother, seated directly behind the Crown table, held a tissue to her eyes. She wore a pale pink Jackie Kennedy suit, but she’d complied with the rules—no pillbox hat covered her dyed white-blonde hair. She delicately dabbed the tissue at her nose before balling it up and squeezing it into a pocket of her purse.

“Max was making the most of his life. His doctors will tell you that his disease spared his organs, which means he could have lived a longer life. Doctors managed his pain with drugs, which means he could have lived a fuller life.”

I gauged Molly’s reaction to this information, but her poker face remained intact.

Twee-dee held a remote control forward like a magic

wand. *Click.* An image of Max, same smiling face, wearing a thin winter coat, snow pants, and snowshoes. He sat on a boulder slightly higher than the surrounding drifts. The trees, mainly bare-branched poplars among evergreen spruce and fir, suggested a sub-alpine trail. Maybe Bragg Creek? Or Kananaskis? A small campfire burned in front of him. Hug and I had stopped taking Fella along those trails after a bear safety course. Apparently, pets, with their assembly of tags on their collars, chimed like a dinner bell for grizzlies.

"Max Taylor was fifty-three years old when he was murdered. Robbed of his remaining time."

Click. Twee-dee scrolled to the next image—a robust man, handsome in his jeans and grey golf shirt, leaning casually against a polished Porsche convertible.

"He was murdered by the very woman who swore an oath to 'have and to hold, for richer or poorer, in sickness and in health.'"

Click. An image of Max, chin up to avoid the slurped kisses of a cradled lapdog.

"Max loved life."

Click. An image of a tanned, shirtless man wearing fluorescent green basketball shorts and flip-flops, surrounded by water, and proudly holding aloft a puny fish.

"Max had plans for the rest of his life. He planned a trip with his wife to Europe for their twenty-fifth wedding anniversary. But she murdered him four months before he could go. He planned to host a party for his father's seventy-fifth birthday. But he missed that celebration by six months."

Click.

I gasped and covered my mouth. An image of a man laid out in a morgue, a white sheet pulled up just past his waist. Conspicuous sutures showed the coroner's handiwork. I winced at the matching healed scars on each side of his chest, presumably from a double mastectomy. I crossed my arms instinctively, protecting my girls. His eyelids were slightly parted, revealing lusterless eyes. His teeth looked too large for his sunken face.

"I and my colleague, Ernest Standish, will prove that Molly Agnes Hopewell murdered her husband, Max Taylor, by giving him a lethal dose of prescription medication that caused Mr. Taylor's death last January."

The show-and-tell was over, but the Crown left the last photo up. I couldn't look at it, so I focused on doodling my notes instead.

"You will learn that Ms. Hopewell planned the murder carefully, exploring several methods before selecting commonplace prescription drugs as her murder weapon." He enunciated each syllable and spoke a tad too loudly. "Ms. Hopewell first sought help from doctors, legally, under the MAID legislation. But even his doctors cannot confirm Mr. Taylor's wishes for his end-of-life."

Molly flinched, but her lawyers didn't interject.

"And Mr. Taylor was not a candidate under the assisted dying legislation."

Twee-dee strode, arms pumping, the few steps back to his table. He picked up a glass of water and drank it down, full to empty, in three loud gulps. "My apologies," he said, after returning to the podium.

"The Defence will tell you that Mr. Taylor was dying. That he was in pain. All that is unfortunate and true. No one denies Max was very ill. What the Defence does not share is that Max continued to fight the disease, accepting every treatment his doctors offered, hoping to prolong his life and even to cure his disease."

Sounded like Max never gave up. Better than I could say for Hug.

"Ms. Hopewell murdered her husband, a man who loved her and trusted her with his life. Ms. Hopewell disregarded the rules and took matters into her own hands, administering a lethal overdose of drugs in the middle of the night when there were no witnesses. When there was no one around to aid Max, to reverse the consequences of her treachery. Her Judas kiss. She killed Max at a point in his life when he was most vulnerable. When he could no longer speak for himself. Could no longer defend himself." Twee-dee exhaled loudly. "Ms. Hopewell showed callous disregard for her husband's life and wishes. Why, you might ask? Why did Ms. Hopewell kill her husband?" He shook his head sorrowfully. "Ms. Hopewell accumulated significant debt—debt she could not repay. Her husband's life insurance policy was a way out for her. Greed motivated her. She was impatient and unwilling for nature to take its course. Ms. Hopewell is a ruthless murderer. Once you hear all the evidence, we are convinced you will find her guilty of the charge of first degree murder." He picked his papers up with a flourish and strode back to his table where Tweedledum stood, waiting to shake his hand.

Like a teeter-totter, when the Crown sat down, the Defence popped up.

"Thank you, Your Honour. Mr. Parker." He bowed deeply, respectfully, toward the judge and less formally to his opponent. "My name is Frank Dodge." Such a fine name for a Defence attorney. Frank, as I creatively dubbed him, moved from behind the table set up for the Defence lawyers and slowly strode, alert and calm, over to occupy the podium. He carried a neat assortment of papers, and he laid them out, rearranging some before satisfied. I was grateful he spared our ears and left the microphone in its stubby position. He seemed to remember his venue, his purpose, and angled himself so he talked straight to us in the jury box.

"I apologize for that." He stretched to grab the remote from his opponent's table and clicked off the image of poor dead Max. "I am sorry Max Taylor died, and died too young."

Keening sobs echoed his condolences. I turned to witness Max's parents crying and embracing each other. The dad was the source of the lament, and no amount of dabbing could rescue the mom's makeup. I'd learned about raccoon eyes the hard way too. Frank waited while Max's parents collected themselves. It didn't take them long, only a few seconds. Brave people.

"I am sorry for your loss," he said to the couple.

She met his eyes and mouthed "thank you." Her grace, fraternizing with the enemy, surprised me.

Frank turned back to us. "Thank you for your time and your focus. In the Canadian legal system, the Crown needs to prove its case beyond a reasonable doubt. A shadow of a doubt. And it is you, the jury, who decides whether the evidence proves the Crown's case." He held his right arm out, circling it expansively like a grand gesture of welcome. Of course, he was wooing us, so I braced myself.

"Molly doesn't have to prove anything. To anybody. We already assume—indeed, must assume—she is innocent of all charges. But I will defend her vigorously regardless. Why? Because, through their accusations, they have defamed her fine name, damaged her upstanding reputation. Molly wants you to hear and judge all the evidence, and to find her innocent." Frank waved his arms when he spoke, particularly as he wound himself up.

"You are the centre of our focus for the next few weeks. We will show you pictures and videos. You will hear testimony from Max's and Molly's friends and family. There will be technical information too. From some of Max's doctors. And the coroner."

The Crown whispered something to his co-counsel. I liked his smile.

"We do all of this so you can learn more about what happened. Then you tell us what you think. You decide what happens next."

I watched Frank's colleague, whom he hadn't introduced yet. She sat at the Defence table and memorized his every movement, nodding her head in time with his points like a bobblehead toy.

"Molly Hopewell is a fifty-two-year-old woman who lost her beloved Max, her husband of nearly twenty-five years, almost a year ago." He paused and scanned the audience. "To cancer."

Rustling and some punctuated thumping startled me and threatened to overwhelm Frank's words. I couldn't identify the source of the commotion, but guessed it was the protesters in the corner rattling their gear. The judge confirmed my hypothesis when I caught him glowering in their direction, silencing them with his stare.

"Yes, you heard me right." Frank glanced toward the protesters. He raised the volume of his voice but maintained his measured, folksy tone. "Cancer. Cancer is an evil disease, and Molly's husband suffered terribly from it. But Molly did not kill Max. She did not inject the malignancy into his body. Or force his cells to multiply uncontrollably, metastasize, and take root in his bones, lungs and brain." He scanned us to make sure he had our attention. He certainly had mine—he could've been describing Hug and me. "No, Molly tried to save her husband. To cure his disease. Molly didn't kill her husband. Cancer did." Frank gripped the podium with both hands.

He moved his gaze, letting it linger just behind the Crown's table. I couldn't gauge his exact focus, but I thought he talked mainly to Max's parents. "Instead of getting to mourn her husband, to rebuild her life, Molly was charged with his murder." Maybe I should count my lucky stars Stanley only evicted me.

He swivelled on his heel and pointed at the raised platform where the accused, Molly Hopewell, sat quietly. I couldn't see her body from about the elbow down, as she too was fenced in by an oak pony wall like the one surrounding us.

Frank pointed. "Molly is innocent. There is absolutely no evidence supporting the charge against her. Instead, considerable evidence proves Molly Hopewell did everything humanly possible first to cure her husband's disease and then, once all hope abandoned them, to improve his life. Any different story the Crown tells is circumstantial, with a lot of make-believe connecting the dots."

Now I was confused. Did she or didn't she?

I studied Molly. She looked worn out, with bags under her eyes and deep creases around her mouth. Still, she'd made herself presentable for the trial today and wore a coral lipstick and a peach blush, colour choices that intensified her blue eyes.

"You will hear a lot about assisted dying, and the legislation that regulates these practices. That's a lot of technical language, and I will try to make it as straightforward for you as possible." He smiled, apologizing in advance. Hug would say, "he led with his chin."

"Some secrets will be laid open for you to examine." He stage-whispered to us, mock-scanning back and forth for eavesdroppers. "The Crown doesn't want you to know that Max was an activist, an advocate for assisted dying, merciful death."

The crowd behind the Crown renewed their commotion. The judge glared them into silence for a second time. I needed to learn that stare for my more recalcitrant clients. Dogs correctly interpreted body language, but we humans often needed remedial lessons.

"Max expressed himself clearly on this issue, and repeatedly. You will hear recordings of Max early in his disease, where he expressed his desires. But then, his health declined. His financial situation changed. And he ran out of options." Frank paused for a moment and studied his now-stilled hands.

When he raised his head again, his eyes were soft, sympathetic. "Molly is a victim here too." He murmured these words. "People want to blame someone for Max Taylor's death. I get it. I did not have the good fortune to meet Max in person. From all accounts, he was an extraordinary man. Smart. Funny. Kind. His parents and his community loved him. His wife loved him."

Frank didn't use the microphone to amplify his voice. "Molly is innocent." She sat primly, head bent, shoulders straight, hands out of sight. "The Crown's evidence is flawed. Full of holes and fancies. She doesn't deserve her portrayal as a heartless villain, a cruel murderess." I nearly laughed at his word choices. "I hope you will serve justice by finding Molly Hopewell not guilty of all charges."

I paused for a moment to make sure Frank had finished, and then I raised my hand to get the judge's attention. The judge saw me but turned his head and ignored me. I knew enough not to wave my arm wildly or call "Yoo-hoo." The judge nodded at Clemence, and once she deciphered his silent communication, he nodded in my direction.

Clemence looked down the line of chairs past the row of knees and I caught her eye. Her jaw muscles clenched and she mimed writing.

I followed her instruction, noisily ripping a piece of paper from my notepad, and writing, "What if we have questions about the case? Or the evidence?" I folded up the paper into a square and handed it like a schoolgirl down the line. When Clemence received the paper, she carried it to the clerk without first opening and reading it. The clerk handed it up to the judge. I refrained from rolling my eyes at the rigamarole to ask a simple question.

"A juror has asked, 'What if we have questions about the case? Or the evidence?'" He handed the piece of paper back to the clerk. "Madam clerk, please enter this into the transcript."

He paused for about thirty seconds. "Thank you for your question. I will define some of the jurors' rules and put them into a better context." He pushed his glasses up his nose using his middle finger. Was the gesture a gibe or coincidence?

"Jurors need to be silent in the courtroom. Remember, your job is to pay attention to the evidence and mine is to pay attention to the law. The lawyers will each present their cases in the best way they can, then you process and sort the information. I am pleased you have questions. Jot them down and continue to take careful notes. When each side rests, after you've seen all the evidence, you will begin your deliberations. Raise your questions then, with your fellow jurors, so you make sense of the evidence together." The judge paused again, and sipped water from a glass placed on his intimidating desk.

"But I need to warn you. All the pieces will not necessarily fit together. Sometimes you will have to interpret information, but you won't know all the details." He paused again. "But please be patient. The evidence will unfold, day by day, witness by witness, and you will incrementally form an understanding of the events of this case."

With that, a different bailiff boomed her, "All rise." We did—the lawyers and the audience, but not the judge. We did our duck-waddle out of the jury box, out of the courtroom, down the hall, and into our jury room.

"Don't get seated," Clemence said. "We're recessed for the day. Collect your things. You know the rules. Do not discuss the case outside this room." She met my gaze. "Be back here at 8:45 sharp tomorrow morning. Don't be late."

CHAPTER 23

Musical Chairs

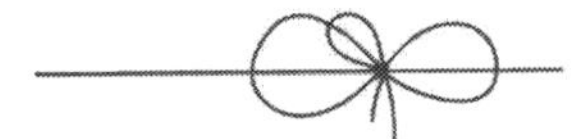

#maidissin

Impartial Jury? (Mobile post)

Justice Forrest better take a closer look at his jury.

Will Max get justice when most of the jurors are atheists? Non-believers? Only one juror was sworn in using a Bible. It gets worse. One other juror is himself dying of cancer, another is involved in law. But the best? How can a retired palliative nurse be impartial?

The jury, so far, has been a bit like musical chairs, with different players every day. Last week, the judge excused one candidate after she discovered her own mother had applied under the MAID legislation for euthanasia. The candidate was understandably upset, but—shame on her—admitted to supporting her mother's decision. The judge dutifully excused her.

But the juror filling her boots is more to our liking. Unfortunately, she'll probably get excused too. And might get charged criminally. Turns out: her husband's brother—yes, her very own brother-in-law—is a bailiff at the courthouse. Today, I caught this same relative handing said juror a packet of very official-looking legal papers.

But while she lasts, by my count, that's two jurors on Team Max.

Will it be enough for Max to get justice?

Comments

L'eagle - *Are you trolling? There's nothing precluding your first three examples from jury duty. But tell the court what you know about the relationship between that juror and the bailiff.*

Olivia - *You get all the best dirt. I don't know how you do it.*

Axel Spinnewyn - **Wink* Thanks, Liv*

L'eagle - *Court officials read all the trial news, even rinky-dink blogs like this one. You just ratted out your source.*

CHAPTER 24

Zane

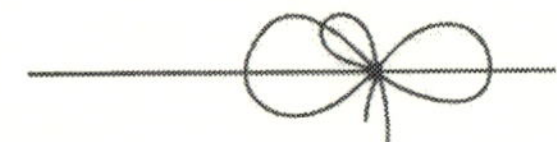

The first thing I noticed about him, after his grave expression, was his cowboy hat. I'd lived in Calgary nearly all my life and had never seen so much cowboy paraphernalia in one place, on one person. Outside of Stampede, that was—when all the urban cow folk hauled out their embroidered snap shirts, boots, and fringed jackets. Universally, every ensemble was topped with a cowboy hat, often the cheap plastic or straw kind available from pop-up souvenir stands.

But this man's hat looked expensive and, following the rules, he tucked it under his elbow.

Someone, perhaps himself, had crisply ironed his white shirt. Creases were visible on the back of each long sleeve. Chunks of turquoise fastened his cuffs together. A bolo tie clasped his collar tight, its turquoise centre the size of a credit card and framed in heavy silver. The witness's boots squeaked amusingly, like frightened mice, when he strode across the carpet to the booth.

This witness opted for the Bible when he pledged to tell the whole truth. When asked his full name, he bellowed, "Zane Angus Taylor." A solid Wild West name.

"What is your role in this trial, Mr. Taylor?" Sometimes Twee-dee was the king of the obvious.

"I am Max's father." He laid his hat on the podium and then placed his palms flat, as though propping himself up.

"As in the deceased?"

"Max is—was—my only son." He rolled his eyes when he corrected himself, as though he deserved a reckoning for getting his facts wrong. I, too, had struggled with grammatical accuracy after Hug died and still hadn't settled on the right verb tense.

"Do you also know the accused, Molly Hopewell?"

Zane squinted at the space Molly occupied, part stage and part corral. Twee-dee stepped to the left, and the witness focused on him again. "She is my daughter-in-law. Known her for about thirty years. They eloped right out of university."

"Do you and your daughter-in-law get along?"

"I thought so, but I found out the hard way that she doesn't respect me or my wife, Beulah." Here, he nodded toward the audience where his wife sat starched and rigid behind the Crown lawyers. She could've walked out of a time machine from the sixties, with her olive-green suit and matching dyed-satin purse, and blonde bouffant. A pair of white gloves clasped in her lap would've completed her ensemble.

Frank and his no-name protégée watched the testimony closely.

"Please elaborate," Twee-dee said.

"Molly excluded us from everything. We complained only when she stopped discussing Max's care." Here, he talked straight to Molly, and cried, "We loved him too. You should have given us a say."

No lawyers objected.

Twee-dee stayed on point, and I drew him as a bloodhound sniffing out the clues. "When was that?" he asked.

"About the time she asked us for money."

"Why did she need money?"

This entire exchange looked scripted. "Witness prep," TV called it.

"She'd spent their savings, every cent on some crackpot cure. Snake oil." He snorted loudly, a sentiment amplified by his mic.

"What was the health regime?"

"I don't know the details. She gave him smoothies with spices every day, things like cinnamon, turmeric mixed with wild—had to be 'wild'—blueberries and other fruit."

I was starting to get miffed. I made similar drinks for Hug.

"Sounds disgusting."

Zane stood with his thumbs stuck behind his ornate belt. "I tasted it once and it wasn't too bad. Max drank it dutifully, even when he vomited all the time from chemo and radiation."

"That doesn't sound expensive. Mostly groceries."

"She mailed away for other stuff, a liquid she mixed with orange juice." Zane frowned, remembering. "So-called alternative medicine. She tracked it down and bought it, even though it was expensive, untested. Some conspiracy hogwash surrounded it, but I don't remember the details. Something about the inventors saying no lab would test it because there was no profit to be made. Max had to take it every few hours, night and day." He waved his arms in exasperation. "How could he get better if she woke him twice a night to drink some hare-brained concoction? He needed his rest."

I administered lots of Hug's medicines, even in the middle of the night. Doctors said waking him was better than missing doses.

"What other expenses did Ms. Hopewell incur?" Twee-dee was wise to divert this witness. So far, his testimony only proved Molly loved her husband. What was it about in-laws, always assuming the worst.

"She tried to take him on a trip. He wanted to go to Europe, fulfill a lifelong dream to explore battlegrounds and their monuments. Places like Vimy Ridge. He was a history buff."

"Tried?"

"She bought open tickets. Expensive first-class tickets. I never travel first-class." He held his head demurely, before adding, "And I have the wherewithal to do so." That tidbit didn't curry my favour, and I suspected Zane ad libbed. "She cancelled everything when his doctors wouldn't clear him to travel. She probably paid penalties, didn't get all that money back."

Twee-dee steered the conversation back to neutral turf. "When was this? What date?"

"I don't remember exactly. But it was not long before he died. A couple months."

"Thank you, Mr. Taylor." The Crown walked toward his table.

"She had no business killing him," Zane blurted.

Twee-dee turned on his heel faster than a speeding bullet. No, that was Superman. What was Spider-Man's tag? Never mind. If looks could kill, Zane Taylor'd be a goner.

"I know he was sick," Zane sniffled. "I'm not an idiot. She could have waited until we were with him too. She stole our son's life, and we couldn't comfort him as he died." Gulping sobs came from the audience, and I turned to watch Max's mother ugly-crying into a monogrammed handkerchief.

Twee-dee contorted his face into a close-mouthed grimace. He performed for a refined audience with only a vaudevillian repertoire. "Would you like a tissue, sir?" he asked. He didn't have one in his hand, and I'd already deduced lawyers weren't allowed near the witness box, so I wasn't sure how he'd get him one.

Zane saved him from that bit of problem-solving by declining the offer. "No, I'm okay. Thank you."

"Was your son able to voice his wants and needs?"

The witness glanced at the floor. "No. He had a stroke during a surgery she signed him up for. Afterward, he couldn't speak clearly, and he couldn't write at all. He pantomimed for the rest of his life."

The Crown paced and avoided eye contact with his witness while stealing glances at us in the jury box. "Mr. Taylor, why do you think Ms. Hopewell murdered your son?"

"Because she's an activist. She lobbied the government, helped get that damnable legislation passed. I know she disapproved of many of the restrictions—so-called safeguards the government imposed. She wanted something more lenient. She started showboating and used my son's murder as a stunt to get the rules relaxed."

I blinked several times, like a computer cursor failing to process.

No-Name half-stood and lazily said, "Objection. Now the witness is showboating."

She was a feisty one.

The judge didn't look up from whatever held his attention on his desk. "Sustained. The jury will disregard the witness's last statement."

Twee-dee bowed formally. "I'm sorry, Your Honour." To his witness, he asked, "Please be specific. Which legislation did your daughter-in-law help get enacted?"

"The euthanasia legislation. Oh, sorry, they don't like that word. The medically-assisted dying nonsense."

Twee-dee nodded then rifled through his folder of papers.

Zane filled the silence. "The law requires the victim to confirm he wants to die immediately before doctors help him kill himself. Max couldn't even speak to complete his application, let alone the rest of it."

This law complicated dying. It was supposed to ease a dying patient's suffering and instead it created fraught family tensions difficult to negotiate from a deathbed.

Frank and No-Name both jumped up like synchronized cuckoos chiming the hour. But No-Name sat again, deferring to her boss. "Objection. Mr. Taylor is not an expert on the Medical Assistance in Dying legislation, its application, or its safeguards. Besides, his information is out of date. Audrey's Amend—"

"Sustained." The judge sounded bored when he cut off the lawyer. "Jury members, we will need to excuse you for a few minutes."

From the back corner, a hoarse voice sounded, "All rise."

Everyone stood to attention, like we sang the anthem. Clemence motioned us, her little ducklings, to follow her out. And we complied.

Eventually, we returned to the courtroom, and the officials behaved as though nothing was amiss. No squabbles. Everyone remained inscrutable so I couldn't gather any insights into the drama.

Once we were all seated and acknowledged, Twee-dee resumed without missing a beat. "Why do you think Ms. Hopewell forced your son to die? Without his consent?"

Zane, who seemed suitably chastened by whatever happened in our absence, answered. "Because he never would've left us of his own free will. Not without saying goodbye. She killed him in the middle of the night. She didn't let us comfort him." His quivering chin betrayed the cracks in his composure.

The attorneys on the opposing teams passed the podium, like barrel racers at a gymkhana. When Frank reached the podium, he offered the witness a faint smile. "I'm sorry for your loss, Mr. Taylor."

The witness regarded the lawyer as though he had rabies. "Thank you," the old man mumbled, his words more gracious than his tone.

"Did Ms. Hopewell pay you back the money she borrowed?"

"Not all of it."

"Is she paying you back now?"

"Slowly."

"Even since she was arrested? Impressive. Do you have a loan agreement in place?"

Zane no longer seemed interested in answering questions. "Yes."

"Is she up to date in her payments under that

agreement?"

"Yes."

"Did she give you an accounting of how she spent the money?"

Zane brightened a little. "No."

"Would it surprise you to learn that she used the money to make mortgage payments on the house she occupied with your son? And she paid for essential car repairs so she could transport your son to his medical appointments?"

"She's Max's wife. It's her duty to look after him."

Frank moved to mosey away again, but turned abruptly, as though remembering something important. "Are you charging Molly interest on that loan?"

"Yes," Zane whispered. I thought he was suitably ashamed of himself, but then he banged the podium, and blurted, "I'm entitled. It's a business arrangement."

Frank kept his composure. "Max was your son. Family?"

"Yes, of course."

"How did you help your son during his illness? Besides loan them money? At a profit."

Zane's face reddened, the areas on top of each cheek plum purple. "I did many things."

Frank rolled his hand. "Yes? Like what?"

"We visited him, at home and in the hospital."

"How often?"

"A couple times a week."

"Did you know Molly was there every day? Every single day."

Zane spewed. "It was her duty. What else was she going to do?"

I glanced to Stanley's corner to gauge his reaction to the testimony. Had he expected the same from me when I cared for Hug?

"What do you mean, Mr. Taylor?"

Beads of sweat glistened on Zane's forehead. "I already

told you." He got quiet. "She..." long pause, "was..." another pause, "his...wife." He spat out the last word.

Frank slouched, non-threatening. "I don't understand your point."

His act fooled Zane, but not me. "That's what she signed on for. That's her job." I looked over at Zane's wife and felt sorry for her.

Frank rested his elbows on the podium. "Your son had a stroke?"

Zane nodded curtly. "Yes, it was terrible. We almost lost him."

"You were there?" Frank asked.

Zane held his chin high. "No one could find Molly, so the doctors talked to me about Max's care."

"I understand they resuscitated Max?"

"He was gone for a couple minutes. We got him back before he suffered any brain damage."

Frank stared at the witness. "You mean, any more brain damage? Max couldn't speak after the stroke, right? Aphasia?"

A sad smile crossed Zane's face. "He still communicated, pantomimed. It wasn't perfect, but if we guessed right, he nodded. And if we guessed wrong, he shook his head. When we repeatedly guessed wrong, he shook his head vehemently. Probably in frustration."

"Did you guess wrong a lot?"

Maybe Zane suspected a trap. "Max never got the hang of charades."

"Did everyone guess wrong?"

"Yes. Sometimes."

"Who guessed right more? You? Your wife? Ms. Hopewell?"

"Molly," Zane said.

"Of course, all those charades, all those miscommunications, could have been avoided if you'd let nature take its course," Frank said. "You could have spared your son a world of hurt."

I thought Zane would climb over the witness box and go for Frank's throat. "How dare you, sir."

Frank remained nonplused. "Actually... how dare you, sir. That day, when you convinced doctors to resuscitate your son, you violated Max's 'do not resuscitate' order. Your Honour, I'd like to enter Max's DNR into evidence."

A shuffling and organizing of papers followed, and within ninety seconds, I examined my copy of Max's DNR, written legibly, with a couple exclamation points emphasizing his decision.

"Your, uh, *showboating* caused considerable pain and suffering, Mr. Taylor. Max couldn't work anymore. After his stroke, Molly stopped even part-time work because Max needed care every moment of every day. The couple's bills piled up. High enough, eventually, to ask you for a loan. Meanwhile, the disease that ultimately killed him ravaged his insides, causing discomfort, debilitating pain."

Tweedledum—Ta-dum—half-stood, leaning on the table. "Objection. Mr. Taylor is not on trial." He sounded weary.

"I'll move on," Frank said. The lawyer leafed through his notes. "You mentioned your son's cancelled trip to Europe. Where were they headed?"

"I can't remember," Zane said.

"I posit that you can't remember because they hadn't decided. Molly and Max considered several locations. The Netherlands. Belgium. Colombia. Do you know what those places have in common?"

Zane shook his head.

"No?" Frank continued. "I'll explain. Some form of euthanasia is legal and available in all these jurisdictions. Your son, sir, wanted to travel somewhere where he could end his suffering."

"You have no proof," Zane snapped.

"Actually, I do." Frank handed the clerk a small stack of stapled packages, and she worked her magic. When I leafed through my copy, I skimmed email communications between

Max's email address and a half-dozen end-of-life facilities in Europe, one American state, and Colombia.

"One last question," Frank said. "Who's paying for the protesters outside?"

Zane shook his head, unwilling to spill his beans.

The judge intervened. "Mr. Taylor, please answer the question."

"Some lobbying groups." Zane frowned. "And me. I am."

CHAPTER 25

Proposal

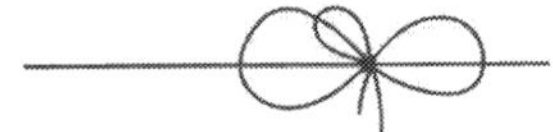

I selected the most likely overstuffed box, dragged it from the corner, and set it on the bed. I flopped down next to it and heard some of its contents rattle as it bounced. After I unfolded the lid and revealed its contents, I had a little cry. There, on top of the detritus of my life, I found the heart-shaped key ring. I thought I'd lost his present to me. I picked it up, breathed on it, and rubbed it on my shirtsleeve. Once dusted, the fake gems shone in the light, proclaiming again how poorly he knew me. Imagine: bling, for me? Too bad my favourite colour only came in gaudy. A part of me—a sizable part—hoped he'd selected it for its heart-shaped symbolism. A token of his love. I wished I could ask him now.

I reached over to my night table and pulled out my journal.

Dear Hug,

Moving into your house was an unhappy occasion. Your timing was never great, but that day was a doozy.

You perched on the gurney, your legs swinging almost childlike over the side. "Well, then. I guess that's that," you said.

The doctor had just left, pulling the curtain behind himself to afford us some privacy. His pronouncement—you had "weeks to months" left to live—still rang in my ears, tolling your death knell.

You stood, your shod feet slapping the shiny marmoleum floor, before you swooped to one knee right in the hospital treatment room, your movements illuminated by the flickering glare of the overhead lights. I was shocked and delighted at the same time. At last.

"This isn't how I planned this," you said, and reached your hand into your pocket. "I wanted it to be more romantic."

The overhead lights reflected on your glasses, obscuring your eyes, so I couldn't even tell what you were thinking.

"It's okay," I said. I felt my face flush with anticipation.

"I know we haven't talked about this. Not really. I planned our future so differently."

I gulped. Me too. I grabbed a tissue and sopped up my tears.

When he'd pulled his hand out, I'd beamed. His fingers were closed around something precious. I moved my left hand toward him, my fingers curled in feigned relaxation. He took my hand gently in his, turned it palm up and kissed it in the convergence of my palmistry lines. He opened his hand over mine, but nothing dropped out. I laughed, nervous enough for both of us. He shook his hand up and down, and still nothing fell. He used my fingers to lever the contents from his palm. I felt something hard, metal, warmed by his touch and glued in place by his sweat, and bulkier than I expected. I felt something give and then a key plopped into my outstretched hand.

"I need you," you said. "I can't do this alone. Please move in with me?"

What could I say to that? You offered no declarations of everlasting love. No promises to cherish or even honour.

I smiled at you while pretending to study the key. Pretending it was enough. I blinked back tears and hoped you didn't see my disappointment. "Yes." What kind of person would I be if I abandoned you when you needed me most?

"Oh, thank you, Heddie," you said, and plucked the key from my still-open hand.

From his other pocket, he pulled the heart-shaped key ring. He wedged open the ring and strung on the key. "I know it'll be a total disruption for you. I'm sorry. We'll make it work."

I sucked in my breath. "You know what?" I tried to sound upbeat, but the squeak in my voice betrayed my anxiety.

Hug studied me. His confused expression suggested he'd celebrated prematurely. "What's the matter?"

I shook my head, afraid my words would come out all wrong. I could already tell his dollar store gift would be around longer than he would.

How could I explain I wanted a key to your heart rather than to your door?

"Did you choose the keyring?" I asked.

He smiled, pleased. "Yes. It's your colour."

I smiled thinly.

I moved my stuff to his place over several days. The hardest part was giving up my apartment. I'd called that flat home for over twenty years, since my university days. The rent was reasonable, the building clean and secure, the apartment sufficient, so I had stayed put. Hug was too weak by then to make room for me in his place, so he supervised while I cleaned and sorted his belongings so I could claim one of his closets, a dresser, and part of the bathroom vanity as my own. The Diabetes Association hauled away my furniture—old, unfashionable, but still functional. I only kept my laptop, a few books, and personal sundries. I'd packed light.

CHAPTER 26

Excuse Me

"All rise," Clemence shouted the command.

We waddled in, this time more like stuffed turkeys after our repast. Someone in the queue had eaten garlic at lunch, and I had to walk through it. I coughed my way to my seat, living my fate to be a one-woman spectacle.

"Welcome back. I hope you had a pleasant lunch. I note you are all present. Mr. Parker, would you like to begin?"

But it was the second seat for the Crown who popped up and walked to the podium. "Thank you, Your Honour, I have the pleasure this afternoon. I would like to call Detective Sabine Nasri to the stand."

The courtroom was silent except for the rustling of 200 people turning in their seats to watch a compact young woman gracefully cross the courtroom. The audience was lopsided again, crowded behind the Crown and deserted behind the Defence. Frank held the pony gate open for the Crown's witness and she crossed the barrier separating the legal insiders and the public. He smiled at her like a welcoming host, and she briefly acknowledged his questionable attention.

I zoned out while the clerk did her thing again, swearing in the witness, clarifying her name and rank. I probably suffered a food coma from the mushy cheese sandwich I'd packed for lunch.

"Detective Nasri, you were the arresting officer in this case?"

"Yes. My partner and I arrested Molly Agnes Hopewell on the charge of murder." The witness stood. Maybe that's why they called it a "witness stand"?

I was drawn to her accent and the husky musical quality of her voice. She dressed in the tailored skirt-suit of the Western professional woman, though she clearly originated somewhere else. Possibly Iran. Her ruby-red blouse was both stylish and flattering.

She'd arranged her shiny, thick hair into a complicated bun coiling her head. I wished, not for the first time, I had smooth, shiny hair.

"When was that?"

"Detective Mark Stokes—my partner—and I arrested Ms. Hopewell at 9:15 in the morning on August nineteenth."

Wow. Molly had rotted in jail for three months. I studied Molly, who sat upright, head high, watching the witness. Her face bore a cryptic expression I couldn't interpret.

"Did Ms. Hopewell resist arrest?"

"No. She came willingly enough. I understand she's also been a model prisoner, causing no trouble." The detective wore a richly detailed gold necklace, all loops and swirls and disks—the one visible nod to her heritage. It lay at the base of her neck and waggled at us whenever she spoke.

"Was she alone?"

"No one else was present. Ms. Hopewell was moving, though. A 'sold' sticker was plastered across a 'for sale' sign on her front lawn. The household contents were all boxed."

I nicknamed this officer Sherlock.

"Was there anything else unusual about the arrest?"

"Yes. Although the details of the arrest were confidential, someone leaked information to the press. About a dozen reporters, with some photographers and camera crews, were present on the sidewalk leading to the property."

"Does that happen often?"

"No, our track record for confidentiality is stellar. Journalists usually photograph suspects at booking, not arrest."

"Can you please walk us through the details of the arrest?"

On a blank sheet from my notepad, I drew the rectangle board table from our jury room—a little more accurately than the person who'd originally drawn our seating chart. I marked down our jury numbers and then tested my recollection of everyone's names: Phillip, Steve, Pat, Brad...

"Excuse me." The judge's tone was strident, firm.

Uh-oh. Busted? I covered my doodle.

Stanley stood behind the judge's podium. Where did he come from?

"We will need to evacuate this room immediately. Detective Nasri, thank you for coming in today, but you are excused. Someone will contact you about when and where to finish your testimony." The judge spoke loudly, and I thought I heard an edge of panic. He nodded at Stanley, who walked off stage left. "Guards, this is not a drill. Jury, please follow the instructions of Clemence—your jury guard." He pronounced her name correctly: two points for the judge. "Leave now." He turned to the lawyers, clerk, and audience. "We are adjourned for the day. Please return tomorrow morning at nine o'clock."

Clemence held the door open, and we rushed out, disregarding our usual order. Other guards beckoned their own charges through different doors. While I waited for a gap to step off our riser, I watched two guards help the lawyers collect their belongings and hustle them out. The clerk and the court reporter both fitted and locked cases over their desks. I heard another guard at the far end soothing, "This way, folks. Stay calm."

We collected our belongings, quick like rabbits, from the jury room. "Wait for me," Clemence said. "Get your phones first." No way I'd forget that.

We assembled without too much commotion.

"We will take the stairs."

"Uh, Clay-mints." Phillip's tone suggested a toddler

demanding a chocolate bar. "I won't make it. It's too far."

"They already shut the elevators off," Clemence said. "But, if you wait here, I can send an emergency crew back to carry you down."

Phillip studied his feet. "No, I'll go on my own."

Clemence waved her arm overhead like a commanding officer summoning troops to battle. "When you get to the ground level, go outside, turn right, and cross the street at the corner. You'll find our muster point."

Once we hit the stairwell, it was a free for all. Traffic flowed opposite to roads, with the slower lane next to the railing and the speeders hugging the concrete wall on the right. Mandi was first to race down the stairs.

"Impressive," I said. "You can really run in those shoes."

"Tons of experience," she said without breaking her stride. One of her heels needed a new tip and paced us with its metallic scrape at every second step.

Ingrid jogged past with a stern-faced nod.

Jim politely accompanied me for a few steps. "You got this?"

"I think so. Go on." I sounded more confident than I felt.

"See ya at the bottom." He descended the stairs two at a time, jumping the last few steps to the landing. Show off. He grabbed the railing at the landing and swung himself around to the next flight like a kid playing helicopter.

Ahead of me, people detoured around Phillip even as I narrowed the gap between us.

When I reached him after hoofing-it for another flight, he was red-faced and perspiring. Some hair escaped his newly donned cap and was spackled to his forehead.

"How you doin' there?" I asked conversationally.

"Not great. Twenty floors is a long way."

"Meetcha down there," Ruth said, and left me alone with Phillip on the stairs.

I peered into the opening between the railings and saw hands, usually two per flight, zigzagging down to the ground floor. The fastest were almost at the bottom, as we reached a metal sign reading, '16.'

"Can I help?"

"Dunno," he said. "My legs are wobbly. I'm afraid I'm gonna fall."

"I'll go ahead of you. If you faceplant, you'll have a soft landing."

He laughed mirthlessly.

Disembodied voices echoed off the concrete walls. As each minute passed, the sounds from below diminished and I imagined my colleagues safe outside, bundled against the cold.

"Not really smart to put the bulletproof courtroom on the twentieth floor," I said, mostly to myself.

"Bulletproof?" He breathed in deep, chest-wracking gasps. At least he could still speak.

"Didn't you know? They moved us the first day."

"No. Why?"

"Dunno." I'd wondered the same thing myself. "But you'd think if they feared violence, they'd want to evacuate us at some point, even if it's just a drill. A lower floor would be easier."

"Are we in danger?"

"Dunno that either." I glanced back at him to make sure he was still doing okay. "You look a little green."

"I think I'm going to puke."

I stepped into the now-empty speeding lane, out of harm's way. "Not on me, you don't. Let's stop here. Get your breath."

"You don't have to wait." His panicked eyes betrayed his brave words.

"You'd do the same for me."

"No, probably not." At least he was honest.

I let his comment slide.

His breathing was still fast, but no longer like he was at the triumphant end of a marathon.

"You ready?"

"Not really."

"Let's keep going. But slow it down. Know any marching songs?"

"I was in the army. A long time ago. I know rude songs."

I could imagine. "So, not marching songs." Our chatter was enough to distract him, and he slowly increased his speed until we travelled at our original pace.

I heard the fast rhythmic slapping of feet. I peered over the railing into the gap between the flights of stairs and saw a hand sliding its way toward us.

"We got company," I said to Phillip just as Stanley turned the corner.

"Hurry," Stanley said. "Where's Clemence?" He probably thought she'd found a hidey-hole in the spartan stairwell. "You shouldn't be on your own."

I was in no mood for his rebukes. "We're going as fast as we can, and Clemence is waiting for us at the bottom."

"You're not my responsibility," he said, disgust distorting his expression. "You're on your own."

He shoved past me, hip checking me out of his way.

"I'll tell Clemence you're still up here," he said before disappearing around the corner.

"Nice guy," Phillip said once we were alone again.

"He's a peach," and I relayed the story of my recent humiliations at Stanley's hands.

We arrived at the bottom level and stopped to catch our breath. It took him longer to find his.

"Thank you, Heddie. Without you, I'd be collapsed on those stairs somewhere." He leaned on the railing, his chest heaving like he needed a paper bag over his head.

"You're welcome, Phillip."

"Please call me Phil."

Yes, okay. He'd earned that. "You're welcome, Phil." I smiled before opening the door to safety.

Clemence waited outside, resembling an impatient bull when she stomped her feet to keep warm. "You're the last." She pointed across the street. "Go join the group."

I switched on my phone once I found the muster point. *Quack. Quack. Quack.* Several texts in a row loaded, all from Leah.

You okay? H, text me.

Tick Tock.

Text me the very second you get this.

Wowza, Leah. Don't get your under-roos in a knot.

I texted back. *Hello. How are you? Anything exciting?*

Quack—Ha-ha. What took you so long? You worried me.

Didn't have phone. Jury duty, remember?

Quack—That's no excuse. A smiley face emoji disclosed her tease.

They evacuated us. Know why?

Quack—Bomb threat.

To Phil, who still hovered at my elbow, I repeated Leah's insight. That explained the scene in front of us. Something had cleared the road of protesters, parting them like the Red Sea and separating them safely behind orange barricades. Paparazzi jostled for prime positions, their camera lights competing with the disco of flashing lights from emergency vehicles. Fire, police, and ambulance personnel rushed between cars, vans and trucks. Four heavily armoured officers followed their equally sheathed German shepherds into the building. People spoke but with hushed voices, like we were in a cemetery. I hoped the dogs stayed safe.

Clemence stood nearby, using her index finger to practice her numbers—counting us off, one through twelve. "Can I get everyone's attention?" she shouted above the din, and only continued once we all focused on her. "We're done for the day. See you tomorrow morning at 8:45."

I thumb-typed, *We're done for the day.*

Quack—Can you get kids from school?

Why, yes, I can.

Sure.

I bid farewell to my new friend, Phil, and walked home.

At least I'd get more exercise today. The stairs didn't count. Too slow to get my heart rate up.

CHAPTER 27

Arrested, Reprise

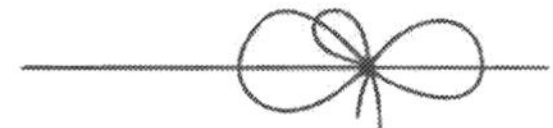

No one explained our rude interruption yesterday. I asked Roy at the security desk. He ignored our earlier bonding with an unconvincing, "Dunno." Clemence remained tight-lipped when quizzed. Even blabbermouth Stanley stayed mum. Of course, I knew, and I immediately informed my fellow jurors once we'd all gathered behind closed doors. Leah had uncharacteristically shared the late-night news report of it all being a false alarm.

The news miffed Ruth. "They need to protect us better. I barely slept a wink last night. Them not explaining what's going on, especially when we can't check the news ourselves? That's just cruel." She sucked in her cheeks to emphasize her point.

Phillip—er, Phil—dismissed Ruth's fears. "Don't be silly. We weren't in danger. Clemence got us out okay." He neglected to mention my important role in his rescue.

"I wasn't worried," Mandi gushed. "Plus, I got a last-minute appointment for a manicure." She fluttered her hot pink fingernails for us all to admire. "I made the rhinestones." Her bedazzled thumbnails glittered.

I was genuinely curious. "How?"

"Trade secret," she demurred. Then she brightened. "I'll show you sometime."

Pat rolled next to Mandi to admire her handiwork. She twisted Mandi's hand to different angles, as if they starred in a Palmolive commercial. "Fine work," she pronounced, placing Mandi's hand on the table.

Norman ignored the chatter. "I knew it was an explosive or something when I saw the dogs. Impressive animals." I noted our shared interest.

Brad crossed his arms. "It's all a big to-do about nothing."

"See. That's what I'm saying," Phil added. His lopsided grin suggested he had finally found a winning team.

I repeated Leah's late-night tidbits. "It was a hoax. They found no bomb, so we were safe."

"Safe from a bomb, yes," Toni said. "Several of us might've had heart attacks." She patted her own chest. "Me included."

The bomb threat turned out to be the glue we needed to turn our mismatched assortment of jurors into a team. What did you call a group of jurors? Today: a bonding of jurors.

Clemence knocked on our door like a countdown clock, giving us our one-minute warning.

——— o o o ———

The judge stated his rote greetings, like some legal version of *Groundhog Day*, but with no sign of Andie MacDowell. No official report about yesterday's frights. No apology. The clerk, the court reporter, the guards—none of them met my gaze.

Once the judge completed his formalities, Ta-dum resumed his questioning almost in mid-sentence, like the judge had released his pause button. "Can you please walk us through the arrest?" He rubbed the stubble on his head while waiting for his witness to answer.

"May I refer to my notes?" Detective Nasri retrieved her folder from a shelf beneath the podium. Today, she wore an emerald blouse, and a matching comb flashed in her hair. Her changed outfit proved I hadn't imagined our previous day's misadventures.

"Did you make the notes at the time of the investigation?" the judge asked.

I understood the need for notes. My brain also struggled with the increasingly dense thicket of details. I vowed to make my notes more meaningful. My solution? I added keywords to my doodles.

She smoothed her hair back from her forehead with her palm. "Yes, I did."

"Do you need those notes now to refresh your memory?" the judge continued.

"Yes, please."

"Then you may consult them. Please cite page numbers for the recording."

She flipped through several pages. Her unpolished, stubby nails suggested her poise was a costume, something she adopted for court days. "The information is on page seven. On August nineteenth, Detective Stokes and I knocked at Ms. Hopewell's residence at 9:15 a.m. Within a few moments, Ms. Hopewell answered, and we arrested her for culpable homicide. I read Ms. Hopewell her rights, put her in the squad car, and took her to the processing centre."

"Did she resist arrest?"

"No."

"How were you first alerted to this case?"

"We received a 911 call early on January twenty-first at 3:44 a.m., less than thirty minutes after Max Taylor died. The caller, Beulah Taylor, Max's mother, reported Max's murder. I responded to the call and became the investigating officer."

I counted the months in the trusty detective's chronology with my fingers. Max died in January, but they arrested Molly in August? Why wait seven months to arrest her?

"Your Honour, I have a recording of the call we're discussing. May I enter it as exhibit two?" Ta-dum said.

The clerk collected a thick, plastic envelope from the Crown and walked it to the judge. She stood on tippy toes to deposit the envelope on the judge's desk. The judge inspected, then returned it to the clerk's still-outstretched hands.

"Madame clerk, please enter the recording as exhibit two."

The clerk returned to her station, where she typed a few keystrokes before stashing the envelope into a worn plastic bin.

The process baffled me—an incomprehensible tribute to inefficiency.

"May I play this recording for the jury?" Ta-dum continued. He glanced at the Defence table. "If there are no objections."

The Defence half-stood. I noted cyan stitching in his boots today. "No objections."

After a couple false starts where the clerk and one guard manipulated the controls for the audio-visual system, a voice played over the speakers at different volumes throughout the room. The sound quality was poor, like their recording studio was inside a submarine.

Static created a digitalized stammer in the operator's voice. "911. What is the na-na-ture of your emer-mergency?"

"He's dead. We need help. The police!" the caller cried. I heard a man yelling in the background, but I couldn't make out his words.

I watched Molly across from me in the prisoner's box, flanked by her usual two guards. She must own the world's largest collection of twinsets, each in their own subdued shade. Today's was beige, and she almost blended into the woodwork. She didn't make eye contact with anyone in the room and instead examined the floor.

"May I have your name please, ma'am?"

Her sniffling sounded like fallen leaves crunching under heavy boots. "I'm Mrs. Zane Taylor."

This family had found their style and stuck to it. Max's mother wore a different Chanel suit today, this time in black tweed. Her posture, ramrod straight with fingers intertwined in her lap and eyes pinned on the back of Mr. Parker's head, suggested she knew she was the centre of attention. Her husband sat next to her, equally ramrod, but leaning forward with his hands resting on his knees as though shielding his wife from scrutiny.

"Are you safe, Mrs. Taylor?" the overhead speakers screeched. The sound was as piercing as metal scraping concrete and a gazillion times louder.

"Yes." She tsk-ed her impatience. "We need the police. Not an ambulance. She murdered him."

"Who is dead?" The operator's tone was competent, matter of fact. Not fanning hysterics.

She sniffled loudly. "Max. My son. My only boy." The last word came out like a howl.

"Is he breathing?"

"No!" she shouted. "I told you already, he's dead."

"Okay. Thank you. I just want to see if there's anything we can do to help him. To revive him."

"He's dead. He's not breathing."

I heard a man speaking in the background. "I can't believe she did it."

"Are you alone, Mrs. Taylor?"

"No. My husband is here."

I glanced at Max's father, who jutted his chin as he joined his wife on centre stage.

"Can you please tell me where you are?"

She wailed. "I don't know the address. He's been here for weeks, and I can't even remember the gosh-darn address."

"That's okay. I can get it." The clatter of typing confirmed his assertion. "Looks like you're at the hospital."

She started sobbing again.

"If you're already in the hospital, can you get a doctor's help?"

"I told you. He's dead. My daughter-in-law, Molly Hopewell, murdered him. We need the police. Besides, a nurse was just here. He pronounced Max dead and left to call the funeral home." She wailed again.

"I have officers on the way, Mrs. Taylor."

"Okay. Thank you."

"Please stay on the line with me. Until the police arr—"

The clerk clicked off the recording. The resulting silence made the room feel hollow.

Ta-dum rocked, heel-toe, at his microphone. "You were the first officer to arrive, Detective Nasri?"

"No. Uniformed patrol officers arrived first and secured the scene. At oh-4:15. My partner, Detective Mark Stokes, and I arrived twenty minutes later, oh-4:35. Mr. Taylor had been dead about seventy-five minutes."

"Who was present when you arrived on the scene?"

"Mr. Taylor's parents waited for us in the hospital lobby. We went to Mr. Taylor's room together." The detective's voice was strong, her tone neutral.

"Was Ms. Hopewell present?"

"No. Their daughter-in-law called the Taylors at oh-3:30 to inform them of their son's death. The head nurse met them when they arrived on scene about twenty minutes later. That's when the victim's parents phoned 911."

"Were Mr. and Mrs. Taylor present when their son died?"

"No."

Max's mother sniffled into her handkerchief.

"Was an autopsy performed on Mr. Taylor's remains?"

"The autopsy provided us with the best evidence of foul play."

"Please be specific. What evidence did the autopsy uncover?"

The second Defence attorney bounced up like a jack-in-the-box, raising her right arm as she stood to her full height. "Objection, Your Honour."

The judge looked up from whatever papers he'd been reading.

The Defence explained, "Detective Nasri is not an

expert on the coroner's report, and we will hear directly from the coroner."

Seemed reasonable.

"Sustained," the judge said before returning to his reading.

"I'll rephrase," Mr. Standish said. "Detective Nasri, what did the coroner list as Max Taylor's cause of death?"

"Anaphylaxis." She moved her hand to her throat.

"As in 'allergic reaction'?"

"Correct."

I still didn't get it.

"Thank you. Your Honour, that's all I have for this witness." Ta-dum returned to his station and slumped into his seat.

"Mr. Dodge, would you like to begin your questioning?" The judge peered over his half-moon glasses.

No-Name rose. "Yes, Your Honour. Detective Nasri, thank you for coming in today. Two days out of your busy schedule is a lot." Hers was the first official, albeit oblique, reference to yesterday's escapade. "Can you please tell me how you know precisely what time Mr. Taylor died?"

The officer didn't consult her notes. "The head nurse in charge of the wing, Mortimer Baldwin, noted Mr. Taylor's time of death as oh-3:20 in the morning."

"Did you encounter any difficulties investigating the crime scene?"

"Yes."

Whaaaat? Here we go. I flipped my doodle pad over and leaned forward in my seat.

"Please elaborate." Yes, please do.

"By the time uniformed officers arrived on the scene, a funeral home director had retrieved Mr. Taylor's body. The coroner recovered Mr. Taylor's remains from the funeral home to complete the autopsy."

"Is this normal procedure?"

"No." The witness avoided No-Name's gaze.

"So when you say your officers 'secured the scene'? What exactly do you mean?"

The witness squared her shoulders. "Well—"

"On second thought, don't answer that."

Nasri stared at the lawyer, open-mouthed and silenced.

"Try this instead. Did you get any important evidence of a crime from the items you secured?"

"No." Nasri looked away again.

"Any crime?"

"No."

"Hm. How long did it take for the coroner to collect Mr. Taylor's remains?"

"Eleven hours."

"Eleven hours? So, what? About noon?"

"14:30—uh, 2:30 in the afternoon."

"Had embalming started?"

"No."

"You sure?" The witness glared at her inquisitor as Twee-dee burpeed from his seat. "Oh, never mind." No-Name read the room. "What was the funeral home director's name?"

"May I refer to my notes?" Nasri asked the judge, who nodded his permission. She flipped through a few pages before finding the information she wanted. "On page fourteen, I note Mr. Keith Jenkins and Mr. Barry Fromm from Living Memorial."

I blinked at the reference. Leah had chosen that place for her mom, and I wished Stanley had done the same for Hug. They planted trees—one for each of their clients—in local parks and held a memorial for the bereaved every autumn. I'd attended one of their events with Leah after Charlie died. I found it somehow cathartic caterwauling among thousands of strangers in a sapling forest. The home was smart about these living monuments and put the names of the dead on a central plaque rather than individual trees. I'd feel terrible if a tree labelled with Hug's name died.

No-name nodded like she was marking down a point for her team on an invisible scorecard. "Who called the funeral directors to inform them of Mr. Taylor's passing?"

"May I refer to my notes again?"

The judge nodded his assent. "Provide the page number."

"On page sixteen. Mortimer Baldwin made the call."

"Molly didn't phone the funeral home?"

"No."

No-Name nodded again, marking another point. "How did Dr. Baldwin know which funeral home to contact?"

"May I refer to my notes again?" This time, she didn't wait for the judge's permission. "Mr. Taylor—Max Taylor—prepaid his funeral arrangements."

"How did you know it was Max Taylor?"

"I interviewed Mr. Fromm, who also owns the funeral home. Mr. Fromm produced a copy of the sales contract, and I confirmed Max Taylor's signature."

"Mr. Fromm will testify later. Your Honour, I would like to enter Defence Exhibit A into the record. It is a copy of the contract signed by Max Taylor with Living Memorial." No-Name turned back to her witness. "When did Max make his own funeral arrangements?"

I'd wondered the same thing. I was already skilled at this jury stuff.

"Nearly one full year before he died."

I wished Hug had shown similar foresight. Things would've been tons easier if he'd made his own arrangements rather than leaving the hardest decisions to me and Stanley.

"Thank you, Detective." She stood poised to step down from the raised witness stand, her pedestal, when No-Name turned, Perry Mason style, and said, "One more thing, Detective Nasri. How many times did you close this case?"

Detective Nasri squirmed like an earthworm on a hot sidewalk. "Twice."

"In fact, didn't the coroner originally rule Max's death as 'natural'? Your Honour, I'd like to present Exhibit B, the original coroner's report dated March fifth." No-Name handed a paper to the clerk, who relayed it to the judge and back again.

The clerk marked down the information in her log before she ferried the document to the witness box and laid it in the witness's open hand.

No-Name continued, "What was listed as cause of death?"

The witness winced before asserting, without consulting the report in front of her, "Complications from cancer." She knew, and she would've stayed mum, except for the Defence's question.

"So, not murder?"

"No."

Wow, that was unexpected.

"Not even anaphylaxis?"

The witness, this hardened detective, blushed. "No."

"And yet you reopened this case a few months later?"

"Correct."

"Why?"

"We received new persuasive evidence that Ms. Hopewell murdered Mr. Taylor."

"What was the source of this information?" No-Name's tone was sickly sweet, like a decaying carcass left too long in the heat.

"Zane Taylor."

"You mean, Mr. Taylor's father?" No-Name affected her disbelief, and I covered my mouth to muffle snickers at her ham acting.

Max's dad sat frozen. Unblinking.

"Correct."

"Is that a usual practice? Do the police normally reopen cases based on evidence supplied by relatives of the deceased?"

So cheeky. I loved this gal.

Ta-dum didn't appreciate the antic as much, and half-stood from his chair. "Objection, Your Honour."

"Sustained." The judge seemed sluggish. To him, it must be same-old, same-old.

"When did you receive this so-called evidence?"

"May I check my notes?"

I didn't believe her. I was certain she remembered exactly when good ole dad visited her.

"It was in July. Mid-July."

No-Name nodded. "Now, turn your mind please to the evidence you collected."

The detective's pinched face showed she didn't appreciate this line of questioning.

No-Name continued, "Did you find evidence of Procheerol in Ms. Hopewell's home?"

What's Procheerol? I quickly flipped through my notes and couldn't find any earlier reference.

"No."

"In her car?"

"No."

"In her purse?"

The detective glared at the Defence before shaking her head.

"Did you find any signs of this drug—any tablets, any residue, any discarded packaging?"

"No, ma'am."

"Thank you, Detective Nasri. That's all I have for this witness." No-Name collected her papers and carried them to her seat.

I examined my doodle of Sherlock's testimony. Molly, in handcuffs, wearing her pearls and twinset—blue, because that's the only colour pen I had—escorted past a 'Sold' sign toward a marked police car surrounded by journalists. In the clouds, I drew busts of Max's parents, grim and severe, with the dad holding a gavel. Plain old words documented the existence of two coroners reports and the drug. I circled "Procheerol" several times, etching a tiny hole in the page. I admired my handiwork, pleased I'd captured everything relevant.

"Redirect, Your Honour?" Ta-dum spoke.

"Go ahead," said Justice Forrest without looking at his

audience.

"Detective Nasri, did you reopen this case based only on the tips you received from the victim's parents?"

She appeared relieved at the invitation to answer questions more thoroughly. "No. The tips were compelling enough to warrant additional inquiry. We followed up, spoke directly with new witnesses, and reopened the case in early August."

"You corroborated all the tips?"

"Correct. Enough so that we reopened the case."

"Nothing further."

The detective stepped carefully down from the witness box and sauntered down the centre of the courtroom, past the gate held open by Twee-dee. She stared straight ahead, shunning No-Name's gaze. I envied her self-confident stride, which she managed even in kitten heels.

CHAPTER 28

Justice Demanded

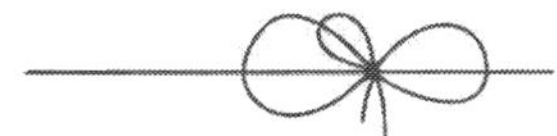

#maidissin

Justice Demanded

By Axel Spinnewyn

Beulah and Zane Taylor demand justice for their son, Maxwell Gerald Taylor, a victim of a so-called mercy killing.

Standing in front of the courthouse today, Mr. and Mrs. Taylor thanked the large crowd of protesters who supported the Taylors' quest for justice.

"We want justice for Max," said Zane Taylor. "The euthanasia legislation changed a half-dozen times in as many years, eroding protections against abuse. Society must protect the weak. Max could not defend himself."

Beulah Taylor said, "The chickens are coming home to roost. About bloody time."

Nearby protesters chanted, "Molly is not God."

Protesters waved signs supporting the Justice for Max campaign. "Suicide and Murder are sins," read the sign held by a man wearing a religious collar. Other signs read, "Let Life Win," "Save Lives, Not Money," and "Trust in God."

If you have any information about this trial, please connect with me on social media. I'll pay a reward for new information leading to a conviction.

Comments

Molly's friend - *Waste of taxpayer dollars. Molly should not be tried. Max was sick and dying.*

Anonymous62 - *Thou shalt not kill. Ever.*

Molly's friend - *His death gave his parents a stage. His dad is a rich mucky muck.*

Anonymous62 - *His dad paid to get justice. Police were oblivious until Zane dropped the evidence in their laps.*

Molly's friend - *Dad should pay for grief counselling. Better use of money.*

Cowboy Gent - *No person has a right to decide when it's time for another person to die.*

CHAPTER 29

A Will and a Way

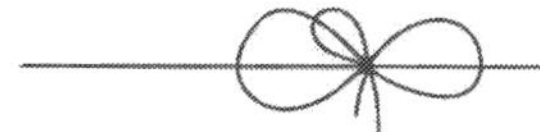

"Do you know what Hugh called you?" Malice lingered in Stanley's narrowed eyes. "Miss Wright for right now. Yup." He flashed me a mocking grin, and I had to admit, Hug had a way with words. "You've spent too much time in your own head, and imagined you were more important to him."

My brother-in-law sucked in his gut, a gesture which puffed up his chest and stretched his navy golf shirt taut. His popinjay hair, sun-bleached or bottle-bleached, I couldn't tell, looked ridiculous against his fake-baked skin. He'd gotten fatter since Hug died, like someone spilled too much yeast into his recipe.

"He didn't lo—"

The mediator raised his hand and stopped Stanley mid-sentence. Lawrence Kingman was an elderly man with thinning white hair. He wore coke-bottle glasses, which I hoped would magnify the merits of my case.

But I wouldn't be silenced. "Do you know what he called *you*?" Admittedly, only when he was angry. "Uptighty whitey, Mr. Stanfields." I turned to my entourage. "Get it? The underwear company?"

Lawrence glared first at me and then Stanley. "I keep things informal in my mediations. And courteous." Stanley met his gaze, and I had to admire his guts. When Lawrence stared at me, I crumpled. "Don't mistake my civility for leniency. I will swiftly censure any misbehaviour."

"You're not the boss of me," Stanley said.

The five of us, including Dee and Becky, sat in a circle of straight-backed chairs that Lawrence had made us arrange ourselves. Lawrence had arrived a few minutes late to find the rest of us seated around the boardroom table. Stanley originally selected the power seat furthest from the door, the spot from where he expected to command the room. But before Lawrence would begin, he forced us to relinquish our expansive and comfy boardroom chairs in favour of the plastic stackable variety he pulled from a closet. Lawrence called his seating plan a talking circle, and made us face one another, all equals, with no table as a buffer.

I squirmed in my seat, already vexed by its unyielding plastic.

"You're right. This is not a court of law, and my findings are not binding. You are here voluntarily, but you agreed to be candid with me and each other, and to follow my rules."

Two three-inch binders, each with dozens of flags, sat atop a square table behind the mediator. A tape recorder leashed to an ostentatious microphone sat next to the binders.

I nodded to renew my vow to get along. Stanley raised his eyebrows and rejected his earlier promise by turning his head.

Becky watched her husband, her thin lips stretched across her face. The burgundy of her lipstick matched the colour of her hair. The quality of her dye job had improved since they started spending Hug's money. "Anywho," she said. "Let's let bygones be bygones."

"But he didn't love her. That's the truth." Turning to me, Stanley said, "Sure, he liked you. He thought you were funny." He tossed his head back and loosed a phony laugh. "Good company. But that's it."

"That's not true." My voice squeaked.

Dog training had taught me to pay attention to people's feet. Dogs predicted their humans' next moves—where they focused, where they were going—by the direction their toes pointed. At the start, Stanley aimed his feet toward Lawrence, but now they pointed straight at me.

As I struggled to decipher the meaning of my observation, Lawrence said, "We're here to establish whether you owe Ms. Wright any obligations under your brother's estate. The rest of this," he rolled his hand in the air, "is irrelevant."

"She's running around calling herself his widow. That's hardly irrelevant. They never married, so she's not his widow."

"We almost got married." I choked my words out.

"Almost doesn't count. Not when it matters." His spittle reached me even across our improvised talking circle. "Horseshoes, remember?"

I was okay with being a horseshoe widow. Horseshoes were lucky.

"He used you. But you used him too. You were selfish," Stanley said, his eyes bugging out of his head. "Selfish and cruel."

"Me? How?"

Stanley crossed his arms. "You know how. You opposed his MAID application."

"Did not!" I yelled.

"Did so." We sounded like children squabbling on the playground. "You wanted to buy yourself more time."

"Time for what?"

He flung up his hands. "You needed more time for him to change his will."

"Whoa, Stanley," Dee said. "You're off base there. I witnessed those conversations too. Heddie's version of events is closer than yours."

The veins on Stanley's neck flexed. "Doesn't matter. He applied anyway. I've got proof." Becky retrieved a packet of folded papers from her purse and flipped them into Stanley's outstretched hand.

Stanley reached across the void to hand the bundle to our mediator. Lawrence skimmed the new document and Dee wouldn't meet my gaze.

"What's that?" I asked.

Stanley placed his hands on his spreadeagled knees. "It's a notarized copy of Hugh's MAID application."

I flushed as a sinking sensation of anger and embarrassment settled over me. "Cancer killed him."

Dee stared at me, then turned to Lawrence. "It's true," she said. "Hugh applied for an assisted death under the new rules. But he postponed his appointment."

"Why?" Lawrence asked.

Dee explained, "Hugh applied as a backup plan, in case things got too bad. He might've proceeded with his application, if he'd successfully arranged his affairs. I know he pushed back his appointment at least once before he cancelled it altogether."

"Who are you trying to kid?" Stanley sputtered. "He went through with it. It's too convenient he died right after that ridiculous living wake she held." He sniffed disdainfully at me.

"His dying was hardly convenient," Dee said. "Do you think Hugh intended this chaos? Do you think he wanted you two to feud?"

Stanley stood and knocked his chair skittering to the floor. "Becky, let's go. This isn't getting us anywhere."

Lawrence walked over, and like a flight attendant, returned Stanley's chair to its upright position. "If you retake your seat, we can resolve this conflict today." Lawrence held his hand out as an invitation.

"What's to resolve? I've got his will. We all know it's real. I've probated the god-damned thing. Hugh left everything to me." Stanley jabbed his own chest with his pointer finger hard, and I hoped it left a bullet-sized bruise over his heart. "He made me his executor. That means I decide."

"Thank you for the lesson in estate law." Lawrence smiled. "Yes, you get to decide. That's why we're here."

"That will was like twenty years old. He prepared it

long before me," I said.

"We all know he tried to update his will," Dee said. "Becky, you were there, too, sometimes. Talk some sense into your husband, please."

Becky's rounded eyes resembled the pug part in pugnacious.

Stanley plunked himself down again. "Hugh was not in his right mind. Don't just take my word for it. Dee, you said so yourself. You called him 'incompetent'." His wattle jiggled.

"You shouldn't have been interfering anyway," Becky added. "This is a family matter." Even seated, Becky was six inches taller than her husband. Her sharp angles and bones contrasted to his plumpness.

"Hugh hired me to help put his legal affairs in order. That's not interfering. It's my job."

Lawrence toddled back to his spot. He arranged his suit jacket under his butt the same way many women smooth their skirts before sitting. "Everyone take a deep breath."

My thudding heartbeat deafened me. "I can help move us forward," I said. "May I read a statement? Leah helped me write it."

"Who's Leah?" the mediator asked.

"She was Hug's death doula, but she used to be a lawyer."

"She's your friend," Stanley said. "Hardly unbiassed."

"Odd career shift," Lawrence observed.

"It makes sense if you know her. She switched jobs after her mom died," I explained. "Charlie suffered locked-in syndrome. Another horrible flipping disease." We'd all been so unprepared for lively Charlie's utter incapacity.

Lawrence nodded. "Heddie's friend doesn't need to be unbiased. Only I do. Please read your prepared statement."

I pulled a folder from my backpack and removed a few pages fastened with a wishbone paperclip. "I brought copies for everyone."

"If you distribute the pages, we can read it for

ourselves. I will add your statement to my record. Does that work?"

What a relief.

A few minutes later, Lawrence looked up from his page. "Thank you, Heddie. This statement is thorough. Let me summarize. You and the late Hugh Fields were in an exclusive relationship for six years. You presented yourselves to the world as a couple, although you never married, have no children together, and each maintained your own households. Two years ago, Mr. Fields was diagnosed with cancer, and he succumbed to his disease four months ago. About ten months before he died, so over a year ago, you gave up the lease on your apartment and moved in with Mr. Fields to help with his care. Do I have it correct so far?"

I nodded, then glanced at Hug's family, who both stared at the mediator, aloof.

"While he was alive, you claim Mr. Fields made you several promises, the most important of which was to leave you his house."

Stanley grunted but offered nothing intelligible.

"That's not quite right," I interrupted. "I'm to take care of Fella. He's more important."

"Fella is Hugh Fields's dog?" The mediator flipped through some pages in one binder and used his finger to guide his eye down a page. "A seven-year-old neutered border collie?"

"That's how we met. Hug—Hugh—brought Fella to one of my puppy classes. He was only about ten weeks old. Super cute." I flushed, and hoped the poor lighting in the windowless room concealed any reddening complexion. "Fella, I mean. Well, Hugh too."

Lawrence smiled. No teeth. "So you're claiming Mr. Fields's primary residence and guardianship of his dog?"

"I guess so, yes."

"Dee, am I right that Mr. Fields—Hugh—did not write these wishes down anywhere?"

"You are correct. Hugh expressed his wishes to each of

us, at various points, verbally." She swept her arm around the circle.

"Why wasn't Hugh able to update his will? He could have saved us all a lot of trouble."

Dee recited the story I now knew by heart. "He tried. I visited Hugh three times, once to take his instructions and twice more to get him to execute his will."

Stanley turned to his wife. "She's talking nonsense."

I couldn't stand them anymore. "She is not. If you'd been around more when Hug was sick, you'd know what he went through."

"Hugh's dead." Becky hurled her pen onto the floor, and it skipped across the surface playfully, unaware of its violent origins. "Deal with it."

I sat open-mouthed, shocked into rare silence. Did she think his death was news?

Dee picked the pen up and handed it back to Becky. "You dropped this."

Becky turned her head and did her best to ignore us. Dee placed the pen next to the microphone.

"We both work." Stanley explained their neglect only to Lawrence. "We couldn't be there all the time."

"I gave up my work so I could be there for him. I was there when he needed me. Every minute. Every day." I twisted in my chair so I didn't have to look at them anymore.

"That makes you a fine nursemaid. Not a wife. Not even a beneficiary, it turns out."

Lawrence clapped his hands once and regained our focus. "Stanley, please show some respect. No taunting one another."

"See what I have to deal with?" I threw up my hands in exaggerated dudgeon.

"Heddie, I understand you're upset. Can you explain what happened? Why Hugh didn't update his will?" I knew Lawrence humoured me.

I'd play along. "Hugh's cancer spread to his bones.

When the cancer cells moved in, they kicked too much calcium out into his blood. It was like his blood curdled, making it harder for his body, including his brain, to work. Thinking, focus, was especially hard. Like he had dementia. The doctors gave him medications to deal with the extra calcium, and the meds helped. But not enough. He'd get better for a few hours, but always relapsed."

Becky sat with her ankles and arms crossed. Stanley stared off at an unadorned corner of the room.

Lawrence addressed Dee. "Why did Hugh hire you? No offence, but you're a bit of a stickler. Someone more, uh, flexible may have accepted Hugh's signatures."

Stanley leaned forward in his seat to better hear Dee's answer.

"Leah believed Hugh's estate was going to be... complicated."

Lawrence glanced at the Fieldses. "Ah."

I hauled out a battered tissue box from my backpack and handed it with both hands to Lawrence. "He wrote a holograph will. I have it here."

Suddenly, all eyes were on me.

"I don't think it'll stand up, though. You know. To the complications. He wrote it during one of his hospital stays."

Shaky handwriting covered the box.

"I can only make out a few words. Are you able to read this?" He passed the box to Dee.

"The relevant parts are on the bottom," I clarified.

Dee turned the box. "Here's what it says..." Her voice lowered as she recited Hug's writing. "'Last will test me Hugh Fields Stan exec cabin Heddie keep Fella house.'" Dee shook her head. "I know what he means here, but only because he told me his wishes. Unfortunately, I think it's undecipherable by anyone else. Besides, he didn't sign and date it."

She really was a stickler.

"Heddie, what are these other notes? 'Justin Trudeau.' 'Wednesday.' 'Egg salad,'" Lawrence asked.

"Hug's cheat sheet." Suddenly, I tired of telling this story, so quickly rattled it off.

Lawrence laughed. "That's ingenious." Silence filled the room. "But it doesn't help us now. Heddie, I'm sorry, but I don't see how you have a legal right to Hugh's estate."

"Yay. Thank you, Lawrence." Stanley slapped his knee with his open hand. "That's what I've been trying to tell her." Stanley seemed too thrilled given the context.

"But he loved me. He said so." I reached into my backpack and pulled my phone from its pocket. I entered the passcode and scooted my chair closer to the mediator. "See," I said. "He says he loves me every time." I opened an email at random, quickly scrolled to the bottom, and tapped the phone.

"What I don't—"

"I have more. Pictures. Hundreds of pictures. Here. I've nothing to hide."

Lawrence obligingly flipped through selfies, proof of our antics. We were all smiles. Full teeth. "Thank you, Heddie. You look very happy together." He handed me my phone, but I used my elbow to block his transfer.

"There's more."

He placed my phone in my hand and wrapped my fingers around to secure it. "It looks like you had something special and loved him very much. I'm sorry for your loss."

"Thank you." I mumbled my rote response to his courtesy.

"I see no evidence here showing Hugh updated his will in a manner acceptable for probate. The tissue box is not enough. Also, Heddie, you have no spousal rights. If he'd lived just a few months longer, you'd be common law spouses." He shook his head. "Why didn't you get married?"

"Hugh considered that option," Dee said.

Given the Fields' matching pinched faces, I suspected this was an unhappy revelation. Stanley crossed his leg over his knee and held it in place with both hands.

"What happened?"

"At first, he didn't think Heddie wanted it. Then he saw how hard she took his illness and decided marriage was the only way he could help her after he passed. But he waited too long. You must be competent to get married too." She peeked at the Fieldses, the Complications.

"I've heard enough," Stanley said. "We're done here." They readied themselves to leave.

"One more thing, please." Lawrence leaned forward and pressed both palms into his knees. "I said Heddie had no legal right to Hugh's estate. At least, none I can see. She still has moral rights."

"What do you mean?" Stanley squalled.

"Your brother planned to change his will to include Heddie. You have an opportunity here to do the right thing."

Stanley bounced up from his chair and strode into the middle of the circle where he confronted Lawrence. "Right thing? Why should I do the right thing?" he shouted. "I'm the injured party here. No one sees that. Tell her to do the right thing. By me. Did you know she didn't call me when my only brother was dying? She didn't let me stand vigil by him. Did you know she hogged the spotlight?" His voice rose to a falsetto and he fanned his face with his fingers while fluttering his eyelids. "Look at me. Look at me. The doctors referred to her in the hospitals—her and him. They didn't even know who I was. That I'm important too. She's only known him for six years. I've known him my entire life." He menaced. "But the worst part, the absolute worst part—because of her, he died in pain. I don't know how she did it. But one minute, he's asking to be put out of his misery, and the next, he's saying he'll buck up."

"That's not what happened, Stanley." I wouldn't bottle it any longer.

Becky patted his shoulder and then handed him a white envelope she'd pulled from her purse.

"I knew this whole thing was a waste of time," he said. "Here. We figured you'd side with her. So this is my best offer."

Stanley dropped the envelope into my lap.

"What's this?" I asked.

"Open it. It's a goodwill gesture. Very generous, under the circumstances."

I used the nib of a ballpoint as a letter opener and pulled out a thin piece of paper. "A cheque?" Their return address was preprinted in the top-left corner. I tried to hand it back, but he wouldn't take it. "You spelled my name wrong."

"How? Henrietta's your real name."

"Yes. But with a Y and a hyphen. H-E-N-R-Y-hyphen-E-T-T-A," I said, like I participated in a spelling bee.

"La-di-da. Your parents were weirdos too," Stanley said. He pointed at the cheque I still held. "Take it or leave it. I don't care."

"I'm curious," Dee said, craning her neck to snoop. "How much did he offer?"

I turned it facedown. "$5,000."

She turned to face Stanley. "That's insulting. We all know Hugh's house alone would net about $250,000. Even in this down market."

I didn't know. Even half of a quarter-million dollars could fund a helluva do-over.

"He was mortgaged to the eyeballs," Stanley equivocated.

"He told me—us—he had mortgage insurance. He said it was enough to pay off all his debt."

"People, enough." Lawrence levered himself from the chair. "We've all heard a lot of important information today, and I encourage you to reflect on it." He reached into his pocket and pulled out a small stack of business cards. He walked the circle, handing a card to each of us. "I'll review the recording of today's session and all your written submissions, but I don't expect my findings or recommendations to change. Before I finalize anything, though, I will review your submissions. I will prepare my final report and email it out by the end of the week. In the meantime, please try to be civil with each other.

Bickering will not resolve your conflict."

"But getting her out of my life will," Stanley said. "Take the cheque. Cash it. Move on. Figure out your life. We're outta here." With no fanfare or even a slammed door to broadcast their departure, Stanley and Becky left the room.

I didn't want to hang out with them in the close quarters of an elevator, so I waited a couple minutes before I hoisted my backpack onto one shoulder. "Thank you. I know nothing changed today, but I appreciate you trying."

Then I left too. Alone. Like how I'd walked in.

At the bus stop, waiting for the bus that would take me home, I checked my email and found no reply from Wendy. Coward. I took out the cheque and examined it. Five grand might be enough to get me on my feet again. Some sixth sense told me not to do it, to stop being so impulsive. Instead, I hauled out my phone and logged into my banking app. With the snap of the camera and a bit of thumb-typing, I deposited the cheque. I felt relief seeing black digits instead of red on my bank balance. Fool's gold.

CHAPTER 30

Two Reports

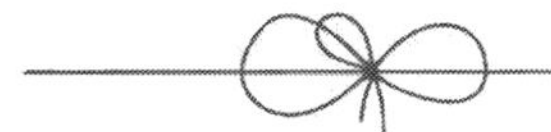

"Thank you for coming to court today, Dr. Butini." Ta-dum bowed his welcome to the elongated man who had towered above the courtroom even before he stepped onto the raised witness booth.

"You're welcome." The witness gestured dismissively.

I sat twenty feet away from him and could smell his aftershave. Why did it have to be Hug's cologne? Paco Rabanne's aroma was thick, heavy, best reserved for intimate occasions. The oak and patchouli notes caught in my throat, and I practised one of Leah's breathing exercises, the box breath, to control my rising panic. I breathed in for four counts, held my breath for four counts, breathed out for four counts, before waiting four counts to start again, but still the courtroom walls crept closer and threatened to smother me. I tried again, staving off the worst of the claustrophobia from gripping my guts and erasing my few remaining brain cells.

The witness—surprise, surprise—was the coroner who'd completed both autopsies on Max. He had earned an impressive assortment of diplomas, degrees, fellowships, and awards, plus he professed considerable experience testifying at other court cases. I studied his curriculum vitae, the document title spelled out fully—a tactic the Tweedles probably considered more credible. My retention of his bona-fides—I can do Latin too—would've suffered without the visual aid. The man's accent was thick, but he spoke impeccable English. He'd taken many of his courses at schools in his motherland, all of which obviously bore motherland-type names. The written CV translated his considerable training and experience, although the English version of the medicalese still remained mostly unintelligible to me.

"Doctor, did you complete the autopsy on Max Taylor?" Ta-dum got right to the point.

"Yes." The coroner flapped his hand at his bangs, which could use a trim and had fallen into his face.

"You completed two autopsy reports for Mr. Maxwell Taylor, correct?"

"I did."

"Your Honour, I'd like to present Exhibit Three: the coroner's report from August. The jurors will remember my learned colleague already distributed a report from March."

The clerk confirmed the exhibit and entered it in her log before providing copies to a bailiff, who then handed a package to each of us. I dutifully jotted my juror and exhibit numbers on the right-hand corner of the top page. I skimmed the report then decided to study it later, on break.

"Why two reports?"

The doctor gripped the sides of the witness stand, readying himself. "I collected Mr. Taylor's body from the Living Memorial Funeral Home, where they'd transported him shortly after his death. I confirmed the funeral director had not yet started embalming, although they had stripped and washed Mr. Taylor's remains before I intervened."

I watched Molly, whose face remained serene. Stanley had spared Hug the indignity of an autopsy.

"I performed the usual tests for the first report, including removing and measuring Mr. Taylor's organs, and drawing blood and other tissue samples to test for chemicals, including prescriptions and toxins. For the second report, my investigation was more thorough because of the allegation of homicide." Here, the doctor broke protocol and addressed us directly. I inhaled sharply. This simple glance shattered my illusion of something like a fourth wall separating us from everyone else in the courtroom. "We rarely perform autopsies when a person was seriously ill and under medical care, unless, with the permission of the patient's family, the treating physician would like to pinpoint the precise cause of death."

I almost laughed, but it would have been a cynical snicker rather than a glad guffaw. Hug's diagnosis had been "unknown primary," a determination apparently given to one in ten cancer patients, and so imprecise that doctors never agreed on treatments. Who knew—besides oncologists—that different chemicals killed off cancer cells originating in different body parts. Different surgeries were obvious—if lung cancer was killing him, don't remove his prostate. But the many tests they conducted to locate the source, the root of Hug's cancer, were never conclusive. All those specialists, and they could only agree he had stage-four metastatic cancer that must've started somewhere.

"And what resulted from those additional tests?"

I drew a mosquito to represent this witness. Blood dripped from its proboscis.

"We found the drugs you would expect for a palliative cancer patient. Antineoplastics, analgesics, cathartics, laxatives. One drug was a common antidepressant, Procheerol, often prescribed to palliative patients on a long decline as a mood stabilizer."

I glanced up from my notes at the mention of this drug again.

"Was Mr. Taylor depressed?"

Dr. Butini put one hand on his hip. "None of my tests diagnose depression."

Hug had certainly been depressed, especially near the end. I'd cornered one of his doctors darting off after a thirty-second visit because I'd wanted him to find a fix.

"Hugh's depressed." I'd reserved using Hug's nickname only with friends and family, and his doctors didn't fit into either category.

"Yes."

"Can't you prescribe him something?"

"Anti-depressants need six weeks to take effect." Then he'd stopped talking, and stood there, arms limply at his sides, staring, his eyes focused and determined. It's like they all went to school to learn how to dribble out parched information. Then I understood, like I'd stepped into a cold shower—this doctor didn't think Hug would live another six weeks.

I'd bawled but collected myself before going back into Hug's room. Even I realized my hysterics were no antidote to Hug's depression.

"Was there anything else, doctor?" Ta-dum's question snapped me back to my job.

"I noted remnants of vomit in Mr. Taylor's esophagus, stomach, and lungs. There was also a small quantity of a liquid, later identified as water, food colouring, and sugar."

"Vomit?"

"Vomit is not an unusual finding—even in one's lungs—when the deceased suffered advanced cancer. Indeed, there was nothing unusual about any of the test results or from my visual examination, and I concluded Mr. Taylor died from complications of his disease. That's what I said in my first report." Dr. Butini arched his eyebrows and leaned into his grip on the podium.

Ta-dum asked in his nasal twang, "What changed?"

"Detective Nasri provided evidence that Mr. Taylor was allergic to the antidepressant my tests found, so I reviewed Mr. Taylor's medical records and realized he was never prescribed that drug."

"Did you perform more tests?"

"No need. It would have been impossible, anyway. Mr. Taylor's remains were cremated shortly after I issued my first report."

I nodded. So many people chose cremation these days. Hug did. That's what I'd prefer too.

"He probably wore a hospital bracelet alerting the

medical staff to his allergies. His clothing and jewellery, and presumably his hospital bracelet, were removed before I received his body. I examined the inventory of his belongings—my staff returned his actual belongings to his wife after my first report." I noted a pattern here, one that allowed Molly to toss any incriminating evidence. "That inventory did not list a hospital bracelet."

"What did you conclude caused Mr. Taylor's death?"

"Mr. Taylor suffered anaphylaxis caused by a drug allergy. Mr. Taylor was a very sick man, and he would have died soon. Certainly, within months, and possibly within weeks. He did not have to die that night."

Molly's poker face remained intact, hiding her secrets.

"Mr. Dodge, would you like to question the witness?" the judge said.

"No questions, Your Honour." Frank's still-nameless second chair half-stood to make this mystifying announcement. She wore cowboy boots today, too, black with white and grey snakeskin inlays along the top and sides of the shafts. The boots were pointy toed, another painful fashion I never understood.

Dr. Butini nodded perfunctorily, recognizing his dismissal. He unfolded his long limbs like a praying mantis, stepped off the podium, and left with no fanfare.

CHAPTER 31

Living Memorial

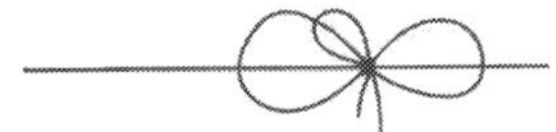

Being a funeral director had to be a hard gig, always witnessing people at their worst. I didn't mean the dead: I meant us, the grievers—the dead's family and friends, the ones left behind. Stanley said I'd been "insufferable" with Hug's funeral director but never bothered to acknowledge the man's contribution to our conflict.

Hug's funeral director, a little man with round glasses à la John Lennon, persistently upsold us. I never bothered to learn his real name, instead dubbing him Ghoul. Maybe he worked on commission. I don't know his motivation. Maybe he suffered an abundant post-pandemic inventory. But I couldn't afford all the trimmings and Hug hadn't planned beforehand. Stanley being Stanley held all his cards too close for me to read.

"We have several packages for you to choose from." Ghoul pulled out a glossy brochure with a comparative chart as a centrefold. Typed matte stickers hid the original prices, which I guessed hadn't been reduced. "The basic package includes preparation, a polished pine casket, cremation, an online obituary and tribute book, and access to our grief support resources for one year. Ten death certificates."

"We don't want a package," Stanley said. "We want simple." He meant cheap.

"Our chapel has openings next week. Would you like to book your own officiant?" The man's voice was dulcet, but he didn't fool me. His tongue was barbed and casting for a sucker.

"We don't need all this stuff." Stanley waved his arm expansively. "My brother wanted a simple funeral, cremation and a small get-together for a toast."

"We have a liquor licence and can supply a bartender."

I shook my head, a gesture Stanley caught. I'd attended too many funerals in funeral homes, with their fake living rooms and cocktail party atmosphere, people standing around visiting and gossiping, even grousing, in the presence of the macabre, flower-ensconced coffin and corpse.

"We'll do our own," Stanley said.

A memorial at Hug's favourite pub was more his style. Our style.

"If you change your mind, just let me know. Please follow me." He stood and moved around his shiny desk. "I will show you our selection of caskets suitable for cremation." We walked down the hall into an expansive showroom where he displayed thirty-ish models in different sizes and colours. "Our cremation caskets are featured along this wall." He pointed with his arm, displaying a fine assortment of wooden coffins with no price tags.

"We want something plain," Stanley said. "I understand we can buy any combustible container. Like a cardboard box."

The man pulled his lips back into a condescending smile. "While these options are dignified, I have others that are, uh, cheaper." He led us to an area hidden behind a pillar. These lower-rung models still featured polished woods in various casts and colours, but with fewer doohickeys and gewgaws.

That's when I lost it. "What do you think we'll do with it afterward? Turn it into a flipping coffee table?"

I threw his coffin brochure onto the floor, stomped on it, and ground it into the probably hand-knotted carpet. Littering, I'm such a rebel. But Hug got his cardboard coffin.

o o o

In the here and now, I noticed my jaw clenching and realized I hadn't been paying attention.

Max's funeral director, Mr. Keith Jenkins, seemed a better choice than Ghoul had been. Jenkins looked like he was about to become his own client, red-faced and sweating, still panting from the exertion of travelling to the witness stand. "I confirmed that Mr. Taylor was deceased. He reclined on a hospital bed, but someone had placed pillows behind him to raise his head and torso. A rolled hand towel was under his chin, and a blanket covered his body to his chest. His arms and hands rested at his sides on top of the blanket."

"Is that posture normal?" Ta-dum asked.

"I see it often. Usually when a person dies in hospice, the nurses use supplies to arrange the body so it appears normal. You know, less dead."

I winced. Nobody had been around to teach me that trick. Hug had laid on his rented hospital bed for three hours before Stanley arranged for his body to be collected. I used the time to help Fella say goodbye to his human. I let him jump onto Hug's bed once Hug was beyond pain. Fella sniffed him, licked Hug's cheek, and curled next to his torso. I embraced the pair of them and rested that way for a long time.

Almost immediately, Hug's face had lost all its Hug-ness: his skin slackened and his eyes, visible through half-slitted lids, became dull and still. His mouth hung open, like he got stuck mid-note in some rousing chorus. I'd tried to close his mouth, but it kept popping open. I never thought to wedge something under his chin to keep it shut.

"Was Mr. Taylor in a hospice?"

This testimony stirred up difficult memories. I really needed to find some way to box them up and shove them aside. I practised one of Leah's breathing exercises again, and it helped a bit.

"No. He was in the hospital."

"What time did you collect Mr. Taylor's body?"

"My colleague, Barry Fromm, and I picked Mr. Taylor up

at 3:40 a.m."

"So fast? Mr. Taylor died at 3:20 a.m. Right?"

"Correct. We were on call for another client."

"Bullshit," a male voice shouted from somewhere behind the Crown. Murmurs from his neighbours echoed his sentiment.

The judge stared at them, and when the audience stilled, Ta-dum continued, "What time did the coroner retrieve Mr. Taylor's body from you?"

"The next afternoon. About 2:30 p.m."

"What had you done to prepare Mr. Taylor's body?"

"We removed and inventoried Mr. Taylor's clothing and accessories. Washed his remains. We had not started embalming."

"Thank you. Your Honour, I have finished questioning this witness." Ta-dum sat down.

I smiled at the now-familiar seesaw switch between the Crown and Frank.

"Have you met Ms. Hopewell before?" Frank stationed himself halfway between his table and the podium. I guessed he planned a short Q-and-A.

"I met Ms. Hopewell a year ago January." That seemed like a lifetime ago. "She and Mr. Taylor came in to make Mr. Taylor's final arrangements. I don't think she was happy about being there."

Frank's salt and pepper eyebrows knitted, and he leaned into his podium. "Can you elaborate?"

"Mr. Taylor told her she needed to 'face the facts.'"

Frank's eyes widened in mock surprise. "Mr. Taylor could speak?"

"He did most of the talking. Even joked about the 'euthanasia lobbyist' making his own funeral arrangements. He seemed reconciled to his fate."

Numerous protesters pounded their palms on wooden benches and interrupted the testimony. The staccato drumming of the judge's gavel silenced them.

"Objection." Ta-dum inspected us, trying and failing to read our minds.

"Sustained." The judge consulted something on his desk. "Mr. Jenkins, please report only on what you saw and heard. Not what you thought." The judge nodded at the witness.

"Sorry." The funeral director's hand shook as he sipped his water. "Mr. Taylor said he didn't want to leave her, his wife, with 'a mess.'"

Hug should've taken a page from Max's playbook. Sure, we'd talked about things, but always loosey-goosey, nothing tangible I could point to now that he could no longer corroborate my recollection.

"Who prepared Mr. Taylor's remains?"

My doodle for this witness featured an open casket containing convincingly detailed skeletal remains. But completing it used up my ink. I wrote on my notepad, "Brad, can I please borrow a pen? Mine's almost dry." Several lines in my letters were faint or missing as the ink skipped. I moved the pad over so he could see it.

My neighbour shook his head.

Maybe he didn't understand. I tapped the message twice with my pen.

He shook his head again, more vehemently this time.

Miffed, I pointed to his pocketful of pens and double-underlined beneath my "please."

"No," he whispered in an unmistakable tone.

I ogled his stash nested in their pocket protector and within easy snatching reach, but restrained myself.

I twisted away from Brad, doing my best to present a cold shoulder. The witness's head and torso swayed from side to side. "Mr. Taylor's remains were prepared by a practicum student, Darla Denworth. Ms. Denworth was on her final practicum in her program."

"How can you be certain Ms. Denworth did not begin the embalming process?"

"She followed a checklist. And my colleague—Barry, Barry Fromm—supervised her work."

"Did Ms. Denworth make any mistakes in her techniques?"

"Yes. She washed and rinsed Mr. Taylor's mouth when she washed the rest of his remains. With a hose."

Oops.

CHAPTER 32

Yup, He's Dead

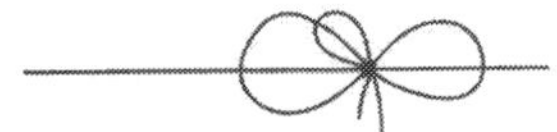

"That was interesting," Ruth said.

Clemence hustled us out of the courtroom as soon as the funeral director finished his evidence. I settled into my seat and rolled close to the table. This necessary manoeuvre allowed others to squish behind me to get to their own seats.

"What do you mean?"

Ruth was about to educate me—us—when Phil interrupted her. "We're not supposed to be talking about the case." He glowered at me, singling me out for his snub. "You're breaking the rules."

"What else are we going to talk about?" I scanned the room for supporters and found instead a roomful of blank expressions, so I continued, "What Clemence said was... we couldn't discuss it if a, we were outside this room and b, we weren't all present." I counted out the details of her instructions on my fingers. "We're all here." I swept my arm dramatically to emphasize my point. "And in the right place." I jabbed with my pointer finger toward the floor to stress this second truth. "So we can talk about it."

"That's right," Jim said, glancing sideways at Phil. "That's what Clemence said." He addressed me directly. "I found it interesting, too, Heddie."

"I was expecting it to be more like TV," Ingrid said.

"I already said that. Days ago." Ruth huffed her indignation.

I laughed, mostly at Ruth's homemade competition. "I know. No atmospheric music. No great reveals. No blown secrets. But mostly, TV prosecutors would never refer to Max's remains as 'body.'"

"You're right," Toni said. "They want us to visualize the victim, connect with them emotionally."

"Hard to get chummy with a corpse," I said.

"Heddie, that's terrible," Ruth said, and I grinned to hail the error of my ways.

Pat ignored me. "I hope we get more definitive information," she said. "The Crown hasn't even told us why they arrested her yet, let alone why they think she's guilty of murder."

Toni said. "How can an autopsy show everything is hunky-dory one day, and then be the basis for murder charges the next? The Defence could sit on his presentable behind doing nothing, and right now, I'd acquit."

We'd all adopted the lingo so quickly.

"How do you know it's presentable?" Ruth asked, then winked, and we six women snickered.

Norman drummed his fingers on the table. "Ladies, really?"

"Like you haven't heard worse coming from your CB radio," Ingrid said. "You could probably give us lessons."

"So far, I don't have a 'shadow' of doubt," Mandi said. "I've got a whole eclipse."

Toni added, "The witnesses only confirmed Max died. Nobody's explained why we're here."

"There were the antidepressants," Brad offered.

"Yes," Toni said. "But nothing showing that Molly gave them to him. That finding raises more questions than facts."

"Like what?" Brad asked. "Seemed pretty damning to me."

"Like, if she did it, how did Molly get the drugs? Did anyone else have them or access to them? How common are they?" Toni said.

"I'm sure they'll explain it all," I said. "But just so we don't forget, I'll make us a list."

"No need for that," Brad said.

I wouldn't follow the advice of a pen-hoarder. I twirled my chair around, went over to the flip-chart stand, and tore off a sheet. Neatly, no ragged edges on my tears. I affixed my paper to a blank part of the wall using the conveniently supplied green painter's tape. On it, using the cinnamon-scented marker, I wrote, "Questions?" Underneath, I swirled a dot followed by "How link Molly to antidepressants?" and another dot with "Anyone else with antidepressants?" afterward.

Brad frowned and turned away from me when I returned to my seat, and I stifled a self-satisfied laugh.

Mandi changed the subject. "I hope they'll change that light above my seat. It's giving me a headache."

Ever helpful, I said, "Let's see if Clemence can get it fixed."

"Let's not," said Phil.

"What's it to you?" I snapped. "Clemence said she'd help with stuff like that."

I strode the few steps where I rapped on the door, and less than a minute later, the jangle of keys announced Clemence's arrival. She unlocked the door and opened it just enough to block any attempted exit.

"How can I help you?"

"Clemence," I started, "Mandi says the light above her seat is giving her a headache."

Mandi waved her hand and smiled brightly to identify herself.

Clemence nodded perfunctorily. "I'll let maintenance know. They'll be quick. The judge doesn't like jurors suffering avoidable distractions." Clemence turned to go, but then she pivoted and gazed straight at me. "Thank you for telling me. Usually, it takes much longer before anyone alerts me to this kind of issue."

I acknowledged her compliment, before addressing my

best gloating smirk to Phil. Maybe we'd find a way to get along better tomorrow.

CHAPTER 33

Tips

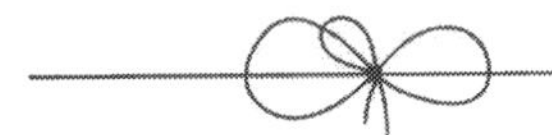

I stepped onto black ice and slid forward into an ungainly lunge. The misstep rattled rather than hurt, another unwelcome reminder that nature always won. I needed my cleats. I'd bought the slip-on kind for a reason: easy-on, easy-off. Tomorrow, I promised myself I'd make the time to wear them.

In the meantime, I baby-stepped around the corner to the courthouse entrance and almost face-planted into a broad back dressed in a black duffel coat. I moved around my obstacle and squirmed through the crowd like a spawning salmon intent on my destination. "Excuse me. Pardon me. Sorry." My apologies marked my slow progress through the crowd, each bump, jostle, and trod toe.

For once, my height was useful, and I spotted a clearing close to the wall, next to the merry-go-round entrance of the courthouse. The concrete, glass, and reinforced steel of the twin towers conjoined by a glass atrium featured bulletproof-this and 9/11-proof-that. I wriggled my way toward the gap and broke through the crowd. When I looked back, I saw nothing but scowls and scorn.

Many in the crowd carried hand-painted signs homemade from scraps and ordinary household items. One masked protester brandished a flattened Amazon box, identifiable by its branded tape, affixed to a metal broom handle. The message on it read, "Lock up your grannies," painted unevenly in what resembled blood but was probably red paint. He wore a shaggy wolf's head mask, menacing canines locked forever mid-snarl. *How do you do, Big Bad Wolf?* I bowed the teensiest bit in his direction. *Sorry you get such a bad rep in the stories.*

Another box, still in its three-dimensional form and painted a bright blue, bore different messages on each side. I could read, "Care! Respect Life," and, "Thou shalt not kill." Their holders pumped other signs up and down like oil derricks. "MAID is murder." "Suicide is a sin."

Across the road, only a few feet away and cordoned by asphalt, a more sedate crowd milled. Judging from their signs, they formed the opposing team. "MAID—Flawed Law." "Choose Mercy before Justice." I considered Dee's cats and wondered if she had a role in this display. She probably wouldn't admit it, at least not to me, at least not now.

I turned my back on the anger and the angry and halted mid-pirouette. Two dozen well-worn empty shoes flanked a backdrop of more protest signs. Some were scuffed sneakers, with soles unevenly worn. A couple were stilettos. The leather curled on the gouged heels of one pair. Hand-painted signs propped behind the shoes created a photogenic tableau for journalists and protesters' selfies: "I had no support," "I was forced," "I didn't want to die."

Some construction boots choked me up, too closely resembling a pair of Hug's favourites. Hug had jammed his abundant collection into the foyer closet and on the floor of his wardrobe. Most of them still had life in them, even as he no longer did. Hug had enormous feet—"skis for feet," he'd said too often—and literally no one could fill his shoes. I hoped Stanley hadn't just chucked them.

A thump followed by guttural groans interrupted my rumination. I pivoted in time to see a man convulsing on the sidewalk and keening in discomfort. To my uneducated eye, I determined he was seizing. White foam around his mouth mixed with droplets of blood from his nose. What looked like dried sick stained the front of his hospital smock; a faded black logo was visible under the white trim around his collar. Why was he wearing a hospital smock? Fortunately, the rest of his clothing, jeans, and brown hiking boots, was suitable for the weather. One flailing foot scattered the nearest displayed shoes.

A line of uniformed police, white Stetsons shading their faces, stood guard in front of the building entrances.

"Hello?" I said, waving my arm widely over my head, hoping to attract the attention of the nearest cop. But he stood, stern, at attention, my summons falling seemingly on deaf ears. "Hello?" I persisted. "This man needs help."

The cop's eyes darted in my direction, but he didn't move toward me or unfasten his radio to call for help.

"You know first aid?"

I'm sure the cop jutted his chin further out as confirmation of my dismissal.

"Come on, man. Don't just stand there."

Refracted sunlight shone through his blonde chin stubble.

I forced myself to swallow through the clenched knot I called a throat and jogged the few steps toward the flailing man. I knelt next to him, soothing him with my words. "There, there," I said. "I'll help." I reluctantly patted his arm, disregarding any worries about herpes or scabies or some other contagion.

Poor schlep, I wracked my brain to recall how to help someone seizing. All I could remember was not to restrain them: something about their thrashing causing injury. There was some advice about sticking something hard into their mouth, like a bit. But someone had shovelled the sidewalk, and I couldn't find any sticks. Bingo, walking poles. I slipped off my backpack and it thudded on the ground. That's when I noticed that my writhing patient had stilled. Oh, no. He passed out? Died? I looked at him and he stared back at me. Baby blues full of life. And contempt.

That's when I recognized Axel.

"Can you get away from me?" he said, forgetting his manners.

Too dumbfounded to react, I stayed put.

"You're interrupting my performance," he continued.

"Whaaa?" My monosyllabic response was ineloquent but understandable.

"My performance," he repeated, as if repetition would help me unravel his meaning. "I'm an artist."

Huh? This kid had an identity crisis. He was supposed to be a journalist.

He fished out a stack of folded lime green paper from his smock pocket, thumbed one out from the middle, and handed it to me. "Fine Art of Protest" seemed to be his company name. Underneath the inexpertly written heading was a more skillful drawing of protesters, more caricature than portrait. I recognized the artist's inspiration in the nearby assembly.

I marvelled at the man's commitment. It took dedication to roll around on cold, slushy pavement to further one's craft. "Well, you fooled me."

"Thanks," he said. "I aim for authenticity."

I used my hand as a prop to wipe around my mouth. "Your makeup is smeared."

He ignored my implied advice. "Whatever."

"Well, sorry," I uttered the refrain of my life. I levered myself up from the ground, inwardly adding creaking and groaning sounds to my movements. Sound effects always helped. When I stood upright again, I brushed off my hands and knees—and spotted fresh salt stains where I'd knelt next to my defiant patient.

"Do you have a tin?" I asked.

It was his turn to be confused. "Pardon?"

"A tin," I repeated, unintentionally mimicking our earlier exchange. "For a tip."

"You're a funny woman," he said, clearly displeased.

"Not really. I consider myself more of a truth-teller."

He pursed his white-lined lips and squinted his eyes. "Go away."

I turned away from the actor and his antics. That's when I spotted phones pointing in my direction, and realized, too late, I'd been videoed. I pulled my scarf closer around my face and moved to stand in front of the blond cop. Indignant, I said, "You could have warned me. Saved me the trouble."

His smirk widened ever so slightly.

CHAPTER 34

Fired

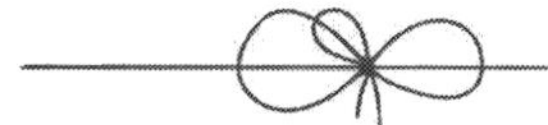

"Can we go over the medical evidence so far? I don't know about you all, but I've heard too many foreign words. I need help deciphering them."

That wasn't entirely true, but people had spouted enough gobbledygook over the last few days for me to miss important details.

We sat behind closed doors again, technically on a break. Everyone else got to do whatever they wanted during these thirty-minute recesses. Us? We got stuck sitting in close, airless quarters where we entertained ourselves. At least they offered us decent snacks.

Phil surprised me when he didn't object. "I know, I know," he said. "We're all here, present and accounted for." He was living proof: you could teach an old dog new tricks.

Mandi said, "Can we start with the doctor? That oncologist?" She enunciated carefully.

"The one who fired him?" Ruth's unattractive scowl emphasized her age. "Yes, let's. I'd like to say a thing or two about her."

"Everybody okay if I write our comments out?" I loaded my notepad onto my chair and wheeled it over to the flip-chart without awaiting their permission. I folded over the first blank sheet on the pad; I'd flip it back over to cover any notes if Clemence marched in. She'd made it clear she had no desire to hear, or probably see, our discussions.

"Oh, yes, please," Mandi enthused. Oh, to be eighteen again.

"I found her distracting," Toni said.

"But she knew her stuff," I added. All Hug's doctors were men. I didn't want to malign the first female oncologist I'd encountered.

"She moved around a lot."

"True," I said. The good doctor had gesticulated not just with her hands and her face, but also with her arms, shoulders, even her torso. "What do we know about her?"

Ruth flipped open her notepad and rifled through the pages before landing on the section entitled, "Dr. Delia Babich, oncologist. Specializes in breast cancer."

I peered over her shoulder. "Wow, I wish my notes were so tidy." I flipped to my own notes for the doctor's testimony and held it up for people to see. The drawing was a personal best, almost a masterpiece, with the doctor's vein-popping anger, and "You're fired!" shouted at a terrified Molly and Max.

"You certainly depicted the salient points," Toni said.

Ruth took charge of our conversation. "We'll get to that, I promise. In the meantime, what else do we know? Can we go around the table?"

I chose the cinnamon and apple-scented markers to jot down people's comments. Maybe I'd pick up an apple crumble on the way home. It would be a nice surprise for Leah and the kids.

"I'll start," Phil said. "She specializes in breast cancer. Max was her patient for about two years."

"He was her only male patient," Mandi added. "She probably crushed on him."

Interesting observation. "How do you figure?" I doodled a heart on the flip-chart while awaiting Mandi's answer.

Mandi stared off into the corner of the room before meeting my gaze. "The way she talked about their conversations."

"I don't remember that."

Mandi licked her index finger and flipped through her notes. "Here it is. The doctor mentioned the so-called 'obvious topics.'" Mandi used air quotes. "They talked about his 'disease,' its 'origins,' 'treatment options,' 'progression.'"

With so much finger-scrunching going on, I could've added a dance track to Mandi's boogie.

"They also talked about 'philosophy, religion, music.'" Mandi laughed. "Oh, yeah, I remember this. She called him an 'articulate and cultured man.'" Mandi's eyes were bright, and her mouth fixed into a silly grin. "The doctor was definitely crushing on him."

"She mentioned 'enjoying' their conversations," Pat added.

My two cents? "That meant her firing him was more like a breakup." I struggled to add insightful observations while fulfilling my scribe role.

∘ ∘ ∘

"I fired him as a patient." The doctor had whispered this showstopper.

Ta-dum placed both hands in the pockets of his robe. "Why would you do that?"

The doctor huffed, indignant. "Because he took so-called alternative therapies, plus the treatments from me. He doubled-up, and the alternative treatment cancelled out the benefits from the protocols I administered." She shook her head, as though attempting to dislodge the image of his betrayal. "He could have one treatment or the other, but not both. He chose the alternative option."

"I don't understand." Ta-dum glanced at his colleague. "Wasn't Max already declared palliative? Why would you care which therapies he took to cure himself?"

The doctor fidgeted and Ta-dum's widened eyes stilled her. She responded to his silent rebuke by raising her neck to a haughtier angle. "I informed Max there was nothing more I could do for him beyond comfort care about six months before I fired him."

"So why did you care which therapies he took? Wouldn't you want your patients to try anything? Anything to find a cure?"

"If it didn't interfere with treatments I ordered."

I was miffed: Max had fought for his life, while his doctor preserved her ego. Hug's doctor knew all about the various remedies I'd found and tried. He wasn't thrilled about us experimenting with them, but also did nothing to stop us.

"Those treatments were dangerous and expensive. Can-cure. Malarkey. I couldn't sit by and watch him poison himself."

I sat forward in my seat, needing to hear more. Hug tried Can-cure too.

The doctor scrunched her nose, and all her exquisite features collapsed in on themselves. "Can-cure is nothing but toxic heavy metals suspended in fish oil. I personally paid to have several bottles tested, and the ingredients were never consistent. That concoction will kill faster than any cancer."

———— o o o ————

"I gave Hug Can-cure," I blurted, and eleven heads turned my way. "Did I kill him?"

Ruth filled the astonished silence. "Oh, Heddie. Who knows?"

"What about those heavy metals? That's bad, right?"

"Yes, generally," Ruth admitted. "But chemo is poison out of context too."

"I learned about it in the hospital library. If it's so bad, why'd they promote it?"

While I had waited during one of Hug's many surgeries, I paced stress-relieving laps around the hospital. One day, I came across a hospital library. I opened the glass door and immediately felt like an intruder. Everyone else sported white coats and stethoscopes. I turned to leave, thinking I'd stumbled into a private resource room for medical staff, but a young woman strode over and blocked my exit. Not intentionally, of course. She was just being helpful.

"Is this room open to the public?" I asked. "May I sign out books?"

"Of course," the woman replied.

I fished my driver's licence out from my collection of credit and loyalty cards. After answering a few questions and completing a single page form, I held a library card still warm from the laminator.

The doctors scheduled Hug's surgery to last ninety minutes, so I headed into the stacks. But I didn't venture far before I found a prominent display—like what bookstores reserve for bestsellers and staff favourites—of books focusing on holistic cancer therapies. I thought it serendipitous, almost magical, that I'd encountered those books just then. Since his diagnosis, I'd asked, prayed, begged the universe, whomever, to save him, and I wound up in front of this stack. I grabbed up the books, checked them out, stuffed them into my already-laden backpack, and headed back up to Hug's hospital room to await his return.

His surgery took far longer than planned. I sat in the hospital room and tried to distract myself from my anxiety and worry. I discovered that reading, especially anything technical, was impossible. So, I played an endless cycle of stupid games on my phone until it rang, startling me when it interrupted the strangling silence.

I didn't recognize the number. "Hello," I answered, my voice suspicious.

"Is this Heddie? I'm Jane McKee, the nurse in the recovery room. Hugh wants to speak with you."

I was so glad, relieved. Hug slurred his words but sounded jubilant. "You got the Clamato ready?"

The doctors had postponed his surgery a half-dozen times when tests revealed snowballing bad news. They'd kept him on the surgical rotation with no food or drink. They even rationed water, allowing him only one Dixie cup of ice chips a day. Of course, an IV hooked him up with nutrition and hydration. Kept him alive. I meted out infantile portions of those chips.

For reasons that still mystified me, he'd fixated on Clamato juice. So, I made him a deal: if he behaved with the ice chips until after his surgery, I'd buy him a lifetime's supply of Clamato. We both kept our ends of the bargain. Unfortunately, I didn't get to fulfill my part for very long.

Over the next few days, satisfied that he was safe again, I devoured the library books, and even took notes—with real, actual words. I injected their ideas into his regimen, including vitamin D—because it was a cure-all, for everything from Covid to depression. Even cancer. I bought reishi mushrooms, resveratrol, bromelain, and omega-3. I subtracted all sugar and even fake sugar.

Still, this once-vital man wasted away before my eyes, as the cancer ate his muscles and the radiation caused him to throw-up.

I ordered Can-cure for him, even paid a premium for fast delivery. The solution itself was expensive. Add international shipping and duty, and the price tag was exorbitant. A one-week supply cost the equivalent of running a six-week puppy class. Totally worth it if it worked.

Hug played along, but I think he'd given up by then. He drank it every four hours, as instructed. I set my alarm so I'd wake up, even in the middle of the night. The coppery taste made him retch, so I masked the liquid first in juice, then smoothies, and finally a soup. I followed the instructions precisely, and it didn't do a damned bit of good.

∘ ∘ ∘

When Twee-dee finished questioning the doctor, Frank stood. He brushed off invisible lint from his wrinkled robe and strode to the podium. "I just have a few questions, and then you can be on your way. I know you have a busy schedule." I sniffed sarcasm.

Dr. Babich nodded.

"Who discovered the lump in Max's breast?" So much for pleasantries.

"Max's wife. He had noted the growth, as well, but ignored it. She was the one who insisted he get it checked."

I wished I'd spoken up sooner, louder at Hug's earlier symptoms. Maybe the outcome would've been different. I'd piled up so many regrets, but that was the biggest. I began to consider that Molly loved Max after all. Maybe even as much as I loved Hug. I studied her, and realized Molly looked as lost as me.

"Objection." The Crown stood, knocking his table and spilling water from his glass in his haste. "Hearsay."

"Sustained." The judge remained serene as he quietly made crucial decisions.

Frank smirked. "Let me rephrase. Who first asked you to examine Max Taylor for breast cancer?"

She fanned a sheaf of papers. "His wife, Molly. I have it in my notes."

"I'd like to reference page three of the doctor's notes. Doctor, please read the highlighted section."

She flipped the page over and then, in a clear voice, read, "GP—that's shorthand for Max's family doctor—referral, biopsy abnormality from left breast tissue. Wife provided history."

"Do many spouses accompany patients to their appointments?"

"In oncology, yes. I even encourage it. Information and options often overwhelm the patient. They need someone else there as support."

I nodded, recognizing Hug in her description. He'd needed me as a note-taker, memory, interpreter, and sounding board. Occasionally, advocate. I had carried a notebook with me and jotted down his random questions and theories, rattling them off to doctors at his appointments. Stanley and

Becky tagged along infrequently and greeted my questions with rolled eyes and exaggerated sighs. But they didn't see Hug at night, console him during his nightmares, or soothe him after another bout of vomiting. They only saw him when he donned his brave face, his public face. Shame on Hug for not defending me. He could have, probably should have, but his ambiguous silence egged them on.

No-Name watched me, her twisting lip a sign of confusion. I cleared my expression into something like attentive neutrality.

"When exactly did you fire Mr. Taylor as your patient?"

"February twenty-third."

"Eleven months before he died. Why did you do that?"

The doctor inhaled deeply. "Max took an untested alternative therapy. He refused to stop it and I refused to condone it. We were at an impasse."

"You'd already told Max he was dying?"

"I told him he was palliative, yes."

"No cure for his disease?"

"No."

"Dr. Babich, do you prescribe Procheerol?" Frank changed the topic.

She examined him warily. "I prescribed it to Max early in the course of his disease, but he suffered an allergic reaction. The allergy was severe enough that he wore a medical alert bracelet."

"Did Max have any pills left over when he stopped taking the prescription?"

"Probably not," the doctor replied. "I only gave him some samples to try. Besides, Molly always brought in his unused meds for proper disposal."

Frank nodded. "Tell me more about those samples."

The doctor's face was bland. "What's to tell? Pharmacy companies distribute small packets of their drugs so patients can see if they improve their condition. If yes, doctors write a longer script. If no, doctors test another drug."

"Is Procheerol common? Do you have many samples of this drug?" Frank asked.

"It's very common. I expect every medical clinic in the country has a significant sample inventory."

"One more question, doctor, are your samples locked up?"

"At night, yes, all the cupboards are locked. But not during the day. Samples are stored in a central cupboard next to the examination rooms."

"Thank you, doctor."

She took that as her permission to leave and moved to step off the witness stand. "Not so fast," Frank said, and smiled. "What time estimate did you give Max?"

She settled back into her spot. "Weeks to months." She blinked repeatedly.

"Why couldn't you turn a blind eye to the alternative therapies?"

"I've treated breast cancer for nearly twenty years. My track record is sterling."

"He jeopardized your stats?"

She muttered something incomprehensible.

"Oh, never mind," he said. "Try this one. Were you aware that Max applied under the Medical Assistance in Dying legislation for a hastened death?"

"We discussed his options."

"Did you know he started that application on February seventeen?"

"Yes, but—"

Frank held up a pencil like a conductor, marking the beat of a well-rehearsed score. "Doctor, how many patients have you helped over life's final threshold?"

"None," she whispered again.

"Isn't that the real reason you fired him? You fired twenty-six other patients days after they each applied under MAID for relief from their suffering. That's quite a record, doctor, especially since the government enacted the legislation only a half-dozen years ago."

She growled. "I help the living. Not those who've given up. I have rights, too, and I can choose not to—what did you call it?—'hasten' Max's death? I don't have to defend my choices to you or anyone else."

No, she didn't. But it still didn't make her right.

———— o o o ————

"I think she's a coward," Phil said.

"Why?" Toni asked.

Phil sounded more irritated than usual. "She abandoned him."

Toni persisted, "you think the 'alternative therapies' was an excuse?"

Phil took a sip from his coffee cup, leftovers from an earlier break, and nodded.

"Me too, Phil." I said, delighted we finally agreed on something. "She said herself that he had 'weeks to months.'" I could never have abandoned Hug, even if I found it hard to concede that he had to decide about his own treatments.

"Can someone explain the 'weeks to months' thing?" Mandi asked.

Ruth had become our resident medical translator. "Doctors don't want to predict how long someone has left to live. Not precisely. Too many variables. So they use a scale. 'Months to years' is the most favourable, indicating that while there's no cure for whatever ailment, there's still a decent amount of living a person can do. 'Weeks to months' is not so encouraging, suggesting the disease has gotten the upper hand. 'Hours to days,' well, that person will die anytime."

"What does 'palliative' mean?" I asked.

She looked at me quizzically. She knew I knew. I raised my eyebrows at her and pointed with my eyes toward Phil. Understanding washed over her. "That's when there's no cure for the disease. Lots of people think that means they're going to die, like tomorrow. Not true. Many patients live superb and full lives for years after they're told they're palliative. Palliative just means the medical focus switches from trying to cure the disease to making the patient as comfortable as possible. Comfort care, end-of-life care."

She used too much medical code, too many euphemisms. I'd earned my own decoder ring helping Hug as he lurched through his disease. Regardless, I feigned ignorance. "End-of-life? Comfort care?"

"Dying from cancer is often painful. 'Comfort care' means the doctors help reduce pain and even manage mood."

Phil shimmied his shoulders in an unbecoming taunt. "Are you an expert?"

"I doubt I'd pass your tests, but yes, I'm an expert. I worked as a nurse for nearly forty years, thirty-three of them—in palliative wards." Ruth maintained a neutral expression. "I was very good at my job."

"Well, once they confirm you as an expert in that courtroom," he hitched his thumb over his shoulder, "you can interpret our evidence."

"That's mature," Toni heckled, not her shining moment as peacekeeper. "Interpreting the evidence is our only job and we'd be foolish to ignore any of the resources in this room. We have experience, and yes, whether you like it or not, expertise."

He didn't look chastened. Instead, he inhaled deeply, readying himself for a fight. "It's hard enough keeping details straight without everyone throwing in their two-bits."

Finally, we got to the crux of his problem. "So let's work out a system to keep it sorted," I offered.

Phil didn't comment and I couldn't tell whether his silence meant agreement or acquiescence. Without his contribution, I labelled the tops of individual sheets from one notepad with the names of the witnesses and passed them around. We all took turns jotting our key observations, questions, concerns to share our memories and analyses. When we were done, I posted everything on the walls, careful to fold each sheet in half to expose only a blank side of the paper and hide our notes from prying eyes.

CHAPTER 35

Dee: Stop, Thief!

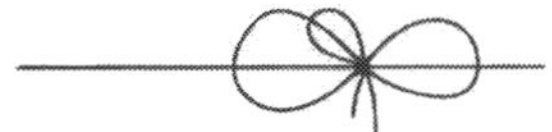

Dee turned the corner, the sheaf of photocopies hot in her hands. The photocopier had not collated the packages properly, and she contended with organizing the pages manually by using her fingers as dividers.

"Hey!" Dee startled the rumpled man standing behind the reception desk. She wasn't expecting anyone, and today's meetings wouldn't start for several hours.

He glanced up and grinned, his innocent countenance at odds with the jimmied cabinet drawer and its jumbled contents strewn on the floor. With a practised one-handed movement, he stuffed a thick binder into his half-zippered ski jacket. Then, without a word of explanation or apology, he shoved past her then dashed out the suite door and down the hallway toward the exit.

"Stop!" Dee ordered, as she ran after him. But she did not move fast or far in her stockinged feet. By the time she got to the hallway herself, he'd already reached its far end and entered the stairwell leading to the main floor and the street below.

She gave up her chase and returned to her desk. She fingered down the contact list pinned to a nearby cork board, then punched-in the number for building security.

The phone rang several times. "Hello?" The security officer sounded out of breath.

"Hi, Bob? It's Dee from Dixon Law."

"Oh, hi, missus." Dee could almost hear the smirk in his voice. She hated to be called by anything other than her name and yet he found it amusing to persist. One of these days, she should complain to the landlord about their security's lack of professionalism.

"I don't have time for your jokes right now, Bob. I've been robbed."

"Big guy, blond hair, blue coat?"

"Yes, that's him. Where is he?" Dee asked, pleased this situation could be corrected so easily.

"He just ran past me. Almost knocked me over." Bob sounded indignant.

"Can you catch him?"

"He's already outside. But I'll try to get his plate number." Bob disconnected the call. Now all she could do was wait.

She dialled 911. The operator answered the call on the first ring. "911. Please state the nature of your emergency."

"I've been robbed." Dee relayed her story, then awaited the police. She reassembled the files and piled them alphabetically. She took stock and found only one missing: Hugh's.

She picked up her phone again and scrolled through her contacts until she reached Heddie's name. She texted, *Call me. 911.* After hitting send, she rethought her message and wrote, *It's an emergency*, just in case Heddie didn't understand her original code.

Heddie called rather than texted Dee back.

"What's up?" she asked.

Dee explained the situation. "That binder contained notes from our work together. Plus, all the materials I prepped for your mediation." Dee expected easygoing Heddie to take this in stride. She'd been through far worse.

There was a long pause and Dee wondered whether the call had dropped. "You wouldn't even let me see that file," Heddie said, too quietly. "I hate that some stranger will see all my faults. Worse, see Hug's faults."

Heddie disconnected the call without saying goodbye.

CHAPTER 36

Twins

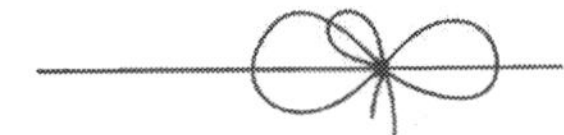

We agreed to meet in the middle of the day, because high noon was a great time for a heist. I'd considered the middle of the night for this liberation, but hiring workers for a midnight expropriation proved logistically challenging. Plus, who dug up trees in the dark?

I parked Dimples around the corner from Stanley and Becky's place, sandwiched between a couple cars and well-hidden behind a cotoneaster hedge. The bright sun shone like an oversized searchlight on my target. I craned my neck, my whole torso in fact, to surveil Hug's tree and their front door. Most of the snow from yesterday's storm had melted, although remnants remained in drifts and the shadows. The snow around my prize was gone, leaving it centred in a dark patch of earth surrounded by a yellowed lawn. Like a bull's eye.

I checked my watch. They should be leaving soon, but they were always pokey. I hoped their flight wasn't delayed. I'd debated offering to drive them to the airport but decided against it. Self-absorbed Stanley would've considered it a peace-offering, a placating gesture, even an owed service, but Becky already smelled a skunk.

At last, a car pulled up and honked. The pair's door opened, and they wheeled suitcases, hers large and his pint-sized, down their driveway to the curb. The driver timed his exit from his upscale sedan with their arrival. He opened the trunk and waited. I snickered at the standoff between the driver and Stanley, as neither rushed to stow the luggage. As usual, Stanley won. The driver picked up each suitcase and levered them into the trunk. He brushed his hands together twice before placing one out—palm-up. Stanley ignored him.

I waited a few more minutes before I made my call. My plan had no give in it, no tolerance for any last-minute returns while Becky checked to ensure her straightening iron was off or Stanley confirmed he'd locked all the doors. I wanted this liberation to be invisible, leaving no signs or evidence.

At first, I'd tried to find an arbourist to help, and had encountered several roadblocks. They wanted pesky details, like why I didn't know where underground wires and cables were located, or why my name wasn't on the property title.

Then I found a Kijiji landscaper willing to do the job. Not bad, considering I only just learned about the twosome's buying trip. I booked Kijiji-guy with a false name and agreed to pay cash for his services, half up front and half on delivery. Paying cash was a pointer I'd learned from TV crime shows, and I followed the advice even when the withdrawal returned my account into overdraft.

I pulled up to their house and parked in their driveway. I figured I had fifteen minutes before the landscaper arrived and brought a replacement tree with him. I was okay with them having a tree, even a Hug-memorial tree. They just didn't need or deserve Hug's ashes. They got everything else of his and wouldn't share. If they'd been reasonable, fulfilled what Lawrence called their moral obligations to me, I wouldn't need to resort to such unconventional measures. Plus, I finally knew how I'd use his ashes to create a fitting memorial for him.

I was going to turn them into a diamond. The process was expensive and took about six months. But the company only needed 200 grams of pristine cremains to create the gem.

I lost any hope for a discreet operation when I first heard and then saw the landscaper arrive. His giant pickup grumbled down the road like it spoiled for a fight. A long trailer hitched to the truck carried a construction yellow tractor with matching tree spade. A tiny cottonwood sat perched in the spade, looking like a toothpick riding atop Big Bird.

I examined the cottonwood and felt better about my endeavour. Sight unseen, the landscaper—who introduced himself as Abe—found a twin in size, shape and colour to the one in the ground. I considered changing the tree to something more suitable for Hug, a specimen that wouldn't aggravate his allergies. A lovely lilac, with its rich blooms and aroma joining to celebrate his birthday. Or a sweet larch, rare with its deciduous needles and cones. Or a plump ponderosa pine, because its shaggy needles amused me and were evergreen in a way he was denied. But, if I changed the tree, I'd get caught for sure.

"Good morning." I hoped I sounded jaunty rather than nervous. I waved. Were my gloves conspicuous? I didn't want to leave fingerprints everywhere.

He grunted his greeting. "Actually, good afternoon." He walked gingerly across the lawn to the planted tree and inspected it. "This tree was just planted. Why we diggin' it up?"

"I'm giving it to my sister." I didn't have a sister.

"What about the tree I brought?" He pointed to the lookalike that was still comfortably cocooned in its burlap wrap in the pointy spade.

"She wants this one." My mind raced. Breathe. The truth wasn't an option. People were weird about dead bodies, even stolen ashes of a dead body. "It's—uh—sentimental. It came from a sucker off my dead uncle's tree. He lived up in Canmore, way up higher than the reservoir. The one overlooking the town. Moved there during the gold rush. But he died…" Shuddup, already.

"Got my money?" I didn't think he believed one smidgen of my horse manure.

"$200, right?"

"Plus fifty for that one. Lookin' 'round here," he studied the neighbourhood and houses, "I should charge ya more."

"No, sir. We agreed. Even fifty bucks for that scrawny

specimen is steep." I removed a $100 bill and a $50 bill, and snapped each before handing them to him. "Down payment. You'll get the rest when that tree," I hitched my thumb toward the one in his truck, "is in the ground and that one, is in my car."

"You're haulin' the tree away in that?" He actually snorted.

Dimples might not be handsome, but he was functional. "I measured." Another lie. "It'll fit on the passenger seat."

"You need a new measurin' tape, lady. No way it'll fit."

"I'll open the sunroof," I said.

"These real?" He held the $100 bill up to the light and examined it. "Got anything smaller?"

"No. Sorry."

He turned to face the job. "My spade will ruin the grass."

"I brought, I mean—got, planks for you to drive on." The hardware store had even cut them to size so they'd fit across my back seat.

He raised his eyebrows and gazed at me suspiciously. "Your, uh, uncle's tree's gonna die." So much for plausibility.

I hoped he was running out of arguments, as I was running out of rebuttals. "This is the second-best time of year for transplanting."

"Is the sprinkler system off?" He pointed to one sprinkler head with his booted toe. "Never mind. We'll lay out the planks to avoid them." He paused again. "Sign this waiver." He'd already partially completed the form using my fake name and neatly fastened it to a clipboard. He handed me the ensemble, and the dangling pen, strung with chartreuse yarn and duct tape, whacked my hand during the transfer. I skimmed the contents of the waiver before duplicating my alias in cursive writing at the signature line and handed him back the signed form.

He scanned the document before dropping it through the open window on the passenger side of his truck. "Where're those planks?"

"Just over in my car."

He groaned and shook his head. "That vehicle ain't a workhorse."

Mind your beeswax, I thought—but thankfully kept to myself.

We off-loaded the planks. I had bought the widest ones I could find, at ten inches each; I hoped they'd accommodate his tires, but just in case, I had enough to span the distance between the driveway and the tree twice. The piled boards had blocked my rearview during my drive, and once, when I'd slammed on the brakes, the stack toppled and smacked into the back of my seat. Not the safest setup.

Despite my mishaps, I remained proud of this solution.

We laid out the planks, the first layer end to end and the second layer parallel to the first. Abe inspected our progress and nodded his head once. He stepped onto the trailer, lowered a ramp, climbed onto the tractor, and started the engine. If the arrival of Abe and his truck had gone unnoticed, the tractor's rumbling would alert all the neighbours.

Abe engaged the tractor, grinding the gears, and drove it carefully off the trailer. He opened the pointed shovel, which now resembled a monstrous Venus flytrap enticing its prey. He carefully drove down the planks toward Hug's tree, where he lowered the boom with its pointy end down and slowly released the lookalike tree in a splatter of dirt. Damn. Maybe they'd blame the mess on gophers.

Next up, getting Hug's tree. The open prongs of the shovel swooped down onto the tree in slow motion. Mechanical gears ground noisily, obscuring the sound of my breath. The maw stopped short of the ground and hesitated. Abe stared at me, seeking a final confirmation. I gave him an A-okay thumbs-up and he drove the points into the earth. The sound of machine wrestling prairie clay thundered. Abe manhandled the levers, jostling the shovel back and forth, up and down. I heard a loud crack and feared Hug's tree had snapped. But the shovel slowly emerged from the ground with the tree embraced in its steel cone.

Planting the replacement was easier. I'd brought some premium topsoil and compost with me. I dumped the contents of the plastic bags into the bottom of the hole and spread it around. I wanted the replacement tree to thrive but remain dormant for the harsh winter freezing. Trees were like bears; they needed to hibernate. But unlike bears, nourishment poked a tree rather than making it drowsy. Not enough nourishment in the soil could kill it too. Right now, I needed just the right balance, but I vowed to sneak it proper fertilizer in the spring.

If I wasn't in jail.

I stood in the driveway, inspecting our handiwork. We'd accomplished a lot and left little evidence anything was amiss. Then, behind me, I heard clapping. I pivoted toward the sound and spotted several families watching our spectacle from their driveways.

One of their neighbours waved her arm overhead, and the sun glinted off the phone in her hand. "Hello, Heddie."

I waved back and even smiled hello before remembering I worked under an alias. I paused just for an instant and watched Abe's reaction. "Heddie's my twin." He shook his head. "I'll be back in a sec."

I walked to meet her halfway, out of Abe's earshot. "Howdy, Mary. What's up?"

"Stanley's on the line." She waved her phone as proof. Her finger covered the microphone.

Uh-oh. "Yes?"

"He wants to know what you're doing."

"How does he know I'm doing anything?" How had he found me out? So fast?

"He spotted your car around the corner and got suspicious. He looked at his security cameras when he got to the airport."

In my head, I bonked my forehead. Best laid plans, et

cetera.

"Are they coming home?"

"They asked me to see what's up. I guess they'll decide based on what I tell them."

I fished for more details. "Can't they see what I'm doing?"

"The camera angle isn't right, so no. Not really."

We stared at each other and I struggled to come up with a credible explanation.

She saved me the trouble. "I'm glad you fixed that planting," she said. "I told Stanley—Becky too—human ashes are bad for trees. They never listen. We've got too much salt in us and trees don't like salt. I saw you amend the soil."

She'd just handed me a get-out-of-jail-free card. "Please explain that to Stanley." I fidgeted with the cord cinching the hood on my hoodie. "It was supposed to be a surprise."

She moved the phone to her ear. "He can't complain about that. You're saving him the time and trouble. But you won't be able to save the other one." She pointed to Hug's tree, with its roots—and his ashes—now carefully enveloped in a plastic tarp.

"I'm going to try." But first, I planned to comb through the soil to separate Hug's cremains.

I wasn't paying him by the hour, but Abe still helped me stomp down the dirt around the replacement tree. He kicked loose clumps off the driveway while I raked the grass upright. Together, we removed the planks, placing each one carefully into my backseat. Now that I had no need for the lumber, maybe I'd donate it.

"Thanks, Abe. I appreciate it." I handed him the rest of his cash. The sadness that threatened to overwhelm me as he drove off surprised me.

Mary strode over to me, her phone nowhere in sight. "They're not coming back, but Stanley didn't sound impressed. He said he'd call you next week."

I thanked Mary and drove off with my loot. The wind

picked up, and the tree swayed in the open sunroof, so I stopped the car and secured it with the passenger seatbelt. I'd accomplished the hardest part. Now, on to part two of my plan.

I drove to Charlie's memorial forest. I dragged Hug's tree behind a tool shed in a quiet corner of the parking lot, gave it a small bit of bottled water, and left it there until I could sort what to do next.

CHAPTER 37
Claim Denied

"My name is Sally Rice, and I supervise the claims department at the North Star Insurance Company." The lenses of the woman's black-rimmed glasses reflected the lights of the courtroom and obscured her eyes. That's probably why I considered her shifty.

"Can you describe your role on a disability insurance claim submitted by Mr. Maxwell Gerald Taylor?" Twee-dee asked.

"I was the adjuster assigned to that claim. He was a client who bought two insurance policies with us. A disability policy and life insurance."

"And did Mr. Taylor make any claims under these policies?"

Her hands flapped like dying birds and she restrained them in a net of fingers she placed in front of her. "A disability claim."

"When was this?"

"He applied last year, January fifteenth. Our conversation about his denied claim occurred on February seventeenth." She punctuated every answer with a head nod.

Twee-dee paced like a jewellery box doll, pivoting back and forth in front of the narrow podium. "So, eleven months before he died?"

The witness blinked rapidly. "That's right."

Frank raised his eyebrows at the witness's answer and

jotted down a note. He tapped at the page with his pen, and his tablemate leaned over and read it. No-Name's leg jiggled under the table, and she barely contained a satisfied smirk.

"What happened to that claim?"

"It was denied."

"Why was that?"

"Because Mr. Taylor stopped paying his premiums."

The Crown turned to face the judge. "Your Honour, the North Star Insurance Company records all its calls. I have a recording with Mr. Taylor, Ms. Hopewell, and Ms. Rice that I would like to enter into the record and play for the jury."

"Madame clerk," the judge said, "what number are we at?"

"Eight."

"Please enter the telephone recording as Exhibit Eight."

I plugged my ears, anticipating a deafening squeal. Murphy's Law, the recording played with no additional sound effects.

"Good morning. Sally Rice speaking. Claims department." I glanced at the witness who stood statue-still. "This phone call is being recorded for quality assurance purposes." Ha. More like evidence.

"Hello. May I have your name again, please?" Molly spoke, her voice husky and soothing. I'd gotten used to everyone else doing her speaking for her.

"Sally Rice. R-I-C-E. Like the food."

"Hi, Sally. My name is Molly Hopewell. I am calling about policy number 432619D." Molly's tone seemed polite, almost chummy.

"Thank you, Ms. Hopewell. May I ask you a few security questions to confirm your identity?"

"Please call me Molly. And, yes."

"Alright, Molly. Thank you. What was the name of your first pet?"

"Spike."

"I'm sorry," the woman said. "Is there another name?"

"Spike was the name of my first pet. A hedgehog."

"Is there another name that begins with…say…B?"

My perspective of the witness was morphing. She sounded helpful. Messing up my own security questions had become my daily condition. They asked, "who was the first," "what is your favourite," "where is the best." I had lots of firsts, favourites, and bests, and rarely remembered which one I preferred on any day.

"My husband's first pet's name was Buster?"

"That's the correct answer. If this is your husband's policy, I will need to speak with him."

"He's right here. I'll switch to speakerphone." The sound quality disintegrated.

"Hello, Sally. Max Taylor here." His voice was clear, friendly, but with a don't-mess-with-me edge. "My wife and I are calling about my disability insurance claim. The doctors diagnosed me with cancer and now I can't work. I put in the claim about a month ago, but we received a letter today denying it."

"I'm sorry to hear about your health problems and wish you a speedy recovery."

I wondered if all customer service people memorized bland scripts of pat responses to life's worst difficulties.

Clackety-clack: quick keyboarding sounded in the background. "I just need to locate your file. There is a reference number in the bottom left corner of the letter. Can you read it to me, please?"

"I've got the letter here. Is it 0215438A?" Molly said.

"Yes. That's it." *Clackety-clack*. "Looks like your policy was discontinued. January fourteenth. Your invoice for the annual premium was not paid."

"What do you mean?" Max's composure cracked. "I sent two cheques on the same day. One for this policy and one for the life insurance."

"What's the life insurance policy number?"

"Same as the disability insurance, but with an L at the

end." Molly's voice sounded colder.

Clackety-clack. "Here's the explanation. I have both files open. We received two cheques. One payment cleared, and so your life insurance remains up to date. The bank returned the other premium payment due to insufficient funds."

"That's not possible," Molly said. "I transferred money to cover both cheques."

"I'm sorry, Ms. Hopewell." They were no longer on a first name basis. "I can only tell you what our records show."

"Can we renew the insurance now?" Max asked, hopeful.

"Yes, I would be happy to help you apply for disability insurance."

"Apply? What do you mean?" His voice quavered.

"We must start a brand-new policy."

"That was a rigamarole the first time. Max was mostly self-employed. Until he got sick." I imagined Molly pacing the room with tight fists at her sides.

"Yes, I understand. We will base the value of his insurance on his income. If he was self-employed, tax returns serve as proof. Three years should be sufficient."

"He doesn't have income at the moment," Molly yelled.

"We cannot insure a zero income, ma'am. Also, please be aware, we don't insure pre-existing conditions."

"What do—?" A loud rattling rendered the rest of Molly's response incoherent.

"Can we reinstate the former policy? I've been a client for more than a decade." Max sounded calmer than his wife, more self-controlled.

"I'm sorry, Mr. Taylor. The window for reinstatement has lapsed."

"How long is that window?"

"Fourteen days."

"I just missed it."

"Your premium was due December thirty-first, sir. It's now mid-February. Your payment is over six weeks late."

"If we called a month ago, when I first applied, the payment might still be in the grace period. Oh, never mind. Can you bend the rules? I've paid my premiums faithfully for over ten years. Surely someone on your end could have figured out this was—like a clerical error."

"I'm sorry, sir. There's nothing I can do. I don't make the rules." Uh-oh, Ms. Rice was going off script.

"Can you please confirm that I paid the life insurance policy premium? And just so you know, I'm recording this call too." Molly sounded snippy.

"The life insurance policy—432619L—is fully paid for the year."

"And can you please give us the contact information for your supervisor? We will pursue the disability—"

Click. The clerk stopped the playback, cutting Molly off mid-sentence.

"I have nothing further for this witness," the Crown said.

No-Name bounced up from the Defence table. "Your Honour, can we please hear the rest of that recording? My honourable colleague stopped it at the best part."

Another loud click and the playback resumed.

"—issue further. We will lodge a formal complaint. *W5* might be interested in this story. They can sort this out."

"I am the supervisor for this department," Sally Rice said. "I can give you the contact information for senior management. I'm really sorry—based on the information you've given me today, I have sincere doubts anyone will reinstate your previous policy."

The pause after her pronouncement was long enough, I thought we'd suffered another equipment malfunction.

Max took over the conversation. "My diagnosis is terminal. So let's focus on the life insurance. The news about the disability claim leaves us with a major problem and I have no intention of making my wife pay for my gaffes for the rest of her life."

"I understand, Mr. Taylor."

"I'm considering my options. Can you tell me, please, what are the reasons you wouldn't pay out my life insurance?"

"There are only a couple of exclusions. Foul play, at the hands of your beneficiary. So, if your wife murdered you."

"Ha," Max laughed, but it sounded hollow. "Fat chance."

"If you committed suicide, your life insurance wouldn't pay out then either."

"What about medically-assisted suicide? Under the MAID legislation."

"If you qualify for a medically-assisted death and you follow all the steps in that process, your life insurance would still pay out."

Max was unflappable when discussing his own death. "I'd better get on that, then."

"Thank you, madame clerk. That's all we need from that recording." No-Name was the first, besides the judge, to show respect to the administrative staff. "Ms. Rice, when was the last time you interacted with Mr. Taylor?"

"May I check my records?"

No-Name looked up at the judge, who raised his usual questions before voicing his permission.

Sally rifled through her sheaf of pages until she found what she wanted. "That day. February seventeenth."

"Eleven days before Mr. Taylor had a stroke and developed aphasia?"

"Yes," she said. Assertively. Head held high. Confident in her answer.

"Did Mr. Taylor finish his application for a medically-assisted death?

"No, I understand his application was incomplete. Because of the stroke."

"He'd started the process, though? In the week and a half between talking with you and suffering a stroke?"

"Yes."

"How do you know that? How do you know about

Mr. Taylor's medical records after you declined his disability claim?"

She paled like a kid caught shoplifting from a candy store. "Um."

The Crown possessed the excellent sense to avoid her gaze by studying something suddenly fascinating about his notepad.

"Did you read or watch any news or reports about this story, Ms. Rice?"

"Yes." She pressed her hand over her heart.

But the Defence wasn't finished. "Is that the only reason?"

The witness remained on high alert. "No." She whispered her answer so softly that the court reporter looked to the judge for help.

"Please speak up, Ms. Rice," the judge said.

"No," she said more firmly, standing defiantly with perfect posture.

What was No-Name getting at? "How did you learn the details of Mr. Taylor's medical history?" Her voice boomed.

"I learned them when Ms. Hopewell made a claim against Mr. Taylor's life insurance."

"What is the value of that life insurance policy?"

"$500,000."

"That's a tidy sum." No-Name turned to the jury to weigh our reaction. Me? I was a tad jealous. "What is the status of that claim, Ms. Rice?"

"It's pending," she whispered again.

"Pending? What does that mean?"

"We don't yet have enough information to pay out the claim."

"But Mr. Taylor died ten months ago."

"There were limitations on his policy."

"Yes? We just heard you explain all that." No-Name circled her arm in the air.

The witness squared her shoulders defiantly. "One of

those limitations is murder."

"How long does it normally take you to process life insurance claims?"

"Somewhere between three to six months," the witness said.

"Ms. Hopewell was only arrested seven months after her husband died. What's your excuse for that delay?"

The witness scowled. "I stopped the process in July, when police informed me they were reopening the case. We only received the coroner's report, the first one, in March, and so we were well within our standard timeframe."

"Alright," No-Name said. "Moving on. We already know you respect a MAID death."

"That's right. The legislation is clear."

No-Name smiled. "And what if a patient travelled to another jurisdiction for a humane death? Some place like Belgium or Luxembourg?"

The witness frowned. "Such a case is not as clear-cut. There'd be an investigation into the circumstances of the claim. Plus, it's more expensive. There are the travel costs. The procedure itself. And the family would probably want to transport the body back to Canada for the funeral. It's not a risk I'd be taking with my family's future."

"Thank you for being so forthright," No-Name said. "Back to the disability policy. You denied Mr. Taylor's claim when his premium was six weeks late, even though he paid his previous bills fully and punctually."

"Yes."

"Let's just look at the timing of that denial, shall we? His premium was due when? December thirty-first, right?"

The witness turtled her head into her shoulders. "Yes."

"When was the claim submitted?"

"We started processing it January sixteenth."

"So, sixteen days later. Only two days after your grace period when he could have reinstated his original policy."

Ta-dum jumped up. "Is there a question in there

somewhere?"

"Ms. Askew, please ask your question," the judge said.

At last, I'd finally learned her name.

"Yes, Your Honour." The lawyer returned her gaze to the witness. "What was the date on his submission? Not when you started processing it. The day he hit 'submit.'"

Sally Rice didn't need her notes. "January thirteenth."

Ms. Askew's tone was placid. "So...one day before the end of the grace period. How was it submitted?"

"Online."

"Your company received it—what?—instantly?"

"Yes."

She showed remarkable restraint. "Was there a timestamp on Mr. Taylor's submission?"

"Yes."

Ms. Askew rolled her hand, encouraging the witness to elaborate. "What time was that?"

"5:20 in the morning." The witness whispered her answer, earning another over-the-glasses glare from the judge. "5:20 a.m." She projected her repetition.

"Help me with the math. That's during the grace period, and, what? Two full business days before it lapsed?"

"Yes."

"Were you sitting on his claim like a golden egg? Sit on it long enough, and your company profits?"

Twee-dee jumped up, and the judge patted at the air for him to sit down again. "I know, Mr. Parker. Ms. Askew, please."

"I'm sorry, sir." She didn't look contrite. "How long had Mr. Taylor been making payments on this policy?"

"Just over twelve years."

"Whoa. Mr. Taylor paid you for twelve years, he was late with his premium, and you denied a claim he made within your grace period?" Her tone oozed condescension. I liked No-Name, Ms. Askew. She didn't wait for the witness to answer. "Moving on. Did you know Ms. Hopewell declared bankruptcy in March?"

"I heard."

"Are you proud of yourself?"

Twee-dee jumped up again.

Ms. Askew smirked. "Enough of that topic. Next up, Mr. Taylor also had a life insurance policy. Fully paid up."

"Correct. His life insurance account was up to date."

"But his wife's claim under this policy is pending?"

"Yes."

"Why exactly?"

"Because the police charged her with his murder."

"Oh, boy. Your company has a lot to gain if Molly gets convicted. You'll also lose a lot when Molly is declared innocent, when she's free to leave and pick up the pieces of her shattered life. You knew Max was palliative? Stage-four metastatic breast cancer? Right?"

The Crown stood, nearly knocking over his chair. "Your Honour, please."

"That's all I have for this witness, anyway." Ms. Askew rolled her eyes and huffed in disgust, dismissing her literally and figuratively.

CHAPTER 38

Leah: Dragonfly Centre

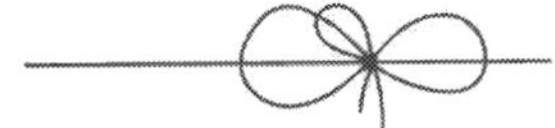

Heddie stood with Fella in the open doorway to Leah's bedroom. "Whatcha doin'?"

Leah sat at her vanity and watched her friend in the trifold mirror before she motioned for her to take a seat on the bed. She frowned when Fella jumped up next to Heddie and made himself comfortable.

Heddie addressed her concern head-on. "Why do people need help committing suicide?" She paused. "If they're intent on it, I mean. Why can't people commit suicide on their own?"

Leah twisted around in her seat. "Oh boy. Committing suicide is not as easy as it sounds. Mom couldn't accomplish it, for example."

Leah considered her mother's final weeks, alert, yet propped on an inclined bed, unable to control any part of her body except her eyes. Tubes fed her, intravenous drips hydrated and medicated her.

"But Charlie didn't apply under MAID."

"Her illness was too sudden, too debilitating. It's only a narrow window where MAID is an option." Leah had seen too many people miss their opportunity, wait too long before asking their hesitant questions, before considering their options. These days, she always broached the subject early with her clients and their families, when patients remained well enough to voice their decisions. Just in case. "What's this really about, sweetie?"

Fella shifted his head to Heddie's lap, and she absent-mindedly petted him, leaving puffs of fur on Leah's quilt. "I'm just trying to make sense of it all."

Leah stood and moved toward her closet. She chose a white padded hanger, slipped her jacket onto it, and hooked it on the closet door. "Lots of people mess it up, making their lives more difficult, unbearable even. The outcome is unpredictable. What if they kill someone else in the process? What if they don't kill themselves and wind up in a coma instead, leaving their family to foot the bill?" She softened her tone. "Are you suicidal?"

Heddie stopped her study of Leah's bed linens, and glanced at Leah, eyes rounded in shock. "No," she scoffed. "As if."

Leah nodded, convinced. "Grab my purse?"

Heddie found Leah's bag, mauve stitching coordinating with her blouse, on the hope chest—"hopeless chest" they'd called it as teenagers—at the foot of Leah's bed.

Leah levered the clasp open and pulled out a folded page. "I think I've found a space for my new grief group. Here, look."

Heddie unfolded the paper and studied the advertisement for a spacious downtown office in a retrofitted high school.

"It's not glamorous. But it'll do," Leah said, eyes bright. "I'm calling it the Dragonfly Centre. I'll help people struggling with complicated grief. Help others answer questions like the ones you're raising."

Heddie straightened to her full height. "Too bad you can't interrogate the dead."

"Interrogate?" Leah asked. "What am I missing?"

"Hug made me promise stuff. But he didn't keep his own promises."

"I don't understand."

"I found evidence he was having an affair, okay?" Her

words escaped in a rush. "Some woman named Wendy. Is that why Stanley's the executor? Even on his tissue box will, Hug chose Stanley. Did Hug hope I'd never find out?

"You must have it wrong," Leah said. "Hugh loved you. He was all in."

"He kept lots of secrets." Heddie shifted her weight and turned away.

Leah sat next to Fella on the bed and placed her hand on top of Heddie's. "He wasn't trying to keep secrets. He was trying to protect you."

Heddie pulled her hand away. "From what?" She worked at untangling burrs from Fella's coat, carefully ripping apart the seed pods before she teased them from his fur and pocketed the evidence. "You're as bad as him."

"We both just did our best, Sweetie. You were—" Leah shook her head as though chastising herself, "are just so vulnerable. Truth is, I still don't know how to help you. Everything I try doesn't work out."

"Does that mean you'll stop inviting Stanley over?" Heddie smirked.

Leah smiled, a quiet acknowledgement that Heddie had been right about that one.

"Why 'dragonfly'?"

Leah was relieved to discuss something more neutral, but knew full well Heddie would pick up their conversation thread again later. "It's symbolic for change, self-realization. Most people won't get the symbolism, but I do and it's just my private reminder anyway."

"Like a vision statement?" Heddie asked with a pinch of attitude.

Leah detoured around her gibe. "Maybe. With some wordsmithing." Heddie handed back the sheet which Leah stowed again in her purse. "You made this possible."

Heddie met her friend's eyes, surprised, but with the beginning of a smile. "How so?"

"By taking care of the kids." Leah stood and finished

undressing. She swung her skirt around so the zipper faced the front. She unzipped it, slipped it off, and inspected it for dirt. She shook it once before she reached for the hanger and secured the skirt on its clips. Next came her blouse, which she loosely rolled and placed into one of her colour-coded hampers. Blue was for washing, green was for handwashing, red was for dry cleaning. The shirt went into the green hamper. She stood almost naked, mauve lace underwear chosen to match her blouse.

"I hate my utilitarian undies," Heddie pouted. "I need to go shopping."

"I'll take you," Leah said. "We can go on Black Friday and hit all the sales."

"You know, Hug wasn't suicidal either."

Leah smiled sadly. "Not in the normal sense, no. He was dying though."

Annoyance flashed across Heddie's face before she ducked her head and started to cry. "Why didn't you tell me?" she wailed.

Leah crossed the room in two steps. She sat on the bed and wrapped her arms around her friend. Fella licked Leah's hand, so she included him in the embrace. "Tell you what?"

"Don't play dumb." Heddie started to hiccup. "Everyone else knew he applied for a MAID death. Why would he do that? Why would he give up? I never gave up on him."

"Ah, Sweetie, you're such a hot mess. Hugh didn't want to leave you. Certainly not before he'd arranged his affairs. His disease caused him considerable pain, and yet, he wouldn't end it until he resolved the situation for you."

"Why didn't he talk to me about it?"

Leah frowned. "He said you shut him down. He tried waiting for a better time to discuss it, to get your okay."

Heddie rested her head on Leah's shoulder and returned the embrace. "Hug didn't need my permission."

Leah shifted to meet Heddie's eyes. "He didn't need it, but he loved you and wanted it."

"I loved him too." Heddie's face distorted as her self-control waned. "I couldn't let him go. He wanted me to decide for him. He wasn't like a sick dog. Why did he try to make me decide?"

CHAPTER 39

Guest Post

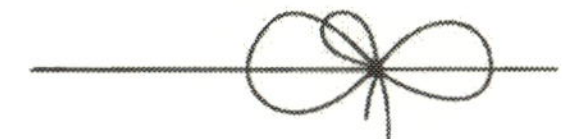

Dear Mr. Spinnewyn,

I was long-term friends with Max Taylor and Molly Hopewell, and I am writing about the travesty of justice occurring right now in our own city.

Max and Molly were high school sweethearts. Theirs was a fairy tale romance, with "happily" for twenty-nine years, but alas, not for "ever after." Their love for each other never flagged, never waned.

After Max discovered he had terminal cancer, Molly and Max found themselves in a no-win situation. When his euthanasia application was denied—frankly, on a technicality—one or the other of them had to take matters into their own hands to end his suffering. Max talked to me about ending his life, committing suicide, but he didn't want to jeopardize the life insurance Molly needed to get out from under the mountain of debt his disease, and yes, his poor decisions, had created. Similarly, Molly couldn't end Max's suffering without losing both her freedom (prison is no place to grow old) and her inheritance.

Molly shouldn't be on trial today. If she killed Max—and it's a big 'if'—she only stepped in where the MAID legislation failed them both. If she killed Max, it was an act of mercy, of true love.

Stand with Molly. She's already suffered enough.

(Name Withheld on Request.)

Comments

Olivia - *Why did you post this garbage?*

Axel - *I said from the beginning that I wanted fair representation.*

Superhero – *It's a slippery slope. Especially with matters of life and death, people must follow the rules precisely. There's no coming back from the grave if somebody changes their mind.*

Cowboy Gent - *I repeat: Molly did not have the right to make this decision.*

CHAPTER 40

Fifty-Fifty

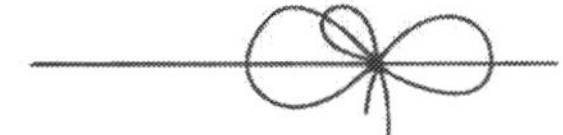

Ruth started the conversation. "Next up. What did you all think about that Sally Rice?"

"They really put them between a rock and a hard place. No wiggle room," I said.

"Last February was definitely a bad month for them," Norman added. "The worst."

"How so?" Ruth asked.

"I'll explain," Phil said. "Max started to apply for MAID, a legal—uh, insured—suicide, but couldn't finish the application. No easy or 'hastened' death there." He used air quotes. We were rubbing off on him. "She couldn't help him die, or she'd get charged with murder plus no insurance money. He couldn't kill himself, because she'd still get no insurance money."

"It was lose-lose," I added. "He had to die in pain, and she had to watch."

"Yes, but our..." Brad hesitated. "Our victim died a horrible death."

"You're too young to know this," Ruth said, "but almost all death is horrible. Especially cancer deaths. Max's was no different. There's often terror—whether it's just as the car crashes, or the excruciating pain of an aneurysm, or the suffering and creeping incapacity of cancer."

"I watched Hug slowly die over the space of months, and couldn't stop it, or even slow it down." I swallowed through my constricted throat.

"My husband died of Covid. His death was cruel. Blood clots killed him, but he was drowning in his own phlegm before that," Ruth admitted.

"My second husband," Pat said. "Diabetes-related kidney failure. Not a good way to go."

"My husband died of a heart attack. It was quick for him, difficult for me," Toni added.

Mandi's mouth fell open. "You're all widows?"

"Half of all spouses—at least when they don't get divorced—wind up wearing my—our—shoes." I leaned forward in my chair, a seated version of putting my hands authoritatively on my hips. "Actually, women have a better than fifty-fifty chance. We live longer. No one ever explains that part of the Cinderella story."

Phil pushed himself back in his seat and sat up straight. "I survived cancer on my own. My wife didn't stick around. My kids helped some, as much as they could, but I still had to give up my ranch."

"When Hug was in the hospital, I saw lots of people abandoned by their so-called loved ones."

"Yes, your... what do you call him? Ampersand? He was a lucky man," Phil said.

Wow. "Thank you. That means a lot." I studied the dents on the table as I edged toward actually liking him.

"But hear me out," he continued. "I considered a MAID death. My chance for a, you know, recovery wasn't great. I left things too long, and prostate cancer in young men spreads fast."

I bit my tongue, not literally, as I held back any retort about his self-description.

"My point is... After I got information about MAID, I felt more in charge. I got my affairs in order, made sure my kids knew I loved them. I wanted them to remember our good times."

Is that why Hug applied? Was Stanley right? Had my

selfishness caused Hug's horrible death? I had so much to answer for. I moved over next to Phil and gestured for him to stand. He wore a bemused expression as he complied. I pulled him to me in a big embrace. “Thank you, Phil. You helped me understand something important.”

Phil returned to his seat, still confused. “The person who talked me through it assured me my death would be dignified, pain-free.” He shifted until he got comfortable. “My point is, dying doesn’t have to hurt. Be so scary.”

“Glad you’re better.” Steve patted Phil’s back. “New topic. That grace period stuff was BS. I think they deliberately delayed processing his claim, sending them that letter.”

“They should be on trial. Not Molly,” Mandi added.

“The in-laws too,” Toni said. “They carried their tiff too far.”

“I dunno,” I said. “I’m beginning to understand that everyone was just doing the best they could.” Maybe I could afford the grace for Molly that I didn’t allow myself.

“Insurance isn’t a charity. They have a bottom line to consider. And shareholders.” I hadn’t pegged Ingrid as a cheerleader for corporations.

“Oh, come on. How can you defend them?” Toni said.

Ingrid clasped her hands on the table in front of her like one of her best pupils. “I’m not, but Molly Hopewell was disorganized. Cancelling the policy was the inevitable consequence of not paying their bills. Life 101.”

CHAPTER 41

Mercy is Formed

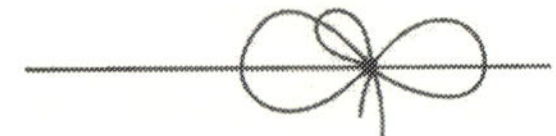

Crabby's Diner was more crowded than usual, with people queuing to gain entrance and then jostling for service. We waited our turn, stomping our feet and clapping our hands to keep warm.

"You're back," Crabby/Sondra said. I smiled, impressed, despite myself. This woman served hundreds of people each day but still recognized me, the newbie. "Grab your seat in the corner."

I swept the room with my arm to remind her of her other guests. "What about everyone else?"

"They're here for takeout."

I'd invited Phil to join us, so the six of us crammed onto the specified wraparound bench, leaving just enough room so our butts didn't touch. I handed out the menus.

Yesterday, as we all left for the day, Phil had geriatric-jogged after me. "Can I walk you out?"

Ever-circumspect, I said, "Sure."

"I need to apologize," he said, as he pulled open the exit door, blasting us both with wintery air. "I never gave you a fair shake."

I cinched my hood around my face. "Okay." I had to agree, even if I wasn't yet ready to admit our two-way street. "Why now?"

"Because you're brave," he said, not meeting my eyes. "And loyal."

I laughed. "You'll have to explain that one."

"You know I had cancer, prostate cancer. They think they got it all, but they ruined me, down there, curing it." He waved at his nether region. "That's partly why my wife left."

"Because you couldn't get an erection?" I shocked even myself with my candour.

His face flushed. "Let me say my piece. You talked about Can-cure... admitted you got it for Hugh, even after what that doctor said."

I stood still enough for fallen snowflakes to melt on my cheeks. "I wasn't brave, Phil. More desperate. I would've tried anything."

"See, that's my point. I heard about Can-cure too. Wanted to give it a go. My wife's response?" He fell silent and swirled circles in the snow with his scuffed boot. "That's when she left me. But I was lucky. Turns out I didn't need it."

"Sounds like your ex is a shallow, selfish person who doesn't deserve the likes of you," I said, meaning it. I started to bawl. "I made other mistakes. Bigger ones." When Phil didn't interject, I continued, "I got stuck. I couldn't let him go. He suffered because I never faced facts."

Phil ignored my confession. "Point is, you stuck it out, tried, and you weren't even married."

——— o o o ———

Crabby/Sondra dropped off our cutlery, mismatched utensils rolled neatly in white paper napkins, and took our orders.

"Oh look, there's Stanley." Ruth's face brightened, and she waved. "Yoo-hoo."

I looked over my shoulder, and sure enough, there he was. "Don't call him over." Her hurt expression encouraged me to add, "please" as an afterthought. "I don't want to see him today."

"But he's by himself."

Crabby/Sondra arrived with our meals and skidded

them across the table. "Bon appétit," she said before moving on to her next task.

After glancing around to confirm I had no eavesdroppers, I spilled my guts. I shared all the gory details, starting with me as a couch surfer and then on to Stanley's misuse of Hug's ashes. I even told them about Hug's tree, the roots still nestled in its green tarp, secreted behind a gardener's shed in Fish Creek Park. By the time I finished my story, their plates were half-empty and my soup was cold.

Toni spoke first. She scooched closer to me, put her arm around my shoulder, and squeezed me in a one-armed embrace. "Stanley's a scum-sucker." She gave his back a withering look.

"Why yes, yes he is," I said, relieved to have one more person on my side. I watched Stanley's face in the mirrored tiles on the opposite wall.

"He must think you deserve it," Phil said.

"Really, Phil? We were bonding." I shook my head. "I can't believe you. Do all you men take classes or something? Siding with each other? You don't even know him and you've acquitted him." I'm sure my face reddened to the same shade as the ketchup bottle on our table.

"I'm not saying he's right. But sounds like he's trying to hurt you. He's kicking, aiming for your Crown jewels," Phil said as he squirmed.

"Knock it off, you two," Ruth said in her best Nurse Ratched imitation.

Mandi changed the topic "What will you do with Hugh's ashes?"

"Make a necklace." Toni pulled a tiny, corked vial strung on a gold chain from beneath her blouse and dangled it in front of us. "Here, look. Meet my husband. George, meet the best of my fellow jurors."

I cringed, before nodding my greetings. "Nice to meetcha, George."

"Are those George's cremains?" Ruth wrinkled her nose.

Toni returned the vial and patted it into place. "I keep him next to my heart."

I nodded, appreciating the symbolism. "I want a ring," I admitted. "There's a place that compresses human ashes into diamonds. It's expensive, but I already put down a deposit. Next step? I send them his ashes." I'd used Leah's food scale last night and measured out 200 grams of baking soda, just to get a sense of how much I needed. It was a lot. I found out too late that ten grams of Hug's hair could've worked too. I'd brushed Fella, who basked in the grooming, and collected his abundant fur for that measurement and proved the hair-option was also unviable.

"How will you do that?" Pat asked, a chip prominent on her shoulder. "How will you sift his ashes from the dirt?"

"I've encountered a few obstacles." Truth is, I'd set myself an impossible task. "No DIY YouTubes for that job."

"I could help," Phil said, his eyes bright, hopeful. "We could go to the park tonight. After court."

"Why would you do that?" I asked.

"Like you said early on—you know, bomb threat day—you'd do it for me."

I wouldn't look a gift horse in the mouth. Another Huggism.

"You're both wasting your time," Pat said.

"I need to keep trying." I ate the last of my soup and scraped the bowl clean. I collected everyone's empty dishes, and placed them on the edge of the table, careful to keep my sleeves out of the way.

More of Stanley's colleagues joined him. "Now he's got a retinue. Time to go?"

"You have a right to be here too. Stand your ground, girl," Ruth said. Then she smiled. "What do you call a group of jury guards?"

"Is that a joke?" Phil asked.

Ruth indulged him. "No, just play along. I'm changing the subject."

I examined them through half-closed lids. "What animal do they look like?"

Ruth contorted her neck to various angles to get just the right perspective. "How about badgers? Nasty creatures."

"That'd be a cete."

"What does that even mean? We can do better." Ruth studied the group again. "How about sharks?"

"A shiver."

"That works. From now on, we'll call them all," she pointed at the guards shuffling through the takeout line, "a shiver of bailiffs."

"Do you know names for all animal groups?" Mandi seemed impressed.

"Test her," Ruth said. "She's amazing."

"How about parrots?" Mandi asked.

"That's a good one. Pandemonium."

"Ha. Fitting," Ruth said.

"Ravens? Is that a murder?" Mandi continued.

"No, it's a murder of crows and an unkindness of ravens."

"Those names are mean."

"We reserve the best names for ourselves. Like 'humane.' Think about the word's meaning and then think about all the despair and destruction wrought by humans."

"Maybe it's aspirational," Toni interjected. "But what did ravens or crows ever do wrong?"

"How do you know so many?" Mandi asked.

"I like animals, and this game amuses the children in my life."

"What's your favourite?"

"I prefer those that just fit. Like a soar of eagles."

Pat looked like she'd caught me wrong-footed. "I thought it was an aerie of eagles?"

I smiled. "Eagles have lots of group names. Aerie. Congress. I like a jubilee of eagles too."

"Everyone knows things like a pod of whales, a gaggle

of geese, a school of fish, a pride of lions," Mandi said. "What are gorillas?"

"A band."

"Giraffes?"

"A tower."

Pat finally joined the game. "Hyenas?"

"A cackle."

"Excellent," Pat acknowledged.

"I like that one too," I admitted. "I'm also amused by a bloat of hippopotami, a smack of jellyfish, a prickle of porcupines. Are you trying to stump me?"

Mandi hung her head and peered at me, her mischievous eyes partially concealed by her thick bangs.

"I accept your challenge. But I warn you, you're treading a well-worn path where all others failed."

"Okay. Loons?"

"An asylum of loons is funny. But a water dance of loons is poetic."

"Turtles?"

"Bale. Or nest."

"Tigers?"

"An ambush or a streak. Both apt."

"Skunks?"

"Ha. A stench." I glanced at the clock behind the counter. "Holy macaroni. Let's hustle. Can't be late. Very important date." I signalled Crabby for our bills.

"What's a group of rabbits?" Mandi asked, advancing my reference.

"A herd."

"Boring."

"I didn't say they were all perceptive."

We paid our bills in cash.

"I got one you won't know. What's a group of widows?"

"We don't get a collective noun. I still win." I smirked at her, defying her to deny my victory.

"Make something up," Mandi insisted. "One of my profs

says there's something like 5,000 new English words every year. One could be yours."

"Okay. I'll try," I said, even though I was the wrong person for this assignment. "How about something like... an ostracism, or an invisibility, or an impoverishment of widows."

"A solitary," Toni suggested.

"Too true, all of them. But sad. And they might give the bullies and trolls ideas. Try again," Pat said.

"Go for something more likeable," Phil added.

"Suggestions?" I asked.

"How about a hardiness?" Ruth said.

"A loyalty," Pat brainstormed.

"Yes, I like that. Or a resiliency." I chuckled without feeling.

"A mercy of widows," Phil said. "I like that one. It's not too fancy—as in, I can pronounce it. And it's something all the widows I know have in common."

Another compliment.

"Phil, you and me, we'll be honorary widows," Mandi said.

I was about to disabuse them both of that terrible idea, but Mandi slipped her arm through Phil's and his face looked so sunny, I couldn't interrupt. So I just nodded, and together, we walked out into the cold.

I guessed that's how we make friends.

CHAPTER 42

Treasure

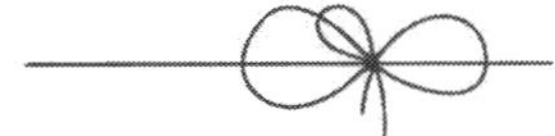

"I don't know all about Max's situation, but based on my experience, Peter Parker's off his rocker." Phil made small talk while he carefully sifted through the dirt, his headlamp shining brightly on our work.

The tarp that protected the roots of Hug's tree was already ripped and spilled its contents into the back of Phil's hard-used Toyota pickup. It had taken both of us, sweating and swearing, to drag the tree from behind the shed and into the truck bed. Mud and grit splattered the truck, itself a patchwork of rust and gouged panels. I couldn't believe the vehicle was actually road-worthy.

"I found more," Phil exclaimed. I'd decided against borrowing Leah's kitchen scale to measure my treasure. My friend was quite tolerant, but I expected that would be beyond even her limits. Instead, I bought a small one at a dollar store. Phil placed his discovery on the scale, which nudged up to 113 grams. So far, he'd proven more adept at our task, but we were almost out of dirt and still short of the requirement.

Our process had been Phil's idea, something he modified from a method for panning for gold. I'd bought two fine sieves at the same dollar store, and we sifted through the dirt about a cup at a time. For once, I was grateful for Ghoul's incompetence. Hug's funeral director had cut corners, and his sloppiness left small bone fragments in the sieves.

"Phil," I said. My mouth was dry and hot, like I chewed

the dirt we sifted. “After you applied for MAID, how did you resolve things?” I needed to know the answer.

“The hardest part was telling my kids.” I was temporarily blinded by his headlamp when he looked up at me. “My daughter was really pissed, but we talked a lot, talked it through. Eventually, she came to terms.”

“How did she accept it?”

“I told her how I felt. I told her I didn’t want to be a burden, didn’t want to suffer. Didn’t want to lose my marbles.” He tapped his head. “I also told her I loved her. Loved them both. I told them again and again, every time I saw them. I wanted it to sink in.” He chuckled. “They thought I was going funny in the head after all.”

“Hug expressed his love too. Toward the end,” I admitted. “He wasn’t super-demonstrative before though.”

Phil paused. The only sound came from the distant traffic whooshing past on nearby MacLeod Trail. When he finally spoke again, he enunciated his words carefully. “Have you thought about the timing of that?”

I squinted at him, daring him to explain.

“When did he start?”

I had to think about it. I clearly remembered his first utterance. He’d been sitting up in a hospital bed in a room where a framed poster of Peyto Lake, its turquoise waters shaped into a wolf’s head, hung on a cream-coloured wall. He was in and out of hospital so much in his last few months, I tracked our chronology based on my recollection of the decor of his rooms. “About four months before he died.”

“He’d already applied,” Phil asserted, and nodded emphatically. “He wanted you to know what you meant to him. My MAID administrator called it ‘closure’. Hugh tried to create closure for both of you.”

Chances are, we collected some of Hug’s remains. But even my inexperienced eye identified soil mixed in. And probably manure and potato compost. Besides, we were fifty-eight grams shy of the company’s minimum requirement. I really tried, but some problems are impossible to happily solve.

We planted Hug's tree again on the edge of Charlie's memorial forest. After Phil left, I crawled beneath the memorial sign, and wrote Hug's name on the underside in blue sharpie. It was not exactly a headstone, and the ink would fade, but I vowed to go back periodically and touch it up. Maybe, down the road, I'd doodle some fanciful decorations for him.

CHAPTER 43

Fifteen Minutes

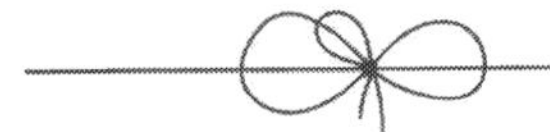

Clemence stood framed by the open door. "Henry-Etta Wright."

My mouth formed a round O of surprise. I felt guilty without knowing what I'd done wrong, but two things tipped me off to brewing troubles. First, Clemence never called us by our names. Only our numbers. Second, she singled me out when everyone knew jury duty was a team sport.

"Number Nine, come with me."

I obeyed her without question or commentary.

"Bring your notepads. All of them."

I pointed to the square foot of the table where I diligently stacked my notepad and exhibits. "It's not here." I raised my arms in exasperation. "It was here last night."

Her jaw muscles flexed. "You've only got the one? Follow me."

I trudged like I headed for the gallows. Numbers Six and Seven—Ingrid and Brad—were no-shows, so only nine people, excluding Clemence, witnessed my censure. Clemence led me into unfamiliar territory, the direction opposite our usual paths to the courtroom or the elevators.

"Where are we going?"

"The judge wants to see you."

Uh-oh. Did Stanley tattle on me about the tree? Probably not, I guessed. I ransacked through the clutter in my brain and tried to recall and catalogue my other misdemeanours.

There was the time I had accidentally read a few headlines about the trial. I'd hauled my phone out while waiting for Leah for something or other. Immediately, my feed was full of news about the case. I was all thumbs trying to clear it and only made it worse, with more headlines filling the screen—part tease and part torture. *Parents Fight for Justice. Mercy or Murder—Hopewell Trial Begins. Flawed Legislation on Trial.*

Then something more alarming distracted me. I squinted and held my screen inches from my face to examine a photo accompanying one article. When that didn't work, I used my fingers to expand its size. Yup, a photo of me, my butt stuck in the air like a bottom-feeding goose. I examined the more photogenic surroundings and twigged that some snap-happy onlooker had taken my picture when I saved the fake-patient, Axel, from his convincing mock seizure.

Leah caught me red-handed, nose in the news, disobeying a juror commandment. I shoved the phone toward her. "Fix it so nothing pops up." I added, "Please," too hastily, a sure sign of my guilt.

She snatched the phone and tried to open it, but was blocked by the screensaver, an image of healthy-Hug holding about a six-month-old Fella.

"Passcode?" she said.

"0-5-2-6."

"Really? Hugh's birthday?"

"Yup." I stood, hands on my hips.

She fiddled for a minute, flicking fingers over the screen like some hocus-pocus. "I turned off your notifications. Now, it's your fault whenever you see the news."

No, it couldn't be that. Leah'd never rat me out.

Maybe they'd found out about that time at the coffee shop. I didn't intend to eavesdrop, but I didn't walk away either. No rules against stopping on route to the courthouse for coffee. Plus, a caffeinated me was always an improved version.

The shop had been crowded when I ordered my straightforward coffee. Once in a blue moon, I splurged for a skim milk latte. But not that day. A two-dollar expense was almost in my budget, but not five bucks. The barista seemed relieved by my simple order and flashed me a shy smile when she handed me my drink. The cup burned my fingertips even through a cardboard sleeve, so I wrapped it in napkins before carrying it to a free table in the farthest corner of the room.

I walked past a bank of TVs, each turned to the local news with a rolling news ticker. *Protesters Rally on Euthanasia Trial. Max Taylor Poisoned, Died in Agony. Hopewell Murdered for Money*. Once seated, I turned my back to the screens and thumbed through my phone until I found my preferred dog training blog.

My seat afforded me a prime view of the café. I sat opposite a vestibule defined by glass doors on each end and leading to the outside world. Two doors seemed redundant, but I was wrong. Spaced several feet apart, they worked together to keep cold air out, with the outermost door closing shut before the inner door opened. The design worked well until selfish protesters propped open both doors as they swept into the restaurant on a blast of cold air.

The group travelled in a pack. They looked predatory, eyes darting about, their placards dangling from crooked elbows or hanging loosely from clasped hands.

"I'll be in the courtroom today," said an older woman wearing a brown button-up coat that resembled a refashioned potato sack. A plush-brimmed hat perched on her head. Her placard, clutched close to her chest, read, "Protect your grannies. Euthanasia is murder." The words were carefully but crudely drawn with red and black lettering on abused cardboard, with bent corners and a few grimy smears. "I'm going to wear this." She spoke too loudly, enjoying her limelight. I craned my neck to snoop but my angle was wrong and she restowed her prop quickly.

I didn't need to see his face to recognize Axel. "Where will you put it?" asked the fledgling journalist wearing his now-familiar peacock blue down jacket.

"Over my mouth, silly." She emitted a girlish titter.

Axel seemed impressed with the old fart. "I can't wait to see that."

I leaned in to listen. From the omniscient perspective of hindsight—twenty-twenty and all that—I shoulda packed my things and headed to the jury room. A heads-up to Clemence might've been smart too.

The old gal placed her free hand lightly on Axel's arm. "I need more allies. You could wear one too," she simpered at him.

Axel reached into his pocket and pulled out a card. "The stunt will make a fantastic visual. Check out my site. This story will be a big deal. Maybe hit mainstream."

The senior batted her lashes. "I'm ready for my closeup, Mr. DeMille."

Barf.

"We've got decent cameras in there. Sit behind the Crown, close to Max's parents, and you'll get in the shot."

I'd heard enough and stood to go. I located the lids and fastened one securely atop my steaming coffee. I used the cup to keep my fingers toasty as I left the shop and walked the last block to the courthouse.

———— o o o ————

Clemence and I arrived at a closed door, an arrival that mercifully truncated my fretting. A brass engraved sign read *Justice Solomon Forrest*. Could knocks sound different depending on the knocker's intent? Here, Clemence's knock sounded deferential. On our jury room door, it sounded commanding. When this door opened, Frank stood there, even more handsome closeup. Flecks of caramel highlighted his brown irises. Blonds were so lucky, as their hair colour hid all the grey. I avoided eye contact with him and wished I'd dressed up more today.

"Thanks, Clemence. Ms. Wright. Please come in." His voice was quieter when he wasn't playing to an audience of hundreds. He held his arm open, a welcoming gesture under different circumstances.

The entire waddle sat in the judge's chambers. The judge sat behind his luxurious desk. Dust-free rectangles suggested someone had recently cleared the surface. All four lawyers—the Tweedles, Frank, and Ms. Askew—sat paired off in matching armchairs. A five-foot gap separated the two sets of chairs like a no-man's-land. Stationed along the far wall, the clerk and the court reporter sat at temporary desks, the kind with fold-up legs. Molly was behind her Defence team, plopped like the bad kid into the corner. Her chair back rested against an enormous bookcase overstuffed with mostly leather-bound volumes. Some perched precariously, like they'd topple with the slightest nudge.

Clemence stood behind me. I inched further into the room to make space for her, but she stayed put.

"Thank you for joining us." The judge wasn't wearing his glasses, and I noted he had two different coloured eyes, one brown and one grey.

"Heterochromia iridium."

An angry look crossed his face before he composed himself again. "That's right."

"Sorry. That's my inside voice." I needed to get out more.

I examined the art behind his desk, less intimidating than gazing into the judge's eyes. I decided the gold-framed piece was from one of the lesser-known Group of Seven artists. Purples, greens, blues, and greys layered the artist's view of the land's history. Tree stood atop the cliffs, tall and gnarly, swept almost bare by the wind. I felt like those trees, standing unprotected and unappreciated before succumbing to the persistent blasts.

"Stanley, can you please find Ms. Wright a chair?"

I twirled in the direction the judge addressed and saw frog-face, smug in my surprise.

Confusion with a hint of anger infused my words. “What the heck is he doing here?” Maybe now wasn’t the best time to assert myself.

The judge looked discomposed and working up to angry. “Mr. Fields works here and has a job to do. Do you two know each other?”

Stanley cut my answer off. “We’ve known each other a couple years.” Nearly seven years, I corrected mentally. “She was my brother’s caregiver.”

I bristled at his description. Once again, Stanley had squashed my relationship with Hug into something unrecognizable from the original.

But I didn't correct them after the judge said, “That’s fine.” He scowled at Stanley. “No more surprises though.”

My brother-in-law wheeled my chair into the no-man’s-land between the duelling lawyers so I sat facing the judge. I leaned backwards to position the legal teams just inside my peripheral vision.

Justice Forrest got right to the point. “How do you know Axel Spinnewyn?”

I let out a sigh—of relief rather than exasperation. So, not the tree then. “I don’t actually know him,” I said. “We only met a couple times.”

“Don’t split hairs with me. I’ve already excused two jurors today. Would you like to join them?”

“What? You fired Six and Seven? Why?” No wonder they were late. “What did they do?” Must’ve been serious. Brad had seemed dotty over his kids and a little too needy, but everything suggested Ingrid was right on the ball. Why did she risk her retirement full of grandkids, gardening, and no golf?

The judge sounded truly miffed. “I will ask the questions here, Ms. Wright. I repeat, how do you know Axel Spinnewyn? Blogger, activist. Private investigator. Fancies himself an actor.”

"I only met him the other day. I tried to help him, but he gave me a hard time because I interrupted his 'performance.'" I used air quotes. "I thought he was seizing or something."

The judge seemed to accept my explanation. "Had you met this man before the trial?"

"We first met at the selection."

"Have you talked with him at all, beyond what you've already explained?"

"Not exactly talked. I've seen him around. He's like a foul smell. I think I saw him in the crowd—among the protesters—a couple times. He wears a blue coat. It's distinctive, recognizable, my favourite shade." I missed a special someone knowing my favourites.

"Anything else?"

"Well, I'm pretty sure I overheard him and others planning the gag day."

Their stunt was, as predicted, impressive, and most of the audience took part. A small group of teenagers, probably high school students on a field trip, hadn't joined in. They too sat, mouths agape at the spectacle and their good fortune at scheduling a memorable outing. I'd identified Molly's supporters that day, too, as they'd also snubbed the action. People had fashioned gags out of round fruits like nectarines and plums, stuffed into mouths and held in place with strips of black fabric. Others unzipped their coats to reveal hospital gowns and nooses dangling around their necks. Almost everyone had affixed black electrical tape in Xs over their eyes.

The judge stood and paced. "You should have led with that. Elaborate."

I told him about my stop at the coffee shop.

"You didn't see what the woman held up?"

"No, sir."

"Why didn't you report the incident to Clemence?"

"I just tried to get myself out of that pickle." I paused before adding, "I also haven't gone back. I don't want to be there if that's where protesters hang out."

He opened the top drawer of his desk and handed me a paper he pulled from it. "Do you recognize this handiwork?"

"It's mine. How did you get it?"

"Explain."

"I doodle my impressions of the evidence. But this looks like a photo. Someone must've stolen my notepad. I couldn't find it this morning."

"We'll discuss its whereabouts later. Tell me about this, uh, doodle."

"It's from Max's dad's testimony. Zane."

"I gathered that by the title." He pointed to the spot where I'd written the witness's name in box lettering. "Why are his pockets out?"

"Because he pretended to be poor. I didn't believe him. See? I added dollar signs. His outfit—you know, his bolo tie and cowboy hat—looked expensive." Out of the corner of my eye, I thought I caught the Defence team exchanging looks.

"Please describe the face you've given him."

"It's supposed to be a crocodile." I thought I'd created a decent likeness. "He cried crocodile tears."

"I don't understand."

"He cried too much, too often. He overdid his anguish. I get it. Really, I do. I understand how hard it is to lose someone you love." I worked at ignoring Stanley's hard stare. "Especially to bleeping cancer. But he worked too hard to get our sympathy."

The judge rolled his hand.

"The loan, for one." I pointed to where I'd drawn a fanciful bow around a stack of dollar bills. "Who makes their dying son pay interest on a loan? Kinda like the dad valued his money more than his kid."

Everyone was silent for a minute, maybe absorbing my conclusion. "Sick and dying is expensive." I should know. From the rented hospital beds to the healthier from-scratch meals to the vitamins and alternative treatments. Commodes. Walkers. Doughnut cushions. Compression hose. Home nursing care.

Meds. Even hospital parking. "Max and Molly weren't working. No money coming in but bills still needed to be paid. That phone call for his disability insurance was painful to hear." If I'd been in their shoes, I too would've been sad and desperate. "What father—or even father-in-law, almost like a father once removed—makes money on loved ones in that situation?"

"Emily? Notebook." The judge held out his open hand, and she deposited a notepad into it.

"Is that mine?"

"You tell me." He held up the well-used legal pad, displaying first its front and then its back. I saw the legible nine marked on the cardboard backing.

"That's my number on the back." I wasn't trying to evade his question. I just needed to inspect the item before claiming it definitively.

Someone had affixed sticky plastic flags on a few pages. He pulled at the first tab and wrapped the forward pages around the top. "Do you recognize this drawing?"

He held it up for everyone to see, and I hung my head, suddenly ashamed.

"This drawing concerns me the most. I assume it portrays Mr. Parker and Mr. Standish."

I nodded.

"Please speak up. The court reporter is recording your answers."

I glanced at her and, sure enough, she waited for my audible response.

"Yes."

"Would you care to explain yourself?"

"It's sort of a hybrid caricature. A mashup."

"Let's start with the headgear. What are these supposed to be?"

"Beanies with propellers on top." The acoustics in the room were excellent despite my attempt to whisper. Molly's corner looked inviting.

"As in?"

"Tweedledee and Tweedledum."

"Not very flattering." He paused before continuing. "Have you dressed them like penguins? Like the villain in Batman comics?"

I studied the drawing again and tried to untangle his interpretation. "At one point, I drew you all as penguins. It's the robes. But, here, they're supposed to resemble the bankers statue on Stephen Avenue." The *Conversation* portrayed two portly businessmen frozen in the act of greeting each other. My drawing had included robes instead of trench coats, and they both lacked fedoras to top their comma physiques.

"That's a little more generous. You owe these gentlemen an apology, though."

"Yes, sir. You're right." I twisted in my chair to face the Crown lawyers, and I looked each in the eye. "I'm really sorry." My drawings were supposed to be private. Lesson learned? "I didn't mean to cause any offence."

Twee-dee spoke for them both. "Thank you."

"That topic is resolved," the judge said, clearly pleased to have righted at least one wrong. "Emily, do you have that other printout?"

His clerk, who was like a coiffed poodle amid a pack of mongrels, handed the judge another piece of paper.

The judge leaned back in his chair. "I'm going to show you something and ask you one question. Weigh your answer carefully."

I nodded and swallowed, preparing myself for whatever came next.

"Do you recognize this article?"

I glanced at the paper with its headline, "Biased Jury: Will Max See Justice?" A picture of my beanie-bankers drawing was in the middle of the page. The byline read "Axel Spinnewyn."

"I didn't give that to him, I swear. I didn't give it—anything—to anyone."

The judge continued, "This drawing appeared in a blog.

It's gone viral, as they say. Some others too. Your drawings have caused quite a stir, Ms. Wright. He's even attributed them to you."

"But how? How did he get my name? How did he get my drawings?"

"That's what I'd like to know."

I shrugged my shoulders. "I have absolutely no idea."

"Clemence, has anything been missing from Ms. Wright's nightly inventory?"

Inventory? Huh?

She handed a clipboard directly to the judge with no relay-intermediary. "No, sir. Here's the list. All checks, every day. Both her notepad and exhibits."

"You count our evidence?" My belongings had been tidier each morning. "I thought it was the cleaners."

She gave me an injured look. "Active jury rooms are out of bounds, even to cleaners."

"Learn something new," I replied. I studied the judge's printouts of my drawings again, the ones from the blog. "Something's off with them." I picked up my notepad from his desk and flipped to the drawing of Zane Taylor's testimony. "See here. That's supposed to be Mrs. Taylor in the audience. In my drawing, she's giving Molly the middle finger. Someone's erased it in the blog version."

"I don't understand."

I displayed them side by side for the judge to see. "I labelled the drawing 'no goodbyes.'"

The judge shook his head. "You'll definitely have to explain yourself."

"The 911 call. She got most upset when she thought Molly killed Max without letting them say goodbye. I got the sense she believed Molly timed Max's death on purpose. To hurt her."

"I see." He paused again. "Emily, can you show me those recording devices again?"

The clerk rummaged through her box before handing

the judge a plastic baggy containing a half-dozen pens and a pocket protector.

"I recognize that stash," I said, pointing to the pocket protector. "Those are Brad's. Why do you have them?" Then I finally clued in. "They're recorders? Cameras? Like spy equipment?" No wonder Brad had hoarded his pens for himself.

The judge fingered the pens through the baggy, dividing them up and inspecting each one. "The angle of the drawing might be right. Mr. Stroud and Ms. Wright sat side by side. Still, it's hard to tell." He nodded again, and I got the sense I'd passed his test. "There will be police investigations, and I hope to gain a better understanding of what happened." He glanced at the lawyers. "Everyone agree? Ms. Wright's notes are, uh, unorthodox. But not negligent."

———— ◦ ◦ ◦ ————

Clemence escorted me back to the jury room. As soon as she shut the door, everyone quizzed me on what had happened. But I'd sworn to keep my mouth shut, so I guarded my secrets like *Mona Lisa*, complete with an inscrutable smile revealing nothing.

"I wasn't sure you were coming back. What happened to Brad and Ingrid? While you were gone, guards I never saw before packed up their exhibits and belongings and carted everything away. They okay?" Ruth asked.

"I don't know. I'm sorry." That was true. I didn't know the details of what happened to Six and Seven, although I knew I didn't want to follow in their footsteps.

Jim didn't buy it. "You were gone for over an hour. You came back, but two other teammates don't return with you? What did you do, Heddie?"

"I did nothing. Consider me an aggrieved party here too."

"Well, just tell us what happened," Jim said. He winked at me, as though that would entice me to confess.

"I'm not allowed. I can tell you nothing. Nada. Zip. Zilch." I pressed my fingers together and then flashed them apart mimicking a vanishing puff of smoke.

It was probably my gesture that pushed him over the top. "Clemence can tell us." Without so much as a howdy-do, Jim bounced up and knocked on the door. Under different circumstances, I might've been proud—he'd just pulled a Heddie.

Clemence opened the door, and Jim spoke before she could say anything. "What happened to Brad and Ingrid?"

"I cannot say."

"Cannot or will not?"

"Will not."

He shook his head, frustrated to be at another impasse. "I didn't know a jury could run with less than twelve jurors."

"Fewer. And yes. Under some circumstances."

"Can't you call in the alternate?" Jim rubbed his bristly scalp.

"The jury can run with fewer than twelve jurors. Besides, Number Fourteen already missed too much." Clemence sounded like a broken record.

Stanley poked his head through the open door into the room. "That's above your pay grade." How often did he hover out in that hallway? How soundproof were these walls?

I rolled back in my chair to get a broader perspective. "That's a terrible expression, Stanley. Insulting." Right then, I was angry at Stanley for being so mean to me. I was angry at Axel for stealing my stuff and publishing it, getting me into trouble. I was angry at the secrets all the court people kept, giving me snippets of information but never quite enough to understand. And I remained truly pissed at Hug for dying and leaving me alone in this mess. I might've been angry at the world for a few things too. But Stanley was in front of me now, and so he bore the brunt for everyone else.

Stanley faltered. I liked this facial expression best. Flummoxed Stanley. Chagrined Stanley. I'd climbed onto my high horse and wouldn't dare dismount. I turned toward Clemence again. "What's the lowest number of jurors allowed?"

Clemence glared at me, beady eyes willing me to be silent. "Ask me again after you've handed down your verdict."

"But this is a murder trial." I couldn't believe they'd dilute justice on such an important matter.

"This conversation is over. Ask me again when you've finished your service." Clemence turned to leave, paused long enough for Stanley to move his head out of the doorway, and shut the door.

The other jurors had stayed silent during our exchange. Ruth spoke first. "Today's been the most interesting day yet. I did not know a trial could continue with *fewer*," she emphasized the word, "than twelve jurors. And Clemence's avoidance of people's questions only makes me more curious."

CHAPTER 44

Jurors Fired

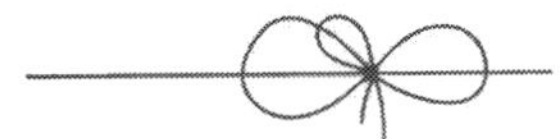

#maidissin

Justice Forrest Fired Two Jurors

By Axel Spinnewyn

Justice Forrest fired two jurors on Rex v. Hopewell today and charged them with contempt of court. The judge announced that the trial will continue with ten jurors hearing the evidence.

Justice Forrest told the packed courtroom, "I have met this morning with the Crown and Defence Counsel on this case, and we have all agreed to proceed with ten jurors. The Criminal Code foresaw this circumstance, and I am exercising my discretion."

But more than half of the remaining jurors have already made up their minds. They even came up with a team name for themselves: a Mercy of Widows. ("Mercy" killing is a euphemism for euthanasia.)

Once this trial is done, we need major reforms in the jury selection process. Currently, too many biases can creep between the cracks.

Comments

Olivia - *Were the fired jurors your sources?*

Axel Spinnewyn - *I plead the fifth.*

L'eagle - *Canada doesn't have the fifth amendment. Your role in this travesty will be investigated.*

Olivia - *Forrest should call a mistrial. Ten jurors? That's not allowed.*

L'eagle - *If he declares a mistrial, it'll be done. They won't try her a second time.*

Olivia - *This trial is a sham.*

Superhero - *Will justice be served if Forrest declares a mistrial on a technicality?*

L'eagle - *Good question, Superhero.*

CHAPTER 45

Concussed

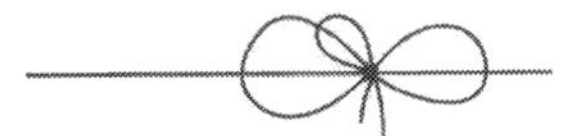

I headed out for lunch, minding my own business. I'd begged off from company today, avoiding the endless natter and forced small talk. We all wanted to discuss one subject, and I couldn't guarantee my self-restraint anymore.

Getting past the front door of the courthouse was increasingly difficult. The new batch of protesters distracted me. Their signs were better crafted with clearer lettering. "End needless suffering." "Good Life? Good Death!"

I brushed against one grandmotherly woman as I beelined toward the door. "Scab!" she drawled and then she walloped me with her sign. I didn't have time to protect myself or explain I hadn't crossed any picket lines. I stumbled into the broad chest of a cop chaperoning the mess and abraded my nose and cheek against the coarse fabric of his woollen uniform coat.

"Excuse me, ma'am." His Stetson shaded his face but I recognized his voice "You again?" my escort from the first day said.

"That's a fine greeting." I attempted a little curtsy. Using my mittened hand, I wiped a warm liquid from the side of my head.

"You're bleeding." My hero was observant. "Let's get you some help." He propelled me through the crowd, fanning his arms like wind turbines while nudging me forward with his chest. Using this method, we made it through the hostile crowd to the front of the building. I hid my surprise when he squished behind me into one spoke of the merry-go-round door. Once safely inside the windowed building, I scanned the crowd, examining face after face until I found the crotchety so-and-so responsible for my predicament. I flashed her a smug smirk, which I amped up when she glowered at me. I turned away when my knight herded me to the separate and faster queue reserved for legal insiders.

"This woman was just assaulted," he said.

I mopped the blood with my now-sodden mitten.

"She might have a concussion. She could need stitches."

I looked up. "Oh, hi, Roy." I smiled as best I could.

Roy examined the source of the blood from the wound somewhere in my unruly hair. He reached under his coffin-like x-ray machine, rummaged through a plastic bin, and handed me a wrinkled cloth. "Apply pressure and staunch the blood before it stains your clothes." My face must have betrayed my doubt about the cloth's hygiene and provenance. "It's clean," he said. He didn't hide his scowl. To the cop, Roy said, "I've got this."

The last I saw of my knight was his hat sluicing through the crowd.

I sat where she pointed, like a docile lapdog. Clemence carefully inspected then cleaned my wound. The judge's chambers were becoming an unwelcome but familiar haunt.

"You're back again." The judge smiled, his kindly expression suggesting this visit would be less onerous. The judge had traipsed into his own office, followed closely by his entourage. I looked from face to face and noted everyone—including Molly—was present. "Should I call a nurse?"

"Ruth is a nurse. Juror Eleven," I said brightly.

Clemence shook her head. "That's unnecessary." To the judge, she said, "My first aid ticket is current, sir, and this wound is superficial. I can clean it up." She stood on tiptoes, even though I was seated and kept my head bent. An icy stream of iodine dribbled onto my forehead and down my cheek. I swatted at it with Roy's cloth, still clutched like a token, and wiped it dry.

"Do you think you suffered a concussion?" the judge asked.

I raised my arms in exasperation. "How could I tell?" I knew little about concussions, other than they addled one's brain.

"Well, for starters, did you lose consciousness?" Frank asked the question.

"No. I stumbled, but I didn't fall over."

A look of alarm crossed Frank's face. "Were you dizzy? Before you stumbled?"

"No dizzier than usual." I smiled, and the judge chuckled. At least someone enjoyed my jokes.

"Say a sentence," Peter said.

"How much wood could a woodchuck chuck... Would you like me to go faster?"

"That's fine. Can you smile?" Peter continued.

I complied with his instruction, then patted my fingers against my mouth to make sure my grin was straight. "See? Even. No, that's for a stroke." I reached for my backpack.

"Sit still," Clemence ordered, pushing my shoulder down with one firm hand.

"But I'll google tests for a concussion," I said. Ever helpful.

"I think you'll be fine," the judge said.

I felt around the wound with my fingertips. The gash was already scabbing.

"Will you be able to resume your duties?" the judge asked.

"You can't get rid of me that easily." I was on a roll.

"We can't lose any more jurors," the judge asserted.

"I've got a question."

They all stared at me like I was a bedbug.

Heedless of their silent warnings, I persisted, "Why do you all travel in a pack?"

Peter was going to answer, but the judge stopped him. "They are all witnesses," the judge said. "To deter any improprieties."

"I don't understand."

"Legal improprieties," the judge elaborated. "No lawyer, no judge, can be alone with a juror during an active trial. All parties are present to protect their own interests and rights."

Peter hovered near me. He brushed bits of my hair aside and clucked like an old hen. "This has gone too far, sir." For a second, I thought he referred to the judge's legal lesson, but he'd just segued to a new subject. "First the protesters, then the bomb threat, now an assault. We must do something about it."

"What do you suggest, Pete? I've beefed up security. If I have the protesters moved, they'll find new ways to cause trouble."

"You could move them across the street. Away from the entrance." I held the cloth to my forehead to stop any more of Clemence's salves from dribbling down my face.

"That could work," Peter said.

The judge stood and held his arm out, inviting his guests to leave his chambers. "I have a better idea. Leave it to me."

Out of the corner of my eye, I caught some movement. Molly rubbed her forehead repeatedly. I imitated her by rubbing my own forehead. She nodded and smiled slightly. Her nodding continued, almost imperceptibly. The behaviour was odd. I smiled back, but this time, Peter caught my gesture. He frowned and moved to stand between us, blocking my view.

––– ∘ ∘ ∘ –––

Clemence marched us back into the courtroom long enough for the judge to excuse us for the weekend. We filed out again, but instead of stopping at our elevator, Clemence continued around the corner and down another long corridor. We grumbled as we followed her. Heedless of our complaints, she didn't slow her pace or stop to explain herself, our mutterings emphasizing every step. She turned another corner, and I spied her destination.

"It's a freight elevator," she explained needlessly.

One look at its scratched and dented features already categorized this device with Darwinian precision.

"This exits through a less-travelled part of the building and avoids the protesters."

Everything about the elevator was filthy. The quilted blankets hanging from grommets hooked below the ceiling bore tears and oily smears. The floor was both dusty and gritty.

We trundled through the open doors in our duckling-routine, and clustered in the middle of the small space.

None of us wanted to touch the dirty walls. I was wearing my best coat, a faux-fur in some hybrid leopard-tiger print. I felt like a princess in its swirling swing style. Sometimes, I playfully pronounced "faux" as "fox," and at least amused myself. I stayed in the centre of the elevator to avoid an unaffordable dry-cleaning bill.

The rickety elevator clanked its way to a subterranean floor. Its doors opened, as expected, into an equally ugly delivery area decorated in gouged linoleum spotlighted under bare fluorescents. They had painted the concrete walls an insipid minty green better suited to an old lady's candy jar.

Off in one corner, I saw a cage, smaller than anything I'd seen in the zoo. About the size of a compact car, but taller. It was a dumb question, because I already knew the answer, but I couldn't resist. "Clemence, what's that?"

Clemence didn't have time to answer, as a door on the backside of the cage opened and Molly stepped into it. Her face was worn, drawn, with pleats of wrinkles lining her cheeks and camouflaging any laugh lines. Molly gestured to me and tapped her forehead. I watched her, still not understanding her message.

"It's a holding cell. Prisoners wait there for transport."

Clemence brightened. “But those cells almost held more exotic guests. During the flood, the zoo nearly sent us their big cats for safekeeping. Lions, tigers, a couple snow leopards. Can you imagine?”

We followed Clemence as she zigged and zagged around crates and forklifts, past huge grey bay doors and windowed offices with scenic views of the loading area. I saw one people-sized steel door with a push bar marking an exit. We went through it, one after the other, in our *Sesame Street* sequence. As juror number nine, I was near the end of the line.

As soon as I stepped outdoors, I walked into a cloud of cigarette smoke and coughed. A ramp led to a paved alley. Despite the smoke and the commotion of the loading dock, it was quiet. No reporters. No protesters.

“Well done, Clemence,” I said. “It’s not nearly as scary out here.”

“Thank Justice Forrest. It was his idea. It was this or sequestration,” Clemence replied. I got the sense she would have voted against the judge.

—— ○ ○ ○ ——

At bedtime, I went into the washroom, ready to remove the day from my face.

I was not one to spend hours preening in front of a mirror, dressing myself up with false lashes and bright lipstick. After Hug died, I’d dolled myself up once for one of Leah’s do’s. I’d applied foundation, but on me, it looked like a chalk outline at a crime scene.

Imagine my surprise when I inspected myself in the mirror, after spending hours hanging closeup to my fellow jurors, Clemence, the judge, the Tweedles. No one had said a thing. I’d chatted with Leah and the kids all evening, and no one mentioned diddly. Leah, I might understand, as she was often distracted. The children, however, were both observant and blunt, and even they never mentioned the iodine-orange stain from temple to chin that clashed with the black and blue bruise from my walloping.

The only person who had tried to tell me was Molly. I was so tired of being the fool.

CHAPTER 46
Ineligible

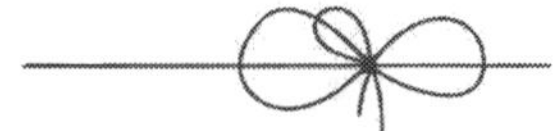

"Mortimer Baldwin," Ruth recited from one of our shared flipchart sheets lining our room. "He supervised the intensive palliative ward." Max's palliative nurse was the one who had picked up after his oncologist fired him, the one who pronounced Max dead.

I snorted, vaguely amused.

"There's nothing funny in what I just said."

I chuckled again. I couldn't help myself. "His name is funny. Befitting too."

Ruth shook her head. "I don't understand."

"Mortimer? Mort?" I spelled it out after she shook her head, clueless. "Mort means 'death' in French. He works with the dying. Get it?"

She nodded but kept watch, as if gauging my sanity.

——— ∘ ∘ ∘ ———

Frank bounced to an upright position and addressed the first witness to present evidence for Molly's defence. "Thank you for coming today, Dr. Baldwin. It is 'doctor,' right?" Frank trod the three or four steps from his table to the podium while he addressed his witness. "Could you please tell us where you work?"

"Yes, I have a doctorate in nursing," the middle-aged, paunchy man explained.

Frank swirled his finger in a minute gesture just before

the witness adjusted his position so we could see him better.

"I work at the local hospital, mainly in the palliative wards. I cared for Max Taylor during his final days." He wore a grave expression, perhaps acknowledging his daily proximity to the dead and dying.

"Were you working the night Mr. Tayler died, January twenty-first?"

"Yes."

Today's boots were black with ox-blood stitching. "Were you present when Mr. Taylor died?"

"No. Molly..." He paused before correcting himself. "Ms. Hopewell, Mr. Taylor's wife, pressed his call button." He glanced at Molly, and then recited his testimony as though by rote, standard procedure repeated too many times. "I attended the patient. I checked his heart through a stethoscope, and it was still. No pulse. I pronounced Mr. Taylor dead at 3:20 a.m."

"Did you notify the coroner of Mr. Taylor's death?"

"No, why would I?" He huffed, as though dismissing a most ridiculous question. "The coroner gets involved when there's something unexpected about someone's death. In palliative wards, death is too common."

Mort was right. I copied his words verbatim. No doodles this time. Instead, I drew and decorated a box around the quotation.

I folded the bottom right corner of the page to bookmark this tidbit. Even I could tell the trial was wrapping up, and we'd soon be deciding Molly's fate.

"Were you surprised by Max's death?"

The witness's hunched shoulders relaxed as though he had finally been asked the right question. He shook his head, slowly at first and then more vigorously. "Not at all. It was sad. Max was too young, but his ordeal was prolonged and painful."

"What medications did you administer to help Max—Mr. Taylor—manage his pain?" Frank rocked back and forth as he talked. Heel. Toe. Heel. Toe.

"So-called 'palliative drugs,' several potent cocktails,

often prescribed at higher doses than if the patient were not dying. Several drugs are addictive, but doctors prescribed them for things like pain, anxiety, nausea."

"Why would doctors prescribe addictive drugs?"

"Dying can be painful and frightening. Palliative drugs help ease the patient's suffering."

"Withdrawal from addictions is also painful, no?"

The witness glanced at the floor in front of him and shook his head, as if trying to dispel the memory of too many ghosts. "My patients will never suffer withdrawal."

"Why's that?"

"Because such drugs are only prescribed when a patient is expected to live a short while longer. Maybe months, weeks. Or days." Mort glanced at the jury, and we held eye contact. "Simply, my patients will not live long enough to withdraw from any addictions."

I nodded and returned to my notes.

"Are these the same drugs used to hasten death under the MAID legislation?"

"Every province's MAID prescription is different, but in Alberta, yes, there is some crossover. Mr. Taylor received smaller doses though. Regrettably, he wasn't a candidate for an assisted death."

"Regrettably? I don't understand. His last doctor fired him after Max applied for an easier death."

"Max got caught between the cracks. I studied his case for a long time. Even got legal involved. He wanted a humane death, but I couldn't prove it. Nor could his wife. Some other family members opposed it." The witness stared ahead, tunnel vision, straight at Frank.

The witness continued, "Max's illness and decline was one of the most difficult I've witnessed in twenty-two years of practice."

I heard a stifled sob but couldn't find its source. I saw only a sea of angry expressions, with clenched jaws, naturally rouged cheeks, and lidded eyes.

Frank waited for the audience to quiet down. "Can you please explain why Max didn't qualify?"

Twee-dee stood. "Objection. Dr. Baldwin isn't an expert on the MAID legislation."

Frank smiled. "No one is an expert in this legislation. It keeps changing. But Dr. Baldwin helped this family navigate the rules and ultimately applied a legal interpretation to their situation. I'm questioning him in that context."

"I'll allow it. Dr. Baldwin, you may answer." The judge waved his hand, like a priest offering absolution.

"Mr. Taylor met all the criteria. He had a terminal illness with no chance of recovery. I signed off on the application. But two signatures are needed, and Max asked his former boss, Dr. James Bell, to be the second. I understand some of Max's family pressured the hospital to deny the application based on a loophole, disqualifying Jim's—Dr. Bell's—co-approval."

I studied Max's parents. I could just imagine this pair calling up the hospital CEO, threatening legal action, and using their son's well-being in a tug-of-war with their daughter-in-law.

"Then Max suffered a stroke, developed aphasia, and could not redo the documentation."

Max had suffered worse luck than even Hug and me.

"Why was Dr. Bell's endorsement suspect?"

"Criteria exist for who can co-sign a MAID application. Dr. Bell's role was challenged because he didn't have hospital rights at that facility, and he wasn't Max's general physician or otherwise involved in Max's care."

"Can only doctors witness a MAID application?"

"No, many healthcare professionals can sign-off. Nurses, social workers. In addition to doctors."

"Was that the only reason Dr. Bell's endorsement was challenged?" Frank asked.

"A witness cannot benefit from the death of a MAID applicant directly or indirectly, according to the hospital's lawyers. So if Molly were a nurse, for example, she couldn't witness her husband's application, as she's presumably a beneficiary in his estate."

"I follow that." Frank examined us, checking whether we shared his understanding. "But how does that apply to Dr. Bell?"

Mort hesitated. "In addition to being a practising oncologist, Dr. Bell is a lobbyist for MAID legislation. He and Max worked together to get the legislation and its amendments passed. Including Audrey's Amendment."

"Audrey's Amendment? Please explain," Frank said.

Twee-dee half-stood, leaning against the table with both arms. "Objection. I repeat, Dr. Baldwin is not an expert on the MAID legislation. Or its amendments."

"Objection sustained," Justice Forrest said. "Mr. Dodge, a new line of questioning, please."

Frank nodded. "Why did Mr. Taylor's MAID application fail? On what grounds?"

"Legal believed Dr. Bell's role as a lobbyist disqualified him from co-signing a high-profile MAID application. They feared he could benefit professionally, that he and Max cooked up some lobbying stunt."

Mort's speech sped up, and he repeatedly glanced at the Crown's table. "There's a tragic irony in that answer. After his stroke, Max knew what was going on. I believe he remained competent—he communicated for most of the last year of his life through devised sign language and charades—but not in the way required to finish his MAID application. He knew his life's work couldn't help him."

"You say that's ironic?" Frank glanced at the lawyers at the Crown table.

Twee-dee stood up. "Your Honour, you've already ruled on this, and my learned colleague is splitting hairs."

"I agree, Mr. Parker," the judge said. He scowled at Frank. "Mr. Dodge, you will refrain from this line of questioning."

The exchange piqued my curiosity. I jotted three notes—incomplete MAID application, aphasia, Audrey's Amendment—on a blank page. I circled the words in ornate ivy doodles and folded the bottom corner of that page too.

"That's all I have for this witness. We will hear from Dr. Bell next." Frank turned to address Twee-dee. "I assume nobody questions Dr. Bell's expertise on these matters."

Twee-dee bounced up for his turn with Mort and ignored Frank's taunt. "Was the accused present when Mr. Taylor died?"

"I think so. I didn't ask."

"Would she have been alone?"

"Probably."

Twee-dee turned to face us, making meaningful eye contact that suggested hanky-panky. I didn't get it. What was sinister about a couple being alone, especially when one of them was terminally ill? After they diagnosed Hug, I couldn't bear us being apart.

"Do you know what goes on in people's rooms when you're not present?" Twee-dee asked, while watching our reactions.

"Why would I?"

I rolled my eyes on Mort's behalf.

"Was Max's bedroom door closed?"

"Probably." The witness's answer sounded flippant. "Most people close their doors." The nurse sipped his water. "We try to keep the ward quiet, so people get decent sleep. Sleep is important for everyone, but especially for the ill. We turn down the lights, but we can't make it totally dark. A closed door blocks out residual light."

Twee-dee ignored the witness's explanation and continued barking up the wrong tree. "Ms. Hopewell was alone in a room, unsupervised, with the victim moments before he died. Correct?"

"Technically, yes." Like me, I think he struggled to understand the point of these questions.

"Who else worked that night?"

"We were short-handed. One nurse was on the floor and the other was on her break when Max died."

Twee-dee nodded. "Did Mr. Taylor swallow his medications on his own?"

The witness's eyes rested on Molly for too long. "Max had difficulty swallowing. For the last couple days, we provided his meds intravenously."

Too casually, Twee-dee asked, "Did you administer Procheerol to Mr. Taylor?"

The nurse shook his head. "No. We were all aware of Max's allergy to that drug. In fact, he wasn't prescribed any antidepressants."

"Any idea how Procheerol got into Mr. Taylor's bloodstream?"

"None whatsoever," the witness confirmed.

The prosecutor turned toward the jury box and examined each of us. By now, I spotted his tell. He willed us to understand his slam-dunk evidence. But I increasingly had my doubts and thought Molly was lucky she and I had shared the same calamity—the dying of our ampersands.

"Thank you, Dr. Baldwin. That's all I have."

The judge moved to dismiss the witness, but Frank stood. "Your Honour, redirect, please."

"Go ahead. Be succinct."

Frank pivoted to face the witness. "Hypothetically..." Frank turned to face the Crown. "Hypothetically, if you wanted to hasten someone's death, would you choose Procheerol? If you knew your patient was allergic to the drug?"

"No. Allergic reactions are unpredictable. A patient is more likely to experience pain, discomfort, disability. Not death. If a hastened, humane death is the desired outcome, I would choose very different drugs."

I glanced at Max's parents. Both perched on the edge of their pew.

"Like what?"

"Opioids."

Frank resumed his heel-toe rocking. "Did Ms. Hopewell have access to any opioids?"

"Yes, certainly. She'd cared for her husband at their home for many months. Doctors prescribed Max morphine and other pain relievers. All so-called controlled substances."

"How are drugs like morphine controlled outside the hospital, in a patient's home?"

"An inventory system, where the home care nurse, patient, and patient's doctor sign off on the prescription count daily."

"Was Mr. Taylor's drug inventory ever off?"

"Never. In fact, Ms. Hopewell returned all their unused inventory each time her husband was readmitted to hospital. She was given a receipt and we placed a copy on file. Nothing was ever off."

Frank leaned against the podium. "Is Procheerol a controlled substance?"

"Not in the same way. You need a prescription for it, but that's it."

"Did Molly have a prescription for Procheerol?" Frank asked.

"That drug has been around for decades and is a commonly prescribed antidepressant," the nurse replied. "Chances are, half the people in this courtroom have old scripts of it in their medicine chests."

"But does Molly have a prescription?"

"I have no idea." Mort shook his head.

What was Frank getting at?

Frank nodded. "Was it unusual for Molly to be in her husband's room?"

"No, she was usually there. I had a cot set up so she could stay overnight and get some sleep herself. She couldn't help him if she couldn't function."

"Did you see any of Max's friends?"

"Yes, sure. He had many visitors. Different people."

"What about his parents?"

"They visited too."

"Who was there more often, Molly or his parents?"

"Objection, Your Honour. This isn't a contest." Twee-dee spoke almost lazily to raise his concern.

"Overruled." The judge nodded at the witness. "You may answer the question."

"I mostly work nights, as I mentioned. Molly stayed every night whenever I worked. I didn't see his parents often." He paused. "They probably visited during the day."

"Do you know how a towel got under Mr. Taylor's chin? After he died?"

"I placed it there."

"That's odd. Why?"

"After a person dies, their body relaxes, including their jaw. The bereaved are calmer, can absorb the information better, if their loved one maintains a dignified pose. I rolled up the towel to keep Max's mouth closed."

"Who did you do this for?"

"Molly. And his parents. She said she called them so they could say goodbye."

Frank paused. "One more thing… Do you think Molly killed her husband?"

"Objection. This witness is not an expert in any of the sciences where he could offer an expert opinion to this question." Twee-dee's tone was forceful. He'd stood fully upright, maintaining the lock-kneed stance of a man on high alert.

"Sustained. Mr. Dodge, you know better."

Frank bowed toward the judge. "Apologies. I'll rephrase." He shifted to face the nurse directly. "Did you see anything to suggest Molly could murder Max?"

"Molly was there every day and left only to get things to make Max more comfortable. Near the end, he only ate popsicles. He liked one flavour—cherry, I think. She kept him well-stocked in popsicles."

What was it with popsicles? They'd been Hug's favourites too. Near the end, his entire face lit up, shoving aside his fear, his pain, whenever I walked into his room with a fistful of popsicles.

CHAPTER 47

Stalked

Fella walked briskly, heeling nicely, though we'd just started our evening excursion. He loved his walks, and I almost felt a bounce returning to my own step.

"Get the news," I said, giving him permission to browse the scents. Fella's nose hit the dirt, lingering at each vertical surface. Fences, trees. Fire hydrants.

We walked maybe a half-block when I noticed a man leaning against a lamp standard by the nearby park. He stood, illuminated on the moonless night at the centre of the streetlamp's glow. He seemed familiar, but I couldn't place him. His cap's brim shadowed his face, camouflaging his features. Still, I recognized something about him. His stance? His shape? His clothes? I couldn't be sure.

"Juror Number Nine," he shouted at me. "Let's talk." He moved toward me, booted feet slapping the pavement with each step. The sound jolted Fella from his odoriferous reverie. "Heddie. Wait up."

Fella was a good dog, but he had a thing against aggressive men—especially those who strutted in brisk, certain movements, heedless of their surroundings and impact. This man strode with such an unearned swagger. Restrained by his leash, Fella started barking and swept back and forth in front of me. I pulled my dog close and patted his head, a gesture designed to silence rather than calm him.

"Fella, shhh." My voice was barely audible. A dog's

hearing was a gazillion times better than ours, and I knew Fella would interpret even my normal voice—still the equivalent of doggy-yelling—as joining his fray.

On command, Fella stopped barking but remained on guard, standing tall with hackles raised.

Undeterred by my dog's warnings, the man continued toward me, and then I recognized him—and particularly his peacock blue jacket. Axel stopped about ten feet away from me, out of Fella's reach. "Can we talk?"

"No," I said. Keep it short. Do not engage.

"Remember me? We met a couple times." He held out his hand, but I didn't reciprocate. "I'm Axel."

How could I forget? "You've got a lot of nerve. You stole my notes, got me in trouble with the judge. Go away." Fella and I started speed walking, backtracking toward home.

Axel jogged after us. "I didn't mean to cause you trouble."

"Well, you did. Leave me alone." I shouted over my shoulder. Fella renewed his barking.

I knew I'd never outrun Axel. So, I did something I'd only read about: I stopped when I neared the next streetlight, strode into the middle of the quiet road, and turned to face my opponent. Fella stopped barking and instead rumbled a deep, low growl, baring his teeth at our approaching inquisitor.

"I only want to talk." Axel slowed his pace and stopped a safe distance away.

Fella clacked his teeth, a gesture he normally reserved for herding exuberant dogs in the off-leash park. I stood in front of Fella, creating a barrier between him and our chaser. This was my cue to him that I could handle the situation. He continued his grumbling, but the teeth castanets quietened.

About this time, Leah stepped out onto her porch, summoned by our commotion, and saw us squaring off fifty metres away. "Heddie, is everything okay?"

Axel turned to face Leah. "She's fine, ma'am. We're only talking."

Leah took control in her usual efficient manner. "You're the only one talking, sir. Heddie, should I call the police?"

"I'm doing nothing wrong." Axel angled himself so he could see both of us. "I'm on a public sidewalk and just trying to have a conversation. I've got rights."

Leah hooted in disdain rather than delight, then waved a perfunctory come-hither. "Heddie, cross the street away from him and then walk this way. Once you're directly across from me, come home."

Axel stepped forward, and pleaded, "No, Heddie, wait. Please don't go. I won't come any closer. But here, take this." He laid a flat package wrapped in a paper grocery bag on the ground. "Consider it an olive branch. I found it in the trash by the courthouse. I flagged some things that might interest you. My card's in there, too, if you want to talk."

"Back up," I said. When he complied, I walked to the bag and nudged it with my toe. Nothing sprang out, so I picked it up and examined the bag's contents. A worn binder encased a couple inches of paper and bore the label "Fields, Hugh Edward." Someone had handwritten my full name on the top of the first lined page. "Heddie" was sandwiched beside it in quotation marks. I scanned the page: "Hugh's widow," "estate conflict with Stanley," "complicated grief?"

I clutched Hug's file to my chest. "How did you get this?"

"I told you. I found it. Listen, I'm sorry about your head." He touched his forehead. "The protesters really took that too far. No one was supposed to get hurt."

"You should be sorry," I exclaimed, massaging my healing wound through my tuque. "She was part of your group?"

"Sometimes Liv takes things too far," Axel admitted. "I'm leaving now. I'll go that way." He pointed in the opposite direction. "But I want to say: I'm sorry for your loss, Heddie. Hugh sounds like an incredible guy." He walked a few more steps, then turned, "Oh, and, check out your office. Hugh left you something important there. I marked several salient points in the file."

"I'm unemployed," I shouted back. "Besides, I've never worked in an office."

"Maybe I got it wrong," he said. "Read Hugh's file. You'll see what I mean."

After we locked the front door and set the alarm, Leah brought me a steaming cup of chamomile tea. "How do you know that man?"

My hands shook, so I placed my drink on the side table to cool. "He's a reporter covering the trial." I didn't itemize our frequent encounters.

"How did he find where we live?"

"From this." I held up the binder for Leah's inspection. "I think we found Dee's thief."

Leah picked up her phone and started texting. "She'll be relieved."

"Dee wouldn't even let me look through it," I said. "But Axel read it all. It's private, and he read it." I struggled to push back tears.

Leah gently removed the file from my hands. "I'll give this back to Dee, and she'll decide what to do next with it."

I shook my head, but she just held on until I relinquished my grip.

Leah curled up on the couch across from me and placed the paperwork next to her. "You'll have to tell the judge about this."

I groaned. "I can't. He already thinks I'm colluding somehow with Axel." I told her about my published doodles and she looked up Axel's site for herself. She didn't look impressed.

"I'm sure you're overreacting." She flashed me the same expression she used with her children when she indulged their nonsense. "What did he mean? Your office?"

"I have no idea. He read Dee's notes. He must know I'm unemployed."

"I'll ask Dee to go through it all and figure it out."

I remained unconvinced, but I picked up the cup and sipped my tea without burning my tongue.

Later, on my own, I researched Dee's diagnosis. "Complicated grief" explained too many of my symptoms. I focused on the cure. All I had to do was face my grief, feel the pain of my memories, accept that Hug was gone. Like everything, easier said than done.

CHAPTER 48

Pawn

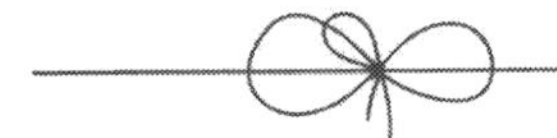

#maidissin

Hopewell Pawned Family Jewels

By Axel Spinnewyn

Today's testimony was from Mr. Chatterjee, owner of the Friendly Pawn Shop, who informed the court that Molly Hopewell sold him several pieces of valuable jewelry.

"I paid her well," Chatterjee said. "More than the pieces were worth."

The court heard that Hopewell received $5,162 for the sale of the jewelry.

Beulah Taylor, the mother of the deceased, reported, "Molly pawned sentimental heirlooms. My great-grandmother's wedding ring, my great aunt's dinner ring, a christening tiara passed down through the generations. We never recovered any of those pieces."

The Crown alleged Hopewell, who applied for bankruptcy nearly three weeks later, sold the assets so they would be excluded from any bankruptcy settlement.

Comments

Olivia - *She is such a Karen. She thinks she's above the law. What did she do with the money from Zane?*

L'eagle - As soon as *Zane Taylor charged his son interest on that loan, turned it into a business transaction, he lost any high ground, including the right to question them on how they spent it.*

CHAPTER 49

Balloon Bouquet

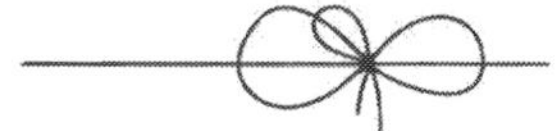

Ta-dum pressed down onto the top of the podium, pinioning himself in position. "Thank you for coming here today, Mr. Wong. How long have you owned your store?"

"Sixteen years."

"What do you sell?"

"Mostly balloons. Balloon bouquets for things like birthdays, anniversaries. We deliver. We use helium in our art."

"Do you sell helium tanks?"

The witness looked first at the jury and then at the audience. "Yes. Not very many. Most people don't want the clunky tanks in their living room." He probably considered himself funny.

"Do you recognize any of your customers here, someone who bought a helium tank from you recently?"

"Yes. The accused." He pointed to Molly, seated uncomfortably on her riser. Today's twinset was sage green.

"When was that?"

"At the start of the year. January."

"How can you remember a single transaction from eleven months ago?"

He paused. "She paid with small bills and pocket change, and didn't have enough, so she asked about layaway. I don't even have layaway, but I made an exception. She came back the next week and paid the balance." He shook his head. "I felt guilty selling her a helium tank when she was so broke. It's not exactly one of life's essentials."

The judge organized the hand-off, and Frank stood and drifted to the podium. "Mr. Wong, thank you for coming in today. Is someone minding your shop?"

The witness appeared surprised by the question. "My grandson is just old enough to be there on his own." He beamed.

"Did Ms. Hopewell mention why she wanted the helium tank?" Frank asked.

"No, she did not," the witness replied. "And I didn't ask."

CHAPTER 50

Suicide

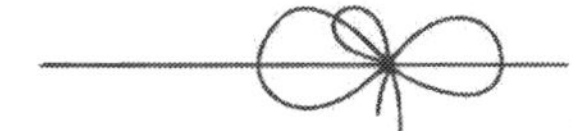

****Trigger Warning: Suicide and Suicidal Ideation****

#maidissin

Suicide Bag

By Axel Spinnewyn

The court heard today that Hopewell purchased a helium tank just days before Max Taylor died.

Earlier testimony indicated Hopewell bought a DIY how-to suicide manual.

Two plus two equals Hopewell planned to murder her husband using a so-called suicide bag, a homemade device allegedly causing a painless death by suffocation. Click here for details (at an unaffiliated link).

Zane Taylor, the victim's father, reported, "The Crown is too cowardly. He's not laying it out for the jurors so they understand how far Molly was willing to go. I didn't even know about suicide bags before. And, for the record, my PI found the evidence, even though the police claimed credit."

Comments

L'eagle – *You need to get your facts straight. That suicide manual was on Max's tablet and was only 11% read. Plus, the coroner's report says he died of anaphylactic shock. Suicide bags cause death by asphyxiation. Both big "a" words, so easy to get confused.*

Olivia – *If Molly loved her husband so much, why kill him so painfully?*

L'eagle – *How many deaths have you witnessed? Assisted death is peaceful, dignified. Not so much, so-called natural death. The obituaries you read to the contrary are lying.*

Good Death – *Coroners can detect helium through autopsy. Max was knowledgeable about euthanasia and would've chosen undetectable (also widely available) nitrogen for his death. Molly too, for that matter.*

CHAPTER 51
Memorial

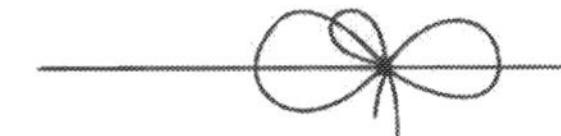

“Mr. Jasperson, can you please describe your relationship with the accused?”

The man could model for *GQ*. His salt and pepper beard was the bushy kind favoured by urban rogues. His shaved head looked like a genetic tonsure, but his baldness, combined with that fabulous beard, grey button-up cardigan and round, tortoise-shell glasses, made him appear cosmopolitan.

“My wife and I have been friends with Max and Molly for years. We all attended university together.”

“Did you ever take part in a conversation with Molly and Max about suicide?” Frank asked.

“Several times.”

“Suicide is not a typical dinnertime conversation.” Frank mentioned the obvious.

The witness’s disparaging look suggested Frank had sprouted a second head. “They were MAID lobbyists. They routinely discussed suicide, death, and dying.”

“Max considered committing suicide?” Frank asked.

“We talked about it after the hospital’s legal team rejected his MAID application.”

I glanced at the culprits for that injustice seated primly behind the Tweedles. Increasingly, I resented their interference.

“What else did you discuss?” Frank asked.

The witness turned and stared at us. “Their options

for a trip. Switzerland. Belgium. Colombia. Other jurisdictions where assisted dying was legal."

Loud thumping from the audience drowned out his words.

"Bailiffs, I've had enough of these interruptions. Please clear the gallery," the judge ordered.

The racket got louder, full of grumbles, swears, and choice name calling, mostly from the troublesome protesters. But all of us on the insider side of the pony wall waited quietly while people collected their belongings and departed.

Near the back, Axel's hand shot up. "Please make an exception for journalists."

Enough was enough. I needed to let the judge know about Axel's questionable actions. I raised my own hand and caught the judge's attention, but he frowned and shook his head. "Jurors will kindly submit questions in writing to your jury guard." I ripped off a piece of paper to do just that, when the judge addressed the entire courtroom. "All journalists with proper credentials may remain."

The judge was making a big mistake.

"I freelance," Axel said. "I'm working on selling my story."

The judge was suckered and allowed him to remain in the gallery alongside his more reputable colleagues.

A few minutes later, Frank addressed his witness in the nearly empty courtroom. "Do you think Mr. Taylor killed himself?"

"Objection," Twee-dee said. "Mr. Jasperson did not witness Max Taylor's final moments."

"I'd like to answer," the witness said, looking expectantly at the judge. The judge was still deciding when the witness continued, "No, I don't think Max killed himself. And I don't think Molly murdered him or assisted his death either."

Frank let the witness's commentary hang for a moment. "I'll rephrase." He pivoted a quarter-turn toward his witness. "When did you last see your friend? When did you last see Max Taylor alive?"

"I left his bedside about nine p.m. on January twentieth. He'd enjoyed his afternoon, with its revolving door of visitors. He'd had another close call but seemed to be rebounding."

Frank nodded. "One last question."

I leaned in, anticipating Frank's usual potent conclusion.

"Did you attend Max's funeral?"

Huh? Frank was losing his touch.

"Max didn't have a funeral. More of a memorial."

"Your Honour, I'd like to present photographs from Max Taylor's memorial. The package would be Defence Exhibit K."

Within about ninety seconds, I rifled through a half-dozen images. I recognized the witness standing next to an equally attractive woman I suspected was Mrs. Jasperson. Molly was there, seated next to Max's parents. They all looked sad. Sad and numb.

"Can you please describe the memorial?"

"Molly rented their community hall for it."

"What are those yellow objects in the photographs?" An image popped up on all the screens, and Frank zoomed in to the relevant quadrant.

"Balloons—happy face balloons that Max bought off the internet. His idea of a joke."

"How were these balloons inflated?" Frank asked.

"Helium."

I let out the breath I didn't even know I'd been holding.

"Is that why Molly bought a helium tank about a week before Max died?"

"Partly." Frank waited for the witness to continue. "Max also said no one could say anything about him, eulogize him, unless they used helium voice." The witness paused. "When you inhale helium and come off sounding like Donald Duck."

I laughed despite myself, and earned harsh stares from everyone, including my fellow jurors.

"Please explain," Frank said.

"He wanted to make Molly laugh." Mr. Jasperson blushed before he looked directly at me. "Or at least smile."

Both Hug and me could've been more clear-eyed about Hug's death. We both should've spoken our minds, our hearts, more. I could've been more like Molly, trudging dutifully through my assigned tasks. But Hug could've done his part too.

CHAPTER 52

Hot Seat

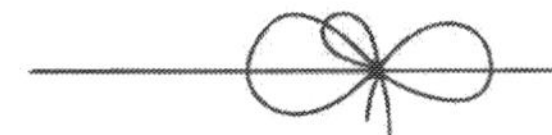

The judge's elbows were planted on his desk, his hands clenched together like odd little bonsais. "Do not ignore my question. Did you do it?" Instead of me, for a change, Axel was the focus of a polite but undeniable interrogation.

Clemence had maintained a stony composure when she'd singled me out again and hustled me into the judge's office alongside the cadre of lawyers, guards, and clerks. I fretted, especially when I spotted Dee. My assessment of the situation became more confused when I recognized Axel in the hot seat in front of the judge's desk.

"Do what, sir?" Axel foolishly asked.

"Don't play coy with me, Mr. Spinnewyn. Ms. Dixon reported that your employee assaulted one of my jurors." The judge nodded in my direction. "Did you also steal materials about one of my bailiffs from Ms. Dixon's office?" With each statement, the judge jabbed his pointer finger into the green blotter covering his desk, where coffee rings and ink spots resembled an ill-conceived Rorschach test.

I moved to protest, explain that the stolen file was also about me, my personal life, my love life. But the judge continued, "I have a mind to simply turn this matter over to the police. Let them deal with it. But first, I need to know how compromised my courtroom is." The judge's pupils were so dilated, I could barely discern the different colours of his eyes. "How many other personnel have you investigated?"

"Only one, sir," Axel admitted. "Well, two, if you include Heddie. She's in the file too." He pointed at me.

I'd observed the judge throughout the whole trial, inspecting and interpreting his expressions and gestures. Not one of the protesters' outrageous outbursts had threatened his composure, and yet Axel's confession nearly undid him. "I am confused," the judge said. "Dee, you said the file belonged to Hugh Fields. Stanley's brother."

I moved to explain all the intricacies, but Dee raised her hand to stop me. She was like a crossing guard managing verbal traffic, and it wasn't my turn. "The bulk of the information related to Hugh, but I also amassed materials for a mediation where Heddie challenged Stanley's administration of Hugh's estate."

The judge narrowed his eyes and inspected first me and then Stanley. For his part, Stanley stood still and camouflaged against the judge's bookshelves. "I need to understand this. First off, Mr. Spinnewyn, you are excused." As Axel collected his belongings, the judge continued, "I will report your transgressions to the police, and I'm sure they will be reaching out. In the meantime, you are not welcome in my courtroom."

After Clemence closed the door behind Axel, the judge turned to me. "Ms. Wright, I thought we had a rapport, an understanding." He flipped his hand between us, including me in the inner circle. "Why didn't you report this?"

"I tried, but you shut me down. Told me to tell Clemence." Dee pressed her hand against my thigh and the judge glared at me, both silencing me in their own ways.

"You need to try harder."

"But you just did it again. You all need to let me say my piece. I'm a victim here too. That guy read my personal information, notes about me," I exclaimed.

The judge replied, "No one here wants a mistrial. Ms. Wright, please elaborate."

So, I did.

The judge's eyes nearly popped out of his head. "Stanley

is your brother-in-law?"

"Yes, the same," I said.

"Why have I not been informed about this relationship?" The judge was like Jekyll and Hyde, good cop and bad cop, all rolled into one.

"We're not really related," I said.

His usual speech, almost languid in its boredom, was replaced with sharp, enunciated syllables. "You either are or you're not. Which is it?"

"Your Honour, I can explain," Stanley said.

"Please do." Any hospitality vanished from the judge's voice.

"Hugh was my brother, yes. But Heddie and he only dated. They never married."

"That's true. I call Stanley my 'bother-in-law,' but that's mostly honorary." My audience did not appreciate my joke. "Truth is, I've seen Stanley more in the last few weeks than in the last four months. Since Hug—er, Hugh—died. Before this trial, I only saw Stanley twice, and once was Hugh's memorial in July." I didn't mention my unceremonious eviction.

"Were you Mr. Fields's—Hugh's—what was the term, Emily—'caregiver'?"

Emily rifled through her notes, but Ms. Askew jumped in. "That was the term, sir."

"Thank you, Stella." The judge nodded. Finally, I knew her full name.

"She was far more than a caregiver, Sir." Dee spoke up in my defence.

"Ms. Dixon, please explain. Everyone else, be quiet."

"Hugh and Heddie dated for several years," Dee started.

"Six," I interjected, ignoring Dee's glare.

"Hugh brought his new puppy to her to train. That's what Heddie does. She's a dog trainer."

"Were they a couple?"

"Yes. They attended parties, his work events, everything—always as a couple. I know Heddie dated no one else besides Hugh, and I believe Hugh was also monogamous."

The judge addressed me. "Have you seen Mr. Stanley Fields outside of this building during this trial?"

When I hesitated, Dee jumped in. "As I mentioned, Heddie and Stanley are in a dispute over Hugh's estate."

The judge rolled his hand for her to continue.

Dee heaved a great sigh. "Stanley probated an old will—one he knew was outdated. Hugh provided new instructions, verbally. But as Hugh's lawyer, I decided he was not competent enough to execute an updated will."

"Does Stanley Fields benefit more or less from his brother's old will?" the judge asked.

"More. He was named sole beneficiary and executor in the old will. In his new will, Hugh planned to share his estate between them."

"Sir, I think you have no choice but to declare a mistrial?" Frank probed tentatively.

"You're like a broken record," Peter Parker jeered.

Frank angled himself to address the Crown directly. "A mistrial doesn't clear my client's name. But if Justice Forrest declares a mistrial, you'd probably never get this farce going again. Public opinion is already changing on this topic, despite the crew outside." He hitched his thumb over his shoulder, and I realized he referred to the protesters. "Molly wants—indeed, needs—to prove her innocence."

The judge silenced the lawyers mid-debate. "Gentlemen, continue this later. We are not alone." The judge nodded in my direction, and it was the lawyers' turn to shut up.

I twisted in my seat to look at the corner where Molly sat. She stared at the floor, hands clasped in her lap. I wondered how she felt, everyone else doing her speaking, her deciding for her.

The judge bounced steepled fingers against his lips. "Stanley, we could have avoided this situation if you'd mentioned your relationship with Ms. Wright earlier. You know the rules."

Stanley looked chastened but he didn't fool me. He'd find some way to blame this on me too.

The judge swivelled his gaze to me. "Have you and Mr. Fields discussed this case?"

I smirked at Stanley, feeling vindicated.

"Of course not," Stanley claimed.

"That's not quite true," I said hesitantly. "He told me I didn't belong on this jury."

The judge pursed his lips. "That's not the same thing. Have you discussed any of the evidence, the witnesses, the law?"

Stanley and I both said, almost in unison, "No."

"Have you shared any of the jury's discussions, any details about the jurors themselves?" the judge continued.

"No." We repeated our answer.

The judge sighed. "Again, we have averted a mistrial. No rule prohibits relatives of courthouse employees, such as security, from serving as jurors. Counsellors, are you both satisfied on this issue?"

Everyone nodded, except Molly, who'd composed herself again and maintained the same staid face she wore in the courtroom.

"But, Sir, she's against MAID, assisted dying," Stanley said.

Silence followed his statement.

"She talked Hugh out of a MAID death, and he suffered because of it."

I moved to stand, and Dee reached over to hold me in place. But I was done with people misrepresenting my views. "How would you know? You were never there." I addressed the rest of my audience. "Hug fought his disease. He never gave up. He wanted to get better."

"My brother's death was painful. Frightening. Because of her." Stanley squinted his eyes, full of hate. "He would've qualified, but she opposed peaceful deaths. At least for humans."

"I'm not a sadist." Hug should've given me the benefit of the doubt. He "protected" me, coddled me, but instead should've helped me understand.

"What are your views on medical assistance in dying, Ms. Wright?" The judge's tone was soothing.

"Your Honour," Dee spoke like she avoided a bear trap. "A juror's political views are irrelevant. No one would've asked her that question during jury selection."

The judge appeared chagrined. "Thank you, Ms. Dixon. You are correct. My real question is: has she been compromised? Is she working to undermine this trial?"

"No, sir," I asserted.

Stanley hissed dismissively. At least I knew his views.

I twisted in my chair so I could look at Stanley squarely. "Why are you being so mean to me?"

Stanley opened his mouth, presumably in surprise, but possibly to inhale enough oxygen to form a rebuttal.

To the judge, I said, "Do you know the whole story?"

Even I could tell the judge didn't want to hear more of my sob story. Too bad for him.

"I'm jobless because I gave up my work to help Hug during his final months. Twenty-four hours, seven days a week. So no income. Plus, Mr. Thoughtful over there kicked me out of Hug's house a month ago."

I winced when the judge slapped his hand on his desk with a loud crack. "It sounds as though things have been very difficult for you. Regardless, you two will take your personal feud elsewhere. It has no place in this trial or my courtroom. Do you both understand me?"

Stanley nodded before studying his shoelaces. I met the judge's eyes before also agreeing.

"I expect I'm seeing only the tip of the iceberg here, and I recommend you two see a counsellor."

"We already went to mediation. It didn't help. But I don't care what he thinks anymore," I said. Stanley's actions almost corrupted my memories of Hug. It had to stop.

On my way out of the judge's chambers, I said, "Not that it matters, when there's no hope, a MAID death is a good death. I'm glad for the safeguards, though, that the dying person decides for themselves. It's hard enough making that decision for an animal. I can't imagine making it for a spouse." I glanced at Molly, who studied the ornate carpet, her quivering chin evidence of her fraying self-control.

Before his office door closed again, I heard the judge say, "Stanley, can you please stay behind? Emily, can you please call his union rep?"

CHAPTER 53

Fella, Fella

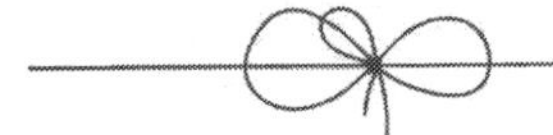

About two hours later, at the end of an exhausting day, I picked up my phone from Clemence and turned it on.

Quack. Sam from Fella's daycare had texted, *Heddie, Stanley's here to get Fella. Please confirm.*

What was going on? Sam had sent the message over an hour ago. What was Stanley up to? A sick feeling roiled my guts.

Quack—*Heddie, please confirm it's okay to send Fella home with Stanley.*

No, it was not okay.

Quack—Heddie, please reply.

I told you, they take my phone away when I'm on jury duty.

Quack—Stanley is impatient. Please reply.

Don't do it, Sam. She knew the protocol, she wrote the damned thing. No dog was to be given to any human without written permission. I did not permit it.

Quack—I'm sure it's okay. Stanley showed ID. Hugh's brother.

I pushed the dial button, and after four rings, got Sam's voicemail.

"Sam, it's Heddie. Do not—I repeat, do not—give Fella to Stanley." I could barely catch my breath and hoped I expressed myself coherently.

Next, I called the daycare itself. "Lucky Dog, Aster

speaking."

"Hey, Aster. Heddie here. Sam around?" I tried to sound casual, relaxed.

"No, she left a while ago."

"Is Fella there?" I hoped against hope.

"No." She stretched out the vowel and raised its end like a question. "He went home with his uncle. We texted you."

"Yes, but I didn't text back. I'm on jury duty, remember? They don't let us have our phones." I paced the cracks on the pavement, pivoting soldier-like at every corner.

"Fella left already."

"Damn. Damn. Damn." I felt like saying far worse.

"Is everything okay, Heddie?"

"Damn, damn, damn. No, definitely not."

"What's wrong? What can I do?"

"Stanley just stole Fella. Dognapped. We're fighting lately, and now he's taken Fella."

"I—we didn't know."

My pacing switched to stomping. "I'm sure you didn't. It doesn't help that you didn't follow your own rules."

"I'll call the police. We have camera footage."

"It won't help. Save the footage, but don't bother calling the police." What would they say except that Fella wasn't my dog? Technically, he belonged to Hug. Who was dead. And I had no legal rights to him.

"We didn't know." Aster repeated herself.

"I know. Now I have to fix this." My heart thumped so violently, I could barely hear our conversation, let alone my own thoughts.

My next call was to Leah. So far, her promise of better days was not working out.

"Join me at Jake's clinic. And text me Stanley's number."

I did as asked, and then marched the couple klicks, pounding my heels into the pavement. I probably gave myself shin splints.

Janet, the afternoon receptionist, looked up from her

computer screen. She flashed me a welcoming smile, and I did my best to be polite. She opened a drawer in the chestnut credenza flanking the wall under the silver embossed letters spelling the clinic's name, pulled a plastic key card affixed to a metal clip from the drawer, and handed it to me. "Leah asked me to give this to you. She said she'd meet you out back, by the crates."

I took the card and clipped it to the drawstring for my hood. I was well-versed in routing the maze of back rooms. I unlocked an exam room and walked through to the back storage and lab areas. Leah prepared meals for Jake's various charges, and the enthusiastic clamour of hungry pets overwhelmed the clatter of kibble in the steel bowls.

Leah spotted me. "Glad you're here. I'll ask Janet to finish this up."

She returned less than a minute later, dressing herself in winter gear. "Ready? Let's go."

"Where?"

"To Stanley and Becky's."

"Why?"

"Because, Stanley plans to sell Fella. He's got a buyer lined up. We must get there first."

"What? Leah? How can he do that? Hug asked me to be Fella's guardian. Hug gave Fella to me."

"It's our word against Stanley's. Come on. Keep up." She slapped her thigh like I was an errant puppy, and I matched her pace.

——— ○ ○ ○ ———

Leah raced down Deerfoot, hopping between lanes to pass slower cars. She pulled a legal document from the top of her unzipped purse and shoved it my way. "Read this. If you're okay with everything, sign. When we get there, let me do the talking."

I unfolded the document, and quickly flipped through the six pages. *Bill of Sale*. She'd handwritten my and Stanley's names, and added Fella's description to the pre-printed template. A yellow sticky affixed to it bore a price tag. "$3,000." I whispered the words, part shock and part horror.

"Stanley claims that's a fair price for a well-trained purebred."

"Well trained? Who bleeping trained him? Leah, I can't afford three grand. I live in your basement, for Pete's sake. My only income is from jury duty. Not even minimum wage." Stanley's cheque had temporarily cleared my overdraft but I had nudged my bank account back into the red again. "I can't afford to buy Fella. I'm going to lose him."

"Listen. I talked it over with Jake and we agreed. Getting Fella back will be our gift to you. Call it a birthday present."

I buffeted from side to side, clutching the grab handle, as she so-called drove. I nearly panicked when she narrowly missed rear-ending a semi, but she zigged in time and avoided any mishap. Out of the truck's blind spot, traffic in both lanes inched along, bumper to bumper, a mechanical millipede creeping south.

We arrived at Stanley and Becky's in record time, despite the traffic snarls.

Leah parked the car. "Stay here. I mean it, Heddie. Right now, this is a financial transaction. You show up, and it'll get emotional." She honked the horn twice to tell Stanley we'd arrived.

She exited the car, slammed the door, pushed her shoulders back, and strode across their yard, all five-feet-two inches of her ready for action. I watched her progress, and rolled the window down an inch so I could hear, if not witness, their exchange.

Leah knocked on their ornate door, all glass and brass in a thick wooden frame. Inside, I could hear Dagwood barking, although, oddly, Fella didn't add his voice to the chorus. A minute passed, and no one answered. Leah turned the knob and opened the door. Dagwood raced free from the house, barking and circling, half-play, half-protector. He inspected the vertical surfaces to complete his toilette. The first thing handy was the lookalike for Hug's tree.

The garage door rolled up and Stanley stepped outside. "What are you doing? That's break and enter. Dagwood, here, boy."

The dog ignored his human and continued checking out his world with his nose.

"Dagwood, here." Stanley patted his thighs with both hands, and the dog continued to ignore him.

Fella still didn't chime in. I decided to find out the truth for myself, confirm Fella was still there. I stepped out of the car, and projected my voice so it would carry through any walls. "Fella, speak." Silence. I tried again, "Fella, speak." Still no reply.

Across the street, another dog sounded an alert, a brief sequence of staccato barks. Dagwood's hackles raised and he pointed in the interloper's direction.

"Dagwood, come here," Stanley repeated.

Dagwood started stalking the other dog, and I could predict what would happen next. Sure, Stanley lived in a quiet neighbourhood, with sparse well-behaved traffic. But accidents happened. In my most encouraging voice, I called Stanley's dog to me.

Happily, tail wagging, he headed my way and snuffled my pockets for treats upon arrival.

"Aren't you a g'boy?" I said to Dagwood as I waggled his ears.

"Leave my dog alone."

I decided to give Stanley a taste of his own medicine. I held Dagwood's collar, jogged him around to the driver's side of the car, and coaxed him to hop in. I jumped in right behind him, shutting and locking the doors just as Stanley tried to force open the passenger door.

Thwarted, he pounded on the window instead. "Give me back my dog this instant."

Dagwood sniffed the window and wagged his tail.

"Dagwood likes this game." I ruffled the dog's ears and earned another lick.

My cell phone quacked. I stretched across the seats to fetch my backpack from the passenger side floor. The call display announced Leah, so I answered. I could see her leaning on the pillar outside Stanley's front door and watching me. I switched on the speakerphone.

"I thought I told you to stay put." Her words were stern, but she sounded like she was a few seconds away from laughing.

"Fella's not here," I informed her.

"How do you know?"

"Call it intuition, but I'll prove it to you."

Stanley peered through the passenger window, rivulets of sweat dampening his forehead despite the cool day.

"Trade ya," I said to Stanley, but loud enough for Leah to hear through the phone. "Dagwood for Fella."

His eyes bulged. "How dare you? You are a piece of work, Henry-Etta Wright. Besides," Stanley sneered, "Fella's not here. He's already gone. I dropped him off on my way home."

"What?" Leah said. I heard her through the open car window and from the handset like an unbalanced stereo. "You told me Heddie could buy Fella from Hugh's estate. You reneged?" She shouldn't be surprised.

"I changed my mind." Stanley crossed his arms and hunched his neck, a gesture that stressed his jowls. "Nothing you can do about it, either. It's all legal."

"You are heartless, Stanley," I said. I was so angry, I spat when I spoke, and rained spittle all over the inside of Leah's car. "Are you trying to ruin me? Destroy me? The fact your brother's death cut me off at the knees isn't good enough for you? You've got to finish the job?"

"Let's count up all the trouble you caused me. Let's see..." He held up a finger. "You've been getting me into trouble at work. You almost got me suspended today."

"That's not my fault," I protested. "You know the rules better than I do and should've told the judge the truth."

"Quiet. I'm talking." He clenched his fingers, leaving two upright. "You squatted in my brother's house for months after he died. Like you owned the place."

"Hug told me I could stay," I shouted.

He shook his head and held up three fingers. "You stole my brother's ashes."

"You what?" Leah asked in disbelief.

Stanley turned toward Leah. "She didn't tell ya? She came here like a thief and stole his ashes. Took the tree and everything." He pointed to the lookalike.

"I don't understand, and I don't need to. Not right now. Truth is, though, Stanley, you should have involved her in that decision, anyway." I was glad Leah took my side.

I couldn't let either of them get distracted. "Tell me where I can find Fella. Then I'll get out of your hair. Promise." I forced myself to sound reasonable.

"No." He crossed his arms, and I could see a closed-mindedness wash over him.

"Why are you being so mean to me? Taking away everything that matters? We both know it's not what Hug wanted, even if I can't prove it. Why can't you do the decent thing for once?"

"Decent thing?" He stomped the ground and leaned forward, mouth agape, like a bellowing bear. "You don't want to talk to me about 'decent'. You claim the higher moral ground when you're the one who let my brother die a horrible death."

"Here we go again." I rolled my eyes.

He stepped from one foot to the other, barely maintaining a semblance of civilized restraint. "You treat your dogs better than you treated him. You'd never let one of your dogs suffer the way your so-called ampersand did."

"Alright, this is getting us nowhere." Leah held out her arms and stepped between us. "Heddie, unlock the door." Reluctantly, I complied, and Leah opened the passenger door to let Dagwood out.

"What about Fella?" I squeaked, as she slid into the passenger seat.

"We won't find him today," she said. Thwarted was not a good look for her. "You drive."

I put the car in drive and off we went, me slowly realizing I might never see my dog again.

CHAPTER 54

Flawed Law

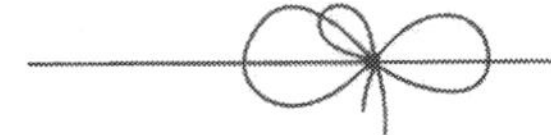

"Dr. Bell, could you please state your full name and your profession for the record?"

I rubbed my eyes and stretched to stay alert. I'd stayed up half the night posting digital "missing dog" flyers on every site I could find. Maybe the people who bought Fella would see them and contact me. I needed to get a grip. I thought it was a miracle I made it in at all, but duty prevailed. The judge was already fed up with me. Plus, I still hoped I could persuade Stanley to tell me where I could find Fella and, with the trial wrapping up, my opportunity to confront him was running out.

"My name is James Patrick Bell. I am an oncologist." The witness turned to face the jury box and gave us a shy smile. I couldn't help myself. I smiled back.

I caught Twee-dee staring at me, thin-lipped and pinched, scolding me for being cordial. He jotted something on his ever-present notepad. Perhaps I'd earned his ire. I was barely paying attention, and all my doodles featured Fella instead of the evidence.

Dr. Bell continued, "I am also the founder and president of an organization called Doctors for a Good Death."

I closed my eyes to soothe the burning gritty sensation that distracted me. After a few moments, fearing people might think I dozed, I blinked them open again. The doctor's outfit was old-fashioned. The button-down shirt, starched crisp, clung to his trim, muscled form, but I decided his polka dot bowtie was one affectation too many.

"How did you become involved in this case?" Stella Askew wore high heels, having forsaken her firm's usual footwear, and leaned one hip against the podium.

"Ms. Hopewell contacted me nearly two years ago, in February 2021, about a year before Max died. She asked me to evaluate her husband to see if he was a candidate for an assisted death."

I caught Twee-dee still studying me. I felt like a science specimen. I carefully arranged my face into a placid but attentive expression. When he turned away, I wiped my mouth in case I wore leftovers from breakfast.

"Ms. Hopewell, and not Mr. Taylor, contacted you?"

I increasingly found the lawyers' failed theatrics tiresome.

"Correct. It was Molly. Ms. Hopewell." He waved his hand dismissively. "We all worked together for nearly ten years, and I cannot refer to them so formally. Molly," he emphasized her first name, breaking down its two syllables, "called me, but Max did the talking once I arrived."

"Could you please explain that last part? Max Taylor still spoke?"

"Yes. Of course." The witness looked at Molly. "They contacted me in February, and Max suffered his stroke in late March. When we first discussed his MAID application, Max was coherent. He knew there was no cure for his disease, and he wanted to arrange an easier death."

"Did you help him with his MAID application?"

"Not on his first visit, no. At that point, Max wasn't a candidate. But legislative changes were imminent, and we all expected them to be finalized within the month."

"Please explain all that."

Dr. Bell nodded. "The MAID legislation, as it was enacted in 2016, required patients to meet several eligibility criteria. One criterion was so-called 'reasonably foreseeable death.' Healthcare professionals who were knowledgeable both in a particular patient's case and his disease had to agree the patient only had days to weeks to live."

"How does that apply to Max?"

"In February 2021, Max's prognosis didn't meet the 'foreseeable death' threshold. Doctors correctly assessed he could live for many more months, maybe even years. Yes, his cancer was incurable, but his disease was controlled."

"What happened?"

"I told Max I'd be back after the legislation changed."

"You knew the changes would pass?" Stella asked.

"More 'hoped.' My organization helped spearhead the changes. Before he got sick, Molly and Max worked on them too."

Stella fidgeted with her pencil and tapped it repeatedly against her notepad. "Please explain what difference these changes made."

"As mentioned, the original legislation included several safeguards. No one wanted someone to die against their wishes. In March 2021, the 'foreseeable death' requirement was removed. This was the most important change for Max. Under the original legislation, a patient could apply only after doctors expected they would die very soon. After the amendment, any terminal patient could apply at any time before that point, wait ninety days, and then proceed with their death."

"So Max could've applied to die early? Even though his doctors said he might live for a year or more?" Stella clarified.

"Exactly."

"That sounds like an important change." Stella gave the Tweedles the evil eye. "Did Max apply again, after the legislation changed?"

"Yes. I co-signed his application, and he was about a week into the waiting period when my involvement was challenged and declared a conflict."

"May I present Mr. Taylor's application for medical

assistance in dying? I believe it will be Defence Exhibit P."

The clerk circulated photocopies to us. Max had initialled and signed in all the right places, albeit with a shaky hand.

"Max's death was not imminent when you co-signed his MAID application on March eighteenth? One day after this amendment became law?"

"That's right," the doctor confirmed. "Doctors predicted Max still had many months to live. Turns out, they were right."

"Max was pretty determined. So why did he apply?" Stella asked.

"Objection," Twee-dee said. "Hearsay."

Stella turned to the judge. "Dr. Bell was part of the conversation on which he will testify."

The judge nodded. "Overruled. Dr. Bell, you may answer the question."

The witness reached for his glass of water and took a long swig. "Max knew he was going to die. Was dying. But living was expensive, costing them money they didn't have. Remember, neither of them worked, and Max's disability claim had been denied about two months earlier."

"He wanted to die because he was broke?" Stella asked.

The doctor scowled and nodded. "He knew his life insurance would pay out, give Molly a nest egg after she repaid the debts they accumulated while he was ill."

"Did the accused agree with her husband's plan?"

Dr. Bell laughed unhappily. "She was dead set against it." I winced at his choice of words. "She believed there had to be another, better, solution to their financial woes."

"What did you think when the hospital legal department considered your involvement a conflict of interest?" Stella asked.

"I'm no lawyer," he said, "but I thought—*think*—me having a conflict was a stretch. But I didn't want to jeopardize Max's application, his wishes, and so I withdrew. Max was working at finding someone else to co-sign. And... well, you know the rest." Dr. Bell sighed.

"Max never completed a new application. He didn't find a replacement co-signor before his stroke."

Dr. Bell turned to face the jury again. I made eye contact with him, directly staring into his golden eyes with their long, feminine lashes. "Exactly. Afterward, he could no longer speak, read, or write. But I believe Max remained lucid. He could still think, understand."

"What did you say to Ms. Hopewell? After Max's stroke?"

"I told both of them that without a complete application, Max was not a candidate for an easier death."

"Why didn't Molly or you fight to honour Max's original application? After it became clear he couldn't redo the paperwork, why not challenge the hospital's legal interpretation?"

"Because Max couldn't speak," Dr. Bell said.

"I don't see why that matters." Stella inadvertently echoed my own thoughts.

"Another of the original safeguards was so-called 'final consent,' where a patient verbally confirmed their wish to die a few minutes before a scheduled MAID provision."

"MAID provision?" Stella asked.

"I know, eh." The doctor flashed his beautiful smile. "That's bureaucratic-speak for a doctor administering the lethal cocktail of drugs that first calms the patient, sedates them, and then kills them." The doctor paused. "But the final consent rule also changed in March 2021. With Audrey's Amendment."

Stella gripped the podium. "What's Audrey's Amendment? We've heard that name before."

"That change allowed some qualified patients to waive their final consent—almost like a pre-consent."

"Why's it called Audrey's Amendment?"

"Lobbyists and legislators named the amendment

in honour of Audrey Parker. That's no relation to your honourable colleague." Stella glanced at Peter Parker at the Crown table. "Ms. Parker had terminal cancer and she used her own situation to raise public and media awareness about some dilemmas with the original legislation. Final consent was her primary concern. Ms. Parker ended her life early, while she still enjoyed some quality of life because she didn't want to lose her ability to speak through a stroke or some other complication of her disease, and thereby lose her right to an easier death. She wanted to die—"

"Objection. Hearsay, plus the witness stand is not his stage." Ta-dum stood to raise his concern.

Stella grimaced at her legal foe. "Audrey Parker's intentions are well documented. That brave woman gave several interviews, all of which are in the public domain."

The judge steepled his fingers. "Overruled. Dr. Bell, please continue."

"Audrey Parker wanted to die on her own terms and didn't want a hard death because of legislative loopholes."

"Like Max?" Stella asserted.

"Objection," Twee-dee said in a bored tone.

"Sustained," the judge confirmed.

"Which part of Audrey's Amendment applied to Max's case?" Stella asked.

The doctor studied the Crown, maybe waiting for them to interrupt. "Max couldn't speak anymore. He couldn't voice his consent, his decision."

That poor man. I started to sob. It was all just too much. I'd lost Fella, and I was slowly concluding I had been inadvertently responsible for Hug's difficult final days. I hadn't brought a tissue, so I sniffled. Clemence examined her charges, concern radiating over her face. When she saw me, my face presumably contorted as I tried to control myself, she stood abruptly and knocked over her chair. I don't know whether it was her movement or the sound that got the judge's attention.

"Your Honour, may we have a short recess," Clemence

said.

The judge scrutinized us all before settling his gaze on me. “We will resume in fifteen minutes.”

It didn’t take us long to exit the courtroom. Clemence admitted everyone else to our room but kept me outside. “Is there someone you can call?”

“Maybe,” I answered. “Can I get something out of my coat pocket?” I shuffled through the door, located my coat in the closet, and rummaged through my pockets. “Got it.” I held up a small rectangle of cardstock.

“No phones in the jury room, but you can sit at my desk. I’ll be right over here if you need me.” Clemence moved to the other table and busied herself organizing her folders.

CHAPTER 55

Axel: Explanation

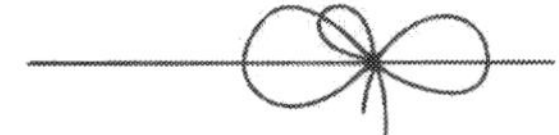

He wasn't surprised when his phone rang. Since the judge's censure, Axel had been inundated with texts, emails and even phone calls. Some were from other journalists looking to interview him, get the inside scoop. Others were from potential clients ready to hire him. He couldn't have paid for more effective advertising.

He was surprised, however, when he saw her name pop-up on call display. He slid the digital slider to answer. "What do you want? Haven't you caused enough trouble?"

Heddie whispered, barely audible, so Axel flicked off the YouTube video he'd been watching. "Listen, I'm on a break." Heddie sniffled. "I'm in the hallway, just outside the jury room. Our jury guard is here, pacing back and forth like a caged animal, and eavesdropping. I need to ask you a question."

Axel paused, so Heddie jumped in. "What kind of information is in that file? You know the one you, uh, found."

"The motherlode. Email printouts. Text message chains. Two transcripts of recorded interviews provided the best insight."

"Dee prepped everything for the mediation." Axel heard a large inhalation of breath. "OK, here goes," she continued. "Did Hugh go through with it?"

Axel didn't need her to spell out her meaning. He sighed, collected himself before answering. "No, I don't think so, Heddie. From what I could tell, Hugh delayed his death mainly so he could get his affairs in order. There's a text message to the lawyer dated June 21 which read, 'Success! Happy summer solstice.' I interpreted that to mean he'd wrapped up his worldly possessions."

Axel heard quiet sobs coming from the phone speaker. "He loved you. That was super-clear. Your name was all over that file. He wanted you to be okay."

"The timing worries me," Heddie admitted. "Hug died five days later, in the early morning of June 26th. For three days in between, he asked for a party, like a living wake with his friends, so he could say goodbye. That sounds like he planned it."

"What difference would it have made?" Axel propelled himself from his chair and headed to grab a beer. He'd bought a case of Big Rock two days ago, and already needed more. "You know he was dying, don't you?"

"I'm not an idiot."

"What does it matter then? He was going to die either way." A long silence followed. "Listen. I'm no doctor, Heddie, but Hugh withdrew the blood transfusions a few days prior to his death. There's your cause and effect. Those transfusions were the only thing keeping him alive. He understood the consequences of stopping treatments and withdrawing them was his final acceptance."

CHAPTER 56
Charades

Stella turned to face us but avoided my gaze. "Let's pick up where we were. Did you meet Max and Molly any other time?"

Dr. Bell answered, "Several times. Together, and just Max on his own."

"Did you record these conversations?"

"I took handwritten notes initially. But eventually, I recorded a video, with Molly's and Max's permission, of course."

"Why's that?"

Dr. Bell pulled his lips back into a sad smile. "I'm not completely sure. Posterity? I thought it might become important. The beginning of a Max's Amendment."

"Your Honour, I would like to present the video Dr. Bell mentioned as Defence Exhibit Q in this case."

The video stuttered and started, the cameraman a little shaky at first, making me seasick. Finally, the image stabilized. Dr. Bell, dressed in a button-down white shirt, open at the neck and hanging loosely over a pair of dark denim jeans, came into view. He looked like he wore a costume, having chosen something professorial for the day's work. Max wore the easy-on, easy-off outfit of the infirm—pull-on navy lounge pants with a matching zippered hoodie. The window behind him cast a bright light that silhouetted his face before someone closed the unfortunate floral curtains and Max's haggard face came into focus.

My blue eyes became green, jaundiced by jealousy. I wished I could find the damned video Leah claimed Hug made.

Dr. Bell continued, "Can you speak?"

Max shook his head, then raised his hand to his mouth and bit into his fist.

"Can you confirm you are Maxwell Gerald Taylor?"

Max nodded.

Dr. Bell spoke more companionably on the video than he did on the witness stand. His eyes conveyed genuine care, even admiration, rather than the guarded visage I'd witnessed in person. "Do you know why I'm here?"

Max nodded twice. Then he pointed straight at the camera, although it felt like he pointed at me.

"We are recording this interview."

Max nodded.

"Why?"

Max pointed again. Right at the camera.

"So people can see you? See you decide?"

Max nodded.

"What do you want to decide, Max?"

After pointing his finger at the camera, he slashed it across his throat. He couldn't speak, but his signing was unmistakable, precise. His head lolled to one side, his eyes clenched shut and the tip of his tongue stuck from between his lips, miming death.

"I don't understand, Max. What do you want to decide?"

Max repeated the gestures twice more, with increasing emphasis, and frowned at the doctor. I imagined Max's internal dialogue saying something like, *Are you dim? I want to die.*

As if reading my mind, Dr. Bell asked, "You want to die?"

Max nodded his head, slowly at first and then more vigorously. He pulled his lips back into a firm line, resigned to ending his future. He raised his hands, steepling them together like a prayer. A plea.

"You are dying?"

Max nodded.

I glanced at Molly. She sat in her assigned seat, this time wearing a coral suit that made her look older and somehow more respectable. She stared at the ground. Meanwhile, his mother held her usual handkerchief and dabbed at her eyes. I rolled my own eyes and hoped no one noticed my breach of decorum.

"Does it hurt?" Dr. Bell asked.

This time, Max contorted his face while he nodded.

"Do you want the pain to stop?"

He nodded again. Emphatically.

"Can I give you different medications? To control the pain?"

Max shook his head no.

I heard Molly in the background. Her voice sounded broken. "Nothing helps."

The camera panned over to her standing at the opposite end of the couch. "It's worse at night. During the day, he pretends. At night, when he's asleep, he thrashes, cries out." Tears welled up in her eyes, but she didn't submit. I'd never managed such restraint.

The camera clicked off.

"Max Taylor was tortured during the last months of his life," Dr. Bell said.

"Can you explain?" Stella asked.

Dumb question. Of course, he could.

Dr. Bell paused, then said, "Max would've been spared considerable pain, but his parents intervened in his care."

Twee-dee half-stood, mouth agape to speak.

"I know, I know," the judge interrupted. "Sustained."

Stella shuffled her feet and swayed slightly behind the podium. "What medical options did his family consider?"

Dr. Bell nodded. "Molly acknowledged her husband

was dying. She opted for comfort care, palliative medicine to ease the physical and emotional stress of dying. His parents wanted a higher level of medical intervention each time Max's condition deteriorated."

Stella shook her head. "Why was that a problem?"

"Max nearly died twice more between March, when he suffered a stroke, and January, when he succumbed. Near the end, Max could barely swallow. Plus, mets—metastases, growths from where his cancer spread—developed in his ribs, making breathing difficult. His chest couldn't move without hurting. Mets also spread to his liver, reducing the organ's ability to remove toxins from his body, slowly poisoning him."

"And?"

"Each time, his father insisted Max be resuscitated. Sure, Max bounced back after each incident, but never fully. He became weaker and needed ever more care." The doctor sighed. "Molly asked the hospital lawyers to weigh in, but they showed more concern about potential litigation than basic human decency."

"That's all I have for this witness." Stella took her seat next to Frank.

Twee-Dee stood. "Did Max Taylor have a personal directive in place?"

"Max's paperwork was in order, including his will, power of attorney over his finances, and his personal directive for healthcare."

"Who controlled Max's personal directive? When Max couldn't speak for himself?"

"It was joint, Molly and Zane Taylor."

"Joint and several, correct?" Twee-dee asserted.

"Yes," the doctor confirmed.

Twee-dee gestured in our direction. "Can you please explain what that means to the jury?"

"Either Molly or Zane could make Max's medical decisions when Max was incapacitated, either together or each independently."

"Zane Taylor was within his rights to order higher levels of care for his only son?"

"Yes."

Even I could see that was dumb. A single document had effectively set up this entire dispute.

"One more thing, you all worked at an organization called Doctors for a Good Death?"

Dr. Bell stared at him, poised and strong. "Yes," he replied.

"What is the purpose of that organization?"

"We lobby the government to develop effective, humane euthanasia legislation in Canada." The doctor turned to face us again. "Euthanasia is a fancy way of saying mercy killing. When a patient has no hope of recovery, when their death is certain and likely to be painful, we at Doctors for a Good Death advocate for quick, painless procedures to hasten the process, letting the patient die more quickly and easily."

"Thank you for the lecture, Dr. Bell." Twee-dee studied us, and I hoped I bore a blank expression. "What was Ms. Hopewell's role in your organization?"

"She led our lobbying efforts."

Twee-dee rolled his hand. "Please elaborate."

"She worked to understand the gaps, so-called flaws in the laws, and then worked with legislators to negotiate improved solutions."

"And what was Mr. Taylor's role?"

"Max was our publicity and events manager. He organized media coverage, news stories, interviews with people like Audrey, Audrey Parker. He helped educate Canadians about the problems with the legislation and rally support for changes, improvements to the law."

"Your Honour, I have some photos here that I would like to add as exhibits."

The judge nodded, and the clerk collected her new bounty before circulating copies to each of us.

The TV screens around the room flashed a photo of a

healthy Max, dressed in jeans and a black T-shirt, five o'clock shadow outlining his chin, mouth open. He held a sign, and I was shocked to recognize the same logo, indeed the same caption, carried by late-comers protesting downstairs. I wished I hadn't made such a fuss, but the other jurors seemed equally surprised by this revelation. When I looked at the tables occupied by the pairs of lawyers, it was the Defence lawyers, Frank and Stella, who stared at me and scowled.

CHAPTER 57

Lobbying Stunt

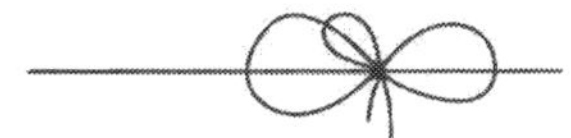

#maidissin

Murder as Lobbying Stunt

By Olivia Newcomb

(Axel has been unavoidably detained, so Olivia Newcomb has stepped in to complete the coverage.)

Today, we learned about a conspiracy to murder Max. His murderers planned Max's death as a lobbying stunt to propel proposed amendments to the MAID legislation to the public's attention, a so-called Max's Amendment.

"Deathly ill people still suffer needlessly in this country," said Dr. James Bell, founder of Doctors for a Good Death, a lobbying organization behind the frequent changes to the MAID legislation.

"Bell is irresponsible," claimed Zane Taylor, the victim's father. "Max and Molly were brainwashed by his silver tongue and charm." Taylor claims Bell's organization single-handedly dismantled important safeguards in the original MAID legislation.

Comments

Good Death - *I never gave you an interview. Where did you get that quote? Thin air?*

Superhero - *Are we watching the same trial? A lobbying stunt is a hypothesis, not a fact.*

Olivia - *A lobbying stunt is worse than greed. Greed is a time-worn sin, totally understandable. But publicity? Advancing her cause? Shame on Molly.*

Olivia - *I still can't fathom their arrogance. Imagine? Max's Amendment. Shocking. They want to legalize murder.*

L'eagle - *You're the minority. Most Canadians support the MAID amendments. This is a classic case where the law has not kept pace with changing public opinion.*

L'eagle - *Juries have a right in Canada to vote their conscience, even if their conscience contradicts the law. Look into "jury nullification."*

Anonymous – *How can I learn more?*

L'eagle - *YouTube it. It's not exactly a secret, although the courts can't tell juries about it ever since the Morgentaler case.*

Anonymous - *What happened there?*

L'eagle - *The jury acquitted Morgentaler, when he was guilty as charged, because the jury felt the law itself was broken.*

Anonymous - *Why haven't I heard about this before?*

L'eagle - *You just have. Google the rest yourself. What do I look like? Wikipedia?*

Onc-doc - *Dismantling safeguards is a slippery slope. I'd rather a thousand people die painful deaths than a single person be euthanized before their time.*

Anonymous - *Anyone dying from cancer is dying before their time.*

Superhero - *Shocking that Axel's coverage is somehow more balanced.*

CHAPTER 58

Tilly

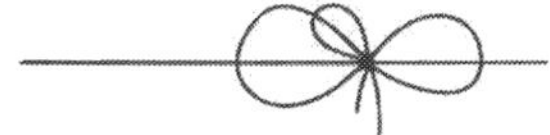

Sundays were normally the days I took Fella to the off-leash park and put him through his paces by practising his commands and playing on agility equipment. I liked to go early, stopping at a Tim Horton's drive-through on the way for a steaming cup of to-go coffee. My favourite park was at the end of 14th. But not this Sunday. Nope. I wouldn't be taking Fella to parks anymore.

I trudged around Leah's kitchen, preparing my morning coffee, wearing my old terry towel ensemble, slippers, and robe. Originally a matching set, washing and use had faded the robe to a tepid version of its original shade. The unbelted robe hung shapelessly from my shoulders. Long snags had pulled from the original weave, leaving mangy bald spots. I rummaged for a pair of scissors in Leah's junk drawer, snipped the longest strands, and tossed them into the garbage.

A towel-turban completed my ensemble. Hug had bought it as a birthday present and then teased me whenever I wore it. It was ugly and dotted with rust stains that resembled dried blood. Not much of a birthday present. I'd seen him more clearly then than later and loved him anyway. He never gave me a vacuum or anything, but bland, uninspired gifts were his specialty. I amazed myself at the number of his failings I'd overlooked since he died. I blurred, blended, and occasionally erased the rough edges of his imperfections.

I untangled the turban from my head and trashed it

too. It was too cruddy to be donated.

Leah raced around the corner, travelling the short distance from her home office to the kitchen. “You’re up,” she said, excitement animating her features. “Get dressed. We need to go.”

“Where are we going?” The tinkle of my spoon as I swirled my coffee sounded like wedding guests cajoling the happy couple to kiss.

“Emm found him. And we’re going to see him.”

“Who?”

“Fella,” she said, giving me a quizzical expression. “Keep up.”

I pitched my cup onto the table, spilling half its contents, and moved to wrap my arms around Leah in a tight embrace. “Oh, whew.” I released her. “You found him.” I squealed in delight. And relief. “How?”

Something about her tone and rigid posture advised me to be wary. “The daughter is in Emm’s class, and she brought him to school. Special circumstances. I met with them, and they seem like pleasant people.”

“Uh-huh,” I said, aiming for noncommittal rather than rude.

“Sweetie, don’t be like that. It’s just—well, it’s going to be hard to reclaim him with a kid involved. It’s not just money.”

“It was never about money. Fella was a pawn in Stanley’s revenge. He sold him to get back at me.” I stood my ground, hands on hips.

“Well, just meet her. Her name’s Tilly, and she’ll give Fella a wonderful home.”

I wondered whether this was the child I’d met a couple weeks ago. How many Tillys could Emm know? “I already give Fella an excellent home.”

“I represented your interests. The family was sympathetic to your situation. Thought we could work something out. Something like visitation rights. They’re looking for a win-win.”

I stomped my foot, the beginning of a tirade. "I'm so sick of always getting the crappy end of any deal. They win and I lose. Stanley stole Fella. My win is getting him back. Unharmed and happy. Why do I always have to compromise? Settle for less than I want?"

Leah stared at me like I was a bug. "Just go get dressed." I turned to go, and she added, "Make sure you put on your big girl pants."

I didn't laugh. I didn't think she was trying to be funny.

I raced downstairs, picked up clothes I'd tossed on the floor yesterday, and pulled them on. I got back upstairs in time to see Leah finish pouring my remaining coffee into a to-go cup.

"Here," Leah screwed the lid on tightly before handing me the cup. "Drink this and try to change your attitude."

"Do I need anything? Besides the coffee?" I raised the cup to honour her.

"Just be prepared, Heddie. There are complications." Leah stared at me, and I tried to box up my hopes, but I didn't throw away the key.

——— ○ ○ ○ ———

"Why the schoolyard?"

Leah parked across from the main gate on 14th, on the opposite side of the uncharacteristically quiet street. She carefully turned her wheels toward the curb and applied her emergency brake.

"It felt like common ground."

"I think I met Tilly before," I said.

In the fenced schoolyard, Fella played fetch with a young girl, unaware of his permanent change of address. Nearby, two adults—presumably the child's parents—watched them play.

"There he is. Fella!" I called. I couldn't help myself. "Here, g'boy."

Fella's head shot up, ears perked like sonar, his tail on

alert. He found me and bolted toward the open gate.

"Yes, here, boy." I crouched, arms opened, ready to embrace him and never let go.

He arrived in an instant, crossing the empty street easily, and we shared a happy greeting, me beaming and cooing, and him dancing, wiggling, and yipping a joyful hello. I think he missed me too.

Our huggle was interrupted by a shriek. I removed my face from the rough of my dog's neck to see the child racing along Fella's path, her parents in distant pursuit. I immediately saw the problem. 14th wasn't so busy on a Sunday but was still no place for an unchaperoned child. In the distance, I saw a pickup truck barreling down the hill, oblivious to gravity's pull toward disaster.

The child navigated the gate like a pro, easily chasing Fella onto the unsafe side of the barricade, heedless of any danger. The compact woman sprinted, her short, dark, curly hair bouncing with each stride. The tall man, silver beard and a brush cut, resorted to calling the child. Neither approach worked.

"Hold," I said to Fella, then pointed with my toes and whole hand toward the child. I mentally estimated the speeds of my dog and the truck. It would be a tight squeeze, but I needed Fella to stop Tilly before she reached the road. "Hold Tilly," I pleaded.

Fella bolted back across the street. Brakes screeched as Fella darted in front of the moving truck.

"Noooo," I said, my hands on my head, my fingers pulling my hair.

When the truck passed, a child of about seven or eight sat on the sidewalk, Fella's neck wrapped in her arms. He panted and she beamed.

The child's parents reached us. "That dog is supposed to be well-trained," the father said.

"He is," I said, indignant on Fella's behalf. "Don't you see that he just saved her?" I held out my hand. "We've met before."

He squinted his eyes before asking tentatively, "Is this the same dog who saved that puppy a few weeks ago?" When I nodded, he said to his wife, "See? I told you."

She seemed underwhelmed by his discovery.

To me, he continued, "That incident was when we placed an ad for a dog for Tilly. He was so impressive."

"But why did he race off today?" the mother asked.

Ah, that. I hesitated for a moment, weighing my options, assessing the likelihood of the consequences of my truth-telling. "That was my fault," I admitted. "I called him. His recall is brilliant." I added hastily, "I had no idea the child would run after him."

"You endangered my daughter," the woman said, face flushed with anger, exertion and probably fear at what might have been.

How was I to know the kid would run after him? "I'm so sorry," I said.

To Leah, she said, "I don't see how this will work. I need Tilly to be safe."

I recognized I'd just blown it. I had no recourse, no legal right to Fella, and now no good will to negotiate some compromise. I felt tears spring to my eyes and worked at holding them back. I moved over to Fella and the child. "So sorry," I said to the child. To Fella, I said, "be a g'boy." I patted his head, waggling his ears one final time before I turned and walked away.

CHAPTER 59

Rested

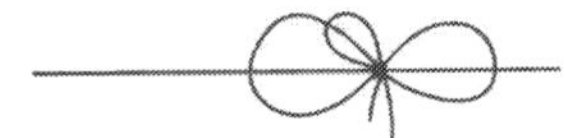

#maidissin

Jury Deliberates in Hopewell Murder Trial

By Olivia Newcomb

Both sides of the Hopewell murder trial rested yesterday, and Justice Forrest provided a summary of all the evidence presented. His summary was impressively unbiased, although we—Alberta's regular Janes and Joes—could've used more help interpreting some of the legal knots.

Zane Taylor, the victim's father, reported, "The evidence was clear. Molly Hopewell killed my son, and he died frightened, in pain, and alone except for his murderer. If the jury doesn't do the right thing, I call on the police and the Crown to fix it. If those ten people don't do their duty, I hope the judge throws the book at them."

Justice Forrest decided not to sequester the jury. We expect he'll regret that decision.

Comments

L'eagle - *Are you threatening a sitting judge? You've got quite a track record. Didn't you already assault one of the jurors?*

Olivia - *No, of course not. I'm peaceful and law-abiding.*

Cowboy Gent - *The judge droned on and on. I'm glad we didn't hear from him too much in this trial.*

L'eagle - *He did his job and summarized the salient points of the evidence. Neutrally. Without bias.*

CHAPTER 60

Reunited

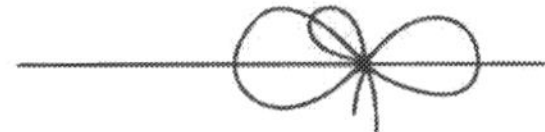

We stood on the porch of an infill in Marda Loop within easy walking distance to Fella's favourite park. I balanced a box of a dozen assorted doughnuts we'd picked up as a price of admission. Tilly opened the door on Leah's first knock.

"Tilly, is that Leah?" a woman's voice called from somewhere inside the house.

"Uh-huh," the girl said, as eloquent as any grade-schooler. Fella poked his head around the child's legs.

I petted him. "Four on the floor," I whispered, so he wouldn't bowl the child over in his enthusiasm.

"Hi, Penny." Leah addressed Tilly's mom. "Heddie's with me too."

Our hostess strode around the corner, drying her hands on an apron bearing a bold Maud Lewis print—the one with the curious, amber-eyed black cat. She glanced at the commotion in her doorway and held her arm out. "Tilly, let our guests in."

The child moved aside, and the dog pushed forward, filling the void.

"C'mon, Fella. Let me in. Nice to see you too." I hoped our host noticed our glad reunion.

"Matt," Penny called. "They're here." To us, she said, "My husband will be here in a minute. Please take a seat." She motioned to the couch, while she moved to an armchair opposite. A coffee table divided the seats, demarcating each team's turf.

"We brought doughnuts," I said, handing her the box.

She made no move to accept my offering. "Thanks."

I sat down and cradled the box on my lap.

The child moved toward me tentatively. "I want a doughnut." She held out a chubby hand.

"Let's ask your mom." I met the woman's eyes, eyebrows raised in a silent question.

Penny half-smiled. "Alright. But just one. And, Tilly, mind your manners. Make sure you thank the lady."

I lifted the lid to show the child the full assortment. She met my eyes before succumbing to the sugar's allure. "Which one?" she asked.

"It's up to you," I said. "You decide." Her hand hovered over the one with maple icing, then the triple chocolate, and finally settled on the one topped in multi-coloured candy sprinkles.

"This one," she said, pointing.

"Unicorn toots," I said, and handed her a napkin.

She giggled, reached into the box to grab her prize, and took a bite, leaving a ring of sprinkles outlining her mouth.

Matt strode into the room and sat in a second chair next to his wife. "Tilly, can you please go play with Fella?" he said. "Grown-ups have to talk."

"Mmkay," the child said, mouth full and still chewing. She tugged Fella with her free hand toward a stuffed toy box in the corner.

"Thanks for agreeing to see me," I said. "Especially after last time." I hoped I looked suitably chagrined.

"Don't thank me," Penny asserted. "Tilly wanted you here. Tilly and your—er—niece..."

"I'm only an honorary aunt. Lucky Emm avoided my genes."

"Fella clearly knows Emm very well. If nothing else, he helped the girls become friends."

Matt got down to business. "Penny said Fella was

stolen?"

"Well, not exactly 'stolen,'" Leah said. "It's more of a custody dispute."

"I don't understand. Is Stanley Fields your husband?" Matt asked.

"Oh, gosh, no," I said, and mock-mopped my brow. "His late brother, Hugh, was my partner. Hugh died earlier this year. Fella was his dog."

"I don't understand. How did Stanley get your partner's dog?"

"It's a long story. He thinks he has a right to sell Fella," Leah said. "Listen, I—*we*—know you paid for Fella. And neither of us," she swept her arm back and forth between us, "want you to be caught in the middle of a family quarrel."

"Tilly needs a companion," Penny said. She pointed to the pair in the corner. "They've already bonded."

"We know he's not trained as a service dog," Matt added, "but he's very good with her. Tilly's school is even helping us get him certified as her support animal."

I watched the child dress Fella using a tutu as an Elizabethan collar. Fella sat obligingly still. "Pink is his colour."

Everyone smiled politely, and a long silence blanketed the room.

"We wondered whether you'd be willing to work with Tilly. Teach her to handle Fella?" Penny asked.

"I don't understand," I admitted.

"Tilly's been coming home from school for the past week, each day with new commands for Fella. Emm's been showing her. Mostly tricks, like 'eight'—where he weaves around her legs like a figure eight—or 'spin,' where he pirouettes." Another silence followed. "Fella listens better to Emm than Tilly." She shifted in her seat and faced me directly. "Heddie, I'm hoping you'll teach Tilly too." She glanced at her husband. "We can't have any more stunts like the last one. Both Tilly and Fella need to be kept safe. No risky showing off."

"I wasn't trying to show off," I said. "I was just saying

hello."

"Maybe so, but your actions put my daughter at risk," Matt said.

I didn't defend myself or mention their roles in the near fiasco.

"I need your assurance, your promise you'll keep her safe." Matt waited for my response.

"Heddie's always been great with my girls," Leah said.

"Yes. I promise," I said. "I can teach Tilly everything. Anything you want Fella to learn? I can teach an old dog new tricks," I said, chuckling. "I can also teach Tilly how to teach Fella."

"Old? He's not that old. Lots of service dogs are four when they're placed," Matt said.

"Fella's seven, though," I said.

Penny and Matt exchanged looks. I interpreted surprise. Dismay. "That's got to be wrong. Stanley said he was 'three or four.'"

"Stanley li—"

"Misspoke," Leah exclaimed, drowning out my harsher assessment. "Fella wasn't his, so he probably didn't remember exactly when he was born."

"I can prove it," I said, pleased for once to have evidence of my claims. I reached into my backpack and pulled out Fella's registration certificate. "Here." I shoved the paper toward them. "This document proves he's a legit border collie and shows his birthday."

Matt studied the document before he looked in the corner at his child and whispered, "How long do border collies live?"

Taking my cue from him, I whispered back, "Ten to seventeen years, depending on his genes." Matt's face fell, so I added, "I've met Fella's parents a couple times. They're both still alive. Healthy. Fella could live a long, happy life yet."

Matt nodded. "But service dogs should retire about ten, right?"

I nodded, adopting what I hoped was a knowing visage while really having no clue.

"Will you excuse us?" Matt said. "We need to discuss some things." The couple stood and walked down the hall, shutting themselves behind a closed door. I could hear occasional syllables but no full words or sentences.

I laid out two napkins on the coffee table and put the box of doughnuts on top of my improvised placemat, then moved to the corner and sat cross-legged on the floor. I wasn't entirely sure how I'd get up again. Fella thumped a greeting, and Tilly said, "Want some tea?" She handed me a miniature teacup and saucer. The looped handle of the cup was too tiny for my fingers, so I rested her gift in my palm. I tipped the cup to my mouth and slurped loudly.

Tilly laughed. "The flavour's unicorn toots," she said, and I knew I'd found a kindred spirit.

Fella belly-crawled a few inches and laid his head on my crossed leg.

"Mmmmm, yum," I said, then slurped again.

Tilly's parents walked back into the room, holding hands. His lips were compressed into a thin line and his jaw flexed. Her mouth and her eyes were both downcast. Both seemed resolute in whatever decision they'd formed.

"You can buy him back," Penny said. "We'll figure out a way to explain it to Tilly. But it's better to break their tie now and find her a younger dog."

Leah moved fast. She opened her purse and rifled through it. "I'll give you a cheque."

I watched the child and dog playing. "Hold up. I've got a better idea." Everyone looked at me as though I'd suddenly sprouted a tail. I finally was getting what I wanted, and still threw a wrench into the works. "Leah, write that cheque, in case my idea doesn't work out. But personally," I squared my shoulders, "I think it's a good one."

I let the silence hang for dramatic effect. Tilly's parents didn't know me well enough to spur me forward and left that job to Leah.

"Spit it out," she said.

"Tilly here," I pointed with my teacup-laden hand, "wants a young dog, and I am a dog trainer with many connections. I've never trained a service dog before, but I'm sure we could figure it out. And I'm not too proud to ask for help from experts if we run into trouble. But my idea is we find a puppy just for Tilly and, together, we all train that puppy to help her."

Matt smiled, seemingly relieved, but said, "Will you excuse us again?"

Penny and Matt returned to their cloister. A few minutes later, they walked down the hallway again, still hand in hand, but this time, wearing matching smiles.

"You've got a deal," Matt said, then shook my hand.

I nodded, pleased with our outcome. "In the meantime, Tilly and Fella can have weekend play dates? I can pop him by after breakfast and his walk and pick him up again when this little one goes to bed. And he can go to school with her too. I can leave him with Tilly in the mornings when I drop off Emm and Bea."

Penny and Matt held their silent commune, studying each other's expressions. Penny was the one who spoke for them. "That would be great, Heddie. Thank you."

"It's a win-win," I adopted my best reasonable tone, and grinned.

CHAPTER 61

Message

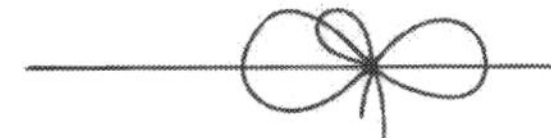

Cheerful chattering and planning occupied me during the ride back home from Tilly's place. Things were finally going my way.

I had decided to leave Fella with Tilly for the day. Her parents could help her understand the play-date arrangement and prepare her for a younger four-legged addition to their family. I was pretty sure my rusty connections could soon find her a suitable candidate.

Leah insisted upon paying for the new puppy.

"I'll get a job, pay you back." I didn't want her to think I shirked our deal, so added, "Another one besides taking care of the kids." In no time, I'd reboot Pawsitive Pups. "Maybe $250 a month. Pay you back within a year. Assuming you don't charge interest." I chuckled at that ridiculous notion.

"No way. Think of it as a pre-present, for your birthdays and Christmases, from all of us, for a year or two," Leah said.

I squirmed only a bit before I accepted her gift.

"I love hearing you laugh again," she said. "Welcome back, Heddie."

"I really feel like I'm back. Thank you, Leah. For everything. I am so grateful for you."

When we got home, I trounced down the stairs to my basement abode, optimistic about my prospects for a change. No more dried-up tumbleweeds of a future for me.

I rustled around the various boxes, shoving aside books

and clothes. Stanley and Becky had clearly never watched *Sesame Street*, as they hadn't bothered packing like with like. Instead, every box contained a jumble of the flotsam from my life. I sniffed the armpit of one sweater and drew back from the assault to my nostrils. I really should've unpacked weeks ago. And done laundry.

Anyway, enough of that. Enough of them. Time to move on.

I located my work backpack and pulled it free from the heap. "Found it!" I yelled.

I carried it up the stairs, skidded to a stop, and plunked my portable office down on the kitchen table. "I've got some breeders' names on my fob in here somewhere. I'll call around to see if anyone has a match for Tilly ready to go."

When I moved in with Hug, to help him out, I'd slowly wrapped up classes with my existing clients. I'd packed all my training supplies—leashes, branded clickers featuring my logo and phone number, handouts for different lessons and bits of homework—into this backpack. Storing everything in one place had seemed sensible. I had used a USB flash drive, also branded, to store important documents, including the all-important contact lists of suppliers, breeders, vets, pet services, and clients.

I unzipped the backpack and started rummaging through its goodies. "Here it is." I hauled out not one but two flash drives, one of which I didn't recognize.

Leah's laptop was already connected to her printer. She took my branded fob, plugged it into her computer's USB slot, and double-clicked to reveal the drive's contents.

"Breeders' info is under that tab, and client emails are under that one." I pointed, leaving fingerprints on the screen.

"It's not a touchscreen," she said, rubbing my prints off with her shirtsleeve.

"Please print the breeders list." A minute later, I held the still-warm paper in my hands. I zipped around the corner to the living room where I'd enjoy the comfort of the couch while I made my calls. Since the Covid lockdowns, puppies had been hard to find—with so many people choosing the companionship of animals to remedy their solitude. I settled in for several hours of phone calls and storytelling. So much had happened since I'd last talked with any of these folks.

But I hit the jackpot on my first call, a breeder in central Ontario who specialized in border doodles—the less-shedding mashup of two smart breeds, border collies and poodles—had one nine-week-old female ready for a new home.

I called to Leah, "Otto's got a puppy he'll give me. No charge. I just need to get her here."

"Who's Otto?" Leah asked.

"Otto Gottlieb. We became friends at the annual Petapalooza conferences." I blathered when excited.

A quick call to Penny confirmed I'd found a suitable match.

"I'm calling WestJet now."

Twenty minutes later, Tilly's puppy had a plane ticket for a trip in two days and I'd arranged her welcoming party at the airport.

I returned to the kitchen. I reached into my backpack and hauled out a mess of papers. They badly needed to be organized, so I started flipping through the pages and making piles.

"What's that?" Leah asked, picking up an envelope shoved into the mix.

I ignored her discovery. "Dunno."

She held the envelope aloft. "May I?"

"Any writing on it?"

"It's blank. But sealed." Leah transported the envelope to a cup of pens and a letter opener she collected on the windowsill. She sliced it open and pulled out a single piece of folded paper and a second, smaller sealed envelope. Unfolding it, she exclaimed, "I can't believe it."

I couldn't tell whether my friend was excited or scared. "What is it?"

Leah scanned the page before answering. "It's Hugh's holograph will. And he's done it right. Handwritten, signed and dated. No witnesses." She looked up at me, eyes bright.

I was afraid to ask, fearful I'd regress so soon in my recovery. "And?"

"We can get it probated, but Stanley's progressed too far with the old will. We'll have to discredit that one first." She handed me the second envelope. "Here. This has your name on it."

I stood, poised to open the envelope, nervous yet hopeful. Maybe Hug and I could finally resolve our incomplete conversations.

"Wait!" Leah shouted. "Take pictures. No, take video. Just in case someone challenges our discovery."

I grabbed my phone and took pictures of everything that could be relevant—the backpack, its pockets, my belongings, the opened envelope front and back, plus the sealed one. Leah trailed behind me, her phone held high, recording. Once she was satisfied, I sat down at the table to open my missive.

She handed me the letter opener, and I slipped the tip of the blade under the licked flap and sliced apart the paper. Inside was a single page, folded in thirds like business correspondence. Hands shaking, I pulled it out and unfolded it. I read, reread, and started to cry.

Leah, still behind the camera, said, "Heddie, read it aloud."

"I can't." My voice cracked.

"Try."

I breathed in deeply and relaxed my vocal cords. "It's dated June twenty-first. Five days before he died." I knew the chronology better than she did.

My dearest Heddie.

I recorded a video for you and shared it with you on this flash drive.

I turned to Leah and squealed. "I looked in all the wrong places. You got that other—?"

She finished my sentence by placing the unfamiliar fob in my hand.

The file password is…

I said "blah-de-blah" instead of the complicated composition he'd written.

I'm sorry nothing turned out the way we wanted. Know that I've always loved you.

"I would've never guessed that password."

Leah peered over my shoulder. "Do you see that password, Heddie? I mean really see it?" A satisfied smile crossed her face.

"What do you mean?"

"Read it."

I started, "Capital H, ampersand, Capital H, Capital T—"

"He's substituted numbers for letters, to send you a message," Leah said.

I glanced at the password again, still not understanding her meaning.

"H and H?" she said.

"Hug and me." Hope edged into my voice.

"Exactly. And this last part—it spells 'true love.' H&HTru3l0v3. He loved you, Heddie. Truly and deeply. I told you he was 'all in'."

I cried again, but for once, they weren't tears of sadness or despair. I still didn't know how to bear the loss, the physical absence of him, the man. But now, there was relief too. I'd been loved. Hug loved me.

"What's next?" Leah asked.

"He wants me to play it. Can I borrow your laptop?"

Leah propped her camera up on the flour canister. I waved at it, smiling despite my tear-stained face. She repositioned the laptop, inserted the flash drive, and I shoved her out of the way—gently, I hoped—before I stole her seat and keyed in Hug's password. A file at the top of the list was entitled: "1 Heddie start here."

I clicked on the file, and the pixels adjusted themselves to reveal my wonderful Hug. He was pale and thin, his hair needed to be cut, and he could've used a shave. But his eyes were clear as he looked straight at me through the intermediary camera. I sniffled and Leah put her hand on my shoulder. I pressed play.

"Hello, my darling. I'm glad you found this. I figured your work backpack was a good place for it. You must've met Dee by now. Leah introduced us and she helped me get everything in order. I've tried a couple of times now to update my will properly, using Dee as my lawyer, but this damned cancer keeps interfering. So this is the best I got."

He held up a blank piece of paper and a pen for the camera. "I'm going to write a holograph will and I'm going to film it." He picked up his camera and did a three-sixty of the room, his den door closed. "See? All by my lonesome. No one's here to coerce me." He held the camera level with his face again. "I'm doing this because I want to."

He used a portable laptop desk as a writing surface, and spoke aloud, slowly, as he wrote. He angled the camera so it also recorded his hand moving along the page, filling it with his words. "I'm of sound mind," he said, and wrote. To the camera, he said, "But my body's a disappointment lately." He held his head back and reached his arms out before touching the tip of his nose with a pointer finger in one hand and the pen in the other. "See?" he said. "Sound mind. And sober." He laughed, and I laughed, too, upon hearing that sound again.

I paused the playback and collected myself before starting the video again.

"I am writing this as a holograph will." He wrote slowly, carefully. To the camera, he said, "Dee told me the rules. I'm handwriting it, no witnesses, and I will sign it. I'm just taping it, too, as a bonus. Mr. Belt and Braces." He laughed, and I smiled reflexively.

"Heddie—Henry-Etta Wright—please take care of my dog, Fella, for me for the rest of his life."

I cried again but remained coherent. "As if I'd let anything happen to Fella."

"Heddie, I know you'll take care of him. He's really your dog, anyway. I just need to make it official. Dee said he's considered property and so I need to set you up as his guardian."

He started writing again. "I appoint my brother, Stan Fields—" To the camera, he added, "like the underwear," and smirked impishly. "I appoint my brother," he started writing again, "to be the executor of my estate." To the camera, he continued, "I don't really care what you do with my body. Stan, you and Heddie decide together. Heddie, I know you want a bench somewhere. I've asked Stan to make it happen."

He started writing. "I leave my house in Calgary and its contents to the love of my life, Henry-Etta Wright, for her sole use. I leave my cabin in Kananaskis and its contents to my brother, Stanley Elwin Fields, for his sole use." To the camera, he added, "Heddie, I've got mortgage insurance, so the house should be free and clear after I go. Once you get your business started again, you can afford its upkeep."

He addressed his comments to the paper. "The End. Signed, Hugh Fields." He added a flourish with his hand and arm. "Heddie, promise me you'll move on after I'm gone. I hope you'll consider me a pleasant interlude in your long and happy life." He fumbled with something off-screen. "Even with all my difficulties, I was happy to wake up to you every morning. You are my love, Heddie. Never forget that. You made my life worth living."

Hug broke eye contact with the camera and pulled forward an orange pad of Post-it notes. "I'll write the password on here too," he said. "Love you, Heddie." Blurred fingers fumbled with the phone, before Hugh called, "Becky, I'm done."

A door clicked open. "That off now?" my sister-in-law

asked. The camera was aimed at the ceiling fixture, but the audio quality remained.

"I think so. Thanks for helping me with all this," Hug said. "Dee said no beneficiaries could be part of it or the will could be questioned."

"Uh-huh."

"Hey, could you put this note on the fridge, please?" An orange blur passed the screen.

Becky paused. "It looks like code."

"Heddie'll understand," Hug replied.

When the playback ended, Leah reached over and closed the laptop screen.

"Becky knew?" All this time, I thought Stanley was the bad guy. "Well, to hell with her." I grabbed Leah and hugged her tight. "She won't ruin this for me. I'm gonna focus instead on what Hug said, what he did."

CHAPTER 62

Roll Call

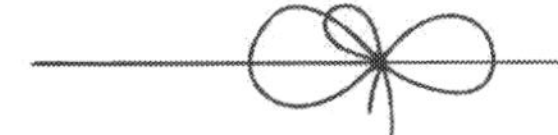

"Let's do another roll call. Everyone say whether they think Molly is guilty or not."

Who had nominated Phil to lead us? Oh, yeah. That'd be me. What had I been thinking?

I glanced around at the flip-chart pages I'd plastered on all the walls. When I'd run out of wall space, I'd affixed pages to the windows with painter's tape. My visual aids had helped us make sense of the chronology and highlighted our unanswered questions.

"Do it aloud," Ruth said. "No more anonymous ballots."

"We've only got three holdouts. Let's talk to them. Explain things," Jim said.

"We all know I'm one," Phil said from his position as emcee.

I braced myself for another tough day and decided to 'fess up too. "Never mind. I'm one too."

"You? Of all people?" Jim said. "You know she's guilty." I set my jaw and he switched his approach. "What can we help you understand?" He sounded reasonable if I ignored his patronizing tone.

I planted my feet, ish, shoulder-width apart. "Maybe she is guilty," I admitted. "Even probably. But don't you think she's already suffered enough?"

Ruth sighed. "That's what's so difficult here. She did the wrong thing, the very worst thing, but for the right reasons."

I grimaced, "And, she's serving a life sentence living without the love of her life."

Mandi raised her hand. "I'm the other holdout. I just don't think she's guilty. Not in any traditional sense. I think the law failed them both."

Jim snorted unattractively. "Now you write the laws?"

Mandi ignored him. "Anyone heard of Robert Latimer?" After we all nodded, she continued, "He killed his daughter, Tracy."

"That poor child endured unbearable suffering," Ruth said. "I can't imagine hearing a child scream in pain for years."

Me neither. I couldn't imagine coping with it for seconds.

"We've been studying that trial in my Social Justice class," Mandi said. "Latimer confessed, and the jury found him guilty, even though everyone agreed his actions were humane, loving."

Jim's furrowed brow accentuated his resemblance to a Neanderthal. "Of course they did. The law—"

"Exactly," Mandi interrupted. "I'm getting there." Her eyes flashed hot. "MAID wasn't available yet, and Tracy wouldn't have qualified anyway. She never talked. Her whole life." She paused. "But here's the thing, the jury didn't want to convict him. They agreed with his choice. Many hoped they'd have such courage, too, in similar circumstances. But they'd never heard of something called 'jury nullification.'" She punctuated her newly-acquired legal jargon with air quotes. "We can make a different choice."

Adam scowled. "What's jury nullif—"

Toni jumped in. "It's a rule that lets us, the jury, decide not to convict someone, even if we think they did it, because we think the law itself needs more work."

"Hopewell should be punished," Jim said.

"Do you agree Max was ready to die?" Mandi asked.

Jim hesitated.

"Oh, come on," I huffed. "Sure, his signing was

improvised, unconventional, but his message couldn't be any clearer. Plus, he filled out a MAID application, for Pete's sake."

"Wasn't good enough for the lawyers and the police," Jim said.

"That's because they must uphold the law, exactly as it's written. We don't," Toni confirmed. "We can send two messages. One, that Molly acted mercifully, and two, that the MAID legislation needs to be updated."

"Whoa," I said. "I don't want to be monkeying around with the MAID laws. Don't misinterpret me. I'm glad MAID exists." I wished I'd known more about it when I could have still helped Hug. "But I don't want to change the rules. I just want to find a way to support Molly, to tell the world she did her best."

I paused, and Ruth rolled her hand for me to continue.

"My main rationale? Even if I think she did it, the Crown didn't prove it. I've heard nothing connecting Molly to the antidepressants. We heard Max was allergic. And they found them in his blood when they tested it a second time. But that's a gigantic leap to say she forced him to take them."

Paper rustled as nine jurors rummaged through their notepads looking for the testimony to fill the gap.

Ruth looked up from her tidy notes. "I can't find anything connecting Molly to those drugs either."

"You're right, Heddie." Toni admitted. "I wonder why the Crown charged her with first degree murder? Why not a lesser charge with a lower burden of proof?"

Jim threw his hands in the air. "They told us it wasn't like TV. They can't dot all the i's."

"The murder weapon is an important dot," I quipped. "Besides, I'm also not convinced about her motive. Based on my experience—"

"This isn't about you," Jim sniped. "She did it for the money. They were unemployed, in debt. No money coming in, except whatever she borrowed. She pawned her jewellery. Her motive was money."

"Yes, but, Max was palliative," I explained, "and Molly knew better than most what that meant. She also knew she'd get a half million dollars in life insurance after he died. She just needed to wait it out, and probably not for long. If it was about money, why risk losing everything just before he'd probably die naturally? She'd already stood by him for so long, through so much."

"I can't forgive her murder weapon," Adam said. "Anyone here got allergies?" He opened his jacket and pulled out a zippered case emblazoned with a red cross symbol from the inside pocket. "I do, and it's horrible. You get dizzy. Feels like a dump truck is on your chest. Can't breathe, can't speak, want to puke."

Jim nodded. "Not a good way to go."

"If she did it, maybe she didn't realize what would happen," I suggested.

Ruth nodded. "Good point. She's not a doctor."

"You're not falling for this too?" Jim asked. "Show some backbone, will ya."

"If she needed to do it," Adam continued, "at least choose something more humane. Morphine, maybe?"

"High doses of morphine are very unpleasant," Ruth said. "Another bad death."

"They just couldn't win," I said. "He should've died—would've died—when he had that stroke. His parents should also accept their part in his suffering. They ignored his wishes."

"I think you're wrong, Heddie," Phil said. Uh-oh, had I lost him again? "His parents loved him, did the best they could."

"But so did Molly. Who else sees that?" I exclaimed.

"I do." Pat said.

"I think the parents were in denial," Phil continued. "Didn't get how sick he was. They just wanted him to live. No different than her with her Can-cure."

I met his pointed gaze. "In the end, I kind of hope she

did do it," I said. "I hope she was brave enough to fulfill Max's wishes, knowing she might get caught, and doing it anyway. You all saw that video. He wanted to die. You all heard Dr. Good Death. He was in pain, suffering, beyond what meds could manage. And his parents—well, they're the ones who should be on trial. Probably not for murder, but for cruel and unusual punishment."

"That's not a crime," Toni said in a huff. Then she stopped herself. "But I understand your point. If they'd let Max and Molly manage their own affairs, rather than injecting their personal values and false hopes into the mix, the doctors would have stopped treatments earlier and at least not prolonged Max's life."

"You know what else?" Mandi said. "They loved each other."

Now wasn't the time to remind everyone I'd just said that. "We all saw her in that video. She didn't want him to die, but she'd faced facts."

"But 'jury nullification' is the ultimate exercise of democracy, even more powerful than voting," Mandi said, and I wondered whether she quoted her prof. "We have a chance to tell the politicians to do better."

"Hold on," I said. "It's a nifty rule, but I don't think we should apply it here." Mandi looked so disheartened, I softened my message. "Have you ever made the decision of life and death for another being?" I asked. "I have. Only ever for dogs, and always when they were deathly sick." I shook my head. "Those decisions were both necessary and heart-breaking. I can't imagine making the same decision for a person, a human being." I looked at Mandi to make sure she understood. "The Crown gave us two outs, first when they charged her with the higher crime, first degree murder, and then when he didn't connect Molly directly to the murder weapon. He needed to offer the best proof and didn't. We got motive—she couldn't watch Max suffer any longer. We got opportunity—judging from that video, he probably would have cooperated anyway.

But Molly's link to the murder weapon is weak."

Toni reached over and touched Mandi's forearm, "Molly gets off either way."

"We can be a mercy of widows after all," Phil stated.

∘ ∘ ∘

We waddled into the courtroom, probably for the last time.

"Have you, the jury, reached a verdict?" the judge asked, his voice loud and crisp.

Phil stood, proud to be our spokesperson. "Yes, Your Honour, we have. We find the accused not guilty."

Molly had stood for the verdict and was steadied by her guards when Phil read it. They both smiled, and one patted Molly on the back, a gesture that confirmed we'd made the right decision.

The judge nodded. "Would anyone like the jury polled?"

Twee-dee stood. "Yes, Your Honour."

Uh-oh. I sucked in my breath and hoped everyone remained convinced.

"When I say your number, please stand and state your verdict." He paused. "One."

Phil stood, and said, "Not guilty." His voice sounded strong, sure.

"Two."

Adam stood. "Not guilty." His chair squeaked when he sat down again.

"Three."

And so, he went down the line. I only balked when the judge called "Eight," but even Jim had been persuaded.

∘ ∘ ∘

The court splurged and paid for my taxi home. We all collected our belongings hastily, and I checked and double-checked I'd left nothing behind. The Mercy hugged and each exchanged business cards, except Mandi—who entered our information into her phone and texted us her number—and Phil, who asked Mandi to add our details into his device.

"We'll stay in touch," Ruth promised. I hoped she was right.

Clemence packed up her belongings to transport them somewhere into the bowels of the building. She'd put the Louise Penny novel aside.

"You done with that?" I asked.

She nodded but didn't elaborate. She looked as tired as I felt.

"Can I borrow it?"

"You can have it. It was headed for a free library anyway," she replied.

"Thanks for everything, Clemence." I reached out my hand to shake hers.

She seemed surprised by my gesture, then beamed a broad, toothy grin. She clasped my hand in both of hers. "You're welcome, Number Nine. You have certainly kept me on my toes."

CHAPTER 63

Two Wrongs

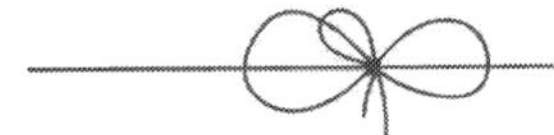

I squinted into the sun before shifting my seat so I could better see my tablemates. We all sat outside, al fresco on this bright chinook day, and huddled over Leah's laptop. I pressed the pause button to stop the video.

Stanley leaned back in his chair with a whoosh of exhaled air. Becky's posture indicated she wanted to bolt. Neither seemed thrilled about their present company or my revelation.

Dee adopted an angry lawyerly tone. "Hugh's video explains a lot, and you screwed up, Becky. Big time."

I jabbed my finger in the air. "You knew. Yet you kicked me out of his house. Let Stanley sell it. Fella too."

I ignored Leah when she booted me under the table. She wanted Dee to do all the talking, but I planned to say my piece too.

"I can't believe you let him probate that old will," I said. "You knew better."

Becky sat, still prune-faced.

"I didn't do anything wrong," Stanley said. "Leave me out of it. I didn't know about any of this." He waved at the black screen. Stanley wrinkled his nose and sniffed in my direction. "Besides, she's no angel either."

"Trying to divert our attention?" I said. "Is the replacement tree still alive?" I fished out my phone, scrolled through some screens, and displayed it for his inspection. "I took this photo yesterday. Looks fine to me."

Stanley hunched his shoulders, and whined, "Hugh wasn't competent. His doctors will testify."

Dee tapped the computer. "Hugh's video is unorthodox, but I'm sure the courts will agree he was in his right mind when he wrote his holograph will."

Stanley convulsed like a fish out of water.

"Heddie could nail you to the wall with this," Dee continued.

I reached down and scratched Fella's head. "You were nasty. Vicious. Both of you. Why should I forgive you?" I liked the vantage from my high horse.

"Your behaviour stank too," Stanley said. "If you use Hugh's video to hurt Becky, me," he put his arm over his wife's shoulder, "I'll use my security camera footage to hurt you." Stanley reached out to pet Fella's head, and I shifted my dog out of his reach.

I didn't appreciate the self-righteous edge in Stanley's tone. "You've lost any right to scold me."

"There's no doubt," Leah said. "Heddie showed questionable judgement there."

Stanley didn't see he'd already lost. "You think? It wasn't just the tree. She stole his ashes too."

"I prefer, 'liberated,'" I said.

"Same, same. You broke the law. Theft. Plus, interfering with a body. Or something," Stanley gloated in false triumph.

Silence followed, and then Leah nodded. "What you did, Heddie, was wrong. At that time, you had no right to Hugh's ashes."

I started to contradict her, and she raised her hand to stop me.

"Hugh's video, and especially his holograph will, both state his wishes clearly. But you didn't know any of that when you 'liberated'..." Her voice trailed off. "And you, Becky, you broke the law."

"We all made mistakes," Stanley said, his voice

wheedling.

"Yes, but Becky's mistake was the worst. And, Stanley, we all knew what Hugh wanted. Dee even showed you his instructions for a new will. Yet, you deliberately ignored your brother's wishes."

"We'd be in a whole different place if you'd shared with me at the start."

Stanley hung his head and looked ashamed. Becky sat, arms crossed and mouth shut.

"Can we fix this?" he asked.

Leah's eyebrows raised. We'd talked through my options and assessed the pros and cons of each. I possessed enough evidence to exact a thorough revenge on Becky, and by implication, Stanley. But all of that would take time. And money. Plus, "two wrongs don't make a right." My favourite Huggism.

"What I want is Hug, and we all know that's impossible. I got Fella back, no thanks to you. I have a very comfortable roof over my head, again, no thanks to you." I fiddled with the chunky ring around my finger. "And, I liberated some of Hug's ashes." I felt my face flush, but I persisted. "Here's what I want. I want you to dedicate a bench to Hug, preferably in Fish Creek Park. You can put your own names on it, I don't care. But include my name on it too. Heddie, not Henry-Etta. And give me an acceptable title. I'm okay with 'love,' 'partner,' or 'spouse,' but I'd prefer 'ampersand.'"

"Why Fish Creek?" Becky asked. "It's so far away."

"Because I said so." I might eventually tell them that's where I planted Hug's tree. Not yet, but some day, when our bygones were firmly in the past.

Stanley looked like he'd chewed off his own tongue.

"Finally, you will sell that condo you bought in Whistler. You can keep some of the proceeds, but you need to share with me. Send Dee all the accounting records for Hug's estate, and she will tell you how much to write on my cheque."

Stanley shook his head. "What will you do with that

kind of money?"

"None of your beeswax," I said. I couldn't have told him anyway. "Don't argue with me on this, Stanley. I'm being generous with you. More generous than you were with me, and more generous than you deserve."

Leah patted my knee, a pat of pride. I could get used to standing up for myself.

"We done here?" I asked.

"I think so," Leah confirmed.

I stood and grabbed Fella's leash. "We're walking home."

With that, we headed out, and I didn't look back.

CHAPTER 64

Darling

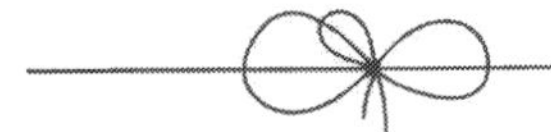

"To Hug," I said, and we all clinked our glasses of Gewurtz together. "I'm so relieved," I confessed.

Leah patted my hand, and I welcomed the touch. "You're right to be."

"Not only about Fella. Not even the money. Well, that too," I admitted. "I can pay you back way ahead of schedule." I chuckled. "But mostly I'm relieved he loved me."

"Of course, he loved you."

"I was worried. I didn't have anything tangible to prove it. But I fixed that." I waggled my fingers in front of them, displaying my evidence.

"Is that what I think it is?" Dee sounded impressed.

I presented my hand so she could have a better look.

"Where'd you get it?" The peacock blue gems shone in the light.

"I wanted a memorial ring, but the diamond type takes months." I never collected enough ashes, but I augmented the sample with ample quantities of Fella's fur and my hair. The company told me I'd get my diamond early next year.

"What are these then? They shine like blue diamonds."

"They're just paste. Or maybe glass. I pried them out of a key ring Hug gave me."

The rest had been Pat's idea. In her salon, she possessed an assortment of resins and glues to affix fake fingernails, and she donated some to my cause. Mandi took the bits and bobs

I gave her—bling from the key ring, some dirt collected from around Hug's tree, a lock of Fella's fur—glued it all together, added a bit of blue dye, suspended it in epoxy. It was her finest work, even better than the accessories she created for herself. I polished it with Leah's Dremel into a bauble and measured and drilled the hole myself, sizing it to fit my ring finger.

I traced a long scratch in the table surface, raising my finger aloft to ensure everyone got a good look.

Leah nodded. "Lots of people fret about what they meant to the departed."

I debated about telling them. I didn't want to spoil the moment. "Well, it's more than that," I said. "I found peculiar things. After."

"Like what?" Dee asked.

I still wasn't ready to admit I'd broken into his online accounts where I found the most compelling evidence. "Cryptic messages on his condolence book."

"Can you show me?"

Could I show her? I had the damned thing bookmarked. Using my phone, I found the offending inscription. "Look. Who signs with their initials?"

Dee inhaled sharply. "I'm sorry, Heddie. That's me."

Leah leaned over to view my show-and-tell. "It's true. I could probably find you a sample." She rummaged through her purse to find her phone.

"Don't bother. I believe you." My last bit of evidence was more damning anyway. "His last email was to another woman. His endearment is irrefutable."

"That doesn't make sense. Hugh loved you," Leah said. "Everyone else knew that. I wish you'd believe it too. In here." She tapped my chest.

"He called her 'darling.'" My tone was hostile, accusatory. "'Wendy Darling.'"

"Oh, dear…" Dee started.

I lost my patience. "You're taking the blame for that one too?"

"It's true," Dee said. "That's me too."

I folded my arms over my chest and waited for her explanation.

"My mother named me after the main character in *Peter Pan*. Hugh wanted to know what 'Dee' was short for. I made him guess, and he came up with some good ones. Delia, Dierdre, of course, Heddie."

I turned away, but she touched my elbow. "I'm not just saying that."

"Uh-huh."

"After he ran out of guesses, I just told him. No one ever guesses a mother would willingly name her daughter 'Wendy Darling.'"

"My mother was sentimental when she named me too," I acknowledged. Then I sat back and considered the chain of events, before I shook my head, unconvinced. "Nice story, but it doesn't add up."

She leaned forward. "I mean it. That's me."

Her insistence made me angrier. "Why didn't you answer me then? I sent you a message." I flicked to show her my email. "Hug did, too, a few days before he died, and you ignored us both."

She shook her head. "That can't be. I reply to every message. Sometimes it's just a receipt, but..." She leaned over and studied my screen. "Oh, I see the problem."

I waited for her to enlighten me.

"See here." Dee pointed to the "to" box. "That's my old firm. I went out on my own about a month before Hugh died." She sat back. "My old employer wouldn't forward my emails, afraid I'd poach their clients. But I gave Hugh my new contact information. I wonder why he didn't use it."

"We'll never know."

CHAPTER 65

A Plucky Rose

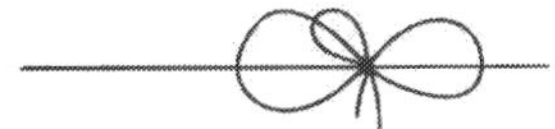

"Heddie, please check those roses and snip off any thorns." Leah picked up a pair of scissors from the bookcase and handed them to me, handles first for safety's sake.

The roses served an important role in tonight's ceremony, a welcoming of her first clients, we intrepid guinea pigs in her first grief workshop. I used some of my inheritance from Hug to help her get her initiative going. She resisted my gift initially. She'd always given me so much, for almost our entire lives. I was glad to be able to help her for a change.

That morning, Leah had hand-picked the roses, selecting blooms barely budding and in several colours. "These'll last," she'd explained. They must've been hard to find on this shortest day of the year.

"Please use that ribbon to tie a bow on each stem." Leah pointed to a white, lacy roll partially unfurled on the coffee table in the centre of a circle of fold-up chairs.

I did as she asked, determined to keep my head down and do my best. I couldn't afford my generosity with Hug's gift. After all, I still cobbled together a living, with my part-time nannying for Leah's kids, role as morning receptionist at Jake's clinic, and a smattering of evening dog training classes.

I lifted a white rose and ran my finger slowly from the bottom to the top of the stem. I only found one thorn and clipped it carefully.

Roses were a favourite, although I didn't love the

perfect cultivated sameness of these hothouse specimens. The flat wild rose should be my personal emblem, with its thousands of prickly thorns dressing it like an angry porcupine. This wasn't some misplaced form of provincial patriotism. I just admired the plant's pluckiness, its ability to survive, thrive, in all the weather the high plains and the mountains threw at it. Plus, it wasn't showy in its success. Its flowers were simple, infrequent.

I placed folders we'd assembled that morning on each chair. Leah'd gotten the folders printed somewhere, each emblazoned with a surprisingly effective logo drawn by her kids: an abstract, Picasso-esque dragonfly. The folders contained several handouts she'd collected and resources I'd personally tested and found useful. I smiled when I spotted my tried-and-true *Doodle Notes* among her recommendations. She listed her website, too, where I knew people would receive helpful reminders of the weekly discussion topics, homework assignments, and a phone number, connected to a twenty-four-hour phone service, in case of any crises.

Leah turned off the overhead fluorescent lights altogether and turned on the table lamps she'd arranged throughout the room. The lower light made the space feel less like an interrogation room. She sidled next to the wall to get the longest vantage on our handiwork. "I think we're ready," she said.

I'd just finished my chores when Leah's first guest arrived, tentatively standing in the doorway, considering the room and her escape options. I recognized her, of course, as soon as she walked in, although she sported an ordinary black tunic over jeggings instead of her usual sweater set. Her hair was a bit longer, casually clipped out of her face with silver barrettes.

I glowered at Leah. "You should have warned me," I said. Understatement of the day, and I vowed to give her a piece of my mind later. She still hadn't learned that lesson.

I strode over to the newcomer, heedless of the alarm

bells ringing in my head. "Hello. Welcome." I held out my hand. "My name is Heddie, and I'm helping out with this workshop."

She cocked her head. "Have we met? You look familiar."

"No," I admitted. Not formally.

Molly put her purse on one seat, claiming it as her own.

About then, I regained some moxie, and said, "We have kinda met before."

She studied me, waiting for me to continue.

"I was a juror. On your trial."

Recognition dawned across her face. "I guess I owe you. Thank you."

"Just doing my duty," I said, before shaking my head to clear out the fibs. "Okay, that's not true. I figured you did it, but not for the reasons they said. I think you tried to help him. We all did."

She examined me, and I'm sure I caught the barest hint of a nod. I knew I should shut up, but I couldn't button it. "My husband died too," I said.

"I'm sorry for your loss."

"Come on. Aren't we beyond that by now? I was gutted by his death. I think you were too. By Max's death, I mean. I started grieving Hug before he died."

Now that I had her undivided attention, I had so much to say. "I didn't have your courage. I couldn't let him go. I held on to him for every instant, too long." She would understand, better than anyone. "If I ever have to do it over again, I hope I'd show your kind of courage," I admitted.

"Funny. I hope no one else ever has to make such an impossible choice," Molly said.

"Hug wanted me to 'move on', but I'm struggling. I don't want to forget him, make him a small part of my past."

She looked at me, maybe really seeing me for the first time. "Try 'carry on', instead. We can 'carry on', leading our lives, doing our level best to live well and fully. But we carry them with us. Max is as much of my present as he is of my past. My memories of him continue to shape me."

"People," Leah said in her best professorial voice, "Please take your seats. Let's begin."

We obligingly complied, with Molly and me choosing seats side by side, our backs to the window and the outside world. Molly leaned over, "Let's get together?"

Yes, let's.

ABOUT THE BOOK

Readers often wonder how much of my novel is true. While the events in *A Mercy of Widows* are made up, they're inspired by things that really happen to people. But this book is a story, and not a record of my own life.

The city of Calgary in the book is the real Calgary. The streets, the weather, the winter roads treated with beet juice, and the courthouse details are true to life, based on what I've seen and researched.

There truly is a secured courtroom within the Calgary courthouse. Despite my inquiries to legal insiders, its exact location remains a well-guarded secret, giving me the creative freedom to place it on the 20th floor—a choice that served as a perfect chance for Heddie to bond with a fellow juror.

I chose to write from Heddie's point of view because I wanted readers to experience her confusion in a direct way. Heddie is grappling with complicated grief, so her journey is marked by erratic impulsiveness, a struggle to navigate life's simplest tasks, conflict avoidance, and some profoundly poor judgment. Sadly, these reactions to grief are too common and too often misunderstood, especialy in our world, where grief, death, dying are seldom discussed.

There's also truth in the progress of the Medical Assistance in Dying (MAID) laws in Alberta, and the impact of Audrey Parker's story.

Why write about MAID in my first novel? I've seen too many loved ones pass away and have pondered how we die. The MAID law offers some peace at the end, but it's not perfect. I wrote to explore my feelings and to understand better what patients and their families go through.

To get the MAID details right, I talked to many people who've dealt with the laws and its practice. And, I read a lot, especially Stefanie Green's book, *This is Assisted Dying.*

As for training dogs, I've done it but always under expert supervision. My dog Bug (on whom Fella is based) is smart and eager, but her border collie nature means she's mostly self-taught.

One great untruth in this book is the dastardly misbehavior of all the inlaws. Unlike Heddie, I have several wonderful inlaws, including the sibling and cousins of my late husband, Tom, and my brother-in-law, Paul, who long ago graduated to earn the honourary title of "brother".

One of the greatest honours as an author comes when readers take meaningful action based on what they read. Beyond updating wills and medical directives, a profound moment for me was when one reader shared that the discussions in my book about MAID guided her and her husband as they navigated his end-of-life choices. This conversation led to her husband applying for MAID, ensuring his wishes were respected for a dignified farewell.

I believe planning for our inevitable end is an act of love for our families, and I thank her for sharing this private and sublime moment with me.

In writing *A Mercy of Widows*, I blended bits of reality with my imagination to tell a story that feels real and, I hope, keeps you turning the pages.

READING GROUP GUIDE

1. Calgary, Alberta, Canada serves as a unique backdrop in *A Mercy of Widows*. How did the cultural and geographical aspects of the city enhance your understanding of Heddie's journey?

2. Heddie's plight and the absence of a wedding ring bring up societal views on relationships and recognition. How does the story challenge or reinforce your beliefs about the significance of marital status?

3. Reflect on Heddie's internal conflict as she navigates her grief and the mercy-killing trial. How do her experiences mirror the complexities of human emotions in times of sorrow?

4. While reading *A Mercy of Widows*, which moments of levity brought you relief or joy amid the heavier themes, and how did these moments influence your connection to the story?

5. Fella, the dog, is more than just a pet in this narrative. Discuss how Fella's presence provides comfort and a non-verbal narrative that supports Heddie's emotional arc.

6. The book delves into the intricacies of Canada's MAID (medical assistance in dying) laws. How did this exploration alter or affirm your views on such a profound aspect of human rights?

7. Marcy Lane intertwines themes of love and redemption with legal drama. Discuss how these elements resonated with you and any parallels you drew from your life experiences.

8. The title *A Mercy of Widows* is evocative and multi-layered. How does it reflect the core themes of the novel, and what meanings did you derive from it?

9. *A Mercy of Widows* is described as an exploration of emotional preparedness in the face of adversity. Discuss how the book portrays the readiness (or lack thereof) to face life's challenges and how it relates to your own life or worldview.

10. Marcy Lane introduces real-life issues into the fabric of her fiction. How does this approach affect your engagement with the story and characters?

ACKNOWLEDGEMENTS

This novel, a tapestry of dreams and dedication, was raised by a village—a community of extraordinary folks whose collective support nurtured it into being.

To Abigail K. Perry, my editor: thank you for your incisive feedback and for helping to mold the early contours of this story. Your wisdom turned challenges into opportunities for growth, and for that, I am ever grateful.

Jess McKeldon: you wielded your editorial scalpel with precision, excising the excess and enhancing the essential. Your guidance has been a cornerstone in this book's foundation.

In the realm of mentorship, Melissa Collings (author of *The False Flat*) was my guiding star. Melissa, your mentorship was a gift that took my writing from raw to remarkable. Your influence is a thread woven through every page.

Penny, you read the genesis of this story with a heart full of hope and patience. Your early encouragement was the seed from which this book grew.

My cadre of volunteer beta readers—Daryll, Bobby, Chris, Dave, Erin, Paul, Kay—each one of you provided vital nutrients through your insights and advice.

To my critique partners—Tyler, Mary, Selma, Morticia, and Anne—your commitment to this work mirrored my own. Anne, especially, you read alongside me through every iteration, your dedication even more unwavering than my own.

My brother is the linchpin of my book's journey—from emceeing launches to mastering audio formats. His persistent nudges, always steeped in brotherly love (with maybe a dash of mischief), dared me to set these pages free. For every visible and invisible task, my sincerest thanks.

Above all, I owe a world of gratitude to my mother. She has been the heartbeat of my writing life. In choosing to self-publish, I was driven by a desire to place this book in her hands while it could still be a shared joy between us, as she was diagnosed with dementia. This book is as much hers as it is mine, a testament to her enduring love and support. She's earned the right, more than anyone, to hold this book and to be recognized as its champion.

This village—my village—has collectively raised this book, infusing it with love, wisdom and tenacity. To each of you, I offer my deepest thanks. Together, we brought this story to life.

ABOUT THE AUTHOR

Marcy Lane

Marcy Lane writes character-driven stories starring ordinary women in impossible situations. Marcy is inspired by the struggles we all face and uses her stories to discover her views on everyday thorny issues.

When she isn't writing, you can find Marcy walking in nearby orchards, or dabbling with messy art media like flow painting and alcohol inks.

Marcy currently lives in a small cottage in southwestern Ontario, Canada with her two dogs, Bug and Lucy.

A Mercy of Widows is Marcy's first novel.

Stay connected with Marcy at marcylane.com

DEAR READER

Thank you so much for picking up *A Mercy of Widows*. I hope you found something in the pages of my book that spoke to you, something valuable that resonated or gave you a new perspective.

If you could take a minute to share a review on Goodreads or social media, it would really help the book reach more eyes. *Word of mouth*, from readers to other readers, is the best way to feature a debut novel.

Also, please join me at marcylane.com. I share news, behind the scenes information about my process and inspirations, short stories, and bad poetry. It's also where I'm shaping up new ideas, and your input could make a difference.

Once again, thank you.

Best wishes,

Marcy Lane

Essex County, Canada

August 2023

Manufactured by Amazon.ca
Bolton, ON

38249404R00231